# RAVAGE THE DARK

## TARA SIM

LITTLE, BROWN AND COMPANY
New York   Boston

Little, Brown and Company
Hachette Book Group
1290 Avenue of the Americas, New York, NY 10104
Visit us at LBYR.com

First Edition: March 2021

Little, Brown and Company is a division of Hachette Book Group, Inc. The Little, Brown name and logo are trademarks of Hachette Book Group, Inc.

The publisher is not responsible for websites (or their content) that are not owned by the publisher.

Library of Congress Cataloging-in-Publication Data
Names: Sim, Tara, author.
Title: Ravage the dark / Tara Sim.
Description: First edition. | Los Angeles ; New York : Little, Brown and Company, 2021. | Series: Scavenge the stars | Audience: Ages 14 and up. | Summary: "After escaping the city of Moray, Amaya and Cayo head to the port city of Baleine to find the mysterious Benefactor and put a stop to the counterfeit currency that is spreading Ash Fever throughout the kingdoms."—Provided by publisher.
Identifiers: LCCN 2020017856 (print) | LCCN 2020017857 (ebook) |
ISBN 9780759555334 (hardcover) | ISBN 9780759555341 (ebook)
Subjects: CYAC: Alchemy—Fiction. | Diseases—Fiction. | Counterfeits and counterfeiting—Fiction. | Fantasy.
Classification: LCC PZ7.1.S547 Rav 2021 (print) | LCC PZ7.1.S547 (ebook) | DDC [Fic]—dc23
LC record available at https://lccn.loc.gov/2020017856

ISBNs: 978-0-7595-5533-4 (hardcover), 978-0-7595-5534-1 (ebook)

Printed in the United States of America

LSC-C

Printing 1, 2021

FOR MY FATHER, WHO INTRODUCED ME
TO THE POWER OF STORIES

WHEN THE GODS HAVE PERISHED
AND THE LIGHT HAS FLED,
WE WILL RAVAGE THE DARK
WHERE STARS HAVE BLED.

—KHARIAN POEM

1

*A sailor needs only two things: a ship and a purpose.*

—ON SAILING AND NAVIGATION, A BEGINNER'S GUIDE

It was perhaps fitting that Amaya was the first one to spot the bodies.

She stood at the railing of the *Marionette*, the naval ship they had sailed out of Moray and northeast along the vast coast of the Rain Empire. She had watched the coastline gradually turn from verdant jungle to flat grassland to craggy peaks as they crawled by, the weather becoming cooler with each passing day.

Roach had traveled to Moray on the *Marionette* in order to figure out what was causing ash fever. To try to find her. He had succeeded in both missions and now had to report back to his officers in the Rain Empire that the counterfeit coins were coated in an alchemical substance linked to the fever.

They had spent a little over a week at sea on their journey to

Baleine, the central port city of Chalier—one of the many territories swallowed by the Rain Empire. It was where Roach had been indoctrinated into the empire's navy. According to the map, they were scheduled to make port that very evening.

But as Amaya gripped the railing of the *Marionette* and admired how the sunset turned the sea to flames, she noticed a rocky little island along their path. It jutted out of the water like a fang, all crags and uneven shelves.

Hanging from the island at the ends of frayed ropes were four bloated bodies, all in various states of decomposition.

Amaya pressed her lips together. The sight of them here, an obvious and blatant warning, seemed too much of an ill omen for her to ignore.

She had her mother to thank for that dose of superstitious dread. *Pray to the star saints for forgiveness and mercy*, she would have told Amaya. *The sight of death brings nothing but misfortune.*

Amaya didn't bother to pray. Misfortune would find her one way or another.

Roach came up beside her and leaned his arms on the gunwale, frowning at the bodies. They were swaying in the sea breeze, and Amaya was grateful the wind wasn't blowing in their direction.

"I take it this isn't new to you?" Amaya asked of him.

Roach shook his head. The late afternoon light gilded his brown hair, kissing his tawny skin in such a way that he almost seemed to glow.

"I saw it when I was brought to Baleine the first time," he said. "The locals call it the Sinner's Shelf. The bodies have been different every time I've passed it, though."

"I assume they deserved their fate?"

2

Roach gave her a crooked smile. "It's where they bring the worst of the lot. Pirates, rapists, murderers. Chalier likes to give outsiders a warning before they come to their shores—follow the rules or end up in the belly of a seagull."

Amaya watched as fetid flesh sloughed off one of the body's arms and landed in the water with a splash. "I don't think they're even fit for seagulls."

Roach glanced at her the same way he used to on the *Brackish*, the debtor ship they had lived on for seven years. It was the look he got when she'd irritated Captain Zharo, or tried to steal extra biscuits from the larder, or signed up for the most difficult diving jobs.

"We won't end up there, if that's what you're worried about," he said as the ship sailed past the Sinner's Shelf. The water churned against the hull, churning like Amaya's insides. "You'll be under my protection."

"That doesn't change what happened," she whispered, staring at the jade ring on her finger. It fit perfectly; she had her mother's hands. "That I'm complicit in what happened in Moray."

It had been a mistake to put her trust in the wrong people. A mistake to bring counterfeit coins to the city, to begin its destruction from the inside out.

"You didn't ruin everything. Being in Moray made you too dramatic."

"Thanks, Roach," she said in a deadpan voice. "You always make me feel better."

He laughed and swept his hair off his forehead, but the wind just blew it back. "Sorry, sorry. And I told you, call me Remy. That's my real name."

"Right." Once a child had been sold to the *Brackish*, Captain

3

Zharo made it a tradition to replace their names with the name of a bug. Amaya had been Silverfish, and Remy had been Roach. It was proving difficult to get out of the habit, to reclaim their personhoods from a man who had done all he could to make them feel like insects, easily squashed under his heel.

A man who was now dead, at least. Amaya had seen the light leave his eyes. Even if she hadn't been the one to do it, there was still satisfaction in having witnessed it, the closing of the worst chapter of her life.

Amaya opened her mouth to ask Remy when they would reach land, but the words stuck in her throat as someone climbed out of the companionway.

Cayo squinted in the bright light, shielding his eyes with a hand. He spotted Amaya and Remy by the railing, and his gaze locked on Amaya's.

She inhaled, her chest flooded with that now familiar cocktail of guilt and shame. There was only so much space you could give someone on a ship this size, but Amaya had tried to leave him alone, to let him care for his sister and talk with the others, until he felt ready to confront her.

But he hadn't. And she was too much of a coward to be the one to approach him.

They conversed mostly in glances and short sentences, emotionless and to the point. It made her shoulders ache with the force of everything she wanted to say, to again tell him she was sorry for her deception, for her role in spreading the counterfeit money, and that he wasn't without blame himself.

Cayo's dark eyes narrowed slightly. Then he turned to the railing, dismissing her altogether.

"Ouch," Remy murmured behind his hand. "I think the point goes to him that round."

Amaya fought against the urge to kick him where it hurt most.

Cayo gripped the railing and searched the water. The sunlight highlighted his cheekbones and nose, the breeze playing with his silky black hair. When he caught sight of the Sinner's Shelf, his eyes widened.

"What in the hells?" He looked to Remy, still ignoring Amaya. "Is this normal?"

"Asks the boy from Moray, where they used to dangle thieves and Landless from the sea wall," Remy pointed out.

"That was a long time ago." Cayo leaned his hip against the railing and crossed his arms. "I'm not bringing Soria up until we've passed that thing."

"How is she?" Amaya asked. Cayo's younger sister, stricken with a grave case of ash fever, had been holed up in a cabin the entire voyage. She had only come out onto the deck a few times, insisting on fresh air even as Cayo hovered nearby like an overprotective nurse.

Cayo's jaw tightened, and his throat bobbed. "Fine," he eventually murmured, still not looking in her direction.

"Another point," Remy whispered to Amaya.

This time she did kick him.

Someone else joined them at the railing: Liesl. The girl was a few years older than Amaya, originally from the Rain Empire, her skin a soft shade of brown and her hair a rich chestnut. Although she normally liked to swathe her generously curvy body in dresses, she had reluctantly agreed to settle for more practical trousers and a blouse while on board the *Marionette*.

"Trousers are so *confining*," she had huffed on their second day at sea. "Honestly, they should all be banned."

"Then what would the menfolk wear?" Remy had asked.

"I've heard of a settlement far to the north where men wear thick skirts," she'd said. "Let's start bringing that into fashion."

The sunlight glinted on Liesl's glasses as she held on to the railing, frowning in the direction of the Sinner's Shelf. The sea wind tousled her curly hair, which she had pulled back from her round, pretty face.

"They don't just hang murderers and the like there," she said. "It's also where they take the dissenters. The revolutionaries."

Amaya was not surprised by the bitter edge in her voice. Liesl was Landless, a sentence decreed to someone who warranted exile. While most Landless were barred from the entire mainland, Liesl was only exiled from the Rain Empire, her former home.

When Liesl had brought it up, Remy had waved the concern away, stating she didn't need to worry.

"I very much do," Liesl had argued. "We don't have papers. I'm a wanted criminal."

"See this?" Remy had held up an envelope, its wax seal broken and chipped. "An official clearance letter from the navy. They gave it to me before I left for Moray, since they knew I'd likely be returning with counterfeit samples. It means I won't be stopped by the dock inspectors."

"That's good news for the coins," Liesl had drawled, "but what about the humans you're bringing back?"

"The officers told me I could bring back any and all persons related to the incident. And that includes all of you."

Liesl had seemed skeptical, and even now her eyes were pinched as she stared at the approaching port. Still, there was a quiet determination in her posture, in the way she held on to the gunwale. As if she had been waiting for this moment a long, long time.

Amaya still didn't know Liesl's full story, only that the girl had joined Boon and the others to try to reverse her Landless sentence. At the mere thought of Boon, a storm brewed in Amaya's chest.

"Did you kill him?" she had demanded, facing off against him between the glaring moonlight and the dark water. "Did you kill my father?"

And Boon had looked at her, and she had known. The brutal tear within her had ripped open further, bleeding fresh.

"In a sense," he'd said, "I suppose I did."

Amaya gritted her teeth. The ache in her jaw fed her helpless fury. Boon had escaped, and they were off chasing a supposed miracle. If Baleine really could offer a cure for Soria, or a lead as to whom Mercado had been sending the counterfeit money to, she supposed this would all be worth it. It still didn't feel like enough.

"This is your home country, isn't it?" Remy asked Liesl, breaking through Amaya's thoughts.

"Yes. I grew up here. Lived through the riots and the propaganda and the scandals. Chalier was one of the last nations to fall to the Rain Empire. We resisted for as long as we could, but..."

She glanced back at the Sinner's Shelf, her expression dark. "Sometimes it's wiser to bend a knee than lose your head," she finished.

Amaya's frown deepened. *I'd rather lose the head.*

"Should we expect some sort of...conflict?" Cayo asked.

Liesl shook her head. "Most of the dissenters were dealt with. They either went into hiding, got turned Landless, or..." She gestured toward the shelf. "The Rain Empire's navy rolled in. They control most of the coastline, and the local authorities patrol the rest."

"I'm sorry." Remy self-consciously plucked at his naval jacket. It was blue with white trimming and possibly the nicest piece of clothing he had ever owned. "My home in the Sun Empire was overtaken, too. But our coward of a prime minister surrendered before we could even try to fight back."

"I don't blame you for taking refuge in their ranks," Liesl said. "This world is a game of survival. You take it wherever you can find it."

Amaya brushed a thumb over the small tattoo of a knife on her wrist. *Survive.*

"Remy's letter might get you through the port," Cayo said, "but you're Landless. You were exiled from your country. From the entire empire. Won't it be difficult to stay in the city?"

"Perhaps, but I've changed since then," Liesl said. "Even if they have broadsheets still up—which I doubt—they'll be hungrier for the bigger catches. And it's not easy to catch me."

"They did once," Amaya pointed out.

"Only because I let myself get caught." Liesl swallowed. "But not this time. This time, I make up for my past mistakes."

Amaya frowned as Remy straightened beside her.

"We should get ready to dock," he said. "Cayo, help me with these sails."

Cayo blinked at him, either confused by what he was supposed to be doing or offended at being given an order. Remy offered him a mocking bow.

"Sorry, I meant please help me with these sails, *Lord Mercado.*"

Cayo pushed away from the railing with a scowl, opening his mouth to retort. Amaya beat him to it.

"I'll do it," she told Remy. "Cayo, you...you go help Soria get ready."

Their eyes met briefly. Just a flash of contact, a light shining off a mirror or a gem. One moment of brightness, of hope, before it went dark and cold again.

Cayo nodded stiffly and descended the companionway. Amaya released a breath, turning to help Remy prepare.

They were here to chase a miracle, but the true miracle would be finding a way to undo all her mistakes.

## 2

A hungry heart is incapable of affection
if the hearts around it are starving.

—REHANESE PROVERB

Cayo's arms were sore, his nose was bleeding, and his sister was
dying.

The first was easy to explain: He had been helping Avi, a Landless man, do chores around the ship. When he was little, Cayo had
wanted nothing more than to steal one of his father's ships and sail
around the world. He hadn't expected there to be so much physical
labor involved, and now his muscles were crying out in regret.

Still, he couldn't help but remember how stubbornly he had clung
to that dream when he was young. To discover forgotten grottos and
hidden depths and legendary treasure.

And then Cayo had grown up, and the world had shown him that
it wasn't full of wonders. It was full of horrors.

He wasn't made for being a merchant, but maybe he wasn't made for sailing, either. Perhaps he wasn't made for anything, which was why he had filled all that empty potential inside him with alcohol and poor decisions.

"Cayo, you're bleeding."

He shook himself at Soria's words and saw a few drops had fallen onto the sheet of her bed. Cayo cursed and reached for his handkerchief before realizing he had given it to Soria.

She handed it back to him silently, watching him tip his head back to make the flow stop. Cayo closed his eyes and pressed the handkerchief to his nose, annoyance humming through him like a struck chord. The others were already moving about and yelling commands on deck.

"I think it's the air," Soria said, her voice weak and cracking. "It's much drier here than it is in Moray."

He'd noticed it, too, when he had stood at the railing. Whereas Moray was always wet and humid, the climate here was cooler, drier. Even the sea was darker.

Cayo swallowed, tasting copper. By the time he removed the stained handkerchief, the bleeding had already stopped.

"Sorry," he murmured, stuffing the handkerchief in his pocket. "I'll find you another one."

Soria smiled and shook her head to say it didn't matter. She tried to speak but ended up coughing instead. Although the sound was familiar by now, it still filled the small cabin like a storm siren, wrenching itself from Soria's chest with ragged inhalations and shuddering gasps.

Cayo held her hand through it. It was the only thing he could do. Dolefully he gazed at the gray splotch behind her ear, creeping its way down her neck and over her throat like a possessive hand.

11

It would strangle the life out of his sister eventually.

He aggressively shoved the thought down, down, into a locked box between the ones he reserved for Amaya and his father.

When Soria's fit was over, he held a cup of water to her lips. Her lips were dry and chapped, her throat struggling to swallow as she took tiny sips. Her silken black hair—hair she had been proudly growing for years, dutifully maintained with coconut oil and sedr— was disheveled and damp with sweat. He would have to cover her head to make sure she didn't get chilled.

"I'm sorry," Soria whispered as he helped her sit on the side of the bed. Her body shook as she tried to support her own weight.

"There's nothing to be sorry for." His voice came out rougher than he wanted it to. "I don't mind, Soria. You're not a burden to me."

She had admitted this particular fear during their week at sea, crying in frustration that she could no longer do simple tasks on her own, that she had to rely on him for almost everything. That because she had done something as silly as running her fingers through the golden coins of her dowry—all counterfeit, all made by their father— she had ended up like this.

"I want to take care of you," he said, gripping her shoulder—as much for reassurance as to keep her sitting upright. "I want to make sure you get the help you need. If you start up that nonsense again, I won't hesitate to cut your hair."

She gasped slightly, reaching for her long locks. "You wouldn't."

"I would. Now let's get you dressed."

He helped her into a plain woolen dress and a pair of worn leather slippers, then covered her with a cloak, pulling the hood up to shield her from the wind. When they were ready, he cast around the room to make sure there was nothing they were forgetting.

But he had left Moray with no possessions. He had nothing.

Nothing except Soria, who was already shuddering with cold as he lifted her into his arms and climbed up onto the deck.

Their small crew was busy with preparations. There was Avi, the Kharian man whose sole purpose in life seemed to be making Cayo do chores; Liesl, the young woman who knew far more than she ever let on; and Deadshot, the half-Ledese, half–Sun Empire sharpshooter who only showed a hint of softness when speaking with Liesl, her lover. There was Remy the naval soldier, a former inhabitant of the debtor ship Cayo's father had once owned and Amaya's oldest friend.

And then there was Amaya herself. Not Countess Yamaa, as Cayo had known her in Moray, but a stranger who had wrapped them together in lies and deceit.

Cayo stood useless and flustered in the middle of the commotion, not quite sure what to do as the ship neared the docks. Remy waved a small blue flag from the prow, which was answered with a similar flag from the docks.

As Amaya helped Deadshot roll out the anchor, Cayo couldn't resist watching her, her movements strong and sure, arms flexing and hair swaying. When she felt his gaze she tilted her face up to meet it, eyes dark and searching. It was a punch to the gut, a shot of confusing, nausea-ridden desire.

Cayo turned his head away. Soria noticed and sighed.

"I know," his sister said, her voice hoarse from coughing. "It was difficult for me to forgive her, too."

Cayo scoffed. "She's the reason we're in this mess."

"*Father* is the reason we're in this mess." Soria shifted in his arms, expression bitter at the memory of Cayo telling her what exactly Kamon Mercado had done to the city of Moray. To *them*. How he had

13

been willing to let his only daughter die to cover up the secret that he was behind the counterfeit currency. "She lied to us. She spread the fake money. But you know as well as I do that she wasn't the mastermind behind this. She's hurting as much as we are. She did what she had to do for her family. You'd do the same."

Cayo tried not to think about how he had gone crawling to the Slum King to help pay for Soria's medicine. "It's not the same. And besides, how do you know?"

"I spoke to her," Soria said, her tone light.

"You—what? When?"

"Does it matter? I like her. I can see why you do, too."

"I don't like her." Cayo forced himself not to look in Amaya's direction again, even as he felt her glance like the too-close brush of a flame. "Maybe I did once, but she isn't the person I thought she was. I don't know who she is now."

"Then maybe you should make the effort to find out."

Cayo frowned, but before he could reply there was a call to haul out the gangplank.

They had officially made it to Chalier. The Rain Empire.

Moray's enemy.

Remy greeted the dock inspector who boarded the vessel and took stock of the ship. Cayo noticed Liesl twitch, as if resisting the urge to cross her arms defensively. A bead of sweat rolled down the young woman's temple as Deadshot stepped closer to her, protective.

Remy took out the envelope from his officers and presented it to the dock inspector, who merely skimmed its contents. The inspector's eyes narrowed on Soria, still held in Cayo's arms.

"Li gres?" the inspector asked of Remy, who nodded and replied in Soléne, the common language of the Rain Empire. Cayo had learned some Soléne as he was growing up and was able to catch a few words: *sick, orders, hospital*.

The inspector shook his head. Remy launched into an argument Cayo couldn't follow. Liesl tensed, and Deadshot grasped her elbow as if to prevent her from leaping over the railing.

Finally, the inspector approached Cayo and Soria. Cayo forced himself to stay still as the man pinned a square of yellow cloth to Soria's cloak.

"It's to let others know she's infected," Remy explained. "They're starting to buckle down on quarantining sick travelers, but they're letting us through since I'm with the navy."

Soria sighed. "Yellow's not my color."

The inspector gave Remy a slip of parchment, no doubt a docking permit. Then they were allowed to descend to the port below, Liesl exhaling in relief.

"At least this is good for something," Remy said to Amaya, tapping the chest of his naval jacket.

"Don't let it go to your head," she said. "It's big enough as it is."

"I'll have you know my head is the perfect shape. Artists come from all over wanting to study its exquisite form."

Cayo tried to block out their easy banter by getting his first look at Baleine. Evening had begun to settle in, the gold of sunset washed away with mellow blues and grays. Cayo was used to the smell of docks—the briny air, the damp wood, the decomposing sea life—but somehow here it seemed stronger, the odor practically attacking his nose.

"What *is* that?" Soria asked as she pinched her nostrils closed.

Once they moved away from the docks, they got their answer: There was a massive fish market up ahead, taking over the entirety of the square that led to the harbor. They gaped at the size of it, at the people rushing to purchase fish for dinner, at the fishermen only just beginning to put out their catches after a long day at sea. Wooden crates and barrels were filled with melting ice, displaying everything from bass to oysters to crabs, all lined up in neat rows. Cayo peered into a barrel full of lobsters that snapped irately at him as he passed.

There were plenty of fish markets in Moray, but none of this scale. Typically fish were bought in bulk there, the majority of the goods purchased from debtor ships.

At the reminder, Cayo snuck a look at Amaya. She glowered at the fish around her, fingers twitching as if longing to hold something— or perhaps simply remembering the shape of a gutting knife.

Past the fish market, the wind picked up and graced them with fresher air. Soria shivered at the chill.

"The military hospital isn't far," Remy said over his shoulder. "Just stick close to me. And...don't stare."

Cayo didn't ask for elaboration. They walked down a cobblestone street lined with shops, lanterns hanging above the doors, highlighting signs and store names in an amber glow. They passed a wine shop, a tailor, and an apothecary, their windows revealing tantalizing displays of what waited for customers inside. One of the shops bore a symbol over its doors instead of a name: a circle containing a star. Cayo stared in curiosity at the hanging herbs and sachet bundles in the window, the jars of black sand and hunks of granite. They told him nothing of what sort of shop it was.

"Oh," Soria breathed suddenly, clutching her chest.

Cayo saw where she was looking and felt his stomach twist. There were people sitting slumped against a store front, their clothes ragged and torn, the hoods of their cloaks pulled up to hide their heads. They held hats and bowls in their laps, silently begging even as wary citizens gave them a wide berth.

Their hands were splotched with gray.

Feeling their gaze, one of the cloaked figures lifted his head. His face was mottled with gray, one of his eyes completely overtaken with veins of silver and black. It was as if he were already in some state of decay, his skin slowly withering and rotting.

Soria shuddered and hid her face against Cayo's chest. Remy shook his head.

"I told you not to stare," he muttered.

"I didn't think it would be this bad," Cayo said, still in shock as they passed the beggars. "I haven't seen any cases of ash fever this extreme in Moray."

"They keep them better quarantined there," Remy said. "That's what they did with the prince before he died. But now that we know the handling of coins is linked to the fever, I'm not sure how much good it will do."

"But you're sure that we can find help here," Cayo said, half a question.

"Certainly more than you could find in Moray. It looks bad on the outside, but the experimental treatments the alchemists are working on do more than the medicine currently being produced in Moray." Remy hesitated, then put a hand on Cayo's shoulder. "Your sister will be in good care."

Cayo still didn't quite trust him, but he hoped he was right.

After another minute of walking, Remy led them down a side street that ended at a wide white stone building. There was a crest above a set of double doors: a cutlass and a bayonet forming an X within a circle of stars. The symbol of the Rain Empire's military.

All along the narrow street hung thuribles that released a sweet-smelling smoke into the air. Cayo, already breathless from carrying Soria, coughed as he got a good lungful of it; it smelled like fermented berries mixed with a bitter herb.

"What are these for?" Avi asked, poking a thurible. It swung on its iron peg.

"Just a preventative measure," Remy said. "The doctors think the incense will help keep the fever from spreading. No idea if it actually works, but at least it's calming." Then he turned to Cayo. "You'll have to go by a fake family name. You and your sister both. I'm afraid of what might happen if the name Mercado gets passed around here."

Cayo and Soria exchanged a look.

"Lin," Cayo said. "It was our mother's maiden name."

"Perfect. Let's go."

Cayo took a deep breath of that sickly sweet air and followed behind him, the others deciding to wait outside.

Except Amaya. She trailed after them, her face unreadable. Cayo almost told her to go back to her coconspirators, that he didn't want her to come, but he couldn't do it. Some part of him knew it would be a lie, his own personal betrayal.

The hospital was completely overrun. As soon as he stepped inside, Cayo was assaulted by the warmth of the place, the oppressive heat of bodies burning with fever. Although the scent of incense lingered in his nose, it couldn't cut through the odor of sweat that permeated the building, carrying undertones of laundered linen and urine.

Dozens of beds crowded the walls, and cots and pallets had been dragged out into the middle of the floor to form haphazard rows. Nurses wandered through the maze as they tended to the soldiers and service members turned patients, reminding Cayo of the gardeners at Mercado Manor as they watered the flower beds. His ears flooded with the din of coughing, groaning, and crying, making him hold Soria tighter against his chest.

He was supposed to leave his sister *here*?

"Remind me why we can't go to a normal hospital?" Cayo asked of Remy.

"The civilian hospitals are even worse than this," Remy replied with a hint of ice in his voice. "Which is why so many of the afflicted have taken to the streets."

"Gods," Amaya murmured behind Cayo. She watched a nearby nurse spoon feed a gray-splotched man. The nurse looked as if she hadn't slept in years, her blue uniform rumpled and stained. "How can it be this bad already?"

"It's a city. What's more, it's a port city." Remy shrugged, but Cayo noticed the worry in his eyes. "It spread with a vengeance."

"Officer Aldano," said a rich, smooth voice. "Welcome back."

The owner of the voice was a large, handsome woman with black skin and her hair done up in a crown of braids. There were small white dots tattooed in semicircles under her eyes, as well as on her knuckles. Although she wore a similar uniform to the nurses, hers bore a badge with that same crest above the archway outside.

Remy pressed a hand to his chest in a sign of respect. "Mother Hilas. You're looking well."

The woman arched a thick, dark eyebrow at him. "I've had two hours of sleep in the last two days and no time to bathe. I look like shit."

Amaya snorted, trying to hide it behind her hand.

Remy didn't falter, putting on a thousand-sena grin. "Always right to the point. In that case, I'm afraid I have a favor to ask of you."

The woman, Mother Hilas, took in Cayo and Soria. She sighed.

"What about your mission?" Mother Hilas said. "When the officers told us you were going to Moray, you promised us results."

"And you'll get them. I need to report to my superior officers, but before that, I had to get her settled." Remy gestured to Soria. "The Lins. Brother and sister. They came all the way from Moray for help." He clasped his hands together. "Don't make them have traveled all this way for nothing."

The woman glared at Remy, muttering something at him in Ledese. Then she sighed again and turned to Cayo.

"How long has your sister been sick?"

"A-about two months, I think." Cayo's voice came out hoarse, but he didn't think it was from the incense. "I've been giving her prescription medicine from Moray, but it only staves off the symptoms. It doesn't cure it."

"Of course it doesn't," Mother Hilas said. "There is no cure. Not yet, at least." She looked pointedly at Remy.

"My findings are going to pay off," Remy assured her.

"If you say so." She turned on her heel. "Follow me."

She led them out of the main hospital floor, up a flight of stairs to a quieter, darker wing. She opened a door for them and Cayo walked in, Soria wheezing and half-asleep in his arms.

The room was small, but at least there was a window facing the street. There were two beds, one in each corner, but only one of them was occupied. A boy a few years younger than Cayo was asleep in the bed nearest the door, his entire chin and lips covered in gray.

"We keep these rooms for afflicted family members of military personnel," Mother Hilas explained, her voice soft so that she didn't wake the boy. "We can place your sister here, as well as care for her, but you will have to pay upfront."

"I could claim her as a family member," Remy offered.

"Even the families have to pay. The hospital needs to keep running somehow. I'll go fetch the administrator and we can discuss."

Cayo wandered over to the bed by the window. He gently set Soria down, arms aching from carrying her through the city. Her eyes were closed, but when he smoothed away her hair they fluttered open.

"Where are we?" she mumbled sleepily.

"In a safe place," he answered. "They'll care for you here while they work on a cure."

Soria struggled to suppress a cough. "But what...about you?"

He took her hands in his to warm her cold fingers. "I'll be fine. We'll figure something out."

A presence at his side made him look up. Amaya had her arms crossed, but she tried to smile for Soria.

"Will you be all right here?" Amaya asked her. "I know it's not ideal...."

Cayo frowned, but Soria gave a weak laugh and nodded.

"Definitely better than the boat," Soria croaked.

"Ship," Amaya corrected, lips quirking upward as if it were a shared joke between them.

Mother Hilas returned with a thin man with reddish hair and a pointed chin.

"I hate to be the messenger of doom here," Remy whispered, "but how exactly are you going to pay?"

Cayo reached into his pocket and drew out his watch, the one his father had given him what felt like a lifetime ago.

He stood and approached Mother Hilas and the hospital administrator. The latter smiled in greeting.

"Hello, Mr. Lin. Mother Hilas has explained your situation to me. We're more than happy to accommodate your sister, but as I'm sure she already told you, we will need payment to cover some of the costlier expenses."

Cayo handed them the pocket watch. "Will this cover them?"

The administrator's eyes widened slightly as he took it from Cayo, examining the fine craftsmanship. If nothing else, Kamon Mercado had an eye for valuable things.

"This will do," the administrator agreed.

"You may visit your sister during the day, but we enforce a strict two-hour visitation limit," Mother Hilas told him. "We haven't been able to determine if the fever can spread from person to person, so it's for your protection as well as the patients'."

Cayo wanted to argue, but one look at her stern face made him think better of it. Sighing, he nodded and returned to Soria, taking up her hand.

"What did you give her?" his sister demanded, her words little more than breath.

He recalled the day his father had given him that pocket watch. Cayo's heart had lifted, thinking he had finally found some way to make his father proud.

If only he had known then how wrong he'd been.

"Nothing important," Cayo told her.

# 3

*The guilt...the teeth-gnashing madness of it...how has
it not laid into you like wolves, like the bitter reminder of
our ancestors' failures?*

—LETTER BETWEEN FACTIONS OF THE CHIHAN COUP, AFTER THE
FALL OF THE REHANESE THRONE

Cayo had wanted to stay the night with Soria to get her settled
in, but Mother Hilas—who oversaw the entire hospital staff—
had firmly put her foot down. Now he was quiet and withdrawn on
their way out, clenching and unclenching his hands, staring at the
cobblestone street as if lost.

Amaya suppressed the urge to hold her nose as they passed the
thuribles. Her mother had used to light sticks of incense on important
days, or when the moon was full, or simply when she needed her
prayers to be heard. The thin sticks would produce ribbons of smoke

23

that smelled of jasmine and warm wood. Amaya's nose would start itching after a while, and she'd always complained.

But now she found that she missed the particular smell. That she would have paid an exorbitant price to relive something she had once found so annoying.

Liesl, Avi, and Deadshot waited for them at the end of the street. And they weren't alone. A tall, lanky boy around Liesl's age leaned against the nearest wall, his arms crossed and one foot propped up, a posture so casual it seemed calculated.

When he noticed them, he broke out into a wide grin, revealing a chipped tooth. He had the same soft brown skin as Liesl, his hair dark and curly. His clothes were rough spun and shoddily mended, the toes of his boots so worn they were likely to turn to holes any day now.

"This is your clever crew, is it?" the boy drawled in oddly accented Rehanese, pushing himself to his full height. Amaya had to crane her head back to look at him, as did Cayo, who seemed particularly displeased about it. "Not happy to see a bluecoat, though."

Remy stiffened. "Who's this?"

Liesl gave the new boy a warning look. "This is Jasper. He's a... friend. Sort of."

Jasper placed a hand to his chest. "*Sort of?* You wound me."

"I *will* wound you if you don't stop playing cute."

"I'll have you know this is hardly playing. You're merely getting the full Jasper Experience, equal parts dastardly charm and roguish good looks." He even posed, puffing out his lips a little as if that's all it took to look sultry.

"I wanna shoot him," Deadshot mumbled, hand hovering over one of her pistols.

"Please don't. Bullet wounds aren't very attractive. A *scar*, though—"

"Jasper." Liesl's voice cracked like a whip.

He sighed and lifted his hands. Or rather, hand—his left arm ended in a stump, the sleeve tucked and pinned. "All right, all right. I see my allure is wasted here. You said you need a place to lie low? I got just the thing."

"Hold on." Remy stepped forward. "I thought I was going to try to get you accommodations at the billet?"

Liesl shook her head. "With my background, it's too risky to stay there. You know that as well as I do."

"So instead you're going to get help from someone who I can only assume is a crook?"

"Hey now," Jasper said with a pout.

"The two of us go back," Liesl assured him. "Trust me, on the outside he's all bluster, but on the inside he's all business."

"That's what I'm afraid of," Remy muttered. "The two of you go back to *what*, exactly?"

"The revolution." She smirked at Jasper, who smirked back. "Let's just say we've been through all the hells together." Hearing the hint of pain in her voice, Deadshot put a hand on Liesl's shoulder.

Remy didn't look convinced. "We have a better chance at cracking the counterfeit problem if we all stay together."

"We'll still be together. Plus, we now have Jasper's resources." Liesl nodded to Remy's pocket. "Show him."

Remy hesitated, but at her insistence he took a handkerchief from his pocket and opened it carefully. Inside was a golden sena coin—or what looked like one. Beside it was a black disc, the core that would only be revealed if the coin were washed of its exterior golden plating.

"Whatever coats these discs is alchemical," Remy said. "And it causes ash fever. After looking through Mercado's finances, we know he's been siphoning money to a foreign investor somewhere here in the Rain Empire. Problem is, we don't know who yet. They're just listed as *the Benefactor.*"

Jasper had been staring curiously at the disc, but then his head jerked up. "Did you say Mercado?"

Remy narrowed his eyes as Cayo tensed. "Is the name familiar?"

"I've heard it here and there when I do underground jobs. It's mostly tied to the currency exchange offices. If you're looking for this Benefactor chump, they'll likely be here, in Baleine."

Liesl's eyes widened. "How do you know this?"

"I got some friends who have contacts in the Financial District." Jasper ran his hand through his curly hair, cocking his hip at an easy angle. "They kept seeing large sums going to and coming from Moray, and wouldn't you know it, there were monthly payments being routed to one K. Mercado."

Cayo frowned. "Routed *to*? You mean my f—Mercado was receiving money as well?"

"Looks like. But at least we can trace the source of it to Baleine."

Remy was still evaluating Jasper. "Can we really trust what this man has to say? What if this is...I don't know, a trap or something?"

"We do have weapons," Avi pointed out. "And in case you've forgotten, we're crooks as well."

Remy opened his mouth, glanced at Amaya, and cleared his throat. "Right. Guess I did forget."

"Which puts you in great company." Jasper slung an arm around Cayo, who started at the contact. "Though I like to think of myself as more of a connoisseur of devious deeds."

Remy rubbed his face. "Fine. But I'm coming with you to see where you're staying."

"I have a strict no bluecoat policy. Even for one as cute as you." Jasper winked as Remy grimaced.

"He comes with us," Amaya said. "He won't run his mouth. If he does, I'll teach him a lesson."

Remy's surprised "Amaya!" came at the same time as Jasper's loud laugh.

"I like you." Jasper pointed to Amaya, his arm still slung around Cayo's shoulders. "You look mean, and I like that. Gives me the shivers."

"Can we please get going?" Liesl demanded as she pushed up her glasses. "My partner has an itchy trigger finger." Deadshot caressed her pistol to further the point.

"Come along, then, clever crooks."

Jasper finally released Cayo and turned to lead the way. Amaya didn't miss the look that Liesl gave her, the slight quirk of her eyebrow.

*For a moment, you sounded like Boon*, that look told her.

Jasper led them to a dark street lined with tenement buildings. Amaya was used to seeing touches of the Rain Empire in Moray, but to be surrounded by an entire city of foreign architecture was something else altogether. Whereas in Moray they used wood and limestone and gold, here they used iron and marble and brick.

Jasper counted the buildings, then opened the door of the third one on the left. "This one should have an empty floor."

"Do you own these?" Remy demanded.

Jasper didn't answer, just laughed as if it were the funniest thing he'd ever heard. Remy's frown deepened.

"It's not for forever," Amaya reminded him softly. "We need all the help we can get."

"*I* could have helped you."

"You have. You are. But you know we can't stay at the billet, not when most of us are Landless." The thought alone of being near so many soldiers was enough to make her shoulders tighten.

Up a flight of rotting stairs and through another door was an apartment, drafty and barely furnished. It consisted of three rooms: a main chamber and two bedrooms, each with two small beds. The center room held a table with a few battered chairs and an ancient-looking stove.

"It's not much, but it's certainly better than what you could find on short notice," Jasper said to Liesl.

"Thanks, Jas. What do we owe?"

"Nothing." Jasper took a step back and swiped his thumb under his nose, grinning. "I still owe you, remember? Consider this reimbursement."

"You just don't want to be in my debt anymore."

He formed his hand into a gun and pretended to shoot it at her. "Right in one. I shudder to think of the interest I've accrued."

Liesl led Jasper to the door, exchanging a few hushed words as Amaya and the others looked around. Amaya thought longingly of her bedroom at the estate in Moray. She had lived for seven years on a ship, sleeping on a hammock among dozens of other children in damp and moldy surroundings, but somehow only a few months of luxury had softened her.

She stole a glimpse at Cayo, wondering how someone with eigh-teen *years* of luxury would adjust to their current situation. But to her surprise, his nose wasn't wrinkled in distaste, and his hands weren't twitching as if longing to wash them. Instead, he was idly tracing the wooden grain of the table over and over with that same lost expression.

When Liesl came back, Deadshot crossed her arms. "What was that about him owing you?"

Liesl pulled out a chair at the table and sat. "The two of us used to be part of a coalition here in Baleine. He got into a spot of trouble, and I helped get him out."

Amaya leaned her hands on the table. The old wood creaked ominously. "A coalition? To do what?"

"What else? To get the Rain Empire out of Chalier. Our nation staved off their forces for as long as we could, resisting total conquest. But in the end..." She gestured to the grimy window that offered a view of the street. "We were plucked up like a grape and swallowed. Now we have to answer to the military and follow the laws of the empire's governing forces. There were riots in the streets. Executions."

Amaya thought back to the bodies on the Sinner's Shelf.

"That was only a decade ago," Avi noted. "I'm amazed the city is as functional as it is."

"The citizens of Chalier aren't easily cowed," Liesl said. "Baleine is subdued because there's a naval base here, but there are still pockets of civil unrest throughout the country. Who knows if the fever's knocked their numbers down, though."

"Speaking of which, I need to go report my findings," Remy said. "I'll come by tomorrow and let you know what the officers say."

"I'll walk with you." Amaya wasn't quite sure why she blurted it out. Maybe she wanted time away from the others; maybe she just wanted to see more of the city and get her land legs again, to reacquaint

29

herself with a sturdy ground and not one that swayed beneath her feet. Either way, Remy nodded and the two of them headed out.

At first they walked quietly, simply taking in the streets limned in moonlight and torchlight, the people tugging their coats closed and pulling their hats down to ward against the wind. Amaya shivered, not used to the chillier weather. She would need to acquire a coat.

"I haven't explored much of the city yet," Remy said. "But Baleine's said to have some of the best luxury shops in Chalier. There's a whole district devoted to them. There's even a district like the Vice Sector in Moray, although smaller and less...intense."

She blinked. "You went to the Vice Sector?"

"I had to. The intelligence officers trained me to investigate every possible lead."

"That's an odd way of saying *gamble*."

"I hate gambling. Why risk losing perfectly good money that you could use for snacks instead? No, it was because most of the counterfeit distribution came from the Vice Sector, so I had to take a look."

Amaya sobered at the reminder. She stuffed her hands into her pockets as she thought back to all those chests of gold at the estate. Fake gold. Fake money.

All given to her by Boon, who had known exactly what it was. He had wanted her to spread it as far and wide as she could.

And she had, damn her. She had fallen right into his plan, so seduced by the idea of revenge that she hadn't even bothered to consider he had been double-crossing her. That him knowing her father's name should have been the first red flag.

"Hey." Remy nudged her side. "The counterfeiting isn't your fault. You didn't know."

30

"I should have looked into it. There was no good reason for him to have that much gold. I thought he'd just...stolen it."

"Like I said, you didn't know. And besides, it's not just Boon who made counterfeit money; Mercado did as well. And this Benefactor is in on it, too."

They entered what must have been the shopping district Remy had mentioned. Amaya spotted more cloaked figures on the street, coughing and groaning as they sat or laid against the sides of buildings. One of them shambled up to a woman leaving a store, their gray hands extended to plead for money. The woman gasped and stumbled over herself to get as far from them as possible.

"If we find this Benefactor, do you think the circulation of counterfeit coins will stop?" Amaya asked.

"That's the plan. Although how to actually achieve that, I have no clue. And it's not just here—we have to think about Moray, too. The city is already bankrupt, except they don't know it yet. It's only a matter of time until the counterfeits are exposed and the city becomes financially dependent on one of the empires."

"What about Rehan?"

"Moray was annexed from the republic a long time ago. Since then it was colonized by both empires. I don't think Rehan would want to get involved in a potential war, especially since they're land-locked between two naval powers and their military presence is mostly directed at border patrol."

Amaya was shaking her head when something caught her eye. She slowly drifted toward a shop display window that was stocked with three headless mannequins in various poses. They each wore a dress, but it was the one in the middle that had snagged her attention.

It was made of deep blue velvet, the sleeves designed so that they hung seductively off the shoulders and left the full width of the collarbone bare. The rest of the sleeves tapered off into a sheer fabric studded with clear, glittering gems that covered the whole length of the mannequin's arms. The bust was similarly encrusted with those tiny gems, the design spiraling across the full, puffed skirt like a star.

She pressed her fingertips to the glass, wondering what it would look like on her. Wondering how many people would bend to her will with just one glance.

"Miss being a countess?" Remy asked at her side.

Amaya was shocked to realize that some part of her did. Not the constant frills and airs, but the power she had felt when she could command a room with nothing but a dress, a smile, and a bit of makeup.

"She was never really me," Amaya said, dropping her hand back to her side. "But she got things done. And she had a nice wardrobe."

"Well, if I ever get promoted, maybe I'll buy it for you."

She snorted. "Sure."

She took his hand in hers, thankful for the chance to have him beside her again, despite the situation they were in.

Remy had found his own path forward, but Amaya had nothing so clear cut. Instead she had a belly full of anger and spite. The weight of the knife at her hip grew heavier with anticipation the more she thought of it, the more she allowed herself to steep in that blistering feeling of betrayal.

They had to find the Benefactor, but she had her own personal mission: to find Boon and make him admit to his crimes. To learn the truth about what had happened to her father.

To pay him back for everything he'd done.

4

*The magician needed a way to reach the stars. He asked the clouds for a chariot, but they drifted off without an answer. He asked the water for a sea foam horse, but its waves pushed him away. Finally, the mountain whispered that there was a way, and that is how the magician found the stairs of tourmaline cut into its side, glittering upward toward the sky.*

—"NERALIA OF THE CLOUDS," AN ORAL STORY ORIGINATING FROM THE LEDE ISLANDS

Cayo woke in a strange bed and tried not to panic.

He had done this his first morning on the *Marionette*, heart hammering in his chest and breaths tangled in his throat. The swaying of the ship had made his stomach lurch, the unfamiliar wooden walls closing in on him like the sides of a coffin.

He had never reacted that way before, not even on the worst

mornings after all-nighters in the Vice Sector. He had woken on top of tables, tangled in limbs, and once in a pile of trash, but now all of a sudden a different bed had him unnerved.

It wasn't just the new walls, or the transition from the ship's hard pallet to the softer yet lumpier mattress—there were new smells, new sounds. His senses were momentarily overrun by the mustiness of the place, the creaking of floorboards from other tenants.

Cayo sat up and found Avi still asleep in the narrow bed across the room, the sheets pulled up to his chin and his black hair tousled.

"This is how it's going to work," Avi had said last night. "You're going to face the wall, I'm going to take off my binder and it's going to feel *great*, and you're not going to turn around until I'm done. After that, I don't care what you do. You can walk around stark naked if it pleases you."

Cayo had obediently turned to the wall while Avi changed. "I won't be walking around naked, trust me."

"Thank the gods for small miracles."

There were no windows in the bedroom, so Cayo fumbled in the dark to get out of bed and slip back into his trousers. He picked up his shoes and crept into the main room, not wanting to wake anyone on his way out.

But someone was already awake. Amaya sat at the stained table, a chipped ceramic mug before her. She looked up, startled, and he couldn't help but stare back. Thin golden light shone through the window, striping the table and the left side of Amaya's face.

"Oh," she said. A simple word, but the way it was said was far from simple. "What are you doing up so early?"

Cayo cleared his throat and began to put on his socks, wobbling slightly as he tried to balance on one foot. "I'm going to go check on Soria, to see how her first night in the hospital went."

"At this hour?" She glanced at the window, the sunlight shifting to the right side of her face. It turned her brown eyes from hickory to cinnamon. "I doubt Mother Hilas will let you through the doors yet. Also, maybe you should sit down while you do that."

Cayo was attempting to shove on one of his shoes while still standing. It was going poorly. But the alternative was to sit with Amaya at the table, and that felt like territory that should remain unexplored.

*Maybe you should make the effort to find out*, Soria had told him when he'd complained about not knowing who Amaya was anymore.

Sighing, Cayo gave up and pulled out a chair to sit across from her, lacing up his shoe. "What are *you* doing up so early?"

"Having tea." Amaya frowned at the steaming mug. "Or what passes for tea here."

"How did you find tea?"

She gestured to the shelf above the potbellied stove, which held some dusty boxes and jars. "There was a canister of it. It's stale, though. And tastes like dirt." Amaya cupped her hands around the mug to warm them. "But it's better than nothing."

Cayo would have killed for Narin, his family's footman, to bustle through the door with a proper tea tray. To savor the aromatic steam and maybe even nibble on a seed biscuit. He nearly said so out loud, then realized Amaya was no longer the countess. She would think him spoiled, unused to life's demands and the sacrifices they required.

And the worst part was that she would be right.

He tugged on his other shoe. Amaya watched him, her gaze steadier and calmer than he expected.

"I doubt the hospital will be open to visitors yet," she said. "We might as well use the time for something productive."

"What, like sharing stale tea?"

"Yes." Amaya lifted an eyebrow. "I can even teach you how to make it."

Cayo flushed. He wouldn't—*couldn't*—admit that he didn't know how to make his own tea. But Amaya took pity on him and got up before he could answer, taking down a second chipped mug and filling it with hot tea from a battered kettle.

"I expect you to do it on your own next time," she said, setting the mug before him. "You'll have all sorts of peasant tricks to learn now, Lord Mercado."

Cayo bristled. Where did she get off with that cold tone when *she* was the one who had betrayed *him*?

"Don't call me that," he growled. "And don't treat me like I'm some...some mindless dandy."

"I know you're not a mindless dandy." She sat back down, her voice and expression solemn. "But your life has been turned upside down, and I know what that's like. So." She wrapped her hands around her mug again. "Ask your questions."

Cayo took a deep breath and sipped at his tea, wincing at the heat and the muddy taste. He had a sudden flashback to the two of them at Laelia's Teahouse in Moray, he as Lord Mercado and she as Countess Yamaa, dressed in decadence and surrounded by extravagance. Now they were sipping substandard dirt water at a lopsided table.

"I guess I just have one question," he said at last. "Who are you?"

It caught her off guard. She sat back in her chair, the beam of sunlight slipping from her face as if she were taking off a mask.

"I'm not sure if I have a good answer for you," she admitted. "Since I'm still figuring it out myself."

"Try."

So she did. She told him about living in Moray as a girl, her Rehanese mother and her Kharian father, how the latter had taken out a loan from Kamon Mercado that he couldn't repay. How her father had been killed for collecting blackmail on Mercado. How her mother had tried to have Amaya smuggled out of the city before Mercado could use her to open her father's Widow Vault, where he stored his blackmail, and how she had been sold to the *Brackish* instead.

Cayo listened in silence as she described those seven years of her life. She hadn't been Amaya then—she had been Silverfish, a Water Bug, an indentured child determined to pay off her family's debt. She had met Remy, and the other children she had later freed, and had had to bend to the whims of the violent Captain Zharo.

"You killed him," Cayo said, the first time he'd interrupted.

Amaya's face hardened. It sent a small shiver through his body, and he wondered if he was catching a glimpse of Silverfish.

"I wish I had," she whispered. "I was going to. But Liesl did it for me. She said I wasn't ready to know what it felt like." Her hands moved restlessly on the tabletop, picking up and setting down her mug. "He abused children, Cayo."

He ducked his head. "I know." If he was being honest, he was glad the man was dead. The thought of Zharo lifting one of those ringed hands to a small child, let alone Amaya, was enough to make his gut boil.

"But I have killed," Amaya went on. "I stabbed Melchor, the man

who sold me to the *Brackish*. I thought it would make me feel better."
She paused. "It did, in some ways. But it wasn't enough."

Cayo glanced at the knife tattoo on her wrist. "Is this a habit of
yours? Stabbing people?"

"Why? Afraid you're on my list?"

"Am I?"

Amaya studied him, and the silence that brewed between them
was enough to get his heart pounding again.

"Not anymore," she said eventually.

Cayo copied her by wrapping his hands around his mug, letting
the heat bite his palms. "My father is, though."

"Yes. He ruined my family."

"He ruined his *own* family." Cayo glared at his reflection in the
bark-colored tea. "He ruined everything. And then he turned around
and told me it was all *my* fault. But...he's still my father. If you try to
kill him, I'm going to try to stop you."

Amaya nodded, as if expecting it. "The situation is different now.
I'm not working under Boon's orders." His jaw briefly clenched at the
man's name. "But I still don't know what I'll do if I encounter Kamon
Mercado again."

He supposed that was fair. Frankly, he had no idea what he was
going to do, either.

"Have I answered your question?" she asked.

Silverfish. Countess Yamaa. Amaya. Three girls in one, and yet
somehow, they were all her. He could see it in how she held herself,
how she regarded him, how she interacted with the world around her.

"Yes," he said, scooting his chair back. "But I don't know how to
feel about it. About...you."

Was that hurt flashing across her face, or had he imagined it? He turned to the door before he could find out, unable to trust himself with the answer. Unable to trust himself alone with her a moment longer.

The sun had risen higher by the time Cayo walked down the street, passing the tattered facades of tenement buildings. This district of the city seemed largely residential, bordering on a slum, but the farther he walked the more the city broadened before him. People hurried past on their way to jobs; he spotted a boy with a chimney sweeper over his shoulder, a woman carrying a large basket of oranges, and a man opening up a hat shop.

There was an older man sitting in a low chair by the street corner, a pile of papers stacked beside him and tied up with twine. He called out phrases that Cayo at first found odd, then realized were news headlines.

"Prince of Moray dead of ash fever!" he yelled, first in Soléne, then Rehanese, then Circíran, the common language of the Sun Empire. "Former colony state in mourning! Cases of the fever spreading into Rhinar and Gregan! The emperor reluctant to call for a state of emergency!"

Cayo's chest tightened until he was far from the man's cries. Somehow having the latest news yelled at him only made it seem that much worse. He lost himself in the growing crowd, passing under stone archways and following the stamped iron street signs as he navigated the city. The sound of spoken Soléne was everywhere, foreign and startling and making him miss home.

He was so used to Moray's organized layout that he couldn't

make sense of the winding streets that bled into one another. Cayo grew more and more flustered as he walked in a large circle, cursing under his breath. He even tried to ask someone for directions, dusting off his Soléne as best he could, but the response was too fast for him to make out properly.

Trudging through the streets, he finally caught the scent of incense and followed it to the hospital. Soria was sitting up in bed, in the middle of brushing her hair. Her skin looked soft and flushed, as if she'd just had a bath. The boy she shared a room with was asleep.

"There you are," she said as her eyes lit up. They were clearer than yesterday.

"Here I am." He sat in the chair beside her bed. "How have they been treating you so far? Were you all right during the night?"

"She did just fine."

Cayo turned to find Mother Hilas entering the room, Remy at her heels.

"Did my sister have any more coughing fits? Tea usually helps—"

"I appreciate your eagerness, young man, but we *are* trained professionals." Still, Mother Hilas smiled at him. "Actually, we come bearing good news."

"I reported to my superiors last night," Remy explained. "I came to tell Mother Hilas that our science officers are working with the local alchemists to make a medicine that should hopefully counter the fever."

"It's not a guaranteed cure," Mother Hilas said, first meeting Soria's gaze and then Cayo's. "But it's all we have at the moment. We can include your sister in the new experimental treatment, if you wish."

Cayo turned to Soria. Although he wanted to say yes, he knew his sister should be the one to decide. She bit her lip, then nodded.

"Yes," she said. "I'd like to be included."

"Very well. However…" Mother Hilas hesitated. "I'm afraid the experimental treatment is going to be costly. In order to procure everything we need, we'll need another payment from you, Mr. Lin."

Cayo's mouth dried. For a second he was back in Moray, in the Slum King's office, pleading for money for Soria's medicine. Needing to do whatever it took to save her.

But the Slum King didn't reign here. He was going to have to obtain the money some other way.

For the first time in his life, Cayo Mercado was going to have to find a job.

# 5

*When Trickster lies, the tree's fruit tastes sweeter.*

—KHARIAN SAYING

A n experimental treatment?" Amaya repeated. "Will it be safe?"

Remy shrugged. Everyone was seated at the apartment table except Cayo, who was still at the hospital with Soria.

"As safe as they can make it, I'm sure," he said. "I have no clue how that all works. I'm just good at following orders."

"You said the substance coating the discs is alchemical," Liesl said. "Did they determine what it is? If it's the cause of the fever?"

"They've isolated it as the cause, yes. And you won't guess what they discovered." Remy sat forward, hands clasped together on the tabletop. "The gold plating on the coins? It comes from a type of sea creature. Brinies."

Amaya frowned. "Those scallop-like things?"

"That's them. You remember how I said I grabbed some papers

from your father's Vault before Mercado burned it all? They mentioned brinies and where to find them, but I had no idea how that could be important until the science officers returned with their findings. Once the brinies begin to die, they start to molt, and the result is the gold-like material that's been grafted onto the discs. The moltings just flake right off their bodies. Unfortunately, once they begin the slow process of dying, they turn *extremely* poisonous. They think the moltings transmit some sort of disease that brinies carry naturally."

Amaya recalled hearing about a group of dinner guests who were poisoned by a batch of brinies gone bad. She also recalled washing up on that atoll where Boon had found her, how the rocks had been studded with brinies.

"Too much contact with the moltings on the coins results in the fever, but they still don't know if contact with an infected person raises the risk of catching it yourself." Remy sighed and sat back. "Cayo might be at risk because of Soria, but I'm honestly more worried about you, Amaya. You were around Boon's gold for a long time."

What he didn't know was that she frequently checked her body for any signs of gray. So far, nothing. "I think I'm in the clear. Something would have manifested by now, right?"

"You have no symptoms," Liesl agreed. "And neither do the three of us. It's a good thing those chests were kept below the estate. But we'll need to keep being careful."

Amaya had told Cicada, one of the older Water Bugs, to take that fake money and use it to get the other Bugs home. She winced, wondering if she had made everything worse, if she had handed him a death sentence.

But she hadn't known then. All she'd wanted was for the children to return to their homes, to finally end this horrible chapter of their lives. She thought of Beetle—Fera—and wondered if she had reunited with the parents who had sold her.

"Now that we actually know what's causing it, we're hoping the medics can work with the alchemists to figure out a cure," Remy said. "But it'll take some trial and error. Hence the experimental treatment."

"Do you think Boon knew it would cause the fever?" Deadshot asked.

"If he did, he didn't say anything about it to me," Avi mumbled darkly. "Why couldn't he have at least told us it was fake?"

"He wanted to spread it among the wealthy in Moray," Liesl said. "Some form of payback for what they did to him. Guess he didn't know that Mercado and the Slum King were simultaneously getting their own cache into the casinos. I doubt they knew about its link to the fever, or else they wouldn't have hoarded so much of it. Thanks to them, it passed through the hands of the poorer citizens, who have far fewer resources to fall back on."

Her voice was controlled yet tight with anger, eyes pinched with the same guilt that dug its claws into Amaya's shoulders. Deadshot took Liesl's hand in silent reassurance, but Amaya had no one to offer her the same.

Until she looked up and saw Remy shake his head at her, eyes soft with understanding. *This isn't your fault*, his look told her. She released a tense breath, thankful, but no amount of empathy could relieve her of the burden of Boon's duplicity.

"Most of the counterfeit coins had been making the rounds in Moray and in the Rain Empire before Boon's gold showed up," Remy told them. "He certainly didn't help matters, but he's not the only one to blame. We need to find out who the Benefactor related to Mercado is and take them into custody."

"We also need to find a way to take the counterfeits out of circulation," Amaya added.

"That'll bankrupt multiple countries," Avi said. "And with tensions high between the empires right now, that would be a disaster, to put it lightly." He got up and stretched, some of his joints popping. "Well, you all have fun with scheming. I'm going to do something productive and get a better layout of the city. If we're going to be here for a while, we need to figure out where to go if our covers are blown."

"About that." Liesl turned to Amaya. "I have an errand, and I'd like you to come with me."

Amaya tried to not let her surprise show; Liesl usually carried out errands on her own or with Deadshot. She had never included Amaya in her plotting back in Moray, simply assuring her that things would get done. Did that mean Liesl was beginning to see her more as an equal, someone who could follow in her footsteps?

Amaya fought down an excited smile. "Sure. Of course."

"I'll go with Avi," Deadshot said. "I'll stake out some escape routes, just in case."

As Liesl gave her a goodbye kiss, Remy pulled Amaya to one side.

"I haven't told my superior officers about you," he mumbled. "They were so happy with the files I brought back that they haven't asked me for more information yet. There's no need to tell them you're here—you won't be questioned by anyone."

A knot she didn't know she was carrying loosened in her chest. "Thank you, Remy."

"To be honest, they were surprised I managed to bring back

anything at all. I was the initial scout, but now that we have more information they'll be sending more officers to investigate."

Worry immediately rose within her. "They're not going to send *you* again, are they?" She didn't like the thought of being separated from him so soon after their reunion.

"No, they cleared me for at least a month of shore leave, so I offered to help with the fever relief efforts here instead."

"I thought you said that was all beyond you?"

"They'll still need soldiers to administer treatments, keep the civilians from rioting, that sort of thing. But that's not why I wanted to talk to you." He pulled a thick envelope from his jacket and handed it to her. "These are the papers I took from your father's Widow Vault when Mercado was ransacking it. The originals are being kept as evidence, but I had a scribe make a copy. I figured you should have them."

Slowly she took the envelope and pulled out the papers, an assortment of letters and notes, one filled top to bottom with equations and numbers. A hand squeezed Amaya's heart as she gazed upon her father's words in handwriting that wasn't his own.

"There's a note on the back of a report about Mercado and his business that reads more like a journal entry. It mentions you, so I thought you might like to read it." Remy pointed it out to her, and she read.

> *When I think of Rin and Amaya, it's as if everything else*
> *falls away into the ocean. Although some will say my home*
> *is Khari, I know my home is with them, wherever they*
> *are. It's a comforting thought. It keeps me working, it keeps*
> *me from going into places that are so dark even the stars*

*can't reach. Rin will make sure Amaya is taken care of,*
*that her legacy may continue. My greatest treasures in this*
*life lie with my wife and my daughter.*

Amaya read the passage again, her heart heavy, longing for the things that could have been. When the pain grew too much, she stuffed the papers back into the envelope.

"Thank you, Remy," she whispered.

*My greatest treasures in this life lie with my wife and my daughter.*

But Rin and Arun Chandra were dead, leaving Amaya an heir to nothing but nostalgia and memory.

Liesl and Amaya were quiet as they headed off for whatever Liesl's mysterious errand was. The streets broadened into thoroughfares, carts and horse-drawn carriages rattling by. Amaya spotted broadsheets tacked up on a board, showing the likeness of a man in his thirties with a beard and a missing eye. The reward for bringing him in read six thousand solstas. Amaya knew from her few months of staying in Viariche that the solsta was worth a little more than the sena.

"Maybe we should become bounty hunters," Amaya suggested. "We can rack up a decent amount of money that way."

Liesl hummed halfheartedly, sparing the broadsheets a wary gaze. "If that's all it took, we should just turn ourselves in. It's a nice boost to my ego, though."

"How come?"

"Because when *my* broadsheets were up, they were calling for

47

ten thousand solstas." She offered Amaya a small smile. "And that's exactly why we're on this little errand."

Amaya dutifully followed Liesl through the city, watching the girl's blue skirt sway as she walked confidently through the streets she had once called home.

Finally, they stopped outside of a squat building with an iron balcony above a large, rectangular sign in Soléne.

"What does that mean?" Amaya asked, pointing to the sign. She only knew the basics of Soléne, such as *hello* and *goodbye* and how to call someone a bastard.

"It roughly translates to *Hall of Beauty*." Liesl's smile stretched wider at Amaya's confusion, and she ushered her inside. "Come on, he'll be waiting."

Once inside, Amaya's confusion vanished. The building looked modest from the outside, but the interior was lavish with dark purple drapes and plush couches. Thick rugs cushioned the floor while a chandelier hung from the ceiling, gleaming in the midmorning light. The air was hazy with smoke and the faint smell of alcohol.

Just as the sign promised, there were people prowling through the den, all of different shapes and colorings. Their clothing was either skin-tight, see-through, or barely there at all.

"Oh," Amaya said, a little strangled.

"To be clear, I tried to get us to meet in a wine shop, but he thought this would be more discreet."

"I wouldn't exactly call this discreet." A girl caught Amaya's eye and trailed her fingers over her own collarbone, then between her breasts. "Or subtle."

There weren't many customers at this time of day, but there was enough clientele to fill the space with the hushed sound of murmuring.

Amaya spotted a woman in her midyears, her skin leathery from a life at sea, who grinned as a Rehanese woman in a silk robe plopped down on her lap. A young, freckled man blushed and stammered under the attention of a dark-skinned woman on his left and a paler man on his right. The paler man wore a leather collar attached to a chain that the freckled man held.

Sitting on a purple chaise in the corner was Jasper. He was currently trying to woo a young woman to come sit with him, but she was playing hard to get. She batted her lashes and opened a silk fan, using it to obscure the bottom half of her face.

"I think she's trying to tell you no thank you," Liesl said as she sat beside him. "I bet I'm more her type."

"Didn't you say your partner was trigger happy?" Jasper said.

"Oh, she is. Why do you think I've kept her away from you today?"

Jasper laughed. The woman with the fan, realizing they were wasting her time, drifted off toward the blushing young man. "Isn't the mean one gonna sit?"

Amaya scowled and lowered herself onto the armchair across from them. "If you keep calling me that, I get to call you the annoying one."

"See? Mean." Jasper leaned forward, resting his elbows on his knees. His left sleeve was buttoned up around the stump of his wrist. "I brought what you asked for, but this stuff doesn't come cheap, Li."

"I know. Let me at least take a look before I decide if it's worth my money."

They waited for a thin young man to saunter by, his expression haughty and his torso bare save for a thin golden chain that crossed over his chest. When he realized none of them would call him over, he scoffed and moved along. Jasper then took a stack of papers from a pocket inside his jacket and handed them to Liesl. Liesl shuffled through them and passed one to Amaya. As Amaya took it, she saw the writing was in Rehanese, not Soléne.

She scanned the document and quickly realized what it was. "This is . . . a fake identity?"

"We'll need to be careful in Baleine," Liesl told her. "Because it's a port city, they're tighter on security. Ever since we were conquered by the Rain Empire, it's not uncommon for checkpoints to pop up randomly so soldiers can verify your identification papers. Everyone needs to carry theirs with them at all times."

"And if you're caught without one . . ." Jasper shrugged. "Let's just say our jail's looking mighty full these days."

"Not to mention you and I have names to bury," Liesl said to Amaya. "Mercado likely exposed you in Moray once he found out your true identity. We can't risk anything."

Amaya read the paper again. Her name was listed as *Yara Sakan*, and her place of origin was a city in Khari, not Moray.

"Memorize those details in case anyone stops you," Liesl warned her. She reorganized the stack of papers and carefully put them into her reticule. "And memorize everyone else's names, too. When we're in public, call me Vivienne."

"Vivi," Jasper said. "I like it. Rolls right off the tongue."

"Is your real name Jasper?" Amaya asked. He only winked in response.

"Thanks for this, Jas," Liesl said. She handed him a coin that flashed gold, but one knowing glance at Amaya told her it wasn't fake. Amaya knew they had a small amount of money, but how long would it last?

"You know," Jasper said, biting the coin before rolling it casually across his knuckles, reminding her of Cayo, "stuff like this usually goes for twice this amount."

"You still have that interest to pay off, remember?"

"Ah, it's always the interest. That's how they get you."

Liesl stood as if to leave, and Amaya followed her lead. A young woman passing by shot Amaya a coy smile, dressed in a slip of sheer gauze and feathers. Amaya blushed and tried not to stare. After living in the close quarters of a ship for seven years, she was comfortable enough with the human body, but the thought of using it for specific things gave her no rush of desire, no lust. It wasn't impossible for her to feel those things—she reluctantly recalled her kiss with Cayo in the rain—but it seemed to take her longer than most people to get to that point.

She was too flustered to notice that Liesl had stopped walking. Amaya ran into her, the girl rigid and tense, blue eyes wide as her face drained of color.

"Li—I mean, Vivienne?" Amaya put a hand on her arm. "Are you all right?"

A man had walked into the den and was speaking with the proprietor not too far away. He was dressed in a finely tailored suit in the style of the Rain Empire, a double-breasted coat with pressed trousers and two rows of gleaming buttons down the front. He was in his midyears, handsome, with light brown skin and threads of gray in his dark hair.

"Shit." Jasper jumped to his feet and turned Liesl around, sitting her back down on the couch. "Mean girl, sit here and don't let him see her."

Amaya did as she was told, too frightened to even snap at him for

51

the nickname. She leaned toward Liesl, blocking her from the man's view as her heart pounded. She didn't know why she was afraid, but anything that could make Liesl look like that was something Amaya wanted no part of.

Finally, Jasper let out a tight breath and nodded. "He's gone. Went upstairs."

Amaya put a hand on Liesl's shoulder. The girl was trembling, her lips pressed into a thin, pale line. "Who was that?"

Jasper plopped down onto the armchair with a scowl that seemed unlike him, glaring at the stairs. There was genuine anger in the burn of his gaze, in the tightness of his limbs, as if he was considering following the man and putting an abrupt end to him.

"André Basque," Jasper muttered. "A politician here in Chalier who's only kept his title because he favors the Rain Empire." He turned his head as if to spit, then thought better of it. "The man who caught Liesl and Adrienne during a coalition raid."

"Adrienne?"

"Her sister."

Amaya's hand tightened on Liesl's shoulder. *Sister?* Liesl had never mentioned having a sister. Hadn't mentioned much about her previous life at all, really.

But Amaya knew firsthand that coming back to the place of your birth was only an invitation to let the ghosts in. To face the things you would have rather left forgotten.

"He's the man that made you Landless," Amaya said. Liesl nodded. "I'm so sorry." Did that mean her sister was Landless, too?

"Let's just go." Liesl stood, the horror on her face overtaken with a manufactured calm. "Before he finishes, which I'm sure will be quick."

"I'll stay here," Jasper said, catching sight of a young man whose trousers hung low on his hips. Jasper flashed the coin Liesl had given him, and the young man sent him a wink. "I'll keep an eye on Basque."

"You'll certainly be keeping an eye on something." The lightness in Liesl's voice was just as manufactured as her expression.

As Liesl turned toward the exit and glanced at the stairs where the man had gone, Amaya felt a chill go through her. There was something unsettling in Liesl's eyes, a coldness that seemed to warp the very air around her.

Whatever business Liesl had with André Basque, it was far from over.

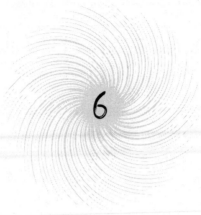

# 6

*Those with wealth make rules and laws for their own kind,*
*understanding little of how they destroy the lives of those*
*whose coffers are lined with dust.*

—POLITICAL PAMPHLET IN THE RAIN EMPIRE, BY ANONYMOUS

Cayo was lying on his back and glaring at the ceiling the next day when he heard the door to the apartment open. The sound was followed by an accented tenor that was quickly becoming familiar: Jasper.

Cayo sighed and turned over. He didn't want to deal with the others right now, not when he finally had a bit of time to himself. Time to figure out how exactly he was going to make enough money to pay for Soria's treatment.

He had never held a paying job in his life. He had worked for his father on the docks, checking inventory and ship records, but that had been an obligation. A way to try to win back his father's favor.

And working for the Slum King...well, that hadn't been a job, not really. Not when the majority of his winnings went into the Slum King's pockets. That had been nothing but a hobby, because for a long time he could afford to maintain it.

And then...

Cayo thought about Sébastien, his long-time gambling partner from Moray who had often worked the tables with him. Unlike his other friends, Bas hadn't come from wealth, so anything he made at the casinos was his only source of income. Bas had been the one to initially discover the counterfeit scheme—the one whom the Slum King had punished by gouging out his eyes.

Cayo clenched his fists as he thought back to the day they'd said goodbye, the feeling of Bas's cheek under his lips. Sébastien had gone to Soliere, a couple of hundred miles to the northwest from Chalier. Cayo wondered how he was doing, if he ever missed Moray. Missed Cayo. Missed their old way of life.

The door to the bedroom opened and Avi stuck his head in. "C'mere."

"No."

"We need you. Also, there's wine."

Cayo reluctantly followed Avi into the main room, barefoot and dressed only in a shirt and trousers. Once he would have cringed at the thought of his hair being this messy, his clothes this rumpled and ratty. But he couldn't afford to think of nice coats and shiny boots and cologne. Not anymore.

Probably never again.

There were, in fact, two bottles on the table. They were a dusky red and unlabeled. Jasper grinned upon seeing Cayo and gestured to the bottles.

"I come bearing gifts," he said.

"We're not paying you back for them," Liesl said.

Jasper put a pinkie finger in his ear and made a motion like he was trying to get water out. "I'm sorry, has the definition of a gift changed in the last few seconds? Must I relearn everything I once thought I knew of this great, terrible world?"

"What's the occasion?" Amaya asked, leaning against the wall with her arms crossed. She kept glancing at Liesl with a worried set to her eyebrows.

"The occasion," said Jasper, yanking a cork out of one of the bottles, "is that I believe I found a lead for you."

Deadshot leaned forward in her seat. "The Benefactor, you mean?"

"The very same."

Cayo pressed his lips together. When they had asked Cayo if he knew anything about this so-called Benefactor, he had told them the truth.

"My father rarely included me in his business. He let me handle the inventory, and that's about it. Whatever this is, he kept it from everyone, including me."

"Feel free to share anytime," Avi said as Jasper poured the pungent-smelling wine into one of the chipped mugs.

"It's not much information, so the buildup's all I have," Jasper argued. "Would you really deny me that?"

"Yes," Liesl said flatly.

"Fine, fine. I told you I first heard about this mysterious Benefactor of yours in connection with the currency exchanges offices, correct? Well, I asked a friend in the Financial District to do some digging, and they found out one of these offices is on Heliope

Avenue. Seems like a good place to check the records, don't you think?"

"And if we check the records, we might have a shot at finding the Benefactor's address," Amaya said.

"More than a shot." Jasper handed her a chipped mug full of wine. "I'd dare say you have a very good chance indeed."

Amaya took the mug, and Cayo watched as her long, callused fingers wrapped around it, cradling it like a newly hatched egg. Her mother's jade ring glinted on her finger. She wore a hint of a smile, as if finding new purpose in the wake of Jasper's discovery. She turned and caught Cayo's eye, that small smile still in place.

Cayo suddenly forgot how to breathe. He stood on a precipice of all things possible, and instead of being afraid of the fall, he relished the thought of surrender. Of tumbling through blank space, knowing he would be all right because there was someone falling beside him.

Then he remembered how he'd felt standing beside her on the ship, learning she was a stranger—nothing but a con artist. He looked away and her smile died. Cayo's breath rushed out, his chest aching.

Falling, as it turned out, was not that simple.

Burning with embarrassment and frustration at himself, he barely registered the mug being shoved into his hands.

"Oh, I don't..." Cayo looked at the contents of the mug, red and smelling of vinegar. His mouth dried. All he wanted was to grab that second bottle and nurse the entirety of it through the night. "I shouldn't."

He'd usually drunk much more than one bottle on a typical outing in the Vice Sector. He could still remember perfectly the moment between sober and intoxicated, that surreal descent into a pleasant, numbing state of being. The world was softer then. He hadn't been as afraid to navigate it like a corridor of daggers, knowing that even if he got cut, he wouldn't be able to feel the pain.

It was only now he could see just how terrifying that descent really was. Cayo forced himself to give his mug to Avi.

"Suit yourself," Jasper said. "More for us."

The others began to talk about ways of finding the Benefactor, sipping at their wine and only occasionally grimacing at the taste. Cayo turned back to his room, then paused.

It was a long shot, but right now, long shots were all he had.

He cautiously approached Jasper, who was leaning against the table as he listened in on the conversation. When Jasper noticed him, he batted his eyelashes.

"Come to charm me?" Jasper asked. "I've been waiting."

"What? No." Cayo crossed his arms, thinking of Soria. He was doing this for her, he reminded himself. "I was wondering if...if you knew where I could find a job."

All talk immediately ceased. Cayo flushed as everyone stared at him, hunching his shoulders as if that was all it took to disappear.

"You," Avi said. "Want to find a *job*."

"It's the only way I can pay for Soria's treatment," Cayo mumbled. "Short of stealing. And I am not a thief."

"I am," Jasper said, brightening. "Want to join me on a heist?"

"Don't rope him into your way of life," Liesl said. "We're on thin enough ice as it is."

"All right, all right. You all are no fun." Jasper looked Cayo up and down. "Got any special skills or talents? Know any sort of trade?"

"Just shuffling cards," Cayo said. "And coin tricks."

"Oh!" Jasper snapped his fingers. "Then you should visit the Casino District. I'm sure they're looking for young, attractive dealers."

The floor seemed to lurch beneath his feet. He had heard there was a small gambling district here in the city, but the thought of going there, of walking through some casino's doors and returning to that world...

His mouth dried again. He had tried to put distance between himself and that bygone version of Cayo Mercado, the one who didn't care about consequences. The one who had savored the high of winning so much it became a drug in his system, slowly polluting his mind and body.

He had vowed never again. He had promised Soria he'd stay out of that life.

The word rose on Cayo's tongue, as tart and vinegary as the wine smelled, when Amaya stepped away from the wall and said it first.

"No."

The room fell silent again. Cayo stared at her, brows furrowed.

"Excuse me?" His voice came out low.

"I said no." Her dark eyes bored into his, crackling and spitting like a flame in the wind. "You know what that will do to you. What it's already done to you. If you go back to that life, you'll probably lose yourself to it again. And we'll be even worse off than we are now, with no chance of catching Boon or the Benefactor."

"Oh, so this is about assuaging your guilt."

The slightest wince told him his arrow had landed true. "No, it's about *all* of us. You're the only one who doesn't get that. You're too busy feeling sorry for yourself and focusing on your own problems when there are people dying in the streets!"

Her voice rose to a shrill scream. She reeled back from him, as if startled by the force of her own rage.

The blood drained from Cayo's face. "My *sister* is dying."

Amaya sighed and rubbed her hands over her face, trying to calm herself down. "I didn't mean...I'm sorry. What you're doing for her...it's admirable. It is." She dropped her hands, the fury in her eyes now replaced with a fatigue that Cayo had never seen before. "But if you really want to help Soria, you won't return to that life. You know that already."

Cayo clenched his jaw, trying to ignore the way the others were looking between them.

"I do know that already," he said quietly. "Which is why I was going to refuse."

She looked as if she didn't believe him, and anger lit him up like a torch. "Is it really so hard for you to think that I can change? Do you really think so little of me, that I'm just a product of my lifestyle who can't think or act for himself?"

But could he really blame her skepticism? He had felt himself teetering between yes and no. One false move and he would be lost again.

Amaya's face turned ashen. "No, I..."

He averted his gaze. The room was deathly quiet, no one daring to move as the two of them stood there, refusing to look at each other. Eventually Amaya turned away, going back into the bedroom she shared with Liesl and Deadshot.

Jasper shifted on his feet once the bedroom door closed, clearing his throat. "Well," he said, keeping his tone down as if afraid Amaya would storm back out, "in that case, I do know of a place that's always hiring."

Early the next morning, Cayo stared in horror at the rows and rows of dead fish spread out before him.

"Are you serious?" He turned to Jasper, who had buried his nose into his scarf to avoid the worst of the morning chill. "The *fish market?*"

"What, don't like fish?"

"It's not that, it's just..." Cayo ran his fingers through his hair, eyes wide with panic. "What...What do I *do* with them?"

Jasper peered at him over his scarf. "You've really never worked a day in your life, have you?" He gestured for Cayo to follow him. "No one's expecting you to do anything with the fish other than haul them around and maybe sell them. No one's gonna ask you to start juggling."

"Why couldn't I do more, I don't know, skilled labor? I can read and write, I know arithmetic—"

"In Rehanese, yes, but not Soléne. And besides, who says this isn't skilled labor?"

Cayo couldn't help the nervous energy that writhed in his gut as they approached a fish vendor near the docks. The sun had only just begun to climb into the sky, a crescent of orange along the horizon. It streaked across the dark water and limned the furled sails and polished railings, fingers of light poking and prodding into dark corners. The smell of salt and fish was everywhere, and gulls crying out in hunger wheeled overhead.

He spared the ships a long glance, wondering what would happen if he simply commandeered one and took off with Soria. To... somewhere. Anywhere he could start over. It was a fantasy he'd often had as a child, but now it seemed like madness.

The vendor Jasper led him to was a large, balding man in a blood-stained apron, with more muscles than Cayo thought any human had a right to possess. He rubbed his own arms self-consciously.

"Victor!" Jasper called cheerily, switching to Soléne to ask him a question. The hulking man, Victor, grunted out a reply. Jasper laughed and shook Cayo's shoulder, switching back to Rehanese.

"We have a mutt who needs a home," Jasper explained. "If I remember right, your last errand boy slipped off the docks and drowned. You'll be needing a new one, yes?"

Cayo tensed. *"Drowned?"*

Victor looked him up and down. When he spoke, his Rehanese was muddled. "You be into a job, then?" Cayo nodded. "Start today. I see what you do. You good, is two niera for a day." The niera was a quarter of the price of a solsta, Cayo remembered. His panic grew, wondering if that would be enough for the treatment.

"Wonderful!" Jasper shook his shoulder again, making Cayo's teeth click together. "Glad I could be of help. Have fun."

"Wait—"

But Jasper was already skipping off, claiming he had somewhere else to be. The young man seemed to always have someplace he needed to be; did he even sleep?

"Name?" Victor grunted.

Cayo hesitated, touching the forged identification paper through his pocket. "Cayo Lin." They had already given his first name to the hospital, and Liesl didn't trust him to memorize a new first name.

"Rehan?"

"Moray."

Victor shrugged like he didn't particularly care and pointed to the stall behind him. It was a large wooden crate slanted on an angle, the better to show off his wares, Cayo guessed. "People here soon. Ice, then fish."

"All right." Cayo stood there, waiting for more instruction, but apparently that was all he was getting out of Victor. "Oh. Um... right. Ice."

He looked around desperately, a hot flush working through him even as the cool wind off the sea ruffled his hair. As Victor checked his business ledger, Cayo walked around the side of the stall. There was an empty bucket, but no sign of ice. Typical—his first task at his first job, and he was already failing.

A noise made him look to the right. A girl a few years younger than him was leaning against her own stall, her dark hair in pigtails and brown skin dotted with freckles. She met his eye and nodded toward the other side of the docks, where the market stretched on and on. Cayo saw a line of workers assembled before a large bin, all carrying buckets.

Cayo thanked her and grabbed the bucket beside the stall. As he joined the line, a group of sailors came in from the harbor, their weary expressions telling of a long voyage finally come to an end. They all wore scraps of green cloth pinned to their coats, but it was clearly not a part of their uniform.

*They're doubling down on who enters the city*, Cayo realized, remembering the yellow cloth they had pinned to Soria's cloak, marking her as infected. It was only thanks to Remy's involvement in the navy that she hadn't been carted off to some quarantine bay.

Once he got to the front of the line, Cayo shoved his bucket into the cold, slushy mess of ice. It got all over his hands and soaked the ends of his sleeves, making him curse and shudder. Why did Baleine have to be so *cold*? He missed Moray's warmth, the balmy breezes and the sweet dampness of the air.

He returned to Victor's stall and poured the ice into the crate. Two men were in the process of setting down nets full of fish, and he watched as Victor handed them each some money. When the fishermen left, Victor scowled at him.

"Go." Victor gestured to the nets of fish. "Put on."

Cayo pointed from the nets to the ice. "There?" Victor lifted his hands impatiently, and Cayo rushed to the nearest net. "All right, all right!"

He pulled open the net and tried not to gag. He didn't recognize this type of fish, but their scales were gray and blue and shimmered in the oncoming morning light. They would have looked pretty if they weren't all piled together in an obscene mound.

Cayo steeled himself, then reached in to grab one. The body was cold and slippery, and he yelped as it shot out of his hand and plopped back among its brethren.

"Fast!" Victor snapped at him. Cayo looked over his shoulder and saw that customers were beginning to flock into the market.

Cayo held his breath and grabbed the fish again, this time by the tail. He carefully stood and positioned it on the ice, where its round, yellow eye stared at him accusingly. Victor clapped at him to keep going, so Cayo moved as quickly as he could, cursing as the fish began to slip down the ice and Victor yelled at him while showing him how to position the bodies just so. To Cayo's ever-mounting distress, a couple of the fish were still alive, and Victor taught him how to smack their heads against the cobblestone.

"God and her stars," Cayo groaned as he placed his new kill upon the ice. "I'm sorry." The fish stared back at him, mouth agape as if it too were stunned by this betrayal.

When he was finally done, his hands were numb and he desperately wanted a cup of tea. He sat behind the stall on a short stool,

taking a break while Victor sold his fish and the sun climbed higher
into the sky. The girl at the stall beside theirs flashed him a smirk.

"You'll get used to it," she said.

Cayo thought his work for the day might be done, but Victor
rounded the stall and shoved a piece of paper at Cayo. An address.

"You, go to delivery. Here." He pointed at a bag nearby. "Res-
taurant, need fish. Go!"

"I—I don't know where—"

But Victor was already turning to a new customer, putting on a
smile that transformed his face from a craggy mountainside to a sunny
hill. Cayo sighed and hauled the bag over his shoulder, staring at the
address he'd been given.

It was going to be a long day.

Cayo got lost multiple times, but eventually he made the delivery
to an irritated cook before trudging back to the fish market. Victor
wasn't shy to tell Cayo how displeased he was with how long it'd
taken, but in the late afternoon when the fish had all been sold and
the pinkish slush left from the ice was dumped into the harbor, Victor
gave him the promised two niera.

"Not good, but you get better," Victor told him. "Come tomorrow."

Cayo staggered away from the market, staring at the coins in his
hand. He had earned them. Not through gambling and trickery, but
through physical labor and effort.

It felt...strangely good. He hadn't felt pride in so long that at first
he couldn't recognize the emotion, but eventually he gave himself

permission to smile, to congratulate himself on achieving something he'd never done before. And what was more, he could give the hospital administrator the first payment for Soria's treatment.

Maybe everything was going to be all right.

"Hey, hey, what's that you got there?"

Cayo froze. He had wandered down a narrow street that would lead him to the hospital, but the late afternoon light formed pools of shadow across the street. From those shadows emerged three figures, two boys and a girl. Their clothes were ragged, their faces streaked with dirt.

"He's pretty," said the girl, sniffing as if she had a cold. "Too bad you can't sell faces."

"I know a guy," said the taller of the boys.

Cayo took a step back, fisting his hand around the niera. His surroundings blurred as he desperately reached for the memory of being taught what to do in this situation, how he had to toss away his wallet or his purse and then make a run for it.

But he had no wallet, no purse, not even his pocket watch anymore. Nothing but the couple of coins in his hand, and he wasn't about to toss them away.

"Leave me alone," he said, hating the way his voice shook.

"Mm, nah," said the girl, stalking closer. They all had knives in their grubby hands, their yellowed teeth gleaming in identical grins. "How 'bout you hand over that money, and we don't kill ya?"

He held his fist to his chest, ignoring all his former lessons on how to deal with thieves. This was *his* money that he had earned. He needed it for Soria.

"Go bother someone else," Cayo said as they began to circle him like vultures. "This is all I have."

"Such drama with this one," the tall boy muttered. "Think he's gonna cry?"

"Bet you I can make 'im cry," said the short boy.

Before Cayo could even try to make a run for it, they pounced. He went down under their fists, trying to curl into a ball while protecting his head from their blows. The girl laughed as she got him pinned, and the tall boy nearly broke his fingers getting him to unclench his fist.

The coins fell out, ringing against the cobblestone.

"No!" Cayo fought back, but one of the boys stomped his boot into Cayo's chest, winding him. The other grabbed his hair and banged his head against the street. The world went spinning as pain exploded through his skull.

"See? Got 'im to cry."

"Psh, I wanted *real* tears."

Cayo curled up on his side, wanting to cough but unable to get a full breath in. He kept his eyes closed, teeth gritted as the ground beneath him tilted. He lay there for a stunned moment, wondering if he was dead or likely to die, before determining the only thing that had expired was the last of his pride.

He eventually got to all fours, his joints sore, his rib cage bruised. "Shit." He took in his scraped skin, the blood on his hand, his torn and dirty clothing.

*Good thing I'm going to a hospital.*

The thought was so absurd that he let out a small, hysterical laugh, resting his forehead against the cool ground as he caught his breath. At least Amaya hadn't been here to see his complete and utter uselessness.

He heard someone murmuring in Soléne as they helped him up.

It was a middle-aged man, his face lined with worry. He repeated his question, which Cayo thought was *Are you all right?* Cayo held his stomach as he looked around, but he knew the pickpockets had long run off with the money.

"No," he rasped. "I'm not all right."

Things couldn't go on this way. He couldn't continue to be the weakest link in the group.

It was time he asked Amaya and the others for help.

# 7

*There came a great thundering noise from the cellar, and Lady Trianh nearly fainted from the insistent pounding and the sweetly malicious voice emanating from within.*

*"Open the door and I will set you free," sang the voice. "I will give you what you desire."*

*But Lady Trianh merely stood with her hand upon the knob, terror in her heart and uncertainty in her eyes.*

—*THE BEAST BELOW*, A HORROR NOVEL FROM REHAN

When she was seven years old, Amaya had gotten stuck at the top of the mast of her father's ship.

Admittedly, it was her fault—her father had warned her not to climb anything without him there to watch her. "A ship is a dangerous place for anyone," he'd said, "including little girls."

It was the ship he used for his business, a long, narrow skipjack with sails that reminded her of a shark's fin. He had asked her to name it for him, and she had chosen *Papaya*, because it was what she had named the doll her mother had sewn for her. He regularly took it out for pearl diving, he and his small team of divers.

That day, though, it had just been the two of them. He had promised her a picnic on the sea a whole week ago, and she had pouted and whined until he had laughed and given in.

"How could I possibly say no to that face?" he'd said as he cupped her cheeks in his large, callused hands, playfully tilting her head back and forth. "What should we have for our picnic?"

"Dumplings!" she'd screamed. "And cake!"

"A girl after my own heart."

"And sweet tooth," her mother had muttered from the corner where she sewed, smiling when her father winked at her.

So they had bought mushroom-and-leek dumplings and a slice of lemon cake and taken to the sea, Amaya watching in fascination as Arun untied the ship from the docks and positioned the sails just so. Her father looked strong and sure as he worked, his broad shoulders straining at his shirt and the sunlight highlighting threads of brown and red in his black hair. Her mother often called him a handsome demon, able to charm just about anybody with a flash of his crooked grin.

"Will you teach me to sail one day?" Amaya had asked.

"Why don't we start now? Here, I'll show you how to use a compass. Navigation is important when it comes to sailing."

But after a while, Amaya had gotten bored and instead played around the ship. Her father had dozed off under the warm sun, the sails furled and the anchor weighed as they bobbed in the ocean's current.

Which was how she had challenged herself to climb the mast—and how she came to be stuck.

"I can't climb down," she'd cried.

Arun had stood at the bottom of the mast, trying and failing to hide the alarm on his face. "It's all right, thikha. I'll be right here, so just jump and I'll catch you."

"No!" she'd wailed, holding the mast tighter. "I'll fall and die!"

"You won't. I promise." He had held his strong arms out, motioning with his hands for her to jump. "I'll catch you."

"But..."

"Just trust me."

She did trust her father. She always had. So Amaya, crying, took a deep breath and leaped from the mast and into her father's waiting arms.

He'd caught her easily, staggering back a couple of steps as he held her tight against him.

"Don't scare me like that again," he had admonished, but there had been no heat in his words, just shaky relief. He kissed the top of her head as she clung to him, feeling safe and protected so long as he continued to hold her. "And whatever you do, don't tell your mother."

Amaya liked to think of her father this way: strong and brave and knowing what to do. Reaching for his hand and trusting that he would never let go of it. It helped to drive away the memory of what had happened a year later, when the debt collectors had come. When her father's life had been taken by the man to whom he owed an unpayable debt, and Amaya had stopped feeling safe.

Stopped being able to trust.

71

"Are you sure about this?" Remy asked, his voice hushed.

"Nope," Amaya whispered back. "But if I spend another minute in that apartment, I'm going to strangle somebody."

"Do I get three guesses who?" Remy asked with a knowing smile. She had told him about the way she'd blown up at Cayo yesterday, how they had been avoiding each other ever since.

It wasn't just that she was embarrassed for the outburst; she had been truly, desperately angry, all the negative emotions she had built up over the last few weeks crashing out of her like a bullet from a pistol. Cayo had insisted he hadn't been thinking of going back to gambling, but she had seen him hesitate. Flirting with the idea of losing himself to the very thing that had ruined him.

Cayo came from wealth. He had always had everything handed to him. After living as Countess Yamaa, Amaya could see the allure of it, the way the rich didn't have to worry about trivial things such as where their next meal would come from, or if they had enough money saved up to buy a new pair of shoes.

She had certainly seen that in him while they were in Moray, but she had also seen who he was underneath the boy that society had molded. She had seen a boy who cared about his family, who would do whatever it took to protect them. She had seen a determination to right his wrongs, even if it cost him more than he was willing to give.

He had been willing to send his father to jail. More than anything, that had shown her the type of person Cayo Mercado was.

But there was still so much more he was capable of being. Amaya just didn't know if he was dedicated enough to find out what that was.

Amaya sighed, her breath turning to vapor in the night air. Remy had gotten her a thicker jacket, but threads of cold stole through the collar and cuffs. "I can't be responsible for him. Besides, my focus is on something bigger."

Remy looked across the street. They were perched on a rooftop above Heliope Avenue, waiting for the last of the workers to leave the currency exchange office. Remy was dressed in dark clothing, his naval jacket tactfully left behind. Amaya's fingers constantly drifted to the outlines of the hidden knives she carried.

Knives that Boon had given her, a reward for learning how to fight with them.

"Make sure you always have one hidden on your person," he had told her, an odd tone in his words that Amaya knew couldn't have been protective. Nervous, maybe, to begin their long con. But she had listened to him, grabbing tightly to any scrap of advice he'd given her.

She had once thought of the gift as high praise—an honor, even. Then the bastard had double-crossed her.

But she would have been a fool to get rid of knives as nice as these.

Finally, when the waning moon had risen completely, the front doors opened and the last of the workers stepped out. They locked up the building and strolled down the lantern-lit street, heading home for the night.

She and Remy climbed down the side of the building—the Chalier style tended toward balconies, which she much appreciated—and hurried across the street.

"I still can't believe you roped me into this," Remy muttered as she jiggered the lock on the back door. She had scouted it earlier that day, pretending to be lost as she wandered through the street, wanting to make use of Jasper's lead. "What if we get caught?"

"Are you seriously the same boy I grew up with? Don't you

remember stealing from the pantry on the *Brackish*, or eating some of the oysters we'd caught before reporting to Zharo?"

"That was different," he whispered back. "And besides, that was mostly you. I was just the lookout."

"Then reprise your role and keep a lookout."

Amaya slipped inside, blinking as her eyes transitioned from moonlight to the shadows of the offices around her. She hunkered down, searching for some sort of alarm system, and stopped Remy before he could walk in after her.

"Wait." She pointed upward, to a thin, nearly invisible string about chest height. "That'll trigger some warning bells, I'm guessing."

Remy cursed and crouched beside her. "You're strangely good at this."

"Maybe I was born to be a thief. Maybe I should take up with Jasper and his crew."

"I know you're joking, but your words just gave me a stomach-ache."

Amaya crawled forward until they were clear of the alarm rigging and stood. They were in some sort of supply closet filled with empty canvas sacks and sheafs of paper and pencils. Through the door, they found a more spacious room with wide, wooden desks lined up on either side. The windows along the walls were close to the ceiling, filtering in sheets of moonlight.

"This is where they take their customers," Remy whispered. "All the coins and notes that come through here will end up in their safes."

"And where would those be?"

Remy pointed to a heavily locked door nearby. "Through the most fortified door, if I had to guess."

There were a half dozen padlocks that Amaya opened only after a great deal of patience and quite a bit of finger cramping, silently thanking Liesl for teaching her these tricks. When she opened the door, Amaya felt a drop in temperature and found a long staircase leading down.

"There's a Kharian myth about monsters that horde their treasures underground," she said as they descended. "The legend goes that if you disturb them, they'll turn you into a golden statue and add you to their collection."

"Well, I wouldn't fault them for their taste. I'd make a pretty attractive statue."

Amaya pointed out a trip wire at the bottom of the stairs, which they smartly avoided. She found a bit of flint next to an extinguished torch on the wall and struck it against one of her knives. The low, flickering light illuminated a row of thick metal doors, all leading into separate safes.

The first safe they opened contained Kharian currency, colorful bank notes and silver coins with cameos of the gods. The next safe was full of money from the Sun Empire, a curious collection from different regions that ranged from brass to agate and even to wood.

"Here we are," Remy said as they pulled open the next safe. There were neatly stacked rows of boxes filled with Rehanese currency, gleaming in the torchlight.

But all she had eyes for were the golden senas. Amaya took out three coins and laid them on the ground. Remy then poured a clear alcohol from his flask, filling the underground chamber with a sharp, medicinal smell. They sat and watched the coins, Amaya lightheaded from the alcohol fumes as her belly squirmed.

None of them turned black.

"What?" Amaya picked one up, finding only solid gold. "But I thought..."

Frowning, Remy opened the next safe, finding solstas and nieras native to the Rain Empire. When they performed the same test again with the alcohol, Amaya's heart sank as the solstas' coating gave way to black.

"Damn it," Remy muttered as the alcohol ate away the gold on two of the coins.

"Did Mercado send these?" she whispered. "Or...do you think Boon...?"

"I have no idea," Remy whispered back, already sounding defeated. "But I'm sure the Benefactor has something to do with this."

"We can't just leave them here," Amaya said. "What if we took them?"

"We've been over this." Remy scrubbed a hand through his hair, eyes tight with remorse. "Taking the coins out of circulation will lead to economic catastrophe. Moray is already on the brink of total collapse. Which would mean that possession of the city state would go to the Rain Empire, now that the prince is dead. And if the Rain Empire faces the same catastrophe..."

"The Sun Empire will attack," Amaya finished for him. "If they've been spared from the fever, anyway. Gods. This...This has the potential to cause a full-scale war."

"One thing at a time."

She reluctantly returned the coins to the safe, pocketing the black discs. The torch extinguished, they headed back upstairs, up another flight of steps leading to a set of double doors. Amaya picked the lock and the doors swung open, revealing shelves and shelves of files.

"Mm, good," Remy said, looking around. "I was hoping this would be easy."

They worked quickly, silently, pulling file after file off the shelves.

Amaya tried to find the word *Benefactor* anywhere—Liesl had written it out for her in Soléne so that she could memorize it—but the words and numbers began to bleed together, making it difficult to focus.

"I found something." Remy rushed to her an hour later, pointing at a file in his hand. "Records from a year ago, with Mercado's name. He was using these offices to exchange the money, but he must have switched to make the trail harder to follow."

"What does it say?"

Remy read silently to himself, brow furrowed. "There's no address. Damn it. Oh!" He pulled the file closer. "Wait a minute...."

He continued to read, and Amaya crossed her arms with mounting impatience. She was about to snap at him to hurry up when he finally met her gaze again, just as confused as he'd been in the vault.

"This doesn't make sense," he whispered. "According to these records, currency was being sent to Moray. There's no record of Mercado sending anything back."

Amaya nearly grabbed the file to read it for herself before remembering it was all in Soléne. "I thought Mercado was sending fake coins here?"

"That's what we all thought. After seeing the coins in the safe, I guessed that the Benefactor might have been grafting the substance onto the solstas. But maybe they had a different arrangement."

Amaya shook her head. They only had bits and pieces of a puzzle that still had not taken shape. It felt as if the more they found out, the further they were from understanding.

"There *is* something useful in here, though," Remy said.

"What's that?"

He lowered the file, grinning. "A name."

A door opened below them. They exchanged a horrified look.

"We didn't trip any alarms," Amaya hissed. "We would have heard them!"

"Doesn't matter, we need to get out of here *now*."

They put the files back and crept toward the stairs. The man who had closed up the offices for the night had returned, muttering to himself as he checked his desk for something.

"Swore I left it here," they heard. "She'll kill me if I lost it."

Then he headed back for the stairs.

Remy frantically pushed Amaya back into the records room, closing the door silently behind them. He pointed at a window in the back, but Amaya's eyes widened and she shook her head.

"We're on the second story," she whispered. "We can't make that jump."

"Who said anything about jumping? We're climbing to the roof."

Remy carefully opened the window, wincing as it scraped a bit. The stairs outside creaked under the weight of footsteps coming closer.

"Come on," Remy whispered, gesturing for her to follow. He disappeared out the window, reaching high above for the roof's ledge and hoisting himself up.

Amaya put her hands on the windowsill and leaned out, greeted with a kiss of cool night air. Her heart beat frantically in her chest.

"Amaya!"

She looked up at Remy, crouched on the roof with his hand extended toward her.

"I won't let you fall," he promised. "Come on."

But she couldn't move. She could only stare at his hand, waiting to clasp with hers.

Remembering her father's hand reaching for her when she had gotten stuck on the mast.

Remembered Boon's hand extending toward her, to help her up from the sand on the atoll.

Behind her, the door began to open.

Panic welled in her throat, choking off her breath. Her mind shut off completely and her body took over, making her dive out the window and hang on to its ledge with her fingers.

The man hummed off-key as he searched the shelves, scraping and shuffling until he crowed with triumph.

"I take it off for one bloody minute and suddenly it becomes the lost treasure of Valens." A rustle, then his voice climbed higher as if impersonating a woman. "'Take your wedding ring off, Belamy, I don't want to see it.' Last time we do that here..."

Footsteps, then the door closing. The creak of the stairs. The slam of a distant door.

Her fingers were already fatigued from all the locks she had picked. She was beginning to slip when Remy reached down and grabbed her, then hauled her onto the roof.

"Amaya, what in the hells?" he demanded. "Why didn't you take my hand?"

She stared at him, lips parted. Swallowing, she looked away as the wind blew her hair back. "I don't know."

She didn't want to say that she felt fractured and unsure, that for one painful second she'd had a vision of him releasing his grip and letting her fall. Just as so many others had let her fall.

Hands were too easy to let go of.

Remy sighed and hugged her. She slowly returned the embrace, missing when this had been easy, when she could just rest her head on his chest and allow it to be a comfort.

"You need to trust me, Amaya," he whispered. "I know we're not the children we once were, but that doesn't change the fact that I care about you. That I want to help you."

She closed her burning eyes, trying not to remember a day on the sea, eating dumplings and cake with her father. The way his arms had felt around her. "I know. I'm sorry."

But she had trusted Boon, and look where that had gotten her.

Remy pulled back, trying to smile. "Well, near-capture or not, at least we got something out of this."

"You said you found a name in the file. Whose name was it?"

"Julien Caver. I don't recognize it, but it's a start, and certainly better than nothing."

Amaya nodded, thinking of the pile of counterfeit coins below their feet, as dangerous and deadly as a monster's horde.

When she returned to the apartment, she thought everyone would be asleep.

She wasn't expecting to find Cayo sitting at the table, an arm wrapped around his midsection as if it pained him.

"Cayo?" She came closer, frowning at the state of him. He was bruised, hair a mess and falling limply across his forehead. His clothes were torn and stained, his posture defeated. "What happened?"

When their eyes locked, he rolled his shoulders back with a wince, sitting up straighter.

"I want you to teach me how to fight," he said.

8

*The hands of the gentry must remain soft and smooth,*
*unmarred by callus or other such visible sign of physical*
*exertion. That is how we tell the elite from the commoner.*
—THE HANDBOOK FOR NOBLES, VOL. I

Cayo regretted his decision as he climbed onto the roof of the tenement building after work the following day. Amaya had found a ladder leading to the flat slab of stone and mortar, deeming it the perfect place to begin training.

Cayo did not agree. There were no protective mats, no practice weapons, no walls to shield his incompetence from anyone who happened to look out a window.

He had woken this morning already sweating with nerves. It wasn't merely the thought of fighting that tangled his intestines into a pit of restless snakes; it was also the thought of being alone with Amaya, of having her instruct him in something so foreign and intimate. Part of him was still upset about her earlier outburst, but it was quickly fizzling away into a singular, heavy block of dread.

Yet when he crawled onto the roof after another frustrating day at the fish market, the wind buffeting his shirt, he quickly realized the two of them would not be alone. Liesl stood waiting, Deadshot on her right and Amaya on her left.

"Um," said Cayo. "What's this?"

"You really think Amaya's capable of teaching you all you need to know?" Liesl said, ignoring Amaya's glare. "She's still green herself. *I'm* going to be in charge here."

"And I'm going to be your sparring partner," Amaya said.

Cayo swallowed and glanced at Deadshot, her expression—as it normally was—stony and unreadable. "And you?"

Deadshot smirked, the tiniest crack in a statue. "I'm here to make sure they don't kill you."

"Before we get started, I need to know what you may have already learned," Liesl said, pushing her glasses up her nose. "And then drill those teachings out of you."

Cayo shifted on his feet. Under the women's stares, he couldn't help but feel woefully inadequate.

"I haven't really learned anything," he mumbled. "Just how to escape muggers."

"That's come in handy, it seems."

He scowled. "That's why I'm here. If I can't protect myself, how can I protect Soria? Or anyone?" Cayo gritted his teeth and looked away. "I know I'm not skilled, or...or useful like the rest of you. I want to change that."

There was an uncomfortable silence as they processed his words. Liesl eventually cleared her throat.

"We're not here to make you feel like you're at a disadvantage," she said, her voice a little softer. "I mean, you *are*, but you're taking steps to strengthen yourself. That's admirable, and perhaps long overdue. Better now than never."

Cayo nodded, grateful for the words. Then Liesl handed him a knife.

"Let's get to work."

Cayo was afraid they would immediately launch into a death brawl and was strangely disappointed when Liesl only showed him the different ways to hold a knife. The hilt felt clumsy and strange in his hand, as if it knew as well as he did that it didn't belong there.

"Feet wider apart," Liesl ordered. "Move the back one more on an angle. Not that far. Do you want to fall over?"

He patiently suffered through it, swallowing his retorts and sighs. He was tired after his second day at work, making him sluggish. Amaya sat against a chimney and watched while Deadshot cleaned her nails with the tip of a dagger. Cayo guessed an hour had passed by the time Liesl got out her own knife.

"All right," she said. "Let's teach you some sparring."

She showed him how to block, how to leap back and to the side when the enemy lunged, how to target the weak points in an adversary's musculature. When she went through the movement with him, though, he was slow and unsure, and Liesl kept tapping the places she could hit if they were actually fighting.

"Wrist—cut. Artery—severed. Chest—stabbed."

"I get it," he grumbled. "I'll try again."

They went through it a few more times, but Cayo's coordination was off. He glanced over to find Amaya still watching, wearing a small frown. Heat rose up his neck under her scrutiny, his shoulders hunching in discomfort.

Liesl switched tactics to offensive strategy instead. She taught him how to lunge, how to slash and how to stab. He held back more than she wanted him to, but he was afraid he might accidentally nick her.

"Stop focusing on that and start focusing on what your body is doing," Liesl told him.

But that was what he least wanted to do, knowing that Amaya was right there, silently judging his every move. When he stepped forward and jabbed toward Liesl's midsection, she easily disarmed him. The knife slid across the roof.

"You're ignoring what I said about how to hold it," Liesl admonished. "Do you actually want to be taught, or no?"

"I do, I just..." He raked a hand through his hair. "I don't know what's wrong."

"Nobody gets it right on their first day. Trust me, I was once just as frustrated as you are now."

"But you had time to learn this stuff. I don't."

"That's why you need to listen carefully to what I'm telling you."

"I *am*, but—"

"I'll help."

Amaya had retrieved the knife. She handed it back to him, hilt first, and he accepted it with a small nod of thanks.

"There are a few things that helped me when I was being taught," Amaya said. "If you'd like me to tell you."

He almost couldn't believe what he was hearing. She was offering to help rebuild the bridge between them, meeting him brick for brick. But there was a flightiness to her eyes, and her jaw was clenched.

He still hadn't forgiven her for lying to him, for deceiving him in Moray. But perhaps the time for forgiveness had come and gone. If he were being honest, he didn't know what he felt anymore; everything had been funneled into a helpless anger, a grim acceptance that what had happened wasn't merely Amaya's fault. It had been Boon's as well, and the Slum King's, and his father's. Especially his father's.

Cayo nodded, not trusting himself to speak. She relaxed slightly.

"I'll watch your form," Liesl said, going to stand beside Deadshot. "Remember what I said about your grip."

Cayo glared down at his hand, readjusting his fingers. It still didn't feel quite right.

"An egg," Amaya murmured.

"What?"

"Think about how you'd hold an egg. Not too tight, because the shell will break, but not too loose because it'll fall and crack."

He revisited a blurry memory of traveling the countryside with his family, how his mother had insisted on buying eggs from a farm they'd passed. He had marveled at the delicate eggs his mother put in his hands, their shells brown and slightly rough against his skin. He shifted his grip on the knife, thinking about those eggs.

"Arm up," Amaya said, lifting her own knife. "Now dodge."

They worked through the same movements, the same lunge and step, the same slash and block. But Cayo found himself far more focused on Amaya than himself; the way she moved like flowing water, in and out like the tide. There was surety in her limbs, in her expression, in the way she flicked her knife like she intended to use it.

It brought a strange moment of dissociation as he staggered back.

For a moment, he saw her in an elaborate gown of flowers. Her face was touched with rouge, her dark hair in elegant coils. She was giving him that small, contained smile, a delicious secret hidden in the curve of her lips.

But no—that was Countess Yamaa, the girl he had found himself pulled to like a raft to shore.

This girl was Amaya, her dark hair frizzing out of its braid, her mouth a thin, grim line. No dresses to hide behind. No title to use as a shield. Just the ferocity in her eyes and the power in her body.

And she was just as beautiful.

Her boot connected with his chest. Cayo grunted as he fell backward, catching himself on the hard roof as the knife went skittering from his hand again.

Amaya stood over him, that concerned expression back. "Maybe knives aren't for you." She turned toward Liesl. "Should we try a sword?"

"One thing at a time," Liesl said. "For now, let's practice some hand to hand before it gets dark."

Cayo laid back with a sigh, half considering rolling off the edge of the roof to escape them. But Amaya's eyes were still on him, and he felt it like a touch, an invisible string pulling at him to get up and try again.

So he got back to his feet and tried again.

Work the next day was its own special hell. Cayo spent the early morning cursing out Liesl and Amaya as his limbs screamed every time he moved. When he crouched to retrieve the fish, he gasped and nearly tottered over as his thighs twanged with pain.

"Why you twitching about?" Victor demanded. "Sick?"

Cayo tried to respond in Soléne so that the man would stop using his broken Rehanese. "I'm not sick. I was...training."

"You were fishing? Why you fish when fish are right here?"

"No, tra— You know what, never mind."

As soon as he was done setting up the display of fish, Victor handed him an address on a slip of paper.

"Delivery," the man grunted. "Special customer. Do not lose."

Cayo studied the address. It was near the shopping district they had passed on their first night here, but it would take some time to find the street, if his past experiences were anything to go by. Victor gestured to a small sack behind him.

"Go before these spoils."

Cayo hauled the sack over his shoulder, grateful to get away from the market. It was loud and cold and smelled awful, although every day he found himself acclimating to it a little more.

Was this how people did it, then? They found a profession they could somewhat tolerate until it simply became routine?

The sky was sunny and clear, which meant more people out and about. Women donned bonnets and kerchiefs to protect from the sun while the men wore wide brimmed hats. Back in Moray, Cayo would have seen a sea of paper parasols.

A surge of homesickness rose within him. He wished he were sitting on the balcony of Mercado Manor watching the sea with Soria, like their mother used to do with them.

Cayo wandered between shops in search of the right address. The store fronts were charming and elegant, paneled with stone and wood and latticework, some with lavish window displays and others with floral designs painted around the names above the doors.

Once Soria was feeling better, he would take her here. They couldn't buy anything—not like they used to—but he wanted to see her eyes light up in glee, trying on dresses and jewelry and cooing over adorable ceramic animal figurines.

He stepped off the main street and eventually found the road he was looking for. The address led him to a shop facade subtler than the ones Cayo had just seen. Above the door was painted a symbol in gold: a circle containing a geometric star.

Cayo had seen this symbol before, on their first night here. When he had asked what it meant, Remy had told him that Chalier—Baleine in particular—had a growing population of alchemists.

Alchemy was a peculiar thing; most seemed to think of it as magic, though in reality it was more a type of science. People in Moray tended to be wary of alchemists, superstitious and unwilling to get caught up in a practice they knew nothing about.

Perhaps they had been right to fear it. After all, the counterfeit coins had been made using alchemical means.

Cayo shoved through the door, and his senses were immediately bombarded. Tables and shelves were crowded with a variety of odd tools and vials, some looking fit to double as torture devices. There were powders and liquids and bricks of herbs, as well as small lumps of clay and charcoal. Symbols had been painted on the walls, and Cayo vaguely recognized them as the symbols for copper, silver, and gold. The smell of the place was reminiscent of metal, a sharp tang with an undercurrent of earthy loam.

There was no one in the shop, so Cayo uncertainly approached the counter in the back. On top of it was a bizarre device supplying a small flame under a glass beaker, the purplish contents simmering with tiny bubbles.

"Hello?" Cayo called in Soléne. "I have a delivery."

A curtain hanging from an open doorway parted. A man in his late midyears peered out suspiciously, glasses reflecting the flame under the beaker.

"Victor Belar?" the man asked.

"I'm one of his workers," Cayo tried to say.

"You're one of his *nieces*?"

"No, I—Victor sent me." He really had to work on his Soléne.

The man came out, brushing off his hands. They were coated with a reddish dust that clouded in the air. He was slightly taller than Cayo and paler, with a head of graying dark hair and a strong, pro-truding chin. He gestured to the sack, and Cayo handed it over.

Cayo checked the name on the slip of paper. "Are you Francis Florimond?"

"Aye." The man bent his head over the open sack, taking a deep whiff. Cayo's mouth twisted; he'd had enough fish smells for one day. "Seems good. Hold on, I'll get the payment."

Florimond took the sack into the back room—his workshop, Cayo guessed. While he waited, Cayo wandered through the aisles of tables, spinning a cog on a tool he had no name for and studying a jar containing a peculiar silver liquid. When Florimond returned, he lifted an eyebrow at Cayo.

"That's poisonous, you know." He had switched to Rehanese.

Cayo smartly took a step back. "Sorry. I'm just curious about… all this." He gestured to the shop around him. "What do alchemists do, exactly?"

Florimond harrumphed and set a small pouch of coins on the counter. "Not an easy thing to explain, boy. Even the basics would make your ears wither."

"I know there's something about…manipulation? Transformation?"

"That's a simple way to put it, sure." When Cayo waited for elaboration, he rolled his eyes. "You got the four main elements—water, earth, air, fire—and everything derives from them. When you rearrange their properties, you get something else." Florimond shrugged, as if that made perfect sense. "In the past, it was thought to be more charlatanry than science. The rich would drink mercury and liquid gold, thinking it would extend their lives. Rather, it did just the opposite. Nowadays it's mostly creating goods. Gunpowder. Medicine."

"Oh." Cayo glanced at the curtain to the workshop. "Why do you need fish, then?"

"You ask a lot of questions," the man grumbled. "I use their guts sometimes. Or grind up their bones. Or just fry them for dinner. Now, if you're done, I need to get back to work."

"Are you hiring?" He cringed as he blurted it, but he would much prefer working in a place like this than the fish market.

Florimond scowled. "I work alone. Besides, I don't want Victor coming in here to yell at me for stealing one of his workers. Or niece. Whichever you are." The man disappeared into the back.

Cayo sighed and took the payment, stuffing it into his pocket. At least he'd given it a shot.

He rushed to the hospital as soon as he was done for the day, trying his best to ignore the heavy ache in his arms and legs and the way his chest felt as if it were about to collapse at any moment. Stumbling through the incense-choked street, he coughed into his sleeve and burst through the doors, out of breath.

A nearby nurse started at his entrance. "Sir—"

"Visitation ends in an hour," he reminded her. She pursed her lips in annoyance before continuing her rounds.

He made his way slowly up the stairs, cursing Liesl with every step as his thighs burned. Before he went to Soria's room, he made a beeline toward the offices that Mother Hilas had shown him.

"The hospital administrator takes care of all the finances," she had explained. "In order to pay for your sister's treatment, you'll need to make payments to him directly."

The door to the office was open, so Cayo knocked and stepped inside. The administrator was seated at his desk and grinned in welcome.

"Mr. Lin," he greeted. "Nice to see you again. I assume you're here to make a payment?"

Cayo nodded and took the two niera from his pocket. He had run here straight from the fish market, going the long way around to avoid the spot where he'd been accosted by those thieves.

His chest tightened as the administrator took the niera with a pained expression. "Ah...Mr. Lin, I hate to say this, but..."

"It's not enough," Cayo finished for him. "I know, but there were thieves, and they..." What was he doing, making excuses? It wouldn't change the fact that he was still short. "I'm sorry."

The administrator rolled the coins in his hand, considering. "I'll tell you what. We can get your sister the medicine tomorrow and see how the treatment progresses, and you can make up the difference later. You'd still be responsible for paying the five niera for the next treatment, though."

"I...Thank you." The pressure in his chest loosened somewhat. "I appreciate it. I promise I'll get you the rest."

When he sat beside Soria's bed, she was asleep. His sister was pale today, the bags under her eyes pronounced, her breath wheezing in her lungs. She would at least be getting the first treatment, but what if he couldn't make enough for the next one? Or the one after that? According to Mother Hilas, she would need a dose every two days at minimum.

Cayo rubbed his hands over his face. They still smelled like fish. There was no chance he could possibly make enough money working for Victor. Could Jasper find another job for him? Could he possibly work two at once?

He thought back to the alchemist's shop. There were several in the city, and he wondered which ones were helping develop the treatment for ash fever. Perhaps Florimond needed those fish guts for a cure. If he went back and begged for a part-time position...if he were persistent about it, if he could somehow have a hand in finding a cure for Soria...

Then again, the opposite could be true as well. Amaya and Remy had found out that the counterfeit money was being mingled in with Chalier currency.

*If I found a way to get in with the alchemists, could I find out who's creating the counterfeits?*

He was thoroughly lost in thought when the door to the room opened and a woman escorted by a nurse entered. The woman sat beside the sleeping boy across the room, murmuring to him in Soléne as she smoothed his hair back. Cayo averted his eyes, giving them privacy.

Soria stirred at their voices, eyes fluttering open. "Oh. Hello.

92

How—" She paused to cough into her fist. "How was self-defense training?"

He had mentioned the idea to her last time he was here. He had expected her to laugh and tease him, but instead, she had nodded grimly and said, "About time."

"It was..." Cayo unwillingly recalled all the times he'd been disarmed, kicked, and pushed. "Well, it could have gone better."

"They walloped you, didn't they?"

"I wouldn't say *walloped*..." She delicately raised her eyebrows. "All right, fine, they walloped me."

She laughed, which turned into a cough. He poured her some water.

"Is Amaya teaching you how to use a knife?" she asked after a couple of sips.

"We've ruled knives out. I'm no good with them."

"Oh?" The corners of her chapped lips twitched. "Were you a little distracted, perhaps?" She cried out in indignation as he poked a spot in her side where he knew she was ticklish. The sound made the woman at the other bed glare at them, and they ducked their heads with suppressed laughs.

In a quieter voice, he told her more about the practice session, as well as how his work at the fish market was going. There was a brightness in her eyes as he talked, the same expression she'd worn when he had renounced his lifestyle in the Vice Sector.

Pride.

A while later, the nurse came back and told him that visitation hours were over. He squeezed Soria's hand and stood.

"I'll be back tomorrow after work," he said. "Let me know how the treatment goes."

"I will."

The nurse murmured to the woman across the room, who seemed stubborn to stay.

"Mrs. Caver, you may return tomorrow," the nurse was saying. "But he will need to rest now."

The woman swore and threatened to speak to the administrator about how she was being treated, and the poor nurse grimaced in discomfort. Cayo frowned, too, but not for the same reason; he frowned because the name sounded familiar.

As the woman finally stormed out, Cayo following a smart distance behind, it clicked: Caver was the name that Amaya and Remy had found in connection with the Benefactor.

Cayo's heart sped up as he glanced over his shoulder at the sick boy, his face splotched with gray.

Could they be connected?

He told the others when he returned to the apartment. Their expressions ranged from surprised to uncertain to excited.

"Congratulations," said Liesl with a smile as sharp as her knife. "You may not be able to throw a decent punch, but you just got us a new lead."

# 9

*We find war in ourselves, as we find war in churning*
*red mud, gunpowder clouds, the cries of sated crows.*
*We walk from a battleground every day.*

—XIN SHE, REHANESE PHILOSOPHER

Y ou're strangling the bread," Liesl told her.

Amaya relaxed her hold on the crusty loaf in her hands, hearing it crackle as the scent of yeast wafted from the fabric Liesl had wrapped it in. "Sorry."

She blamed the fact that they were surrounded by too many people for her comfort, all chattering and haggling across the marketplace in a language she didn't know. Not even the threat of a mysterious fever could stop them from congregating. Amaya and Liesl stood under a red awning as Liesl tested tomatoes, gently squeezing them to determine their ripeness.

Amaya was fascinated by the food here. She was used to the

colorful fruits and produce of Moray: taro, coconut, mango, guava. Moray's cuisine was a curious blend of Rehanese and Ledese, with Rain Empire delicacies. But here the focus was on bread, potatoes, and cheese—and fish, of course—and Amaya wondered how the people here could sustain diets so rich in heavy foods.

It reminded her of being in Viariche during her training with Boon and the others. The way Boon had sometimes bought an entire loaf of bread and ripped hunks from it while walking down the streets at night, teaching her how to steal, how to misdirect others.

The memory turned her stomach cold, and she suddenly wanted to hurl the bread she was holding as far away from her as possible.

*I will find you*, she thought. *I'll put everything you taught me to use and make you suffer.*

"Stop scowling," Liesl said. "You'll attract attention."

Amaya forced herself to take a deep breath. They weren't here to merely shop for their dinner. Amaya glanced down the street, where Avi casually leaned against a building. He affected boredom, but he was keeping a careful eye on their mark, a young woman with a basket dangling from her arm. She currently stood before a stall displaying glass bottles of milk.

"Something's been bothering you," Liesl said as she moved on to the next stall, this one carrying different types of salts. Liesl tested a thick granule of pink salt and hummed in approval.

Amaya began to squeeze the bread again, strangely comforted by its texture. "It's nothing."

"Yara..."

She sighed, partially from resignation and partially from the sound of her fake name. "It's really nothing. Just...thinking about Boon. How to track him down."

Liesl peered over her glasses at her. "And? How far have you gotten?"

Amaya blinked. She had expected a reprimand, maybe even laughter. "Not far?"

"Do you think he left Moray?"

"If he's smart, he would have."

"Do you think he has ties to the Benefactor?"

"I..." Amaya stared at the girl, wondering how much time Liesl had devoted to this particular train of thought. "He might. He probably does, doesn't he?"

Liesl nodded. "Then that means Boon is either in hiding, or somewhere within the Rain Empire. Or both."

"When were you going to discuss this with me?"

"We're discussing it now, aren't we?"

Amaya gritted her teeth against a retort. Still, she felt better knowing she wasn't the only person who planned to find him again. The others were just as hurt, just as ready to spring into action. Even Cayo was doing his part by asking them for training.

"By the way, you're going too easy on Cayo," Amaya said. "He's already been pampered all his life. He needs to learn faster."

Liesl thought it over as she filled a small pouch with the pink salt and paid the vendor. "Maybe I am being too lenient. But people like him tend to break if they're pushed too hard."

"He won't break." She didn't know where the acidity in her voice came from. "He's not as strong as he'd like, but he's not weak."

Liesl's lips quirked up in a smile, though Amaya wasn't sure why. "Noted. I'll go harder on him. Poor lad."

"See? You're doing it again." Amaya rolled her shoulders back, trying to get rid of some of the tension. "You were never that soft with me."

Liesl paused before a cabbage merchant, a curious expression crossing her face. She took in a breath as if to speak, then let it out as a sigh. After a moment she said, "You're right. I suppose...I suppose I was harder on you because you remind me of someone."

Amaya's frown dissolved. "Your sister."

Liesl nodded. She picked up a cabbage head, pretending to study it as her eyes grew distant.

"The first wave of the Rain Empire's military swept through Chalier about ten years ago. It was...bloody. The country had resisted for as long as it could, but in the end, it fell because of dirty politicians and the cowardice of the wealthy class. They were allowed to keep their manors and their titles so long as they signed off the land to the empire."

Liesl took a short, controlled breath and set the cabbage head down. "Naturally, the common folk took the brunt of the invasion. They fought back in whatever ways they could. They refused to simply hand over all they had to an empire they wanted no part of." Her jaw clenched, the muscle jutting out. "My parents were part of the rebellion. There was a horrible riot, what people refer to now as the Courser Day Massacre. They both died that day."

Amaya hugged the loaf of bread to her chest. She had guessed that Liesl was also an orphan, but knew it couldn't have been an easy thing to say aloud. The gods knew she had trouble even thinking it. "I'm so sorry."

"I was left alone to care for my little sister, and as a result she had to grow up much faster than she should have." Liesl shook her head. "She'd been such a sunny child, and after that...well. Neither of us were the same.

"As we grew older, my sister and I did the only thing we could to avenge our parents—we joined the rebellion ourselves, to one day claim our independence again." Liesl lowered her voice even more. "Although now, as you can see, it's more of an underground coalition. Too many of us have been caught or killed to risk being exposed."

Amaya nodded. "Jasper's in it, too."

"Yes. It's why he has so many contacts, knows his way through the city better than anyone. He and Adrienne became inseparable. He taught her how to get information, and she taught him how to decode messages. It was kind of terrifying, seeing them work so efficiently together."

"Are you gonna buy some cabbages or no?" snapped the merchant.

Liesl cursed at him in Soléne before they moved on to a cloth vendor. "She was there when he lost his hand. They were caught on a ship during a mission to steal some naval plans. The captain retaliated by taking Jasper's hand. Probably would have taken more had I not come and dragged them out of there."

"So that's what he meant by owing you," Amaya murmured. "And why he didn't like the sight of Remy's jacket."

"It's always been dangerous, what we do. But the chance to get back at those who betrayed us . . . it was worth it, to me." Liesl touched a bolt of satin, rubbing it between her fingers. "Until we were caught."

"By André Basque?"

Liesl nodded, that cold, hard look returning to her eyes. "We were on a mission to get correspondence from his home office, but Adrienne was captured, and I ran back to try and save her. I'm sure you can guess how that went. I thought I was going to hang, but apparently because I'm a woman, they were too squeamish to sentence me to death." She scoffed. "So they made me Landless instead."

"And your sister?"

"I don't know." Liesl's cold expression collapsed into one of such despair that Amaya felt it like a crack in her chest. "They kept us separated, and they refused to tell me what they'd done with her. Not even Jasper knows, and he practically tore the city apart to find out. I've searched for her, but it's like trying to find one fish in an ocean." She dropped the fabric and turned to Amaya. "But I haven't given up. I swore that if I ever came back here, if I ever encountered Basque again, I would make him tell me where she was. I would finally get my vengeance—for myself, for Adrienne, and for our parents. Now that our path has led us here, I have to make the most of it. I have to find her."

Amaya studied the ground as Liesl led her to the next stall. Some bell inside her had been struck by Liesl's words, as if Liesl were a distorted mirror reflecting back the very thing that had driven Amaya to this moment. She brushed her thumb over the knife tattoo at her wrist, the ink no longer as stark and vibrant as it had once been.

*Survive. Revenge.* These were the pillars upon which she'd built herself, the promises that had given her a reason to fight, a reason to deceive and harm and kill. But even though she had taken strides to fulfill these promises, they had left her colder and emptier than before. She had ruined lives, including Cayo's. Including her own.

What form of ruin would Liesl's revenge take?

"That's why you were happy to stay in Baleine," Amaya said. Liesl nodded. "I'll help you find your sister, so long as you don't lose sight of our mission."

She would be there for Liesl just as Liesl had been there for her. And, hopefully, there would be less of a mess to clean up afterward.

Liesl was solemn as she reached out and squeezed Amaya's wrist.

"Thank you," she whispered.

A soft whistle caught their attention. Avi stood nearby, feigning interest in a glassblower's wares. He nodded discreetly in the direction where the young woman with the basket had gone.

"First things first," Liesl muttered as she and Amaya began their slow, careful chase.

They followed the young woman through narrow alleys and streets, being mindful not to get too close or make much noise. Finally, she arrived at a handsome homestead, the front made of white stone and the windows sporting planters of red geraniums. It was by no means the nicest house Amaya had ever seen, but it was far from the worst.

Amaya ducked around the corner as Liesl hurried on ahead and pretended to trip over her skirts. "Oh, drat! Excuse me? Um, miss?"

The young woman turned, the front door open behind her. Her dark eyes were wide with surprise. "Yes? May I help you?"

It was easier for Amaya to hear Soléne than it was for her to speak it. Liesl had given her lessons when they had trained in Viariche, and even Boon had given her tips, although his accent had always made Liesl wince. But, just in case, Liesl had given her the gist of what she would say.

"I—I'm so sorry to intrude on your day," Liesl stammered, clutching at her skirts, "but I'm afraid I'm lost. I'm waiting for my brother to pick me up. He said he would be somewhere on Malene Street, but I haven't seen him yet. You haven't seen him, have you?"

"I . . . don't believe so," the young woman replied, confusion threaded through her words.

"He works for an affluent family somewhere nearby. A family by the name of LeRaine. This wouldn't be the LeRaine residence, would it?"

"No, it's the Caver residence. LeRaine is that way." The young woman pointed down the street.

Liesl brightened. "Oh! Thank you! Truly, I would lose my own head if it weren't attached to my neck...."

The young woman gave her a nervous smile and disappeared into the house, closing and locking the door behind her.

Liesl returned to Amaya as Avi joined up with them. "Let's wait for nightfall before we continue. You know what to do, Avi?"

He looked offended by the question. "What do you think?"

"Then let's get this food back to the apartment. Deadshot will start whittling the chairs into spears if there's nothing for dinner."

At midnight, Amaya, Liesl, and Deadshot met Avi down in the basement of the tenement building. Tied to a chair was a barrel-chested man with a gag in his mouth and a cloth over his eyes. He was sweating profusely, filling the damp, mildewy basement with the tang of salt and fear.

Liesl set her lantern on a dusty crate and clasped her hands together, all business. "Julien Caver?"

Avi removed the gag but not the blindfold. The man's rasping breaths filled the dim basement, the shadows created by the lantern flickering across his square face.

"What do you want with me?" he growled. "Is it money? I'll give you money, just let me go!"

"Money of a sort," Liesl said. Her voice was cool and proper, and even Amaya found it intimidating. "We know you've been dealing with counterfeit currency, Mr. Caver. Or would you like us to call you the Benefactor?"

The man leaned back—or tried to, in his restrains. He bared his teeth, lips red from the gag.

"What are you talking about? Who's a benefactor?"

Liesl exchanged a look with Avi, who stepped forward and smacked Caver across the face. The man cried out, and Amaya's lips thinned.

"We don't like playing games," Liesl said. "Is it true that you frequently visited the currency exchange offices on Heliope Avenue to deposit large sums of gold?"

Caver gaped, speechless. Sweat rolled down his temples, dampening his blindfold.

"I...I used to. But that was months ago."

"You changed offices, you mean. To stagger the trail."

"What are you talking about? No, I..." Caver gulped, trembling now. "For a while I was hired by someone to go to the foreign currency exchange and put my name down on the transaction papers. Once a month, I'd go to pick up the stash and deliver it to the offices. Then I was paid a percentage from the exchange."

Amaya frowned, as did Liesl. Deadshot made a questioning motion as to whether or not she should hit him this time, but Liesl shook her head.

"And how exactly did this work?" Liesl asked.

"I would get an address delivered a day before the exchange. I'd go to the address, and the money would be waiting. Then I took it to the offices, had it exchanged to Rain or Rehanese currency depending on what was in the bag, and took eight percent for myself. I'd go back to the address where I found the money and leave the exchanged money in its place. Then one day, the money just...stopped coming.

I wasn't given a reason why, just told that my services weren't needed anymore."

"But who hired you in the first place?" Liesl said.

"That's just it—I have no idea. I felt like I was being followed for a week before I got a letter in the mail with the job offer. I needed the money bad, so I wrote back and accepted."

Liesl removed her glasses and pinched the bridge of her nose. Deadshot had begun to pace.

"So you're not the Benefactor," she said flatly.

"I told you, I have no idea what that means!"

"And you have no idea who hired you." Liesl returned her glasses and fixed him with a glare he couldn't see. "I'm sure this all seemed perfectly legal to you?"

"You don't understand." Caver's voice began to tremble. "At first it was to pay off some debt, but then my son, he...he got the fever. Paying to keep him alive is taking everything from us. If my brother wasn't military, I don't even know how we'd be able to get him into a hospital. Every hospital in the city is overrun by the rich who can afford treatment."

Amaya looked at Liesl. The girl looked back, frustration in her gaze. They had to let Julien Caver go.

Their lead had led to nothing.

"Very well," Liesl said, signaling Avi again.

"Wait!" Caver shifted, and Amaya wondered if he thought they were going to kill him. "I know a fellow like me who was hired in the same fashion. Except he doesn't go to the offices, he goes to the casinos."

"The casinos?" Liesl repeated.

"He gets a cache of solstas and distributes them by gambling

104

throughout the city. My guess is the money's dirty. Spread out like that, it'll be harder to track down, right?"

Amaya curled her hands into fists. If only he knew just how dirty that money was.

"And what's this man's name?" Liesl asked.

Caver hesitated, but eventually cowardice won out over loyalty. "Trevan Nicodeme."

"What does he look like?"

"I...Just a regular man, you know? He's got thick muttonchops. Bit of a belly. Likes to wear a pocket watch. I—I don't know what else..."

Liesl nodded to Avi. "Thank you, Mr. Caver." Avi quickly choked Caver into unconsciousness before reapplying the gag. "Get him back into his house before anyone realizes he's missing."

"The records at the offices said that Mercado was the one receiving the gold, not sending it," Amaya pointed out. "Maybe they used a different office for Mercado's payments?"

"That could be the case," Liesl said slowly, "or else we're missing some crucial connection."

"What do we do now?" Amaya asked as Avi hauled the man over his shoulder, grunting at his weight.

"I was hoping for a different outcome, but I suppose a name is better than nothing. We'll just need to find this gambler and see if he knows more." Liesl took a deep breath. "And while we work on that, there's someone else I can set my sights on."

Amaya's stomach squirmed. "Basque."

"Adrienne," Liesl corrected. Deadshot took her hand, and Liesl gave her a small smile. "While we search for the distributor of the counterfeit money, we might also be able to find out where they took my sister."

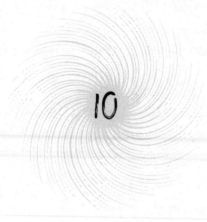

## 10

If only we could see each other's worth,
The death of our demons, a new star's birth.

—KHARIAN SONG

Cayo hid a yawn in his elbow, grimacing as it allowed a fresh wave of fish stink to enter his mouth. It was dawn at the docks, and Victor was going through his business ledger as Cayo set up the fish on ice, their own little routine.

He'd been doing this for a week now, but it had only gotten marginally easier. He still dropped fish, misjudged how much ice was in the bucket, and got lost during deliveries. Victor barked at him when he messed up, clapping his hands to make Cayo hurry and muttering to himself in Soléne. The man didn't know that Cayo's Soléne had been returning to him more and more and that he could actually understand what the fishmonger was saying, curses and all.

But Cayo was determined to keep at it. Just the other day he had visited Soria and noticed the difference the treatment was making, the way she was able to stay awake longer, the way she coughed less frequently. He still had to make up the difference for the treatment's cost, but if he found a way to keep making payments, then maybe... maybe she really could be cured.

Besides, it was now a matter of principle. Yesterday he had walked into the apartment to find Deadshot handing Avi a couple of coppers.

"What's that for?" Cayo had asked.

"We had a bet that you wouldn't last a week at the fish market," Avi had explained. "I had the utmost faith in you, though. This one didn't." Deadshot smirked.

"Take a bath before we start training," Liesl had told him, not even looking up from the news sheet she was reading. "You smell like a merman's balls."

"Do mermen *have* balls?" Avi asked.

Amaya, drinking tea, had looked Cayo up and down. "So? How does it feel, working with fish all day?"

He recognized the sting of a barb when he heard one. Cayo had tried to meet her stare, but in the end he'd muttered something about washing up and escaped to his bedroom.

He held a fish in his hand now, gazing at its pale underbelly. He imagined Amaya sinking a knife into its flesh and scraping out its insides, repeating the process for hours on end. Day in and day out. For seven years.

On board his father's ship.

"Where you gone?" Victor clapped loudly beside Cayo's ear, making him jump. "Move!"

Cayo kept his head down as he piled the fish onto the ice. Customers were beginning to trickle in, the first rush before the midmorning lull, which was usually when Victor made him do deliveries.

His task done, Cayo stood and stretched out his back. Between working at the market for hours, followed by training, followed by running to the hospital to see Soria before visitation ended, he was completely exhausted. By the end of every day he was usually out as soon as his head hit the pillow. He couldn't remember when he'd last been this tired.

He took refuge behind the stall, sitting on his usual stool and bracing his elbows on his knees. Victor typically dealt with the customers, not trusting Cayo's shaky Soléne to get him through an encounter. Cayo was all too happy to let him, giving himself an opportunity to people watch.

He'd noticed more sailors and visitors entering the harbor with those green squares pinned to their clothes. Cayo wondered what happened to those who didn't pass inspection, if the quarantine bays were full and if the infected were now being forced to turn back around.

Victor swore suddenly. Cayo immediately thought it had something to do with him, but Victor was glaring at a woman browsing the eels nearby. She was tall and willowy, and wore a fine pink dress that flared over her hips. Her brown curls were nestled under a wide-brimmed hat, her hands covered in gloves of white lace.

Cayo didn't see what the fuss was about. He had seen plenty of women like this in Moray, out for a stroll under Rehanese-style parasols. But the girl who worked the stall beside theirs was also glaring at the woman.

"Who is she?" Cayo asked her. He needed an excuse to practice his Soléne.

The girl blinked at him. "How should I know?"

"Everyone seems to be...I don't know...targeting her." The other vendors made a show of putting on wide smiles for her, exchanging pleasantries as she passed, but as soon as she turned away their faces fell into scowls.

"We don't need to know her name to know she's part of the nobility." The girl crossed her arms, a defensive pose. "A beautiful, rich traitor."

"I don't understand. What makes her a traitor?"

"Chalier was incorporated into the Rain Empire because of people like her." The girl turned and spat. "They got to keep their precious wealth while the military stormed in, beating and herding the rest of us."

Cayo bit the inside of his cheek, thinking of Moray. Now that the prince was dead, what would become of his home? Would it be incorporated into the Rain Empire due to the cowardice and greed of the gentry? Would his father be at the forefront of that movement? And what about the Sun Empire, who had always wanted possession of Moray and its trade routes?

"Surely it's not just the gentry's fault," he said. "The empire was the one taking your land."

"The empire took our land, but the gentry takes things from us all the time." Her crossed arms tightened. "My friend got ash fever a few months ago. She tried to be admitted into a hospital, but they were already full of the infected upper class. They bribed the city officials to close off the hospitals just for them. So we cared for her as best we could." Her eyes shone as a tear fell over one freckled cheek. "She was evicted from her apartment—too sick to work. She died on the streets before we could find her."

Cayo averted his gaze. "I'm...I'm sorry." He swallowed, his throat tight and dry. "My sister has it, too."

The girl gave him a look of sympathy, one he didn't deserve. "Then you should understand our hate."

He did. He felt it now, reminded of the injustice of who received treatment and who was left to suffer. The most vulnerable members of society were essentially being told their lives didn't matter. That if they couldn't pay for medicine, they were already as good as dead.

But as the woman came to Victor's stall, as she smiled and pointed with a delicately laced finger at which fish she wanted wrapped up, Cayo couldn't help but yearn for a time when company like hers was normal. When he had been ignorant of the division between the classes, when he could escape into the crowd and pretend to be common for a night.

Then he wondered what Amaya would think of that. Cayo cringed, suddenly embarrassed for himself. She saw him as a child of privilege, something that had once angered him, offended him—but it was true. He had been a part of the problem. Probably still was.

He could work to undo it all his life, but it wouldn't change the devastation it had caused. Money, debt...it ruled the world, and the rich were content to keep it that way.

Victor let his smile fall as soon as the woman moved away. He snapped at Cayo. "You, go to this address."

Cayo reluctantly took the square of paper ripped from Victor's ledger, then perked up when he recognized the address. It belonged to the alchemist, Florimond.

*Maybe I can ask him for a part-time position again*, he thought with prickling excitement.

And that would mean more money for Soria *and* a way to investigate the alchemists—and potentially help find a cure. Smiling, Cayo hefted the sack of fish over his shoulder and took off, the sun warm against his back.

He passed a residential street, watching a woman beat the dirt and dust out of some rugs outside her home. When the street fed into the main thoroughfare, he stopped cold.

A checkpoint had been erected in the middle of the street. Citizens were lined up before the contingent of military guards, whose jackets were a dark blue trimmed in white. An officer was examining paperwork at the front, granting citizens access to the other side once they cleared inspection.

Cayo ducked around the corner and pressed his back against the wall, pulse racing.

He had forgotten his forged paperwork in the apartment. Liesl was going to murder him.

That is, if he didn't get thrown in jail.

But if he didn't get to the other side of the street and make this delivery, Victor would assuredly fire him—and he would lose another chance to convince Florimond.

Cayo gently knocked his head back against the wall. "Shit." There was only one thing he could do, and that was use the cramped, dark side streets to evade the checkpoint. It would take him much longer, and he would certainly get lost, but it was either that or a jail cell.

Heaving a nervous sigh, he pushed away from the wall and found the nearest alley. He was well acquainted with the alleys in Moray, and the ones in Baleine were no different; they ranged from harmless to foul, from laundry hanging out to dry to mounds of trash and... worse things.

The sounds of the crowd disappeared the deeper into the maze he went. He kept his eyes on the ground, not wanting to step in anything he'd regret. Which was how he ran into the three people he least wanted to see.

They jumped down from a balcony, blocking off his escape routes. Cayo tensed as they closed in, tightening his grip on the bag of fish.

"Well, well," said the short boy. "We were waitin' for folks to come by to escape the checkpoint, but this's an unexpected treat!"

"Yeah, I think we're fast becoming friends," the girl sneered. "You're not stalkin' us, are you, pretty boy?"

"I should be asking you that," Cayo said tersely, making sure to keep his eye on their positions. Liesl had instructed him to always be aware of his opponent's body, the way they moved, how even a twitch could give away what they were about to do.

"You know the routine by now," said the short boy, crooking a finger. "Hand it over."

"I haven't gotten paid for the day." They didn't have to know he had some niera in his pocket right now, still short what was owed to the hospital.

"Gotta have *something*," the tall boy said. "What's in the bag?"

"Buried treasure," Cayo said flatly. "What does it smell like? It's fish."

"Fetch a nice price at the market," the girl directed to the short boy. "And make a good dinner."

"No need to tell me twice." The boy grinned, his incisors sharp. "C'mon, friend, let's do it the easy way this time."

Cayo slowly lowered the bag to the ground. The three pickpockets smiled, but their expressions turned to surprise when Cayo raised his fists.

"Oh, you don't wanna do that," said the tall boy. He actually looked pitying.

"Nah, let's see what he's got up his sleeve," said the short boy, bouncing a bit on the balls of his feet as he lifted his fists as well. "Let me have it, pretty boy."

He and Cayo circled one another. Cayo's heart tapped a nervous rhythm against his breastbone, but he couldn't stop to wonder what in the hells he was doing; he had to prove that he could handle himself, that he was capable of learning and adapting.

He was too slow to evade the punch that connected with his jaw.

The other two hollered as Cayo staggered back, touching the spot where the boy's knuckles had barked against his jawbone. Pain lanced up his cheek, a sharp ache that momentarily wiped his mind blank.

"Whew!" The boy shook out his hand. "Again?"

Cayo dutifully raised his fists, and the boy laughed in approval. The other two thieves cheered him on as they circled once more, Cayo trying to drive out the ringing in his head in order to focus on the boy's small yet stocky frame.

A slight twist in his torso. Cayo stepped to the side, avoiding the boy's jab, and rushed in with an uppercut that sank into the boy's stomach.

"Oof!" The boy stumbled backward, wheezing with laughter. "Gettin' better!"

Cayo gritted his teeth at the patronizing tone, then immediately regretted it as pain shot across his jaw again. Making use of the distraction, the boy came at him with a quick series of punches, catching Cayo in the chest and arm as Cayo attempted to hook his foot around the boy's ankle. It was a move he had practiced with Amaya, much to his despair, as it involved quite a lot of physical contact.

But even though he managed to hook the boy's ankle and knock him off balance, the boy quickly turned them around and got Cayo pinned under him. Cayo growled and tried to break free, but the boy might as well have been made of brick.

"Nice try!" the boy said, cheerful. "You almost got me!"

Then he sank his fist into Cayo's stomach, repaying him for the earlier hit. All the breath rushed out of him as the boy rooted through his pockets and took the niera for himself. Cayo curled up on his side when the boy climbed off him, saliva dripping from his open mouth.

"Thanks for the fish!" the girl called as they ran off. "Better luck next time!"

Their laughter echoed down the alleyway as Cayo struggled to his feet. The bag was gone; his money was gone. He would have also said his dignity was gone, but that had been handed over a long time ago.

"Damn it." He held his throbbing head in dirty hands. What good were these training sessions if they weren't paying off? If he still got jumped and taken advantage of?

*Stop feeling sorry for yourself and do what has to be done.*

Usually his voice of reason sounded like Soria, which was why the memory of his father's voice came like a douse of cold water.

They had been sitting in his father's office at home. Kamon Mercado had been pacing, furious, while Cayo had sat slumped and hungover in the chair before his desk.

"I've given you everything," his father had seethed. "Anything you could possibly want, and this is how you repay your family? By going out and gambling away our money, drinking yourself to death, whoring yourself out to whomever you like?"

Cayo had sank farther into the chair, wishing his drinking *had* brought him death.

"You're going to fix this," his father had said, pointing a stern finger at him. "Whatever it takes, Cayo, you're going to do it. Not only for this family and our reputation, but for your own self-worth. Do you understand?"

Cayo had mumbled something about it being too hard.

"Don't give me excuses. Stop feeling sorry for yourself and do what has to be done."

In the present, Cayo sighed and dropped his hands. He supposed what needed to be done was return to Victor and explain what had happened.

But first, he had to take a risk.

When Cayo walked into Florimond's strange shop, the man was dealing with a customer. Cayo waited near some shelves, an arm wrapped around his torso as he swayed on his feet. As the customer left, she gave Cayo a nervous look.

"What's the meaning of this?" the older man barked in Rehanese. "Coming in here caked in dirt and bruised like rotten fruit. You'll scare away my customers!"

"S-sorry." Cayo shuffled forward, and the man adjusted his glasses.

"You're Victor's delivery boy. Where's my fish?"

"I, uh..." Cayo shifted, suppressing a wince. "As my appearance would suggest, I was robbed."

"Robbed." The word was flat, emotionless.

"They took my money, as well as your fish. I'm really sorry."

"So instead of returning to Victor to get it sorted, you came here to track filth into my store and tell me there's no delivery?"

Cayo flushed. "I..."

He remembered all the times he had gotten in trouble in Moray: with his father, with the Slum King, even Soria. Cayo had developed an entire retinue of excuses and methods to find the fastest, easiest route out of punishment, and he frantically searched through them now.

His eyes began to well with tears as his lower lip trembled.

"I...I'm so sorry," he said, his voice thick and warbling. "I couldn't stop them, and I just thought you should know what had happened...."

Florimond took a step back at Cayo's sudden display of emotion. "Well, that's—"

"I'm trying so hard to make money so that I can take care of my sister. But what I make isn't enough, and now these thieves have stolen all I have and your delivery, and I'm afraid..." His breath hitched, and this time he didn't have to feign the agony in his words. "I'm afraid I'll be fired, and that I'll lose her!"

Florimond was visibly sweating as Cayo sobbed, perhaps a little too loud to be believable, but the man seemed convinced as he frantically waved his hands through the air.

"It's fine, it's fine! I'll send along a note to Victor and tell him not to fire you, you can't help it if there were thieves."

"But even then, what I make with Victor isn't enough," Cayo mumbled, sniffing. "If I can't find a way to provide for my sister, she... We've already lost our parents....She's the only one I have left...."

116

Florimond sighed and ran a hand through his hair, making it stick up in the back. Cayo did his best to look as miserable as he felt.

"You asked me last time if you can help me out around the store," Florimond muttered. "I can't pay much, but if it'll get you to stop blubbering, you can come work a few hours each week. But you'll have to move heavy boxes and other such grunt work. You don't touch my experiments."

Cayo immediately stopped crying and wiped a sleeve under his eyes. "Truly? You'll let me work for you?"

"It's only temporary! And only if you do everything I say. If you don't—or if you start blubbering again—I'll kick you out."

Cayo clasped his hands together before him. "Thank you! Thank you so, so much, Mr. Florimond!"

The man grunted something about coming in tomorrow evening before escaping to his back room. Cayo reined in his grin until he was back on the street, his victory nearly making him forget about the soreness of his body.

One more step toward finding the cure—or the counterfeits.

Or both.

Victor was upset about the fish, but the bruise blooming on Cayo's jaw was evidence enough that he was telling the truth. Still, he took it out of Cayo's pay and only gave him one niera instead of two. When Cayo passed by the hospital, he shamefacedly handed the single niera to the administrator instead of the three he had been counting on to complete the payment.

"I'm sorry it's not the full amount," Cayo said. "But I can get the rest to you tomorrow."

The man sighed, as if restraining himself from reminding Cayo that there could be no treatment without payment. Instead, the administrator gave him a weary smile and a nod. "That'll do just fine, Mr. Lin. So long as it's by tomorrow."

He visited with Soria for an hour. She was sleepy today and didn't speak much, so he mostly just held her hand and drank the willowbark tea that Mother Hilas made for him once she'd spotted his bruise. He liked the woman. She didn't ask questions.

Cayo glanced at the bed across the room. It was now empty. The boy, Mother Hilas explained when he asked about it, had been moved to a private ward. No doubt his parents were now paranoid after Liesl and the others had kidnapped Julien Caver.

When Cayo returned to the apartment, Liesl tsked at the sight of his bruise.

"Let's get to training, then," she said. "So that you don't get a matching one on the other side."

"Hold on. Something happened today."

"Other than a thrashing, you mean?"

But when he told the Landless and Amaya about working for Florimond, genuine shock flitted across their faces.

"You..." Avi leaned against the table, peering at Cayo as if seeing him for the first time. "You found a second job, one that gives us access to the alchemists." Cayo nodded. "Who are you, and what have you done with our little lord?"

"This is good," Liesl murmured, eyes already faraway with possibility. "Cayo can keep an ear to the ground in order to suss out which alchemists the counterfeit money is coming from."

118

"Which might lead to the Benefactor." Amaya looked at Cayo with a peculiar mix of confusion and satisfaction, though he couldn't say if it was directed at him or at the situation in general.

"Well done, Cayo." Liesl put a hand on his shoulder. "But don't think this'll get you out of training. Especially now that you've put yourself in an even more dangerous position. You have to be ready for anything."

He was disappointed that their pride hadn't lasted longer, but at least he had shown them he wasn't entirely useless.

They climbed up to the roof. Deadshot took her place against the chimney as Amaya watched on, Liesl going through the basics again with Cayo.

"So when he got you to the ground, what did you do? I'll show you how to break his hold next time. And I want you to start carrying a knife."

But they had tried knives, and a sword, and even a staff, and Cayo had been dreadful at all of them. He had tripped over the staff—which had just been a broom with the end chopped off—and had nearly impaled Liesl with Avi's sword. Hand to hand may have been a slight improvement, but his motions still felt clumsy and slow, and as they worked into the evening Cayo began to feel his frustration boiling.

"Again," Liesl instructed as he squared off against Amaya. "Get her into a headlock."

Cayo took in a breath and blocked Amaya's punch, restraining her arm. But she spun and kicked at his shin, making him curse and let her go.

"Do *not* break your hold!" Liesl barked.

"What in the hells am I supposed to do, then?" he shouted back. "I'm obviously not cut out for this!"

Liesl crossed her arms, a dangerous glint in her eye. "So you're just going to let yourself get mugged every day? Or, now that you're poking through the alchemists' affairs, present your back as an easy target in case you spook the wrong person? What about Soria? How will you pay for her treatment if they keep stealing your money?"

"I don't *know*, I... I don't know."

He sank into a crouch, holding his pounding head. He felt like he was going to throw up, or scream, or maybe both. All his earlier excitement washed away in a tide of that familiar, muddy dread. His breaths started to come quick, his stomach roiling with nausea.

Then came a gentle tap at his shoulder. Cayo looked up, expecting to find Amaya, surprised instead to see Deadshot crouched beside him.

Silently, she handed over one of her pistols.

Cayo stared at it. The muzzle was long and etched with a floral design, the handle gleaming with wood and pearl. Swallowing, he took it from her, testing the weight of the weapon in his hand.

"There's one thing we haven't tried yet," she said.

Liesl seemed unsure, but at Deadshot's small nod, she relented. Amaya regarded the pistol as if it were about to turn into a snake and wrap itself around Cayo's neck.

Deadshot went down to the apartment and came back with three empty milk bottles. She set them on the lip of the chimney, then stepped back.

"Use the sight if you need to," she said. "One foot in front. Don't lock your arms. Watch out for the recoil. Be careful where you point it."

Cayo waited, but no further instruction came. "That's it?"

"That's it."

He took a deep breath, his nerves buzzing. He'd never shot off a gun before. Cayo shook out his arms and lifted the pistol before him, aiming it at the leftmost bottle. The weight of it bore down his hands, but he forced himself to keep his arms up, to line up the sight as best he could.

He thumbed back the hammer and pulled the trigger.

The pistol jumped, the bullet firing with a kick of power that made him gasp and stumble back. The sound rang in his ears, his palms buzzing and warm in the aftermath.

It took a moment for him to realize the bottle had shattered. Glass spread across the roof like fallen diamonds, sharp enough to bite.

They were all silent as they processed the debris. Then Deadshot threw her head back and laughed.

"What do you know? A natural." She grinned and winked at Cayo, who flushed at the praise. "Guess I'll need to teach you how to reload."

"Well," Liesl said. "I suppose we've finally found your outlet."

Cayo looked down at the gun. It made him a bit uneasy, but he couldn't deny the power he had felt. He handed it back to Deadshot, but she shook her head.

"Keep her. I have plenty."

"Her?"

"Her name's Jazelle. You better take good care of her. She's a fine lady—likes to be pampered."

"I'll, uh, try my best."

"And you better not shoot your own foot off," Amaya muttered. "Or aim that thing at me."

"Why would I...?" Cayo shook his head. "I won't."

As he got ready for bed that night, he couldn't help but stare at the pistol gleaming against the bedsheet. It was beautiful, he had to admit. But deadly. He'd need to be careful with it, desperate not to prove Amaya right by accidentally shooting off one of his own appendages.

"Nice to meet you, Jazelle," he murmured. "Please don't get me murdered."

**11**

A ballroom is as dangerous as a battlefield.

—SAYING FROM THE RAIN EMPIRE

Y ou *what?*" Remy roared.

Amaya winced and rubbed her ear. "It was the only way."

"It was *not* the only way!" He groaned and put his head down on the apartment table, fingers digging into his windswept hair. "I was figuring out a way to call Caver in for questioning! You know, *legally.*"

"Where's the fun in that?" Avi asked as he sipped his tea.

Remy had been so busy with the fever relief efforts he hadn't been able to stop by for a few days. Liesl had debated whether or not to tell him about Caver, but Amaya had insisted. She was now beginning to regret it a little.

Remy peered up at Avi. "This is why you're all Landless. You think of the worst possible way to go about things and decide it's the best solution."

"Well, it was," Amaya retorted. "We got the information we needed. Or rather, we found out it was little more than a dead end."

"But now if I try to open up an investigation, there'll be an inquiry," Remy said. "Caver's scared out of his mind as it is after that stunt you pulled."

"But he won't go to the authorities," Liesl said. "Otherwise he'd have to admit to being involved in the Benefactor's counterfeit laundering."

"He didn't know it was counterfeit, though." Remy drummed his fingers against the table. "And now all we have is a new name that might not lead to anything we don't already know."

"Which you'll leave to us, if you're smart," Liesl said. "You would have spooked Caver just as bad had the authorities shown up on his doorstep. Anyone else involved in the scheme will be on high alert."

Remy sighed. "Fine. I'll let you have this one. But please, *please* inform me the next time you decide to kidnap someone."

"Absolutely not," Deadshot said.

Amaya smiled as Remy grumbled. She recalled the times on the *Brackish* when he had helped settle disputes between the Water Bugs, the lectures he'd given the ones who had been behaving poorly. She could see now that Remy had always been fit for authority.

Remy selected a butter cookie from the tin in the middle of the table. "By the way, where's Cayo?"

"At work," Avi said with a smirk.

"Oh, right." Remy gave Amaya a pointed look. "The fish market."

When Cayo came back smelling like fish and the sea, it tended to make her nauseous. It threw her back onto the *Brackish*, to the creaking of the rigging and the squish of fish guts between her fingers.

"Not the fish market," Avi said. "An alchemist's shop."

Remy blinked. "A what?"

"The little lord's gone and gotten himself a second job. One that might help us figure out which alchemists are in on the counterfeit scheme."

"Oh!" Remy glanced at Amaya to confirm this was true. "Well. That's...great, actually. Not the part about having two jobs, but that experimental treatment's not cheap. I don't blame him for getting a second one."

"How has it been going?" Liesl asked him. "Has it been administered to others?"

"The patients seem to be improving, but it's not quite a cure. We compared it to the medicine in Moray and found that it helps counter the patients' symptoms better, now that we know what causes them, but getting them to go away completely..." He sighed. "I don't know. It's not a total cure. They'll just have to keep working."

Amaya was lost in thought when Remy left for the evening, promising he'd report any new developments on his end. She was wondering if she should visit Soria—she had gone a couple of times in the past week—when there was a knock on the door.

Liesl opened it to reveal a Kharian girl, her skin a warm brown and her hair dark as ink. She held a shawl around herself, but Amaya could tell the neckline of her dress was plunging.

"You Vivienne?" the girl drawled.

"That would be me."

"Here." The girl handed Liesl a slip of parchment. "That's from Mona." And with that, she turned and made for the stairs.

"What was that all about?" Avi asked as Liesl returned to the table.

Amaya had been staring at the girl, wondering why she looked familiar. "She's from that Hall of Beauty place, isn't she? The one where we met Jasper?"

"Yes. I went back and did a little snooping. Apparently André Basque, widowed now for five years, likes to frequent a young woman there named Mona." Liesl sat and read the message before handing it to Amaya. "I convinced her to become an informant."

"How did you swing that?" Avi asked with a raised eyebrow.

"Easy. I told her I was going to bring Basque down."

Amaya recognized Basque's name, as well as an address, but the rest she couldn't read. "What does it say?"

"Basque is holding a gala at his manor to raise funds for those affected by ash fever. It's our best chance to get close to him." Liesl's grin was sharp. "And we're going to be attending."

Avi nearly choked on his tea. "Pardon?"

"Rather, Amaya and Cayo will be attending as a young, newly married couple eager to show off their wealth and status." Liesl leaned forward as Amaya shrank back, dread filling the pit in her stomach. "It's time for you to become Countess Yamaa again."

"Absolutely not" were the first words out of Cayo's mouth once the plan was related to him.

He had just come home from an evening of work at the alchemist's shop, weary after hauling boxes all day. Liesl had sat him down at the table and made him tea, asking if he'd learned anything useful, which he hadn't. And then she had broken the news to him.

Amaya tried not to flinch. It was difficult to ignore the acid in his voice.

"Let me ask you a question," Liesl said, all calm and composed. "You would do anything for your sister, wouldn't you?"

"Of course, but—"

"You ran away from home, traveled all the way to Chalier, and are now working a job at the fish market *and* a job as an alchemist's lackey. All for her! So why shouldn't I infiltrate a wealthy politician's home for my sister?"

"Then *you* pretend to be married!" He gestured wildly between Amaya and Liesl.

"I can't be seen," Liesl reminded him patiently. "André Basque knows what I look like."

Cayo rubbed his hands over his face.

Amaya stood up from her chair. "Look, I don't like this, either," she said, "but could you rein in your hatred of me for *one* hour and do this?"

He looked at her as if she'd thrown a vase at his head. Cayo opened his mouth, released a frustrated breath.

"That's not it," he muttered, looking away. "I'm just not comfortable with pretending to be someone I'm not. Not in such an elaborate way, at least. You've had practice at it, but I haven't."

"Which is why your role is minimal," Liesl explained. "Leave all the talking and flirting to Amaya."

"Flirting?" Amaya interrupted.

"Basque is drawn to up-and-comers in the community, and I'm sure your appearance will cause a bit of a stir. Meanwhile, Avi will keep watch outside on the central balcony—it has access to the windows in the ballroom—and I'll sneak into Basque's study while you keep up the distraction. Deadshot will cover my back."

"You really do know your way around this man's house, don't you?" Avi said.

"I still have the blueprints memorized from the last job. The last *botched* job." Liesl finally let her composure crack as she clenched her jaw. "That mission cost me my sister. But this one will help me find her."

Cayo's expression softened, but dread still sat heavy in Amaya's gut—not merely at the thought of having to pretend with him that everything was fine, but at the idea of donning the countess persona again. What if she was out of practice? What if she ended up ruining the entire mission?

A knock on the door sounded before Jasper let himself inside. "Ah, the gang's assembled! Excellent."

"Let me guess," Cayo drawled. "You're helping?"

"Of course. I'd never pass up the chance to knock Basque down a peg or two." Amaya recalled what Liesl had told her in the market about Jasper and Adrienne being close, remembered the fury in his eyes when he had spotted Basque in the Hall of Beauty. "In fact, Li gave me the most important role in all this."

"Which is?"

"Tailor." Jasper lifted his arms, full of two large, wrapped bundles. "One for the mean girl, one for the sad boy."

"Sad boy?" Cayo repeated as Amaya took the topmost bundle from Jasper. It was surprisingly heavy.

"It wasn't easy to get these," Jasper said pointedly at Liesl, who rolled her eyes.

"Stay for dinner, then. We'll need to go over the plan again anyway. The gala is tomorrow night, and we're tight on prep time."

"Are you sure this'll work? Getting information from Basque's own study?" Jasper leaned against the wall with crossed arms, his expression mellowing out to something more somber. "Trust me, I've tried to tap information from Basque for years. He hides his business too well."

"It'll work," Liesl said darkly. "It has to."

Amaya took the wrapped bundle to the bedroom. Placing it on her bed, she kept her fingertips on the crinkly paper, debating whether to open it now or wait until tomorrow.

Curiosity getting the better of her, she began to unwrap the parchment from what it was protecting. It was the dark blue dress she had seen on display while walking with Remy, with the glittering sleeves and the star pattern spreading across the wide skirt. She stared at it as if it would rear up on its own and strangle her, wrap her in those gem-encrusted sleeves and steal the breath from her body.

She touched the fabric with uncertain fingers. The corset was velvety and smooth, the skirt silken and soft. She imagined the tailor who had made it, dedicated to stitching every single one of these gems into the folds. Wondered what her seamstress mother would have said over the craftsmanship of it.

Wondered what Cayo would say about it.

Carefully, she wrapped the dress back up and placed it under her bed. She supposed she would find out tomorrow.

Somehow that made her even more nervous than the mission.

Amaya had gone by several names throughout her life: Amaya Chandra—shisa to her mother, which meant lemur, and thikha to her father, which meant blossom—Silverfish, Countess Yamaa.

Yet when she saw herself the next night in the cloudy mirror hanging by the bedroom door, all she found was the countess.

Liesl, who had helped her into the blue dress, stepped back as Amaya approached her reflection. The skirt rustled pleasantly against her legs, the gems glittering along her brown arms. Her shoulders and collarbone were exposed, and Liesl had decided to curl and pin up her hair to show off her neck. A couple of strategic curls framed her face, which was touched lightly with the makeup Liesl always brought with her.

"If I had my whole collection, I could have done a lot more," Liesl said, sounding wistful. "It's probably gathering dust in that Moray estate. Let's hope the gentry of Baleine appreciate a subtle look."

"It's perfect." Amaya admired the sharp points of kohl at the corners of her eyes. Liesl had brushed blue powder on her eyelids, a bit of rouge on her cheeks, and finished with a touch of red on her lips. Amaya didn't think it was subtle; she thought it was like war paint, declaring her ready for battle.

Her spine straightened, her chin lifted. Being Countess Yamaa had taught her a bit about power: who wielded it, and how, and why. It had shown her that most people thought women only invested themselves in finery and frivolity, but that wasn't always the case. Their clothes, their makeup, their jewelry, their smiles—they were all weapons unleashed on unsuspecting opponents.

Amaya liked these weapons. They were much harder to use than the knives hidden under her dress, and took more time to master, but they were just as effective, if not more so.

She felt dangerous. Unstoppable.

"I wish we had some jewelry," Liesl said as she fretted with Amaya's hair. "Your collarbone looks so bare."

"Because it *is* bare." Amaya was surprised by the smile she wore. "It might be better without, anyway."

"True. You don't need any more glitter to be enticing. Are you all right with that, though?"

Amaya shrugged. "The countess is."

"I see." They shared a small, secretive smile. "To be honest, I'm rather jealous. I wish I got to dress up tonight." She ran a hand over her black outfit. "It's been so long since I've had the chance."

Amaya took the makeup kit from the bed and opened it, revealing the powders and creams within. She chose one of the small containers of lip paint and handed it to Liesl. "Just because you're on a stealth mission doesn't mean you can't look nice while doing it."

Liesl laughed. "You are absolutely right." She accepted the lip paint and approached the mirror to apply it. "Go check on Cayo. He's been nervous all day."

Hearing that made *her* nervous, but Amaya obediently walked across the apartment to the boys' bedroom. The door was already ajar, so she pushed it open farther, only then realizing she still held the makeup kit in her hands.

She nearly dropped it when she saw him. For the past few weeks, Amaya had acclimated herself to seeing Cayo in regular clothing—stained shirts, roughed-up breeches, threadbare coats. He had strangely worn them well, as if the clothing were transformed from ordinary to statement piece as soon as it came in contact with his body.

But he wasn't wearing regular clothing tonight. He stood beside his bed as he did up his cufflinks, gleaming golden at his wrists where a hint of a white satin shirt poked through. His suit was black and hugged his body in the right places, showing off the plane of his shoulders and the slope of his thighs. The lapels on his jacket were a wet-looking silk, the right one punctured by a golden brooch in the shape of an arrow.

Cayo spotted her and froze, face slackening as his gaze roamed over her. Amaya lit up like a torch, stealing all the air in the room.

"You..." Cayo cleared his throat, his voice hoarse. "That dress is..."

"Blue," she said, then cringed.

Movement stirred in the corner of the room as Avi got off his bed and headed for the door.

"I'll, uh, go see if Deadshot needs anything," the man muttered as he made a hasty exit.

Silence settled between the two of them. Cayo nervously checked his cufflinks, something she had only seen in clothing from the Rain Empire.

"Martisse," he blurted suddenly. "That dress. I recognize her style."

Amaya had no idea what he was talking about at first. "Oh, you mean the designer."

He nodded. "Sometimes Soria and I received catalogues from the Rain Empire. We always liked her collections a lot. Soria wanted one of her dresses for her wedding. But that was before..." He trailed off, biting his lip.

Amaya took a couple more steps inside. "You...You pull off the suit nicely. You must have missed wearing them."

His eyebrows twitched, no doubt wondering if she meant it as a compliment or an insult. Frankly, she wasn't sure, either.

He gestured to the makeup kit in her hands. "Do you need help getting ready?"

Of course Cayo knew how to apply makeup. Amaya swallowed

her frantic laughter and came to a swift and startling decision. "No. Sit on the bed."

His dark eyes met hers, just as startled as she was. Amaya added a hint of a smile, already employing her arsenal. Cayo hesitated, then turned and sat on the edge of the bed. She set the kit down beside him.

"Be sure to find something that matches my complexion," he said. His tone was joking, but his nerves made it fall a little flat.

"I'll see what I can do." Her fingers hovered over the different powders, enticed by their brilliant colors. Finally, she selected a compact of glittering red. "Close your eyes. And don't move."

Cayo did as she asked, a rush of satisfaction flowing through her at the obedience. She took a moment to watch him like this, sitting before her, eyes closed, vulnerable. Trusting her, even though he had no cause to.

It was more than she would allow herself.

Amaya swiped one of Liesl's small brushes through the red substance. She tapped it to release the loose powder—something she had seen Liesl do numerous times—and bent over Cayo, putting her face close to his.

His breath caught when she put the brush to the inner corner of his eyelid. His lashes trembled, black and straight so that when his eyes were open, it almost looked as if he had none at all. She swiped the brush cautiously over his eyelid; since there was no crease, she spread the red powder in an arch reaching toward his eyebrow. Then she made it fan out at his outer corner, a mirror to her black kohl daggers.

Her hand shook slightly as she did the other eye. She realized she was standing with one leg between his, that his own breath hit faintly against the side of her jaw. A shiver ran down her spine, almost messing up her work.

Amaya glanced down at the exposed length of his neck, the soft, defenseless skin of his throat. She could have wrapped her hand around it and squeezed, listened to him gasp and feel him writhe helplessly against her, torn between fighting back and allowing it to happen.

It would be a kindness.

"Amaya?"

She realized she had stopped moving, her breaths coming quicker. She stepped back.

"All done," she croaked.

Cayo's eyes fluttered open. He gazed up at her, and she was stricken by what she'd done. The red complimented him nicely, highlighting the darkness of his eyes and the soft tan of his skin. It gave him an air of flirtation, of confidence, an obvious message to anyone who looked at him that he knew what he could do with just a grin and a wink.

She had given him a weapon to use tonight as well.

And if she wasn't careful, one he could use against her.

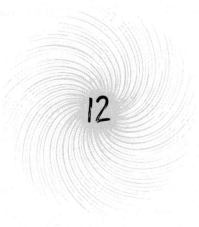

# 12

*The magician climbed the slope of the mountain, the*
*tourmaline glittering and cold under his feet. He peered*
*at the stars high above, wondering when, and if, he would*
*reach them. But the wind blew frigid in his ears, pushing*
*him back, back, cutting through him like a knife. And the*
*magician knew: He had to keep going, or else fall like*
*Neralia had, into the crushing dark of the sea.*

—"NERALIA OF THE CLOUDS," AN ORAL STORY ORIGINATING

FROM THE LEDE ISLANDS

C ayo had debated bringing the gun with him, but Deadshot
advised against it.

"It'll be bulky in your pockets," she'd said, indicating how his
trousers weren't exactly spacious. Then she'd grinned. "Unless you'd
like to make a suggestive statement."

"That . . . won't be necessary."

As the carriage approached the lit-up manor, though, he couldn't help but feel defenseless. His hand kept straying toward his hip, as if expecting to find the pistol's wood-and-pearl handle there.

"Do you think someone's going to jump you in the middle of a party?" Amaya muttered. "You'll be fine."

"You're wearing your knives!"

"Because they're easier to conceal than a gun. But *someone* wasn't very good with knives, was he?"

Cayo actually welcomed the jab; it helped negate the sudden and unwanted flare of desire at seeing her in that dress. When she'd walked through the bedroom door, he had almost thought of her as Countess Yamaa, the disorientation riding on the wave of awe that had struck him down.

But it had lasted only a moment. He had more important things to focus on than the curve of Amaya's collarbone, or the way a curl of hair fell against her neck, or how she smelled of lavender and fresh linen.

"Here's where I leave you," Jasper called from the driver's seat as the carriage rattled to a stop. "Let's start the show."

Cayo's mouth dried when he opened the door and stepped onto the cobblestone outside the manor's open gates. He turned and held his hand out to Amaya, who had been gathering her skirt in her hands, prepared to step down on her own.

Her eyes darted to the partygoers on the lawn. Swallowing, she slid her hand into Cayo's and allowed him to help her down.

"Don't get too wild," Jasper said with a wink as he flicked the reins and the carriage took off.

Cayo presented Amaya with his left arm. She hesitated again before she took it, their sides brushing as they strolled toward the manor. He ignored the tremor that spread across his ribs in favor of getting a good look at their surroundings, wanting to be able to describe it to Soria when he saw her next. She would demand as many details as he could remember.

He had seen his fair share of manor homes in Moray, enough to know that André Basque had not skimped on presentation. The manor lay on the outskirts of Baleine, providing enough space for a winding drive that led from the black iron gates to the manor's entrance. When they passed through the gates, Cayo noticed a crest split down the middle on either gate, a ship and a cloud stamped in gold.

"Basque owns a fleet of debtor ships," Liesl had explained to them yesterday. "That's partly how he came into his wealth. He also rubs elbows with the nobility of the Rain Empire, and he hosts fundraisers like this often to appear empathetic to the civilians."

"Does it work?" Cayo had asked.

"He isn't dead yet, so I'd say so."

"I thought the people here hated the rich." He thought back to the other day in the fish market, how everyone had scowled at the young woman in the pink dress.

"Oh they do, make no mistake. But at least Basque makes a pretense of giving back, unlike the others." Liesl had shrugged, her eyes cold. "They don't know he likes to skim a percentage of the profits for himself. Like scooping the top layer of cream from a bottle of milk."

"The best part," Avi had agreed wistfully.

There were guests milling about on the front lawn, a wide courtyard with a stone fountain in the center and four patches of perfectly manicured grass. Spruce trees lined the property, giving the night air a fresh scent that was a pleasant escape from the usual smells of the city. Light spilled from the windows of the manor, a large stone construction with steep gables. The entrance was held up by marble columns, reminding Cayo painfully of the entrance to Mercado Manor.

The guests were already holding gleaming flutes of golden, sparkling wine. Some of them glanced curiously at him and Amaya as they passed, and Cayo automatically sent them his best grin, the one that showed off his dimple. They smiled back, then resumed their conversations.

"You're far too good at this," Amaya murmured. "I thought you said you didn't have any practice at pretending?"

"This is a different kind of pretending."

They passed through the wide, open doors into the antechamber. The walls were sculpted with exquisite carvings, and standing candelabra burned in every corner, showing off a grand marble staircase. A set of doors was open to the left of the stairs, where most of the noise was emanating.

A servant in livery waited on the threshold. Cayo handed him the invitations Liesl had procured from her contact, and after a cursory look the servant swept a low bow, ushering them inside.

Amaya's grip tightened on Cayo's arm as she took in the splendor of the ballroom. The walls were more gold than plaster, and crystal chandeliers hung in two even rows from a ceiling painted with a wide, breathtaking pastoral scene. The marble floor was crowded with people in flowing dresses and fitted suits, the tinkling of porcelain and the flutter of laughter rising above the crowd like cigarillo smoke.

It took Cayo a moment to realize he was smiling. He'd felt anxious on the way here, but now...now he was in an element he recognized. For the past several weeks it had been nothing but new experience after new experience, and it had worn down his spirit and his confidence. This, though? This, Cayo understood.

But a thread of worry stitched across his chest all the same. Not for him, but for Amaya. Her grip remained tight as they entered the ballroom. They received more curious looks, and a couple broke off from their conversation to join them.

"We need you two on the floor to make sure that André Basque doesn't vanish," Liesl had told them earlier. "If he leaves the ballroom, give a signal to Avi. He'll come and warn me. But don't forget to charm the guests who try to speak to you. Your covers can't be blown."

"Pardon me," one of the men said in Solène, "but I couldn't help but wonder if that's from the Martisse line?" He indicated Amaya's blue dress.

She was making quite the spectacle in it, earning looks ranging from envious to ravenous. The fact that she wore no jewelry, forcing the eye to gaze upon her glittering arms, only enhanced the effect.

Cayo opened his mouth to reply for her, but Amaya took a step forward with a sweet smile.

"It is," she said in her shaky Solène, her accent rough. "I'm impressed with your eye, sir."

The man straightened a bit at the compliment. "And I'm impressed with your taste, my lady. Tell me, are you new to Baleine?"

"Fresh off the ship," Amaya answered. She put a fond hand on Cayo's chest. "We're originally from Rehan, where we were just married. This is our honeymoon."

"Ah, so romantic! Baleine is a fantastic destination for such a trip. The shopping districts are not to be missed."

"Are there any shops in particular we must visit?"

As they continued their chatter, Cayo could barely pay attention.

He was mostly focused on the spot on his chest where Amaya had placed her hand, his stomach curiously light and warm in the aftermath of her words.

"—sure my husband would agree." Amaya's eyes flashed in his direction. "Wouldn't you, dear?"

Cayo started, unsure what was being discussed. "Oh, yes. Of course." *Husband.* He knew it was their cover, but it felt different hearing her say the word out loud.

The couple exchanged a pleasant goodbye with them before moving on. Cayo took a deep breath, fighting not to loosen the collar of his shirt.

"You know more Soléne than I thought," he said with a quirk of his eyebrow.

Amaya's easy smile was gone, but he was sure she was ready to turn it back on in an instant. "It's easier to learn when you're surrounded by it. And Liesl practiced some conversations with me. People like this are so predictable, they're easy to fool."

Cayo stiffened. He had been one of those fools once. She had acted just like this back in Moray, and he had fallen for it.

She felt his tension and let go of his arm. "Cayo…"

But another group of partygoers was making their way toward them. They put on their best smiles and pretended that everything was all right.

The entire time, the spot on Cayo's chest continued to burn.

Cayo watched Basque hold the attention of a group of nobles. They laughed at some joke of his, and a young woman was bold enough to put her hand upon his arm. As a widower, Basque was a prime target for marriage, for alliance. Cayo wondered how many attendees had been ordered by their families to flirt with the man.

Basque was handsome—Cayo couldn't blame them. He was tall and broad, his manner commanding without being overbearing. His dark brown hair was streaked with gray, but it only added to his stately appearance.

Cayo was continually amazed at how the worst of people could appear so striking.

He checked on Amaya, who was holding her own little court nearby. A group of women were fawning over her dress and wanting to know more about Rehan. Amaya kept sending him pointed glances to come help her, but he ignored them.

*People like this are so predictable, they're easy to fool.*

Gritting his teeth, Cayo turned and almost ran into a server.

"My apologies, sir," said the server. "Would you care for a drink?"

Cayo stared at the serving tray, at the flutes filled with that golden, bubbling wine. For an instant he heard Soria's disapproving tone, which fizzled away in a surge of irritation.

*Fuck it*, he thought viciously as he took a flute and nodded his thanks to the server. Cayo stalked the edges of the party, sipping at the wine and keeping an eye on Basque. The man had moved on to a group of men, shaking their hands and patting their backs in easy camaraderie.

Cayo looked up at the window where Avi was stationed. He caught a glimpse of the man in the corner of the window, who gave the signal that Liesl still hadn't finished with her business.

*What's taking her so long?*

The wine on his tongue was bright and potent. He forced himself to take only small sips, to not finish the entire flute, but it was proving difficult. It would be too easy to get another after this one, literally handed to him on a silver platter.

But as he scouted the ballroom for signs of another server, he stopped on the figure of a young woman wearing a lavender silk gown. She was speaking with a small group in the corner, her expression serious as she cradled her glass between two gloved hands.

It was the young woman he had seen at the fish market, the one who had generated so much hate.

Curious, Cayo meandered toward the group, pretending to admire the pastoral artwork on the ceiling.

"—wanted to, but Lady Georgina seems to be stitched to his side," the young woman was complaining.

"Well, you know her engagement broke earlier this year," an older woman said. "She's desperate."

"He won't waste his time on someone like her," said a man with a nasally voice. "Not when you're such a catch, Lady Deirdre. You have a growing empire, after all."

"Bad choice of words, darling," said the older woman.

But the young woman—Lady Deirdre—laughed. "I suppose that's one way of looking at it. I shudder to think what would become of the alchemists' progress without their patrons."

Cayo frowned. *Patrons?* Florimond hadn't mentioned anything about having patronage—but then again, Cayo had only been in the man's company for a solid five hours. Alchemy was an expensive venture, so he supposed it made sense that someone like Florimond would need support.

"Your family was smart to get involved as soon as possible," said one of the young woman's friends. "The investment will surely pay off, considering how the alchemists are improving their craft."

"Indeed," Lady Deirdre murmured with a small smile. "And we certainly have them working hard."

Cayo didn't like the way she said it, her words oily and slick with self-satisfaction. Just how many alchemists did this woman and her family play patron to?

And what was she having them work on?

"Lord Basque would be a fool not to partner with you," said the nasally voiced man. "Or consider you a worthy match."

"Agreed. Now if only Lady Georgina would kindly peel herself off his arm..."

"You're not supposed to be drinking."

Amaya had crept up to his side, startling him. Cayo scoffed and took a sip just to vex her.

"This is what *people like me* do," he said.

He could practically see the angry retort forming, ready to lash him like a whip. Instead, she took a step back and sighed.

"I'm sorry I said that. I thought you'd know I wasn't lumping you in with them."

"I *am* lumped in with them. Or at least, I was."

"You're better than them, Cayo."

"I'm really not. Or rather, I wasn't when you first met me." He downed the rest of his drink in one go, welcoming the tingling, numbing sensation spreading through him. "And you took advantage of that."

Amaya's eyes flitted from the empty flute to his face. She must have seen the rage there, the embarrassment.

"You're right," she said softly. Her eyelashes hovered over her dark eyes, which were searching him as if searching the ocean floor for pearls. "And I'm sorry. I'm sorry for what I did to you."

Cayo stood there, stunned, unsure what to do with the words. Before he could figure it out, music began to drift through the ballroom. A string quartet had set up at the far end of the room, their first stretching notes an invitation for the nobles to dance.

The two of them stared at each other. Waiting. Debating.

Finally, Cayo set his empty glass on one of the chairs that lined the wall and held out his hand with a small, sardonic bow. Apprehension flashed across Amaya's face before she took his hand in her own, allowing him to lead her to the dance floor.

Energy buzzed where their fingers connected, where Cayo placed his hand upon her hip. She put her other hand upon his shoulder, a few inches above where she had touched his chest earlier.

And then they were moving, stepping and twirling through the sea of dancers as music filled the air. They earned stares as they danced, and Cayo wondered what they must look like—a young, handsome couple in a world all their own.

Amaya watched him, and he watched her. He pressed his hand against her hip and felt the indent of one of her hidden knives.

"Did you mean it?" he said softly, under the music. "Your apology?"

"Why wouldn't I mean it? I *am* sorry. Boon…" She shook her head. "He may have been the catalyst for this—and trust me, I still have a blade with his name on it—but this is my fault just as much as it is his."

Cayo appreciated hearing it. He had wondered if she would use Boon as a shield, but the fact that she was owning up to her own mistakes gave him hope. "I understand."

"You were a part of his plan simply because of who your father is. But you're not responsible for what you didn't know."

"I should have been more involved in my father's business instead of going to the Vice Sector. I should have done anything but return to the Slum King. I should have..." He sighed. "I don't know what I should have done."

"Let's just focus on what we're doing now," Amaya said. "Helping Liesl. Finding the Benefactor. Saving your sister—and Moray."

"And my father?" he asked. "What about him? And Boon?"

Her expression darkened to something cold and unforgiving. If her pleasant smile was Countess Yamaa and her prickly frown was Amaya, he wondered if this was Silverfish coming out to speak.

"They'll need to pay for everything they've done," she whispered. Cayo realized then that their bodies were very close; her front was pressed to his, her words warm against his throat. "They killed my father and destroyed my life. Destroyed your life, and Soria's, too. This won't end until they see justice."

A shiver traveled through him. He wanted to protest, but one thought of Soria laid up at the hospital dispelled it. His father was responsible for that. For all of this.

"Do you..." Amaya's voice failed, and Cayo met her eyes again. They were a storm of danger and yearning; not for him, but for the promise of vengeance. It made his heart speed up, his grip tightening at her hip. Her breath caught, like it had at the apartment when she had applied the red powder to his eyelids.

"Do you regret meeting me?" she finished softly.

It wasn't what he was expecting, and he didn't know how to answer. Did he regret meeting her? A week ago—hells, an hour ago—he would have said yes. But it was different when he was facing her, when they were this close and he could feel her heartbeat drumming a panicked tempo.

His gaze traveled down to her collarbone, to the swath of bare skin below. The back of his neck prickled at the idea of bending down and pressing his lips to that skin, at finding out just how warm it was. Amaya shuddered against him as if she had read his thoughts, her fingers squeezing hard into his shoulder.

And then the song ended, and the nobles around them clapped politely for the string quartet. Cayo came back to himself and quickly stepped away from her, gulping down air as if he had been drowning. Amaya's pupils were blown wide, her cheeks flushed as she nervously ran her hands down her skirt, fanning it out. Not looking at him but rather scanning the ballroom.

Basque. Cayo couldn't find the man anywhere.

*Damn it.*

He hurried to the middle of the ballroom and gave the signal to Avi, patting the top of his head as if checking his hairstyle. The man disappeared from the window.

"Liesl's taking too long," Amaya murmured, gathering her skirt in her hands. "I'm going to find her."

"Wait—"

But she was already hurrying out of the ballroom, leaving him to follow behind.

"Ah, a lover's quarrel?" said a tipsy noble with a hearty chuckle.

"Shut up," Cayo snapped in Rehanese. He barely had time to savor the man's affronted expression before he ran out on Amaya's heels.

**13**

*People with something to hide often find ways of
flaunting it to others.*

—EMPRESS CAMILA OF THE SUN EMPIRE

Amaya made her way toward the grand staircase, trying not to
run. Her skirt swished about her legs as she walked, catching the attention of a few partygoers mingling in the entryway. She
gave them a warm smile, pretending she knew exactly where she was
going.

Liesl had drawn them a simple map of the manor's layout, but it
spun through Amaya's head now. As she crested the top of the grand
staircase, she looked left and right, unsure which hallway would lead
to Basque's study.

"Right," said a voice behind her.

Amaya jumped and scowled at Cayo. "What are you doing? You
should stay in the ballroom."

"Is that all I'm good at? Socializing and eating finger foods?"

"This is *not* the time for your hang-ups." She went down the hallway on the right, the red carpet runner softening her footfalls. Cayo followed behind. "You need to stay there so that we don't draw suspicion."

"Everyone's eyes have been on you," he countered. "If they see me without you, it's going to look more suspicious."

"Then tell them the marriage is over!" Amaya picked up the pace now that no one else was around, but Cayo matched it.

"Just admit that you don't think I can be helpful," he snapped.

"What? I never said—"

Amaya stopped and grabbed his arm. She put a finger to her lips and peered around the corner.

The hallways of the manor were elegant and broad, with podiums displaying pottery, busts, and intricately painted plates. The doors were few and far between, but one had opened nearby. Amaya watched as two men stepped out, one closing and locking it behind him.

André Basque.

"You'll have your very own ship in no time," he was saying to the other man, placing a hand on his shoulder. "All you'll need to do is find a capable captain to run it. But I'm more than happy to add another investor to my fleet."

"You're too kind, my lord."

Then the two of them began to walk down the hall. Toward Amaya and Cayo.

Amaya turned, wide-eyed, and grabbed Cayo by the lapels of his jacket.

"Kiss me," she hissed.

He gaped at her. "Wh-what?"

"I said *kiss me!*" she whisper-yelled as the men's footsteps grew louder. But Cayo's eyes were as wide as her own now, his mouth working frantically.

"I—I can't—"

Amaya growled and pulled him close, her back hitting the wall behind her. Leaning up, she pressed her lips to the side of his neck.

Cayo gasped and went very, very still. She could feel him tense against her as she kissed his neck again, his skin warm to the touch, his pulse racing under her lips. The smell of him surrounded her, reminding her of falling rain, a balmy breeze through the leaves of a palm tree.

He started to pull away. She parted her lips and bit him.

A soft, low moan escaped him. It vibrated through his chest and into hers, and a sudden, terrifying pressure grew in her lower belly, spreading fingers of heat through her limbs. It turned her buzzing and weak, and the small, pitiful sound that left her mouth was muffled against his neck.

It dawned on her like a horror, the slow, creeping dread of something stalking from behind, catching her before it was too late to run: She was attracted to Cayo Mercado, the son of the man who had ruined her life.

What god had she angered to end up like this?

A polite cough sounded nearby. Amaya and Cayo sprung apart to find Basque and his business partner standing in the hallway. There was a semi-pained look on Basque's face even as the other man leered at Amaya's rumpled appearance.

"I'm all for having a bit of fun," Basque said with a charming smile, recovering from the surprise. "But the party is exclusively downstairs."

Amaya quickly threw on her silliest smile, even forcing herself to giggle. "So sorry, my lord! I was merely trying to find the amenities and got distracted."

"Easy mistake to make. There's one downstairs, so you know for next time." He glanced at Cayo's disheveled jacket. "I'll, ah...give you two a moment to get yourselves in order."

"Thank you, my lord!" Amaya said.

Basque nodded and left with his business partner, who threw Amaya one last suggestive look. Amaya let her smile fall as soon as they were gone, hurrying toward the locked door.

She couldn't think about what had just happened. She refused to. Similarly, Cayo was stunned and silent at her side, breathing a little hard and eyes still wide.

Amaya pressed herself against the door. "Liesl? Are you in there?" Surely Basque would have called for a guard if he'd spotted her.

The door unlatched and opened from the other side. Liesl beckoned them into the darkness of Basque's study, closing and locking the door again once they were in.

"How did he not catch you?" Amaya demanded.

"Avi signaled Deadshot, who whistled up a warning. I hid under the desk. If they'd walked around and spotted me...well, we wouldn't be having this conversation."

Her voice quavered slightly. Amaya held Liesl's trembling hands in her own.

"It'll be all right," Amaya said. "We haven't been caught yet. Have you found what you needed?"

"In a sense. I've gone through the whole room and barely found anything except this." Liesl gestured them over to the window flooded with moonlight, slipping a ledger out from under her shirt.

"He keeps diaries of sorts," Liesl said softly, glancing at the door every now and then. Amaya had never seen her so shaken. "A culmination of business transactions and the like. It's dated from the year Adrienne and I were..." She swallowed.

"What does it say?" Cayo demanded.

"That's just it. It's all in code." Liesl opened the ledger, showing page after page of a language that Amaya had no familiarity with. Or maybe it wasn't even a language—there were shapes and symbols in odd patterns. "Of course the paranoid bastard writes in code. I haven't cracked it yet, and it'll take time. Time we don't have."

"Then let's copy the pages dated from when you were caught," Amaya whispered. "Quickly."

"I'll do it." Cayo held out his hands. Liesl hesitated before handing him the ledger, then turned to find some loose paper.

"If Adrienne was made Landless like me, it could say where she was shipped to," Liesl said as Cayo sat at Basque's desk and began the work of transcribing by moonlight.

"And if she wasn't made Landless?" Amaya asked.

Liesl glowered at the ledger filled with its strange shapes and letters. "We'll know soon. Until then"—she turned to the nearest bookshelf—"I'm going to see if there's any more dirt I can dig up."

Amaya crossed her arms and paced, occasionally looking out the window to check if Avi and Deadshot were all right. Cayo's pen scratched against the paper, the only sound in the room other than their nervous breathing and the rustle of Liesl's movements.

Then Amaya heard footsteps down the hall.

"He's back," she whispered sharply, gesturing for Cayo to wrap it up. "Let's go."

His pen moved faster across the paper. "I have a few more lines."

"We'll have to leave them," Liesl hissed, her eyes fixed on the door as Basque's voice reached them, muffled through the wood.

"...sure we can reach some sort of agreement."

"That's exactly what I was hoping for." A woman's voice, high and lilting.

Cayo stood from the chair, still writing. As the key scraped in the lock, Amaya yanked the paper away, leaving a long streak of ink in the bottom corner. Liesl grabbed the ledger and put it back where she'd found it as Amaya pushed Cayo toward the window.

"There were two more symbols!" he argued.

"If you want to stay and get thrown in jail, be my guest," Amaya growled. She practically shoved him out the window onto the ledge beyond. Cayo scrabbled at the wall, swallowing a gasp as he tried not to look at the gardens below.

Amaya crawled out after him, turning to make sure Liesl was right behind her. But the girl stood staring at the door, caressing the sheath at her hip where a dagger lay.

"Not today," Amaya told her.

Liesl met her stare. It was a strange reversal of roles, Amaya thought, to be the one to tell Liesl to stay her blade. But Liesl admittedly had more sense than Amaya ever had, as she nodded in agreement and climbed out onto the ledge after her.

She had just closed the window by the time the office door swung open. Liesl pressed her back against the wall as a lantern light glowed softly through the glass.

Amaya exhaled and closed her eyes, leaning her head against the stone. It was cold and rough against her back, and the night air on her bare shoulders made her shiver. Her skirt fanned out around her, fluttering haphazardly in the breeze.

The paper was still crumpled in her hand. She unceremoniously stuffed it down the front of her dress, unwilling to lose it to the wind. Cayo let out a choked sound beside her, though she was unsure if it was because of the height or her lack of decorum.

"I must admit, I've been particularly jealous of your family's business," Basque said, his voice low and muffled through the window. "So I'm willing to learn more."

"Hardly a business," the woman replied with a smile in her words. Amaya recognized the tone of flirtation, having employed it herself on more than one occasion. "If anything, I'd say it's charity. And I know you have a soft spot for that, my lord."

Basque laughed. "Well, I am throwing a fundraiser, after all."

Cayo touched his shoulder to Amaya's. "I recognize her voice," he whispered. "I overheard her in the ballroom. Lady Deirdre. Apparently her family is the patron for a lot of alchemists in the city."

"I believe your influence can greatly help my family's ventures," the woman, Lady Deirdre, continued. The light flickered slightly, as if she were moving closer. "Paying the expenses for alchemists tends to get rather costly, as I'm sure you've a notion."

"Of course," he replied smoothly. "Only to be expected, considering what they can do. I've just seen one of their latest inventions, a lantern that changes color to better spot faded bloodstains. Useful for the city guard, I bet."

"Indeed. And what with them now trying to find a cure for this horrible illness, the expense reports keep racking up. I heard you have an interest in alchemy yourself. With your wealth and reputation, and our business endeavors, I'm positive we can make a true difference. Not only to the city, but to all of Chalier. To the Rain Empire as a whole."

Liesl curled her hands into fists. Amaya was half afraid she would dive back through the window and throttle them both.

"I wasn't aware you were so loyal to the empire," Basque replied.

"Aren't we all?"

"In theory, I suppose." He sounded amused. "In order to keep our status, our titles. But many would spit at the name of the emperor and his underlings."

"I assure you, I am not one of those." A faint rustle; Amaya imagined her sitting on the edge of Basque's wide desk. "And I know you are not, either. Indulge me a moment's speculation, if you will. Consider adding even more weapons to the military's arsenal. To have the power of the alchemists fulfilling the whims of the empire."

Liesl tensed beside her as Amaya's stomach dropped.

"Ah," Basque said. "Which whims in particular?"

"The empire was created with conquest and military takeover. Now imagine if the alchemists and their inventions were added to the equation."

"I see," Basque murmured. "There is a certain appeal in that, yes. It would help with our future dealings with the Sun Empire."

"And dare I say other territories as well? Territories that we've longed to snatch up for ourselves?"

"That would be quite the investment." Basque's words were faraway, as if already envisioning it, drawn to the allure of power. "But I'm sure even my coffers would strain at such an undertaking."

Lady Deirdre laughed low in her throat. "Oh, you have no need to worry about that, my lord. Simply invest whatever sum you're willing to part with, and I will do the rest. You'd be surprised at how far a single solsta can be stretched."

"And you have plenty of solstas, do you?"

"Much more than enough," Deirdre purred.

The three of them waited as Basque and Deirdre murmured some more, Deirdre uttering another flirtatious laugh before the light was extinguished and the office door closed. Cayo let out a long, shaking breath.

"Shit," he whispered. Amaya couldn't help but agree. "Does this mean—"

"Wait until we're on the ground," Liesl hissed.

They shuffled along the ledge, keeping their backs to the wall, until they reached a drainage pipe. Cayo, being the first one in line, threw a panicked look over his shoulder at Liesl.

"Worst-case scenario, you land in a bush," Liesl whispered.

Amaya glanced down and spotted Deadshot and Avi waiting for them below. As Cayo grasped at the pipe, muttering curses the entire time, he managed to get halfway down before slipping. Thankfully, Avi was there to catch him.

"We'll make a burglar of you yet," the Landless man said as Amaya got ready to follow after them. Cayo merely let out a nauseated grunt.

"If you look up my skirt, I'll stab you," she directed to the three below her. She slowly yet steadily made her way down, her slippered feet sliding against the wall. Her heart leaped into her throat until she finally found her way back to solid ground.

They waited for Liesl, quicker and quieter than the others. Deadshot embraced her, and Liesl returned it with a relieved sigh before breaking away.

"What *was* that?" Cayo demanded, pointing up to the office. "The nobles are planning to exploit the alchemists for warfare?"

"That's what it sounded like," Liesl said coldly. "And the way Deirdre was speaking..."

"She could be the Benefactor," Amaya finished.

The others stared at her. Not with confusion, but with grim acceptance.

"Her family is patron to most of the alchemists in the city," Cayo agreed. "And if she's already thinking about using them for weapons, one of those weapons could be the counterfeit coins."

"She mentioned setting sights on other territories," Liesl added. "Obviously she's referring to Moray. The empire's wanted it for decades, and it's already sufficiently weakened thanks to the counterfeit coins. If her family helps the empire claim it, she'd be as good as royalty."

A moment of silence passed over them, Amaya shivering from both the breeze and revelation.

"Cayo," Liesl said suddenly, making him start. "Your alchemist. Florimond. Find out who his patron is, and what exactly he's working on. It could very well be that some alchemists are working on a cure while others are working for the Benefactor. We need to figure out who is who as soon as we can."

Cayo nodded, an odd mix of uncertainty and determination on his face.

"In the meantime, we'll try to find out more about the Deirdres." Liesl glanced up at the window, her expression hard. "And crack Basque's code."

Deadshot and Avi led the way to where Jasper waited with the carriage. Amaya didn't miss how Liesl's hand drifted back to her dagger as they stole into the night, a promise unfulfilled.

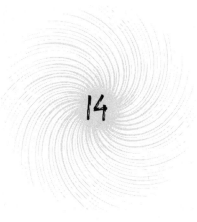

# 14

*When you place a bet, make sure you know your limits.*
*Even the best of men can be ruined within a single night.*

—*THE DEVIOUS ART OF DICE AND DEALING*

Cayo kept his voice down as he told Soria what had happened the previous night. He felt a disturbing amount of satisfaction at the look of shock on her wan face.

"Cayo," she breathed, coughing a little. "You *didn't*."

"I did. Nearly fell and broke my neck in the process, but I'm officially a thief now."

Soria laughed around her coughing. "Don't sound so happy about it!"

"I'm *not*. But after it was all over, I felt this rush of energy. It was amazing. It was like..." His voice trailed off, not wanting to dredge up the past, but Soria already knew what he was about to say.

"Like gambling in the Vice Sector," she finished for him, arching one eyebrow.

He grinned sheepishly. "Exactly. It was the same rush I got when I won big at the tables."

"Oh, Cayo." She sighed. "First a gambler working for the Slum King, now a thief stealing from the rich. You're a regular degenerate."

"There could be worse things," he said. "Don't worry, I'm not about to make it a habit."

"You better not. But if you do, you should at least grab me a new dress." Soria turned and coughed harder into her shoulder, her body seizing up as the contractions racked through her.

Cayo held her hand until it passed, unable to do anything else. As she lay there gasping for breath, he used a cloth to wipe away the saliva at the corner of her mouth, the tears that had escaped her eyes. His gaze trailed down to the splotch of gray on her neck, creeping steadily and surely up her face and down her chest.

"She doesn't seem to be improving anymore," he had said to Mother Hilas the other day after leaving Soria's room.

"It's difficult to predict how certain patients will react to certain medicines." Mother Hilas had put a steadying hand upon his shoulder. "We'll just have to observe and keep administering the treatment until a cure can be found. I know that isn't what you want to hear, but that's the truth of it."

But after what they had overheard the other night, Cayo didn't know how many of the alchemists actually *were* focusing on a cure. Liesl was determined to find out more about the Deirdre family, even going so far as to keep Avi and Deadshot stationed at their manor on the outskirts of the city.

Robin Deirdre was the Benefactor. She had to be. Which meant if they found out which alchemists were working with her—who exactly was making the counterfeits—they had a chance to shut production down.

"Cayo?" Soria frowned. "You look worried. You're not telling me something."

He exhaled and squeezed Soria's hand. She squeezed weakly back.

"I can't tell you exactly what happened," he said softly, glancing around, "but I think we have a lead on how to stop the counterfeits. Maybe. It'll depend on what information we can find."

"Oh!" Soria put her other hand on top of his. Her fingers were cold. "That's wonderful news, isn't it?"

"It is. But it's only a small step toward fixing...all of this." It felt as if he stood at the base of an impossibly high wall, with no other way to climb up other than using his hands. "I don't even know if it *can* be fixed."

Soria's eyes burned. "If I ever see Father again, I'll...I don't even know what I'll do. I've never been this angry before, Cayo."

"I know." He cradled her hands in his. "I'm going to do whatever I can to put a stop to this. To make sure the alchemists find a cure."

She smiled, somehow both sad and proud. "Tell me...about Amaya's dress," she wheezed.

He bit his lower lip. He conjured an image of Amaya from that night, of her in that dress, calling him her husband, dancing with him, pressing him against her in that hallway. When her lips had touched his skin, it had felt like the strike of a lightning bolt, all heat and energy and the promise of fatality.

He still couldn't believe it had happened. Or that they had escaped Basque's manor, for that matter.

"God and her stars, you're blushing." Soria cackled faintly. "Is there something you're not telling me?"

"What? No." But that only brought more heat to his face, and Soria's grin grew wider. "Shut up."

"Must have been a nice dress," Soria murmured.

"Mm." Cayo cleared his throat. "You would have liked it. It was a Martisse."

"Ohhh." Soria gazed wistfully up at the ceiling. "I want a Martisse. Go steal one for me, Cayo."

"I don't think my skills are quite that advanced yet. Besides, I'm still working that fish market job, remember? And a side job for Florimond."

Soria smiled. "I remember. And I'm really proud of you for sticking with it. Thank you, Cayo."

He kissed the back of her hand. "Anything for you."

"Then go get me a new dress."

He laughed and stood, patting her hand. "I'll work on it."

The sky was a brilliant mix of pink and blue as he made his way to the market. He had decided to split his visitation today, an hour in the morning and an hour in the evening, unable to wait a whole day to tell Soria what had happened the night before. That way he could also make his latest payment to the hospital administrator after his shift at Florimond's.

Where he would hopefully learn something new for Liesl.

"You look happy," Victor grunted as Cayo began to set up the stall for the day.

"Do I?" Perhaps it was the residual adrenaline lingering in his veins. Although fleeing Basque's manor had been terrifying, and finding out the possible identity of the Benefactor had been horrifying, he

160

had to admit he hadn't felt this alive in some time. It made him think of the stories he'd read as a child, of the protagonists who braved dangers not only to save the day but simply for the thrill of it.

"I don't like it," Victor said. "Head down, keep working."

Cayo rolled his eyes but did as instructed. He was finding it somewhat easier now to deal with the man and what the workday asked of him, settling into a routine that gave him some measure of stability.

But was he happy? The idea strangely terrified him. Cayo hadn't been able to say he was happy in a long, long time. Perhaps *happy* wasn't quite the word—perhaps he was merely adjusting, finding whatever small things to hold on to in order to make life just the tiniest bit easier.

Like the memory of Amaya's dark eyes on his, the heat of her lips on his neck. How she had actually apologized, reconstructing a little more of the bridge that lay ruined between them.

"What do you think?" Cayo asked of the fish in his hand. "Is this...Are she and I...able to be fixed?"

The fish just stared back at him, eyes wide and mouth agape.

"Yeah," Cayo agreed. "That's how I feel, too."

Cayo nearly dropped the box he was hauling into the back room at Florimond's shop. It was the last of some new shipment, and based on how heavy they were, Cayo was inclined to say Florimond had ordered himself about a third of a stone quarry.

"Careful with those!" Florimond griped. He was leaning over a glass vial that emanated a smell like rotten eggs. There was a whole table devoted to various beakers and containers, as well as barrels, boxes, and heaps of metal under tarps. The room was crowded and oddly warm compared to the chill outside.

Cayo leaned against one of the boxes and wiped sweat from his brow. "What's in them, anyway?"

"Hematite," Florimond muttered, more absorbed in his current experiment than answering Cayo's question.

"What's that?"

The man sighed and set his vial down. "A type of mineral found in sedimentary rocks."

"What do you need them for? Is it to help with the cure for ash fever?"

Florimond peered at him over his glasses, and Cayo affected an innocent smile. He could already hear Liesl's snort of reprimand. Apparently he wasn't very good at being a spy.

"I don't pay you to be curious," Florimond said. "I pay you to do labor. Now go dust the shop."

Cayo hesitated. He wanted to stay in the back room longer, wait for Florimond to become engrossed enough in his experiment that Cayo could start to poke around.

But he was already on thin ice, so he grabbed the feather duster hanging on a hook by the door and entered the main shop. He was tired from getting up earlier to see Soria and from his day's work at the fish market, but that thrum of excitement kept him going, the promise that they were finally on the right track.

A customer came in while Cayo ran the duster over the shelves. Florimond emerged to conduct business, then coughed pointedly once the customer was gone.

"You have to pick things up to dust effectively."

Cayo blinked. He'd been dusting around the items on the shelves, too afraid to move them and mess up their order. "Sorry." He carefully lifted the jar he had seen during his first visit here, the one with thick silver liquid.

"Mercury," Florimond said suddenly.

"Huh?"

"I know you want to ask, so I'm telling you what's in the jar." Florimond leaned against the counter, looking like an old, cranky lion watching its prey tiptoe around the field. "It's called mercury. Lots of properties. It can be used to extract gold, as a component of explosives, even recreate the power of lightning. Extremely poisonous. Folks have gone mad using it."

Cayo swallowed and gently, very gently, set the jar back down. "I see."

"Do you have interest in becoming an alchemist?"

"Ah, I don't think so?" He tried to imagine it, but the very idea seemed ridiculous. Maybe even more so than his childhood dream of being an adventurer.

"Then why do you ask all these questions?"

Cayo shrugged. He had to seem casual, curious, the very opposite of suspicious. The fact that he could feel the outline of his pistol beneath his jacket made the task harder. "I guess, what with all this sickness running around, I'm eager to see what the alchemists will come up with. I've heard you're working on a cure."

Florimond didn't answer, simply returned to the back room. Cayo sighed and finished the dusting. When he went to hang up the duster, Florimond was standing before his shelves, where a small wooden box lay open. The alchemist held a letter in his hand, jaw clenched as he read its contents.

At Cayo's appearance, Florimond quickly stuffed it into the box and slammed the lid closed. Cayo made a mental note of that.

"You said before that you have to take care of your sister," Florimond said. "She has the fever, doesn't she?"

Cayo froze. Perhaps he really had asked one question too many. "I..."

The man gave him his customary scowl, but there was a heaviness in his eyes that replaced his usual annoyance. "Many in the city have it. It's only natural you'd want to know how the cure is coming along."

"And how is it coming?"

Florimond gestured to the notes scattered across his various work stations. "Slowly. Until there is a way to counteract the disease caused by the brinies, we are firing arrows into the dark."

"Is your patron Robin Deirdre?"

Florimond stared as if Cayo had been invisible until just this moment. "How do you know about Robin Deirdre?"

"She came to the fish market the other day." He swallowed, the back of his neck damp with sweat. "I heard others talking about her." That, at least, was the truth.

"Well, she's definitely got the alchemists in this city by the balls." Florimond looked away. "But no, she's not my patron."

Cayo held back a sigh of relief.

"I'm sorry about your sister," Florimond muttered, still not looking in his direction. "We're working as hard as we can to find a cure."

Cayo nodded, not quite knowing what to say to that. "If there's any chance I can help..."

Florimond grunted again. Between him and Victor, that seemed to be their favorite mode of communication. The alchemist made a shooing gesture at him.

"If you don't even know the basics of alchemy, I doubt you can help." Florimond turned back to his experiment. "But I'll let you know. You can go for the day. Your payment is under the counter."

Not a whole lot of information to bring back to the others, but it was a start. At least he now knew that Florimond was one of the alchemists working on a cure, not the cause.

Which left them to figure out who in this city was funded by Deirdre.

With his full day's wages in his pocket, Cayo made his way back to the hospital to pay the administrator. Although the first treatment hadn't yet reversed the effects of ash fever on his sister, and although Florimond said they were still far from a cure, he couldn't help but feel the first blossoming of hope like the gradual crawl from winter to spring.

Then a whistle pierced the air.

Cayo looked over his shoulder. The three pickpockets were following him like wolves on the scent of blood, smiling eagerly.

His stomach sank. They had marked him as an easy hit, someone they could repeatedly target without repercussions. No, it was more than that—this had become a game for them, one where they always won and he always lost.

Cayo hoped the few people on the street would provide a buffer between him and the thieves. But as he picked up the pace, he realized he couldn't lead them to the hospital or the apartment—if they knew his regular route, it would just provide them with more opportunities to jump him in the future. And if he ducked into a shop to avoid them, they would simply wait for him to come back out before resuming the hunt.

He had to confront them—and make sure it was the last time.

Cayo turned into a narrow alley. Their footfalls rang behind him, quickening their pace to match his. Cayo's heart hammered as he navigated the streets, searching desperately for a place where he could make his stand.

He finally came across a small four-way intersection that joined two alleys together, forming a little square. There was a toy horse leaning against the side of a building, as well as some gnawed-on chicken bones. Cayo put his back to the wall and waited.

They each came out of a different alley. The short boy looked surprised to see him standing there, but it was quickly replaced with a hungry grin.

"Look, he's gettin' smarter," the boy said. "He knows to get it over with."

"Aww, but I liked it when he fought back," the girl pouted.

"We could make it more fun," the tall boy suggested. "Three rounds, best two outta three wins?"

"Oh, I *like* that!"

"There won't be any more rounds," Cayo said, his voice firm. "I'm not going to be your plaything any longer."

"Oof!" The short boy pretended to stagger back as if from a blow, holding up his hands. "Such mean words from such a pretty face! Makes me wanna teach you a lesson."

"Teach 'im," the girl growled with excitement, eyes shining as she bounced on the balls of her feet. "And lemme watch."

166

The three of them stalked closer. Cayo took a deep breath, then reached behind him.

Drawing out his pistol, he cocked the hammer back with a thumb and aimed it at the short boy's chest. "Stay back."

The thieves froze. For once, Cayo saw genuine fear in their eyes.

"Hey," said the short boy. "Hey now, that's cheatin'."

"And ganging up on me three to one is fair, is it?" Cayo countered. "You're not taking any more of my money. In fact, I'd say you owe me money."

The pickpockets glanced at one another, silently weighing their options. The girl shifted on her feet. "We got nothin' today. You were gonna be our only mark."

"Then it seems we're at an impasse. I suggest you leave."

The short boy scowled and moved closer, but Cayo aimed the pistol higher, at his head. The boy stopped in his tracks.

"I said *leave*," Cayo repeated.

The short boy spat on the ground between him and Cayo. "Keep your damn money, then. Let's go."

The three pickpockets skulked away, throwing Cayo dirty looks over their shoulders. He stayed in place, barely daring to move until he could no longer hear their footsteps. Then he let out a long, relieved breath and leaned over to rest his hands on his knees.

"I did it," he muttered to himself, laughing slightly. "I did it!"

Although he felt a twinge of guilt for aiming the gun at them, hope rose higher in him with every step he took toward the hospital, Jazelle once again snugly hidden under his jacket. He had fended off his attackers on his own. He had been able to walk away with money for Soria.

Maybe this *was* what happy felt like.

Cayo bounded up the stairs of the hospital, his body light and running on the high of adrenaline. He passed Soria's room on the way to the administrator's office, digging into his pocket for the money that was owed.

He knocked on the door before opening it all the way—and froze.

Instead of the administrator, Mother Hilas sat slumped at the man's desk, staring blankly at the wall. At the sound of his knock, her dark, deadened eyes lifted to meet his.

"What..." Cayo walked inside, looking around as if he could find any clue as to what was happening. "Is something wrong? Where's the administrator?"

Mother Hilas stared at him. To his silent horror, tears began to run down her face.

"Gone," the woman whispered, her voice ragged. "He's gone."

Cayo's heart beat low and hard, a sickening rhythm. "What do you mean, gone? Did he get the fever?"

"No." Mother Hilas took a shuddering breath, covering her face with her hands. "He...He took everything. All the money patients spent for the experimental treatment...all the medicine...He took it and fled. The reason why the patients haven't been getting better is because he switched the treatment with a placebo. No doubt he's planning on selling the real thing through some backchannel market for three times the amount."

The world turned hazy and dark. Cayo collapsed into the nearest chair, struggling to pull air into his lungs.

"But...But there *is* a treatment," he said slowly, his words distant, insubstantial. "They can make a new batch."

"Yes. But the patients who were already paying for it..." Mother Hilas wiped at her eyes even as a small sob escaped her. "All that money, wasted, and for nothing. It'll be more expensive to make a new batch, and now most of them can't afford the real thing."

Which meant he wouldn't be able to afford it, either.

The song he'd sung all his life was that so long as he had enough money, he could solve any problem. A quick exchange of coins, and doors would open for him. The world would bend itself over backward just to keep that flow of currency coming.

He was beginning to see more and more that money didn't solve problems—it created them. So long as it existed, greed would always run the world.

The medicine was gone. Soria wasn't going to get any better unless he found a way to pay for new doses of medicine. But he doubted Victor or Florimond would pay him anything more than what he was already making, and even though the other night had been successful, he wasn't about to become a thief.

Making an honest wage hadn't been enough. And in a city full of the struggling poor and the thriving rich, it was all too clear to him now that playing by his old rules wouldn't work. Those rules had been written by people like his former self, people in power who only wanted personal gain.

*You should visit the Casino District,* Jasper had said. *I'm sure they're looking for young, attractive dealers.*

Cayo gritted his teeth and tried to drive the words away. If he couldn't throw money at his problems, he had to do whatever he could to help the alchemists, help Florimond, with the cure.

If there was even one to be found.

**15**

NIHA: Do not forget the relief that laughter brings.

ARME: And if the laughter will not come?

NIHA: Then you must forge joy in whatever

way you can.

—*THE LADY OF HIRAI, A PLAY FROM REHAN*

When she had been training in Viariche, Amaya had often seen Boon drunk. At first she had let it go—he was a slob of a man whose life was far from easy—but eventually it started to nip at her.

They had been walking back to the *Brackish* one night when Amaya's patience snapped. She'd wanted to go back to the apartment she shared with the other girls, but Boon was too far gone to make the walk on his own. With his luck, he'd burst into the nearest guard station and serenade them with a ballad of his misdeeds.

So Amaya walked beside him as he stumbled and shuffled, alternating between curses and giggles. She wasn't sure she had ever seen him so far gone.

It scared her.

Boon had scratched at his black beard and squinted at her. "Wasser problem?"

Amaya's gaze had been focused on the bumpy road leading to the docks. "What?"

"Your face," he'd grumbled, gesturing to his own countenance, his brown skin already creased with wrinkles. Then he'd cackled, his breath reeking of alcohol. "Used to know a woman'd scowled like that."

He'd put a hand on her shoulder, jostling it in what she could only describe as a fond gesture. But there was no way a man like Boon held any softness for girls like her. Or anyone, for that matter.

"Why do you do it?" She had blurted it out before she could stop herself, but his inebriation had made her bolder, hoping he wouldn't remember it come morning. "All this drinking, stumbling around in gutters."

Boon had scoffed. "Think I like gutters?"

"You certainly like alcohol."

"Aye." He'd lifted a hand as if expecting to find a bottle there, then scoffed when it turned out to be empty. "Helps the mind, y'know?"

"No, I don't know."

"'S like a...balm. Now that's an odd word, huh? *Balm.*" He stretched the word out consonant by consonant. "There's things I'd rather not think, yeah? But when the mind's addled, no problem." He'd pressed a finger to his temple. "No problem."

Amaya still didn't understand, and she didn't think she ever would. There were times Cicada would sneak her sips of lupseh on the *Brackish*, and she had enjoyed those, the pleasant warmth in her belly and the way it helped ease the soreness of her body.

But this excess was different. It was medicine for a sick man who knew he was never getting better so long as he kept taking it.

They'd arrived at the *Brackish*, and Amaya had waited for him to walk up the gangplank. But Boon had just stood there a moment, swaying slightly. Finally, he'd turned and gripped her chin, startling her.

"Whatever 'comes of you, don't be like me." His voice had been low, plaintive. "Not this. This..." He indicated himself: his soiled shirt, his ratty jacket, his bloodshot eyes. "Whatever this is."

Amaya had stared at him, unsure where this was coming from. "I won't. Trust me."

He'd chuckled and patted her cheek. "Aye. Much smarter'n me, aren't you?" He would have normally said it as a taunt. Instead, he'd sounded sincere. Proud, almost.

Amaya had stepped back from him, feeling strange. "Go to bed, old man."

Boon had made a shooing motion at her before navigating the gangplank. Amaya had walked back to the apartment, rubbing her chin.

He'd given her a warning she hadn't needed. But she couldn't help wondering if there was something else to it, if he'd had some inkling of what would befall her in the next few months. If he had known, even then, that she would go against his plans, repaying one betrayal with another.

"Do you realize how many disturbance reports there are in Baleine?" Remy asked around a yawn. It was early morning, the sky a pale gold. The sun, newly risen, was the only thing keeping Amaya from shuddering on the wooden bench where they sat outside a tea shop.

A thin, greasy sheet of brown paper sat between them, bearing a solitary pastry they were slowly working through. It was flaky and buttery, and completely covered with sugar and slivered almonds. She was trying very hard not to inhale the entire thing, considering Remy had bought it for them and deserved at least a few bites.

She had desperately needed to get out of the apartment. Cayo's presence was like a low hanging fog, permeating and suffocating. He was understandably on edge after learning the hospital administrator had run off with the medicine—no doubt to peddle and make himself a small fortune—and that paired with Liesl's desperation made for a heavy atmosphere.

Not that she wasn't empathetic. If she could, she would track down the fake administrator and turn him into a pincushion, returning the medicine that Soria needed. But he was long gone, and they had to focus on what was feasible with the knowledge they currently had.

"We just need one that matches Boon's description," Amaya said as she twisted a bit of the flaky bread away and popped it into her mouth. "If we can find a report that matches his description, maybe we can find *him*. He did all sorts of reckless things in Viariche when we were there. One time I had to save him from a woman with a gun."

"Was he flirting with her?"

"No, he was trying to steal her gun."

When she had told the story to Liesl afterward, they had shared a laugh. But now as she thought back to those days, she could feel her heart hardening. It was easy to consider Boon pathetic, unreliable, foolish—but what lurked beneath was a mind far craftier than he ever let on.

"All right." Remy sighed, pushing the rest of the pastry her way. "I'll see what I can dig up. Don't expect to hear from me for a century. Or at least, not until we deal with the Ghost Ship."

She was halfway to shoving the pastry into her mouth when she stopped. "The what?"

"There's a ship anchored out in the harbor. It just showed up overnight." Remy shrugged, too sleepy to be properly curious. "There's no sign of anyone on board, but we can't lead it to the docks in case there's something dangerous inside. So it has to stay out in the harbor until the navy can dismantle it. But of course, we need the order cleared first, and there's a bunch of paperwork...."

"Why would someone just abandon their ship in the harbor?"

"Probably desperate to get into the city. They've doubled down on the quarantine, sending entire crews away." Remy shook his head. "But leaving your ship in the harbor and swimming the rest of the way to Baleine? That's ridiculous. Surely they could have thought of something better."

Amaya plucked an almond sliver from the pastry and chewed on it, staring at the small brown birds hopping around them, hoping for crumbs. "Thank you, Remy."

"For what?"

"Everything. For getting us into the city. For helping us. For breakfast." She laid her hand on top of his. "Just...thank you. I don't know how we could do any of this without you."

He looked genuinely startled before passing it off with a grin, squeezing her hand in his. "Hey, of course. I know you'd do the same for me."

"I would. I would decimate an entire city for you."

"Please don't do that."

Amaya spent the rest of the day in a strange mood. She felt restless and tired at the same time, her body crying for action even as her mind cried for calm. It didn't help that whenever her mind wandered, it inevitably returned to Basque's manor, to the feel of her teeth on Cayo's skin. She groaned in mortification every time.

She was brought out of her listlessness when Deadshot and Avi returned from their day of investigating Robin Deirdre. Liesl sat at the table, muttering and scratching out words as she worked on Basque's code. She had been like this all day, only surfacing to ask if Amaya was dying due to all her pained groaning. The girl had barely eaten or drunk anything, so fixated on the code that everything else became inconsequential, even gathering information on Deirdre.

When Deadshot placed a hand on her shoulder, Liesl startled.

"What? Yes?" Liesl blinked at them through fingerprint-smudged glasses.

"We found out the Deirdre family's been part of Chalier's nobility for a long time," Avi said. "They rose in power when one of their heirs married into royalty, back when Chalier was still an independent nation."

"But then the empire came along and made the royal family obsolete," Deadshot added.

Avi clucked his tongue. "It's likely her family is doing all they can to get back to the top. Investing in the alchemists and using them for warfare seems like the most direct route into the emperor's pocket."

"But since the empire abolished the Chalier royal family, that would have been a heavy blow to the Deirdres," Deadshot pointed out. "Why would Robin Deirdre be working so hard to help them?"

"Better to have allies than enemies?" Avi shrugged.

"That also doesn't explain why she's focusing on spreading the counterfeits here in the Rain Empire."

Liesl listened but didn't offer comment. She only nodded and turned back to Basque's code, making Deadshot frown.

But Amaya understood. If she had a sister who'd been taken from her, she would be working just as hard to get her back.

In some ways, that was what Boon was to her now: a smaller target she had to strike down before aiming at their true objective. If Liesl's guess was right and he was somewhere in this city, she would find him.

As Liesl poured over Basque's code, Amaya returned to the bedroom and lifted her mattress, pulling out her father's notes. She read them as best she could—he had used his own shorthand in many places—but again and again she came back to that one passage.

*My greatest treasures in this life lie with my wife and my daughter.*

She rubbed a thumb against her mother's jade ring. Why write something so sentimental among all these letters and records? Had he hoped for her or her mother to find it one day?

A knock on the bedroom door made her look up. To her surprise, Avi slunk in, looking exhausted after another day of snooping.

"Hope I'm not bothering you," he said. His voice was hoarse, eyes tight as if in some sort of pain.

"You're not bothering me," she said, setting the papers aside on her bed. She gestured for him to join her, which he did with a barely suppressed wince. "Are you feeling all right?"

176

"Tired," he grunted. "A little sore." He rubbed a hand against the back of his neck; Amaya had never seen him this nervous. "Look, I'm just going to come out and say it. I...I haven't been completely honest with you."

Her chest tightened. "What are you talking about?"

Avi crossed his arms, a defensive pose. "It's about Boon."

Her skin prickled with cold, hands curling into fists.

"What about him?" she asked softly.

"I never met your parents, but Boon knew them. Was friends with them, I think. He would tell me stories about them when he was drunk enough. Stories about...learning alchemy."

A black, oily feeling brewed in Amaya's stomach. *Boon knew my parents?* She recalled the way he had reacted to her father's name on the *Brackish*, frenzied, shocked.

"He...My mother as well?" she asked.

Avi nodded. "He said your mother was a smart woman who helped him with his experiments in alchemy. From the way he talked about her, it seemed like they'd been close once."

No. That didn't sound right at all. Her eyes fell onto her father's papers, but there was nothing in there about alchemy.

"Are..." Her voice nearly failed her as she thought back to those barrels of gold under the atoll. "Are you saying she helped him craft counterfeits?"

"I don't know. He never told me that the gold he gave you was counterfeit, but considering he knows some alchemy, he obviously made it himself. If your mother helped him, knew about the disease that brinies carry, maybe...maybe she knew how to counteract its effects." Avi shrugged. "Like I said, I don't know all the details. I just thought you should know what I know."

Amaya's fingernails pressed crescent moons into her palms. "Why didn't you tell me earlier?"

Avi's face fell. "I didn't think you were ready. Or, shit, maybe I was just scared, or hoped it wasn't true. But at least you know now, before..."

"Before what?"

He shook his head. "Nothing. Sorry." He stood from the bed, wincing again. "We'll find him, Amaya. We'll wring the truth out of him."

*Boon knew my mother.*

*My mother knew alchemy.*

She stared at the ring on her finger. Could she really believe what Avi had just told her, considering Boon was the one who had given him the information? All the things she didn't know was a library kept under lock and key. Somehow, she had to find a way to smash through the doors.

After tossing and turning for hours, Amaya was woken by the sound of footsteps. She had become a heavy sleeper on the *Brackish*—she'd had to, in order to drown out the sound of at least a dozen other children snoring and crying and creaking in their hammocks—but ever since leaving the ship, she tended to be right on the verge of consciousness at any given moment.

She sat up when the bedroom door opened. She could make out Deadshot's silhouette in the faint glow of candlelight emanating from the main room. Amaya slipped out of bed as Deadshot eased the door closed most of the way, which allowed Amaya a small window to peek through.

Liesl was still sitting at the table, surrounded by candles and papers. Deadshot sat beside her and settled a hand on her back. "You need sleep, morija."

"I almost have this one letter figured out." Liesl's voice was monotonous as she continued to focus on the code.

Deadshot sighed and rubbed her lover's back. "You won't get to her any faster if you work yourself to death. You'll be able to work even harder after a night's rest. Right now, your mind is too crowded, too tired."

"Don't tell me about my own mind," Liesl muttered. "I know my limits."

Deadshot gently took her chin, forcing Liesl to look at her. The candlelight gleamed along the edges of Liesl's glasses.

"I love you, but I also know when you're being a stubborn ass," Deadshot said. The frankness made Amaya smile as Liesl sputtered. "We will save Adrienne. But if you're sleep-deprived, you'll be more hindrance than help."

Liesl's lips thinned. Amaya knew her well enough to see the first signs of rage.

Amaya pushed open the door and joined them. "She's right," she said, keeping her voice down so she wouldn't wake the boys. "You'll be able to get more done when your mind isn't overworked."

"Adrienne—"

"Has survived this long," Amaya finished for her. "She can wait another couple of days."

She was taken aback by the crumpling of Liesl's face, the tears that welled in her eyes. "But what if...what if she *didn't* survive? What if she...?"

She heaved a shuddering breath, holding her head in her hands. Deadshot continued to rub her back, whispering soothing words in Circíran. Amaya placed her hand on Liesl's shoulder.

"You helped me in Moray," Amaya said. "Now it's my turn to help you. And you know how you were always ordering me around, saying it was for my own good? Well, here I am, telling you to go back to your damn bed."

That surprised a laugh out of Liesl. Deadshot gave Amaya an approving nod.

"Fine," Liesl said, dropping her hands. "But no one better disturb my work tomorrow."

"We wouldn't dream of it, morija."

Amaya blew out the candles as Deadshot led Liesl back to the bedroom. She lingered a moment in the doorway, allowing them some privacy as she watched tendrils of smoke drift up from the burnt wicks, gray and ghostly in the moonlight.

She was about to close the door when the one across from theirs opened, slow and uncertain. Amaya peeked around the frame, wondering if Avi was coming to check if everything was all right. Maybe she could ask him more about what Boon had told him about her mother.

Instead, Cayo leaned out to make sure that they were gone. He snuck into the main room and closed the bedroom door silently behind him, fully dressed despite the late hour.

Amaya frowned as he headed for the front door. Once he left the apartment, she rushed to pull on her trousers and a jacket.

"Amaya? What are you doing?" Liesl called sleepily from the other bed.

"Taking a walk now that I'm awake. You get some rest."

"All right," the girl said around a massive yawn, snuggling against an already snoring Deadshot. "Don't get murdered."

Amaya grabbed her boots but didn't put them on yet. She left the apartment and silently stole down the stairs, only just catching the sight of Cayo sneaking through the main entrance.

*Where are you going?* She shoved her boots on and followed him into the night, the moon nearly full above their heads. Keeping her distance, she watched as Cayo wove through the cobblestone streets, his hand occasionally flitting to his side where he kept his new pistol.

They kept up their game of cat and mouse for nearly half an hour. Lights shone brightly ahead, and she could hear the raucous sound of people having a good time. Cayo hesitated on the outskirts, gathering his nerve before moving forward.

Amaya's stomach sank as she turned the corner and realized where they were.

The Casino District.

The avenue before them was strewn with hanging lanterns and streamers, the buildings lined with iron balconies and colorful signs. A large building down the way had its doors flung open, people streaming in and out like competing schools of fish. Outdoor cafés and alehouses were set up with wooden tables, their chairs occupied by those already on their way to drunk or those who merely sipped at their drinks as they watched the crowd pass by.

Cayo stopped to take it all in. Amaya took the opportunity to slink up to his side.

"What in the hells do you think you're doing here?" she demanded.

Cayo jumped back. "What—How did you—"

"You're bad at sneaking out. Is it because your manor was so big that you couldn't wake anyone even if you tried?"

Cayo frowned. "Before you get the wrong idea—*again*—I'm here for a reason."

"To get more money for Soria's treatment?"

"No—I mean, I thought about it. I won't lie and say I didn't..." He raked a hand through his hair, agitated. "But I couldn't sleep, so I thought maybe I could try to find that man Julien Caver mentioned. Trevan Nicodeme. He's supposed to be integrating counterfeits into the casinos, right?"

"You..." She couldn't help it; she laughed. The look on his face only made her laugh harder. "You wanted to do this by yourself?"

"I'm tired of wasting time. The sooner we discover who's making counterfeit coins and who isn't, the sooner we can stop this."

She sobered at that, at the steel hiding under his words. Cayo held his body defensively, angled slightly away from her, as if wanting to run.

All too clearly she understood. He had become just as restless as she'd been earlier, and for good reason. It was no wonder he couldn't sleep. After what Avi had told her, she couldn't, either.

What Cayo needed right now wasn't admonishment. What he needed was a distraction.

"All right," she agreed. "But that means blending in to get information, right? I hear two players are better than one. You focus on playing, I focus on listening."

His lips parted in shock, as if unable to believe what he was hearing.

"*You* want *me* to gamble," he said slowly. "To gamble *with* me."

"You said you're tired of wasting time." She set off down the street. "So let's go."

Cayo reluctantly followed her. Admittedly, she had no idea what she was doing. But she felt oddly emboldened by this new side of Cayo, even if it did bring them dangerously close to the things he was supposed to be avoiding. She sent a silent apology to Soria.

Amaya had been to the Vice Sector in Moray; she knew what casinos looked like, how they operated. Still, when they entered the casino's open doors, Amaya had to stop to process all she was seeing. The place was huge, the carpet below their feet stretching out in an ocean of blue and yellow. Chandeliers dripped from a ceiling that was a riot of gold molding, bearing a circular glass dome in its center. The walls were painted a rich blue, studded with veined marble columns.

There were gambling tables everywhere, as well as three different types of bars. The noise of the crowd was like a typhoon, a storm of sound and energy that made her fight-or-flight response kick in. A cheer erupted in the back of the hall while a shriek of laughter cut through the air nearby, raising the hairs on Amaya's arms.

Beside her, the bleak expression on Cayo's face had melted into a grin.

She'd never seen this look on his face before. The tension had seeped out of him, and his eyes held a glint of mischief with the promise that it would soon be fulfilled. He seemed . . . confident.

Surprisingly, she didn't hate it. Didn't hate that she was the one who put it there.

"Where should we start?" she asked.

He turned to her, cupping a hand around his ear. "What?"

She raised her voice. "What's your plan?"

"I thought this was *your* plan?" He looked around again, gaze snagging on a couple of tables. "Like you said, we should mingle with the crowd. Gambling is the easiest way to do that. Ask harmless questions while other players are distracted."

"Like if anyone's seen a man with a pocket watch and muttonchops?"

"Exactly."

She hesitated, hating the question she knew she had to ask. "Do you have enough to put down?"

He slipped a hand into his pocket. "It'll have to be enough."

"What if you lose?"

His expression darkened. "I learned some tricks from the Slum King, if worse comes to worse. But I don't plan to cheat if I can help it."

"I don't want to see your face up on a broadsheet, Cayo."

"Me neither. They'll probably get my eyes wrong." He turned and waded into the crowd, leaving Amaya to chase after.

Although the casinos in Moray ranged from opulent to seedy, there was something uncannily extravagant about this one. Cayo told her it was named the Golden Harbor, appropriate considering the gilded ceiling and walls. Small stages lay scattered across the room, the one nearest them occupied by a young woman in a skin-tight outfit cut off at the arms and legs.

The young woman's brown skin was coated in a glittery substance that made her sparkle as she danced upon her square of a stage. Her head was haloed by a fan of feathers, her feet encased in dangerously high-heeled shoes. As she danced, she threw winks and smiles at the people who came closer to watch, the sway of her curves almost hypnotic.

Amaya was so distracted by the dancer that she didn't realize

Cayo was no longer beside her. She looked around, frantic, then relaxed when she saw he had merely found a game to observe.

She didn't recognize the game that was being played on the table covered in a fine blue felt. There were both dice and cards involved, and the players kept saying numbers and colors out loud. Cayo watched through a single round and sat down before the next one started.

Amaya bent down to whisper in his ear. "Do you know how to play?"

"I've played it in Moray before. It's fairly easy." He turned to look at her, which brought their faces unexpectedly close. They both froze before Amaya leaned back.

"If you're sure," she said, her voice strained.

She anchored her hands on the back of Cayo's chair as he put down one of his silver nieras. The dealer passed around cards, and Amaya peeked at his hand despite not knowing what it meant. When it was his turn, Cayo threw a pair of dice and said *seven* and *blue* in Soléne. The dealer turned a card over and the players groaned while Cayo smiled. They went around like this a few more times until it happened again, and the dealer announced Cayo the winner.

Amaya's stomach fluttered as Cayo gathered the handful of niera toward him, his motions practiced and easy. She took the now-empty seat beside him, watching him transition the coins into a gambling pouch that the dealer provided him, the casino's insignia embroidered on the fabric. No gold coins, thankfully.

"Is it enough?" she asked. "For Soria?"

"No." Cayo gazed at the pouch in his lap, frowning. "Mother Hilas said the next batch of medicine they produce will be even more expensive than the first."

He nervously pressed his thumb into the pouch, as if to reassure himself that there was money inside. Amaya realized this was the most money he had held in a long time.

"Why are you doing this?" he asked suddenly. "Before, you were so upset at the thought of me gambling."

She winced at the reminder of her outburst. "I was. But now… Well, we're ultimately doing this for good, aren't we? To help bring down Deirdre and expose her as the Benefactor." She shrugged. "Besides, I'm here with you."

He paused at the words, thumb digging harder into the pouch. The dealer began to set up the next game, but Cayo stood, abandoning his chair and his place in the round.

"Come on, then." That glint had returned to his eyes. "Let's find some bigger stakes."

# 16

*Sin is always better with company.*

—*A HUNDRED AND ONE VICES FOR THE EVERYMAN*

Cayo, now up by six niera, decided it was time for a drink.

The instinct came as easily to him as breathing. It was in his routine: gamble a little, get on a roll, grab a drink. That was always how he'd done things, until it became habit, until it became a luck ritual.

His friends had all had their own luck rituals. Tomjen's was to kiss someone on the cheek, and Sébastien's had been to hum a bar of his favorite song.

Cayo's was to have a drink in his hand. He told himself he wouldn't actually drink it, but remembering the way the sparkling wine had tasted at Basque's gala, he knew full well he wouldn't keep to that.

"You win money and then immediately decide to spend it?"

Amaya asked beside him, leaning an elbow against the bar and fixing him with an unimpressed glare. "I thought the whole point of this was to get as much as you can while gathering information."

"I'm only getting started," Cayo argued. "Sometimes you have to spend money to make money."

"By betting, perhaps, but not with alcohol."

"So you think. I happen to play even better with a drink nearby."

"If you say so," she muttered. The bartender came back and placed a full glass before her. "What's happening? What is this?"

"Liquid courage," Cayo answered, accepting his own drink and paying the bartender. "To be more specific, it's called a Gilded Lotus."

"You got me one? Why?"

"Because drinking alone isn't fun." Cayo picked up his glass, a rounded tumbler filled with a greenish-yellow concoction, its rim coated with crushed lime salt. He held it out, and Amaya carefully clinked their glasses together before taking a sip. Cayo tasted lemon and orange, as well as the heady, heavy overtone of vorene, one of the Rain Empire's most commonly exported alcohols.

Amaya hummed, pleased with the taste. She licked a bit of lime salt off the rim, and Cayo had to avert his gaze. "It's good. But are you sure you should be drinking? I thought you wanted to avoid it."

"One or two won't hurt."

She didn't look convinced, but he ignored it in favor of staking out his next table. As they weaved through the crowd, Amaya kept glancing at him, taking small sips of her drink.

"You're different," she said eventually. "In here."

"Am I?" He did feel different, standing in an environment he'd come to think of as his sanctuary—before it had become a hell. But even with the distance he'd put between himself and this lifestyle, he still yearned for the nights where living had been simpler, easier, better. To dull pain and chase highs and for once not be afraid.

And it didn't hurt that Amaya was with him. At first he hadn't liked the thought of her sticking by his side tonight, but while he played he couldn't help but want to impress her, to show her that he could be useful, if just not in the way she'd initially wanted.

But what if they could pay for Soria's medicine, as well as find a lead? A night of slipping back into old habits might be worth it.

Cayo spotted a familiar card game called Threefold, one he had played often in the Grand Mariner back home. "All right," he said to Amaya, "I'm going to play a couple of rounds, and you're going to watch. Then you're going to play."

She nearly choked on her drink. "Me?"

"Have you ever gambled before?"

"Only once, when..." She flushed. "When I went to the Vice Sector looking for you."

Which must have been when she'd met Romara. "Then I'm sure you'll be a quick study."

Her eyes narrowed. "You just want to win against me, don't you?"

"It sounds alluring." He flashed her a dimpled smile. "I already know your tells."

"And *you* are predictable. I'm going to win."

"We'll see about that."

Cayo sat and played a couple of rounds, falling back into the routine of the game, the rhythm of the cards. He kept an eye on the other players, noting how a woman scratched her nose, how a young man's tongue darted out between his lips, how another always sniffed right before showing a bad hand.

They were actors in a play, and Cayo knew all their lines.

After he won his second round, the other players grumbled, most of them leaving their seats in search of a more favorable game. Amaya sank into the seat on his left.

"Got the idea?" he murmured.

Her dark eyes flashed in challenge. "Don't you worry about me."

He grinned and subtly pointed at the woman two seats down. "She seems like the sort to know a man with muttonchops. Watch this."

Cayo leaned an elbow on the table, smiling in the woman's direction. What she wore wasn't particularly fashionable, but she had a keen gaze and had been the hardest to read. Which meant she was a regular.

"Can't believe I got lucky," Cayo said. His voice sounded foreign to him, too carefree to be natural. "Other week I was here, I got walloped by a man with muttonchops. Muttonchops, of all things!"

The woman raised a plucked eyebrow at him. "Am I supposed to say sorry?"

"Have you gone against him? His winning streak was maddening."

"Can't say that I have."

"Pretty sure she's telling the truth," Amaya whispered as the cards were handed out. "Nice try, though."

Cayo examined his hand. Not bad—but not the best. His gaze slid over to Amaya, studying her reaction to her own hand.

He'd claimed to know her tells, which wasn't a lie. He'd had plenty of time to observe her in the past several weeks. When she scrunched up her nose, she was dissatisfied. When she chewed the inside of her cheek, she was thinking about something that worried her. When her fingers twitched, she was angry.

But she showed none of her usual tells tonight. Instead, she looked calmly at her cards and set them face down on the table. Noticing Cayo's stare, she winked.

He scoffed and returned to his own cards. Her left eyebrow had twitched slightly, but he didn't know what that meant yet. He targeted the woman on the end instead, swapping a card with her. The game went on, slowly, carefully, the players tense as cards exchanged hands, three times per player.

When everyone revealed their hands, Cayo immediately looked at Amaya's. She had been close, very close, but he ended up victorious again. The winnings were pushed toward him, and he scooped the coins into his pouch before any of the other players could start a fight.

Amaya didn't seem angry, though. At least, her fingers weren't twitching. When Cayo faced her, she surprised him with a wide grin that nearly knocked him to the ground. The rest of the casino was an unsightly blur compared to that smile.

"Again," she said.

They tried their luck at other tables, other games. There had been a bevy of Rain Empire games in the Vice Sector, enough for Cayo to have familiarized himself with a handful. They sat at a table of Twice Scorned, rolling sets of differently shaped dice, and stood around a roulette wheel calling out colors and numbers.

Amaya remained steadfast in her goal to beat him. A couple of times she did, at first shocked and then distinctly pleased with herself.

"Maybe I have to start worrying about *you* coming back here," Cayo joked as Amaya added her winnings to their fattened pouch.

"It's not the game I'm addicted to," she said. "It's the look on your face when I win."

Cayo tried his charm again and again, attempting to weed out anyone who might have crossed paths with Trevan Nicodeme, but so far no one had risen to the bait. Still, he kept his ears open and ended up overhearing quite a bit of gossip that served no purpose, as well as speculation about the supposed Ghost Ship in the harbor.

He had seen it while working at the fish market. It had been anchored far enough away that he couldn't make out any details of the ship, just its outline. People liked to point and mutter about it—"It's abandoned?"; "I heard it was filled with a poisonous gas"; "No, it's probably haunted"—but the navy wasn't able to do anything about it until they got clearance from higher-ups to dispose of it. In the meantime, one of their ships was always lingering nearby, watchful for suspicious activity.

Cayo and Amaya had long since finished their first drink. Going against the faint, worried voice in his head that sounded like Soria, Cayo took them to one of the other bars, where they ordered something called Divine Chance. In order to make the drink, the bartender handed them a pair of dice they had to roll in order to determine what combination they'd get. Cayo got a five and a three, producing a floral mix of lavender and cardamom syrup, and Amaya got a two and a six, resulting in cherry and muddled mint.

"This is surprisingly good," Amaya said after a tentative taste. She pointed at his. "But that's the last one for you tonight."

"Whatever you say, my lady."

Despite Amaya's wariness, he noticed her relaxing as they returned to the card games, her mouth soft and her eyes bright. Cayo thought back to her in Basque's manor, the elegant and untouchable Countess Yamaa. Here she was mischievous and addictive, and Cayo found himself leaning over to make fun of the other players just to hear her brief, husky laugh.

"Do you think that hat was alive once?" he whispered, pointing out the plume of feathers on one woman's head.

"I think it's *still* alive," Amaya whispered back, her breath smelling of cherries.

A drunk man was swaying in his seat and muttering insults to the dealer, his face blotchy and his nose bearing the broken veins of an alcoholic. Amaya gave him a dirty look, one of her hands straying to a hidden knife.

"Just leave him alone," Cayo murmured as the woman beside him took her turn. "He'll probably doze off soon anyway."

But the more they played, the more belligerent the man got. He turned his ire toward the other players, critiquing their dice throws and questioning their choices in fashion.

"You wear *that* to toss the whale bone 'round?" he slurred at Amaya, sneering at her high-collared jacket that had admittedly seen better days. "Hair fallin' all 'round your face like some vagabond."

Amaya's eyes narrowed, but Cayo leaned forward to block her from the man's view. He disarmed the man with a wide smile, emboldened by the alcohol buzzing pleasantly through him.

"I'll make a wager with you," Cayo said. "All your winnings against all my winnings."

Amaya poked him in the back. *"What are you doing?"*

193

"Hah?" The man peered at him with bloodshot eyes while the dealer nervously looked between them. "You're just a little boy. Don't steal from little boys."

"Indulge me." Cayo rattled the dice in his hand. The sound they made was as comforting as rain on a window.

"I win, she's gotta put her hair up or some'n'," the man muttered, pointing at Amaya. "Little bit of makeup, y'know..."

"We'll see what we can do. But if *I* win, you have to answer one question."

"What sorta bet is that? Fine, fine."

Amaya sat back with her arms crossed, brow furrowed. Cayo flashed her a reassuring smile before going one-on-one with the drunk man, each of them taking turns rolling the dice and racking up points. Cayo's heart sped up giddily, remembering what it felt like to be in the heat of the moment, competing with someone across the table as his friends cheered on the sidelines.

Cayo observed the man's form, how exactly he held and released the dice. How his bloodshot eyes flitted around the casino as if paranoid. When the man's next turn came, Cayo timed a fake sneeze at the exact moment the man released his dice. The man jumped at the noise, and the dice barely rolled, showing the lowest score he'd earned the entire game.

Then it was Cayo's last roll. He held one of the die between his thumb and palm, tossing the rest as usual. But the third he let go of at the very last second, making sure it wouldn't roll and that it could land on a six.

"Well, then," Cayo said, leaning his elbows on the table. "Looks like your pretty mountain of coins is mine, and the lady gets to wear her hair however she damn well likes. *And* you have to answer one question."

The man's face reddened even more. "You— What did you—?"

"Trevan Nicodeme," Cayo interrupted. "Where does he like to gamble?"

The man gaped in an almost comical way, and Cayo knew his guess had been correct. Someone this shifty looking surely frequented the sorts of places a money launderer would go. Or at the least, someone this concerned with appearance would undoubtedly have noticed a man with muttonchops.

"Trevan?" The man blinked several times. "I—I don't know! The Crown and Barrel, I think?" He scowled suddenly. "Why d'you want to know? You set this up, didn't you?"

The man stood, yelling and swearing at Cayo until the casino guards came to escort him away. Cayo laughed as the dealer shoved the man's coins toward him. His blood was effervescent, his body crying, *More, more.*

He had done it. He had gotten a lead.

When they left the table, his victorious grin faded when he realized Amaya was no longer smiling.

"You cheated," she said.

Cayo drained the rest of his drink and set the empty glass on the nearest table. "I did what I had to in order to get us information. It worked, didn't it? Besides, I taught that bastard a lesson."

"That bastard," she said, pointing in the direction the guards had taken him, "is who you'll become if you keep this up."

The joy sparking through him fizzled out. "You were the one who thought this would be a good idea. Why are you complaining?"

Amaya drew herself up. "I don't have the right to be worried? One wrong move and we could have the authorities breathing down our necks."

She paused, took a deep breath. "It's not just the cheating, it's...
it's the reminder of the life you used to have, when you'd do things
like this without a second thought. We're not in the Vice Sector,
Cayo. You don't work for the Slum King."

"You think I don't know that?" Cayo mumbled. "I'm doing this
for Soria, not myself. You don't get to shame me for that."

"I'm not trying to shame you. Just no more cheating, all right?"

He glared at her, but she only gazed calmly back. He scoffed and
turned back to the bar.

"Fine," he said. "But I'm getting another drink."

"We have what we need. We can go."

But Cayo didn't want to call it a night. Amaya kept a close eye on
him as he won a few more games, lost a couple others. Since Amaya
refused to let him have a third drink, he found a group of people in
the corner smoking jaaga, and they let him have a couple hits. The
world was bright and pleasant, and Amaya's worry had become unex-
plainably funny.

"Don't move," she warned him before walking away.

He should have felt panicked, but he didn't. He just leaned against
the wall and watched the crowd, and when Amaya returned with a
glass of water, he grinned.

"I didn't move," he said as he took small sips. "I trusted you'd
come back."

"That's nice." Amaya crossed her arms. "Trusting people must
be nice."

"Mm, I don't though," he murmured. "Not really. But you—
you've lied and you've done bad things, but you're still *good*. Me,
I'm—I'm not good." He pressed a clammy hand to his forehead, closing his eyes. "I've never been good. That's why you hate me."

Her eyes were pinched. "Cayo…"

Before she could say anything else, someone approached them carrying a stack of flyers. They handed one to Amaya.

"What does it say?" Cayo asked.

"I don't know, I have a hard time reading Soléne."

He took it from her and skimmed it. He pushed himself off the wall, the water in his glass sloshing.

"What is it?"

Cayo shook the flyer. "An event here at the casino in a couple of days. High-stakes games only. Anyone can compete, but they already have a list of prominent people who'll be there, probably to draw a decent crowd." He lowered his voice. "One of them is Robin Deirdre."

Her eyes widened. "We have to compete."

"We?"

"I mean *you* have to compete. We can't pass this up, Cayo. We can be right next to the Benefactor!"

He should have felt excited. Instead, he felt his stomach drop. "Do you really want me to do this? It would mean putting down the money I won for Soria."

She considered it a moment longer, visibly torn. "It's a risky idea," she said at last. "But it's the best chance we have of finding out more about her. Besides, I saw you play tonight. You were unstoppable."

Cayo couldn't help the flare of satisfaction at the praise.

"It's your decision, though," she said.

He stared at the water in his hand. Everything in him cried to say yes, burying that tiny voice that sounded like Soria. Eventually he nodded.

"I'll do it."

Amaya folded up the flyer and tucked it into her pocket. "All right. But we're doing this on one condition: no alcohol, and no drugs. And no cheating."

"Those are three conditions."

"*Cayo.*"

He put a hand over his heart. "I swear."

"Good." She steered him toward the exit. "Now let's get you to bed before you fall on your face."

## 17

*The beast curled its claws over her shoulders,
steering her ever onward.*

*"Do not look behind you," it whispered in Lady
Trianh's ear.*

*The back of her neck was damp with sweat, the urge
to look over her shoulder a burden that sat heavy
in her heart. But the beast's fangs were a mere inch
from her skin, begging to puncture and tear at the
first sign of betrayal.*

—*THE BEAST BELOW*, A HORROR NOVEL FROM REHAN

*T*hat's why you hate me.

Those words had been haunting Amaya since Cayo had said them the night before. His voice had been slurred yet full of an emotion she couldn't ignore.

Despair.

Amaya had tossed and turned since they'd snuck back into the apartment, anxious and more than a little disturbed. When dawn broke, Liesl got up and went back to her decoding. Amaya went to check on Cayo and found his bed empty.

"Went to work," Avi said as he sipped his tea. "Looked fair wrecked, though."

Amaya had to admit she was impressed at Cayo's determination. With nothing else to do, she went to visit Soria and found the girl partially sitting up against her pillows. She seemed to be dozing but opened her eyes when Amaya came in.

"Amaya," the girl said sleepily. "How are you?"

"Fine, I suppose." Amaya sat heavily in the chair beside her bed. "I'm more concerned about you, though."

Soria smiled. "You know, I'm getting rather tired of other peoples' concern."

Amaya flushed. "Sorry."

"No, no, don't be sorry. I'd just prefer discussing something else."

Amaya nodded, looking around the room as if for inspiration. "I should bring flowers next time. It's so sparse in here."

"That would be lovely."

"Which are your favorites?"

They chatted about small, inconsequential things for the next half hour, and Amaya found that she'd desperately needed the distraction. Still, she couldn't quite shake her memories of last night. After a lull in the conversation, she ended up blurting, "Your brother's a fool."

Soria was startled into laughter that quickly became a cough. Amaya handed her a cup of water.

"What did he do now?" she wheezed.

Amaya explained what they'd done last night. Soria's amusement faded as Amaya explained the change that had come over him.

"At first it was fine, and we were actually having fun." Amaya said the words like she was testing them out for the first time. "But he spiraled a little."

Soria looked down at her hands a moment, a divot forming on her brow.

"Amaya," the girl said at last, "I expected more from you."

Amaya leaned back. A flash of prickling heat filled in her chest, which she quickly identified as shame.

"I've seen him that way before," Soria went on. "When he would come home still drunk or drugged. Sometimes he'd be sweet and happy, and other times he'd be angry and volatile. I hated it." She turned her head away, staring out the window at the bright morning light. "But it was the only way he thought he could deal with his pain. Once in a while he would curl up at the foot of my bed to sleep, because he didn't want to be alone. He fears it, I think. And he doesn't know how to handle that fear."

Amaya closed her eyes tight. *That's why you hate me.*

"But you're not like that," Soria went on. "You know when enough is enough. So why did you let him get away with it?"

Why had she? Amaya licked her dry lips, unable to find a suitable answer. "I don't know. I guess...I didn't know how to stop him. What can I do to make sure he doesn't fall into it again?"

Soria met her gaze, her right eye nearly overtaken with gray. "You ask that as if you care about him. Do you?"

"I..." Amaya peered at the floorboards. "It's complicated, Soria. You know that. And besides, we have things to do."

"I understand there's a larger problem. That it'll take time to fix."
Soria fiddled with the sheet that covered her. Beneath it, she looked
stick thin. "But I love my brother and I don't want him to suffer. I
don't want him to be punishing himself. I just…" A tear fell, but she
was too weak to lift her hand to brush it away. Amaya leaned forward
and did it for her. "I just want him to be all right. I wish I could help
him, but I can't. I can't do anything!"

A sob escaped her, and Amaya quickly moved from the chair to
the edge of the bed. Panicking, not seeing any handkerchiefs nearby,
she grabbed the sheets and carefully dabbed at Soria's eyes.

"I hate this," Soria whispered. "I hate it so much."

"I know." Amaya squeezed her thin shoulder. "I'm sorry. I
don't…I don't know what to do."

"That's all right. I don't, either." Soria shook her head, eyelashes
clumped into spikes from her tears. "I hope you and the others find
out who caused this. I hope you stop them."

"Even if it was your father?"

"Yes." Her dark eyes hardened. "If he really is part of the counterfeit scheme, then he deserves justice."

Amaya took her hand, cold against her own. "I'll stop them. I
promise."

Soria sniffed and tried to smile. "Thank you. Take care of yourself, too, Amaya. Please."

"I will."

She waited until Soria was asleep before heading back to the
apartment, her mind even more clouded than it had been before.
There were so many things outside her control, Cayo included. There
was only so much she could do.

But she had to try regardless.

When she opened the door to the apartment, she was startled by the sudden cry that came from within. Liesl was standing at the table, her chair knocked to the floor behind her.

Deadshot ran out of the bedroom. "What happened?"

Liesl gaped at the sheets spread out before her. She looked at Deadshot, then at Amaya, her glasses glinting with the light that streamed through the window.

"Adrienne," she whispered. "I know where she is."

Amaya's skin prickled at the mix of victory and horror in Liesl's voice. "Where is she?"

Liesl planted a shaky finger on the decoded records. "Basque owns a fleet of debtor ships. He sent Adrienne to one of them. The *Silver Star*."

"Where is it now?" Deadshot asked.

"If this schedule he wrote out is anything to go by, a few of his ships, including the *Silver Star*, should have already come to Baleine to drop off shipments. But they've been keeping certain ships in the harbor for quarantine reasons. Jasper gave me a list of their names a few days ago." Her voice caught as tears filled her eyes. "The *Silver Star* is one of them."

Amaya exchanged a glance with Deadshot. "So that means…"

Liesl nodded. "We have to smuggle my sister from a debtor ship without getting caught."

Jasper went to the harbor and came back looking grim.

"It's there all right," he said. "The *Silver Star*. Are you sure she's on that particular ship? It's been a few years."

"Captains aren't in the habit of trading debtors to different ships. She has to be on it still."

"Can we really trust Basque's notes?"

"It was in code, wasn't it?" Liesl snapped. "Why would it be in code unless he wanted to keep the information to himself?"

Jasper wisely didn't question her again. Liesl was nervous enough as it was, double- and triple-checking the decoded notes, pacing around the apartment, barely eating anything.

Cayo was nervous, too, but for a different reason. With the high-stakes game coming up, he was visibly more tense and had taken to rolling niera coins across his knuckles. Liesl had insisted he go to work at Florimond's as usual rather than join them.

"I don't want your antsy fingers getting us into trouble," she said. As if she were one to talk.

"Fine," Cayo had muttered. "But, um... good luck." He'd glanced at Amaya, extending it to her as well. "I hope you find her."

They still hadn't told Liesl about the high-stakes game. The girl was too focused on Adrienne to concentrate on anything else. But the more nervous Cayo grew, the more Amaya did as well.

Which was why, when they found themselves on the roof of an inn along the harbor, Liesl couldn't help but notice Amaya's fidgeting.

"What is it?" Liesl whispered. The moon was climbing toward its apex above them, the sky a dark swath of fabric. The street at their backs emanated a warm, welcoming light, but the docks ahead were cloaked in shadow broken only by the occasional lantern.

"Nothing," Amaya whispered back. "Just... reliving bad memories."

Which was true enough. The thought of stepping foot on another debtor ship made her insides writhe, and she was ashamed by the fear that Captain Zharo could instill in her even when the man was dead. It was that fear that made her wonder if it were possible to free all the debtors, not just Adrienne, to spare them from a similar fate.

She also couldn't help but remember another confrontation at the docks. Boon gazing at her somberly across the deck of his stolen ship, then the crash of his blade against hers.

*Did you kill my father?*

*In a sense, I suppose I did.*

Amaya closed her eyes, driving his face, his words away from her mind as she twisted the jade ring on her finger. She needed to concentrate if they were going to pull this off.

Deadshot crouched at the lip of the roof, watching the alley below. Jasper had a short spyglass affixed to his eye as he watched the docks. Amaya had asked if they should enlist Remy's assistance, but Liesl had been against it.

"He's been tremendous help, but we can't keep putting him in these positions," the girl had said. "Not when his loyalty lies elsewhere."

"His loyalty lies with us," Amaya had argued. "The navy just gave him a home and structure that he needed."

"He could still get in trouble, and that's the last thing we need. Best to keep him out of this."

"Leave the trouble to us," Jasper had agreed, though his normal joviality had been missing. He seemed as anxious as Liesl, though he had insisted on coming.

Jasper now lowered the spyglass with a nod. "All set."

"Then let's go," Liesl ordered.

They moved quietly across the roof and onto the one beside it, following the curve of buildings along the harbor. The sound of nearby waves was a dull roar under the pounding of Amaya's heart, the din of tavern dwellers below their feet like the humming of hornets.

Avi waited for them in an alley. He leaned against the wall with an arm around his torso, eyes closed tight, but when they dropped down he started and straightened himself. With a finger to his lips, he silently led them toward the docks. The fish market was packed up for the day, leaving nothing but a few empty stalls set up in a half circle, like a ring of broken teeth.

"Dock sixteen," Avi whispered before he slipped away again, heading toward his sentry spot. He would keep a lookout in case anyone approached the ship.

Jasper beckoned them to the opposite end of the harbor, where a dinghy sat bobbing on the water. They climbed in, and he untied the rope from the dock as Deadshot began to row.

"We can't simply saunter onto the ship like we own it," Liesl had explained earlier that day over a crudely drawn map of the docks spread across the table. "We'll need to be discreet. And we'll need an escape route in case someone sounds the alarm."

"This is gonna be harder with that Ghost Ship in the harbor," Jasper had added. "It's guarded night and day by a naval ship. So long as we avoid their detection, we should be fine."

Amaya gripped the sides of the dinghy as Deadshot rowed them farther from shore. Moonlight rippled across the ocean's dark surface like strands of pearls abandoned by careless ladies. In the distance she saw the so-called Ghost Ship, nothing but a black silhouette against the lit naval vessel beside it. Perhaps it was a trick of the moonlight, but it truly did look eerie.

They passed the boats and rowed behind the larger ships. Amaya nervously thought of a story her father had told her about demons in Khari, how some of them slumbered disguised as giant rocks or hills. Wanderers wouldn't even know they were there until it was too late. The massive forms of the ships loomed over them, ready to uncurl and grab her at any second.

"This one," Jasper whispered, pointing to dock sixteen.

Deadshot rowed the dinghy closer, the tiny vessel nodding up and down with the movement of the tide. Jasper helped navigate them into the space between two ships, where the moonlight was cut off and everything fell into darkness.

They tied the dinghy to the old, rusted rungs studding the hull. The ship's name was painted boldly beside them, under a row of portholes: the *Silver Star*. A pretty name for a ship that looked as if it was five years past due for repair.

"The layout of the ship should be simple," Liesl had told them earlier. She'd taken a sheaf of parchment and placed it above the map, sketching as she talked. "It's a barque, which means there'll be two decks above the hold. If I were to guess, they'll have placed everyone on the middle deck toward the forecastle."

Amaya reached for the crusty, cold rungs and ascended the side of the ship. They were wet from sea spray, so she went slowly, taking care not to let her boots slip.

She paused halfway up. A symbol had been carved under the ship's name, a circle containing the shape of a diamond surrounded by ivy. It looked like the crest of a signet ring pressed into wax. For some reason it tickled the back of her mind, as if she had seen it somewhere before.

"What does this mean?" Amaya whispered down to Jasper.

"No clue," he whispered back. "It's not Basque's crest, I know that much. I also know my hand's gonna cramp with cold if we keep dawdling here."

Once on deck, they split up. Jasper went to the stern and Deadshot to the forecastle, keeping an eye out for Avi's signals. Which left Amaya and Liesl to locate Adrienne.

"The captain's quarters are usually in the stern," Liesl whispered. "It should be far enough away not to wake them, but let's not take any chances."

Amaya couldn't stop the sudden memory of Zharo's ringed hand striking her face. "Agreed."

They stole down the ladder of the companionway. Amaya spotted the door to the captain's quarters on the right, and on the left was a hallway leading to what appeared to be the galley.

Liesl pointed at a set of stairs to the deck below. They quietly made their way down, hands pressed against the side of the ship as they descended into the dark. A set of doors with a flurry of locks stood in their way.

"Guess the captain doesn't want them to escape," Liesl said dryly, taking out her lockpicking tools. "Can't imagine why."

Liesl went through the locks like they were nothing, then pulled open one of the doors just enough to slip inside.

A wave of bitter nostalgia washed over Amaya at the familiar sounds that greeted them. The snores, the groans and murmurs, the squeaking of the hammocks. The smell of unwashed bodies was overpowering, layered over the briny, nauseating scent of fish and blood.

Amaya choked and slapped a hand over her mouth. Liesl gripped her elbow, as much a warning as reassurance.

"This isn't your life anymore," the girl whispered in her ear. "Let's make that true for my sister."

Amaya nodded, closing her eyes tight. A deep, relentless tremor had started in her chest and spread to her arms, and more than anything she wanted to run back to the fresh air above and dive off this ship.

But she made herself follow Liesl as the older girl began to prowl through the hammocks. Amaya's gaze strayed toward the bodies they held. They ranged from children to adults, but mostly those in-between, skinny and sickly and most of their hair shorn off. As if the captain wanted to keep them uniform, stripping them of their individuality. Like how Zharo had named all the children on the *Brackish* after bugs.

Liesl made a soft, despairing sound. Amaya's heart leaped into her throat, wondering if Adrienne wasn't here, if maybe she really was on a different ship, or if these conditions had sent her to an early grave.

But her fears were sent scattering as Liesl hurried to a hammock where a young woman was sleeping. She was about Amaya's age, her chestnut hair curling close against her scalp. Her frame was broad yet her skin was loose, as if she had lost a lot of weight in a short period of time.

Liesl's hands shook as she reached for her sister. At the first touch, Adrienne woke with her mouth open, ready to scream or fight. Liesl pressed her palm against her mouth, bringing her face in close.

"Ren, it's me," Liesl whispered.

Adrienne stared at her, breathing heavily against her sister's hand. Her relieved cry was muffled against Liesl's palm as tears escaped the corners of her eyes. They embraced each other and the hammock swayed dangerously, Adrienne's back heaving as she tried to stifle her sobs.

"I'm so sorry," Liesl whispered, cradling the back of her sister's head as her cheeks shone with tears. "I'm sorry it took me so long to find you."

Adrienne pulled back and wiped at her eyes. "Liesl." Her voice was high and scratchy. "You're here to get me out?"

"No, I'm here to throw a party," Liesl snapped, or tried to; her words were still soft with affection. "Of course I am."

Adrienne bit her chapped lower lip and looked around at the other hammocks. "I..."

Liesl's hand tightened on her wrist. "We need to go before any of them wake up."

But Amaya was already noticing a curious head pop up, no doubt woken by the whispering. "Liesl..."

"Adrienne, we *have to go*."

But her sister crawled out of the hammock and stood defiant before her. She was taller than Liesl, and broader in the shoulder.

"I'm not leaving them," Adrienne said, not bothering to lower her voice anymore. "They're all suffering. If I abandon them, I'm no better than those like Basque."

Liesl stared at her. "You can't be serious."

A girl nearby stirred and rubbed her eyes. "Adrienne? What's wrong?"

Amaya's stomach clenched as memories of the Water Bugs assaulted her. She thought back to the looks on their faces when she'd bought the *Brackish* with Boon's false gold, the revelation that they were now free.

"We can do it," Amaya said, stepping up to Liesl's side.

"We don't have *time* for this—"

"Think about how this will hurt Basque," Amaya said. "Judging by the number of debtors, this must be one of his most lucrative ships. It'll be a significant loss to his income."

More and more people were waking and murmuring in confusion. Liesl's eyes widened in panic, but Adrienne took her sister's hands in hers.

"Please, Liesl," she said.

Liesl sighed and looked toward the ceiling as if asking the star saints for assistance. "You know I can't say no to you. This is why you're spoiled."

Adrienne grinned and turned to the others. As she explained what was happening, Liesl focused her glare on Amaya.

"If we end up on the Sinner's Shelf, my ghost is going to haunt yours," Liesl growled.

"We've freed a debtor ship before," Amaya reminded her. "We can do it again."

And truthfully, she wanted to do it again, and again, until no more debtor ships roamed the Southerly Sea. The realization staggered her, this different form of vengeance she hadn't thought of before now.

"What's going on in here?"

The voice shot across the cabin, making the others cry out in alarm as Amaya instinctively reached for a knife. The figure of a stocky woman filled the open doorway, glowering at the prisoners.

"Who did this?" the captain barked, pointing at the picked lock with a sawed-off shotgun. "I'm gonna string you all up one by one unless someone comes forward!"

But Amaya was already slipping through the crowd of prisoners. When the captain noticed her, the woman's sickening grin was replaced with confusion. She swung the shotgun at Amaya the same time Amaya flung one of her knives.

The woman yelled as the knife embedded itself in her side, firing the gun as Amaya dove to the floor. But the aim went high, blowing a hole through the ceiling as the prisoners screamed.

"Restrain her!" Adrienne ordered, her voice carrying over the commotion as if she'd been born for command, just like her sister.

Several of the prisoners leaped forward and grabbed at the captain's arms. One wrestled the shotgun away as the captain thrashed and cursed, getting blood all over the floor. As they began the difficult business of trussing her up, several more prisoners ran through the door, making the most of the distraction.

"Shit," Liesl hissed. "If that shot didn't alert someone, runaways certainly will."

"We can't worry about it now," Adrienne said. "We need to get this ship into open water." She then looked at Amaya. "Thanks for the knife. Are you my sister's lover?"

Amaya blinked as Liesl snorted.

"My lover's up there," Liesl said, pointing at the ceiling. "Or there, rather." Her finger moved to the open doorway where Deadshot had appeared, no doubt drawn by the gunshot.

Adrienne's face lit up. "Look at those *muscles*."

"Yes, I'm quite fond of them." Liesl shoved her sister forward. "But we really have to move."

Deadshot helped haul the captain back to her quarters, leaving Amaya's bloody knife behind. Amaya picked it up and wiped it on her sleeve before sheathing it.

The above deck was a mess of whispering and nervous shifting. Liesl signaled to Avi that the plan was changing as Jasper ran forward.

"How many siblings did you have down there?" he asked, eyeing the others.

"Apparently quite a few. We're taking the ship."

"*What?* Li—"

Then Adrienne stepped forward, and Jasper's voice failed him. Amaya raised her eyebrows at the look that passed between them, stark and yearning. Liesl, oblivious for once in her life, asked the people who had followed Adrienne if they knew how to sail.

Finally, Adrienne moved forward and hugged Jasper hard.

"I'm so sorry," he whispered, holding her tight. "I failed you and Li. I should've done more, I should've looked harder...."

"Don't say that," she said softly. "You did what you could. We were all fighting for the same cause, and we knew what the consequences would be." She stepped back with a watery smile. "And now we're doing all we can to fix it."

"We're going to have to make this quick," Liesl interrupted, watching as some of the prisoners ran across the deck and jumped onto the docks. "Amaya, you take the helm while Deadshot and I take care of the rest."

Amaya gripped the spokes of the wheel as Liesl gave out orders, calling for the sails to be unfurled and the anchor to be lifted. The prisoners knew their duties like a song, making quick and quiet work of it.

Avi, perched on the roof of the nearby ship records office, caught her attention. He was waving frantically, touching his chest twice. The signal that the navy was onto them.

Amaya cursed under her breath and realized the vessel watching over the Ghost Ship was coming to life with scurrying soldiers.

"Liesl!" she called down, knowing the time for stealth had passed. "We have to go *now*."

Liesl barked out orders alongside Adrienne, who knew the others by name and assigned them to their tasks. The wheel jerked beneath Amaya's hands. She turned it a bit to the left as the ship began to move, slow and cautious as it nosed its way back into open water. The hull scraped against the dock and she winced. She had only had helm duty a couple of times on the *Brackish*.

The *Silver Star* gained momentum as Liesl and Jasper rushed to join her. The naval ship was slowly starting to close in from the opposite side, but its pennants flapped halfheartedly, the wind working against their sails.

Jasper took out his spyglass. "Hey, mean girl, your friend's on that ship."

"Remy?" Amaya handed the wheel off to Liesl and rushed to the railing. The closer the ships came, the more she could make out his head of tousled brown hair behind the gunwale.

Hoping it would work, she gave a high, sharp whistle followed by a two-finger salute, the familiar call and response from their days on board the *Brackish*.

They were close enough now that she could tell he'd noticed. When he saw her, his eyes widened and his mouth moved; she could practically hear him cursing her out.

Remy hurried to the helm as the ships began to draw up alongside each other and the naval soldiers prepared to board. Amaya pulled out a knife, more than ready to defend the prisoners from the system that wanted to destroy them.

There was a call and a shout, and suddenly the naval ship veered away, toward the docks. The prisoners gasped as Liesl sighed in relief.

"Well, what do you know," Jasper drawled. "The bluecoat turned out all right."

"I'm sorry, Remy," Amaya whispered. She knew she had a lecture in store, that he might face a suspension or worse for what he'd just done for her.

But then a cheer erupted on the deck, the prisoners of the *Silver Star* throwing up their fists in victory. Adrienne beamed at Liesl, and the sisters hugged tightly, fingers digging into each other's backs.

"You know you can't all stay on this ship," Liesl told her, sobering as they parted. "You should go down toward Leguinne and leave it there, then go on foot to Viariche. Once my business has been taken care of, I'll meet you there."

"What business is this?"

"I'll tell you about it when I come back." Liesl put a hand on her sister's shoulder, squeezing hard as if, despite her words, she wanted Adrienne to never leave her sight again. "Will you be all right? I can go with you."

"Tovi and Hermé know the ship backward and forward, and we'll put the captain in one of the rowboats and leave her in open water. You can use the other rowboats to get back to shore." Adrienne grinned. "We'll be fine."

Jasper cleared his throat. "I'll go with her."

"You will?" Liesl and Adrienne demanded at the same time.

"Just to get you to Viariche," Jasper said hurriedly. "Until Li comes back. If... If that's all right."

Adrienne flushed as Liesl finally looked between them with a suspicious frown.

"That's all right with me," Adrienne whispered.

"What about the Benefactor?" Liesl asked of Jasper. "You've been invaluable to us. Without your contacts, I don't know how far we'll get."

"You'll think of something. You always do. Besides, I don't know how much more help I'll be, since I can't access the Deirdre records."

Liesl hummed doubtfully but caved. "Fine. But if anything happens, Jas, just remember how much you like your remaining hand."

As the ship began to settle and Deadshot and Adrienne finally exchanged a proper greeting, Amaya turned and saw the supposed Ghost Ship looming on the starboard side. It sat dark and brooding on the water, a silent monument to the city's paranoia.

Her smile fell as its features became clearer under the wan moonlight. It was a frigate, small and nondescript, bearing scratches along its hull as if it had undergone a battle and lost. A piece of its railing was missing on the port side.

She had seen this ship before, in Moray. The night Nian and Cricket had died. The night she had realized Boon's true intentions.

She had fought him on the deck of that very ship.

Boon was somewhere in the city.

*18*

*Just as gold is alloyed to give it strength, so too must*
*our findings contribute to a better world.*
—ZANE MUSTAVE, RAIN EMPIRE ALCHEMIST

Cayo was sweeping metal shavings in the back room when the bell to the front entrance of Florimond's shop chimed.

A customer. Which meant Florimond would be distracted for at least a little while. Cayo quietly leaned the broom against the wall and took the lockpicking tools from his pocket.

When he had told Avi about the box of letters Florimond kept in his shop, the man had handed over his tools and told Cayo to make use of them. He still wasn't very skilled at it, but at least he'd had some practice on the apartment's locks.

Florimond was working on a cure, and his patron wasn't Deirdre. There shouldn't be any reason to suspect him. And yet Cayo felt strange about the secrecy around the box; it gave him a prickling sensation in his stomach that he couldn't properly explain.

But as he headed toward the shelves, a man's booming voice cut through the door.

"Francis! Haven't seen you at the meetings lately. What's keeping you cooped up this time?"

A friend? Another alchemist? Cayo used the man's voice to his advantage, slipping the tools into the box's small lock.

"I'm not 'cooped up,' I'm working."

"Same thing. Patron's got you burning more candles than you can afford?"

"I'm fairly certain my workload is none of your business."

The man's laugh was loud and belly-deep. "Same as ever. We miss you at the meetings."

"I'm sure you do. What you want, Avon?"

"Well, Deirdre's got me working a bit harder, too, and I completely forgot to order more goldenseal. Can you spare a few ounces?"

Cayo stopped his attempt to find the lock's tumbler. *Deirdre?*

"She has you using goldenseal?" Florimond scoffed. "That can be poisonous in high doses."

"Good thing we're not using high doses, then, isn't it?" Something creaked, as if the other alchemist were leaning against the counter. "C'mon, I know you have some. The sooner you give it to me, the sooner we can get cracking on this cure."

Cayo frowned. Deirdre was having her alchemists work on a *cure*?

It took a second to realize Florimond was walking toward the back. Cayo yanked the tools from the lock—cursing when one of them momentarily caught—and stumbled toward the broom.

Florimond paused at the door and gave him an odd look. "What's wrong?"

"What?" Cayo's voice was nearly a squeak. "Nothing. I, uh…"

218

He cleared his throat. "I couldn't help but overhear. Is that another alchemist?"

Florimond muttered to himself rather than respond, digging through his various jars of herbs and dried plants. Cayo gripped the broom handle tight enough to warrant splinters.

"Is Deirdre his patron?" Cayo tried again. "Are her alchemists working on a cure, too?"

Florimond found the right jar and headed for the door, giving Cayo that odd look again.

"Want to go work for him instead?" Florimond demanded.

"What? No, I...I'm just curious."

"Everyone's working on a cure. What matters most is who gets there first—and what price it'll go for." He nodded to the broom. "If you're done, you can go home for the night."

Cayo glanced at the locked box as the other alchemist said his goodbyes and the entrance's bell chimed again. Florimond came back and immediately resumed his current project, ignoring Cayo as if he'd become just another piece of clutter.

He'd lost his chance, but at least he'd stumbled on some information. His head spun as he returned to the apartment. It was empty; the others were out on their mission to rescue Liesl's sister.

He was far too anxious to sleep, so he stayed up to wait for them, pacing the length of the apartment. He practiced making the beds—he avoided Amaya's; it smelled too much like her—and even started to dust using one of his socks, at a loss for what else to do. When that was done and the moon had climbed to midnight, he began practicing how to make tea. The cup he poured was bitter and pungent, making him gag.

The door opened as he was tossing out the soggy tea leaves. The others streamed inside, slightly damp and smelling like the sea.

"How did it go?" But one look at their faces told him they had succeeded, and some of his anxiety melted away.

As they filled him in on what had happened—"Wait, you stole the entire *ship*?"—he couldn't help but glance at Amaya's oddly stony expression, the stiff way she held herself. She didn't seem glad or relieved.

She seemed...furious.

"I wish I could have gone with her," Liesl sighed as she kicked off her boots.

"We'll see her again," Deadshot assured her. "And now we can focus on the counterfeit situation."

"Right." Liesl flushed. "I'm sorry for being so preoccupied."

"She's your sister. We understand."

"I'm glad you were able to find her," Cayo said. "I, uh...I found out something. At Florimond's."

The others turned to him. Everyone except Amaya, who leaned woodenly against the wall, staring at the window.

When he told them about the other alchemist and how Deirdre was also trying to find a cure, Avi rubbed his chin.

"Well, now," the man said. "That's an interesting development."

"Why would Deirdre be focused on making counterfeits *and* a cure for the fever she's causing?" Deadshot asked.

"Florimond said something about price. About whoever getting the cure first being able to control how much it goes for."

Avi laughed darkly. "Of course. She accidentally causes an epidemic, and then miraculously finds a cure for it. She could be controlling the whole damn thing to make a profit."

"That would be...ghastly," Liesl muttered.

Amaya pushed off the wall as the others contemplated at the table, heading for her bedroom. Cayo made to intercept her.

"Are you all right?" He kept his voice down.

She clenched her jaw, staring at his chest instead of his face. "Fine."

"You don't seem fine."

"I'm *fine*, Cayo." Her voice turned gravelly and sharp—a hint of Silverfish coming out. "Please move. I'm tired."

He hesitated. Whatever stood between them still felt fragile and brittle. If he dared to say anything more, do anything more, he worried it would shatter completely.

But what they were facing was so much larger than an uncomfortable reconciliation.

"Are you going to be all right for the tournament?" Cayo whispered, glancing at the others.

"Worry more about yourself than me," she hissed before shoving past him and closing the door behind her.

He tried to ignore the cold weight in the pit of his stomach that only grew heavier the more he thought about the game, the chance to sit at the same table as Deirdre.

The pouch of coins he'd won was tucked beneath his pallet, and more than anything he wanted to bring them to Mother Hilas and beg for any and all treatment they could buy.

But Liesl had ignored their mission because of her sister, and he didn't want to stumble into the same pitfall, to remain the weakest link among them. If there was a chance to gain an advantage, he was going to take it.

Even if it meant risking everything he had worked for.

**19**

*Trickster brought the moon three gifts: a bowl of oil,*
*a rabbit bone, and a drop of demon's blood. The moon*
*asked the purpose of these gifts, but Trickster did not say,*
*only instructed the bone to be anointed in the blood and*
*to steep it in the oil. Over time, it grew into a fearsome*
*beast that stalked the moon, terrorizing all who came*
*upon it. When Trickster next visited, the moon demanded*
*why he had done this. I thought it would help you,*
*Trickster said. With what? asked the moon. Isn't it better,*
*Trickster replied, to know your enemy as well as yourself?*

—KHARIAN MYTH

Amaya laid on her bed, twisting the jade ring on her finger until her skin turned red.

Tonight, she and Cayo would go back to the Golden Harbor

in the Casino District. Tonight, they would be in close proximity to Deirdre and hopefully get more answers out of her.

But Amaya couldn't stop thinking about Boon's weathered ship in the harbor. What Avi had told her. She conjured an image of her mother sitting in the corner where she liked to sew, kneeling beside Amaya and pointing out the beautifully glimmering webs of spider silk in their garden.

Boon had known her parents, and he hadn't told her. The weight of her mother's potential betrayal sat like a cancerous growth inside her, and knowing the truth would be the only thing to remove it.

Remy's voice broke through her fugue. At first she dismissed it, thinking it some auditory hallucination. When he called her name again, she sat up with a gasp.

*Remy.*

He was sitting on the edge of her bed, thick eyebrows furrowed. She grabbed his wrist.

"The ship," she rasped. "Remy, I'm so sorry."

The laugh that came from him was strangled yet sincere. "Let's just say you owe me a pastry."

"What happened? Are you in trouble? I've been so worried—"

"After that stunt I pulled to save your ass? Of course I'm in trouble."

She pressed her forehead against his shoulder. He sighed as he rubbed her back.

"It's all right," he murmured. "They only gave me a suspension. The debtors running loose on the docks were a good enough excuse to turn back to port."

She leaned back. "Did they...?"

"Don't worry, they escaped. Although I have no idea how much time they'll have until they're caught again."

Amaya nodded miserably. She thought about how she'd felt on board the *Silver Star*, how badly she wanted to do that again, deposing captains and freeing their prisoners. Saving others from what she had suffered for seven years.

"I know you had your reasons for doing it," Remy said. "But next time, wait until I'm not on duty, all right?"

"I'll try."

He smiled faintly, then dug a piece of paper from his pocket.

"Anyway, that's not why I'm here," he said, "although I suppose I had to show my face so you didn't think I'd been executed for treason. They've been keeping a close eye on me, or else I'd have come sooner. Do you remember when you asked me to be on the lookout for incident reports?"

Amaya's stomach fluttered, thinking back to the sight of that ship in the harbor. "Yes."

"A new one came in. Took me a while to get ahold of it, what with the suspension and all." Amaya grimaced even as he grinned. "It matches. 'Tall, stocky Kharian man, black hair, black beard, drunkenly smashing bottles against the side of an ale house,'" he read from the paper. "'Incapacitated the active officer attempting to fine him and fled the scene.'"

A cold, heavy weight settled inside her.

"That ship," she whispered. "In the harbor. It's his. The one he had at Moray."

Remy cursed. "I thought it looked familiar."

To Amaya, there had simply been no mistaking it. That night in Moray had left a brand within her, down to every horrific detail. The puddle of blood under Nian. The way Amaya's lungs had seared with pain as she'd run through the streets. How coldly the stars had burned overhead.

"Where was the incident reported?"

He consulted the paper again. "Aumerine Street. It's in a poorer district, far from the shops but not too far from the harbor." Seeing the look on her face, he squeezed her forearm. "Amaya, I don't want you doing anything reckless with this information. If you're planning on going after Boon, at least let me go with you."

She looked into his warm brown eyes and wondered how they would regard her after seeing her kill a man.

"I will," she lied.

As the late afternoon sun bled into the ocean and evening began to blanket the city, Amaya donned her knives and slipped out of the apartment without anyone noticing.

Cayo's shift at the fish market had likely just ended. He was probably on his way back right this instant, preparing in nervous anticipation for the high-stakes game that started at midnight.

Amaya would be there. She had promised.

But first, she had other business.

Guilt nipped her heels with every step she took through the chilly streets of Baleine. Her breaths kept catching in her throat as she thought about Remy's earnest face, the anxious twist to Cayo's mouth.

But she couldn't let Boon get away. She couldn't let her questions go unanswered any longer.

It was full dark when she reached Aumerine Street and found the ale house where Boon had been spotted throwing bottles. With a few pointed questions, she learned that after the encounter with the officer, Boon had lumbered off in the direction of a nearby district.

The district smelled of woodsmoke, the streets more dirt than cobblestone, with chickens walking loose and unbothered. The houses here were ramshackle, the bottoms bearing water damage as if they'd been flooded in the past, likely after a bad storm. Compared to Basque's manor, they were little more than plaster boxes.

If the counterfeits continued to circulate, these were the people who would be hit hardest during the economic collapse. They were already so vulnerable; she couldn't imagine what would happen to them if they lost everything.

She gave Boon's description to those she encountered on the street. Most hadn't seen him, but a couple pointed north, saying they'd seen him come and go from Rupin Alley.

She stalked up and down Rupin Alley, but had no way of telling which house he might be squatting in. Just when she was about to start knocking on doors, a shout came from up ahead.

Amaya tensed and crept forward, the gloom helping to conceal her as she peered around the corner.

A man yelled at another in Soléne, shooing at him to get out of his sight. The other man barked a familiar laugh and staggered away, weaving drunkenly in her direction.

Amaya's skin prickled.

*Boon.*

The rage welled up, bright and sparking and voracious.

Silently, she slipped a knife from its sheath.

One moment. Just one moment was all it would take to erase him from this world, erase the source of her grief and her guilt.

It wouldn't right her mistakes, but it would be a mercy for them both.

He stumbled down the street, passing where she'd wedged herself between two houses. Amaya followed, careful not to make a sound, her lungs aching from too-shallow breaths. The hilt of her knife bit into her palm as she tightened her grip.

Just one thrust. One quick flick of her wrist as the blade sang across his throat.

She lengthened her stride. As he reached for the door to a building little more than a glorified hut, she lunged forward and grabbed the back of his collar, pressing her knife to the side of his neck.

Boon stopped but didn't fight against her. Didn't even seem surprised, as if he'd known the attack would be coming.

"Thought it might be you," he mumbled. His words were more slurred than normal, but he didn't smell like alcohol despite his wavering stride. "Come to finish it, then?"

She pressed the knife harder and was satisfied by his grunt of pain. "Why shouldn't I, after everything you've done? I'd be doing the world a favor."

His rough laugh turned into a cough. "Probably right about that. But I got a proposition for you anyways."

She bared her teeth. "I'm tired of your propositions."

"You wouldn't be the only one." He coughed again, and she frowned. "But just hear me out. I won't run. Not in a state to."

"What do you mean?"

He gestured impatiently in front of him. "We can't talk here. Just come in, yeah?"

She weighed her options. Kill him and leave his body in the street for some unlucky person to stumble upon, or listen to what he had to say. But what had doing the latter ever gotten her?

Sensing her reluctance, Boon turned his head slightly despite the knife and froze.

"That ring," he rasped. "Where did you get it?"

She glanced at the band of jade on her finger and her questions all came flooding back. Her mother and father. Alchemy.

Heart racing, she finally released him. Boon stretched his neck from side to side and faced her, frowning.

"Well?" he demanded. "Where did you find it? You didn't have it before."

"That's none of your business," she said coldly. "This ring belongs to me." Brandishing her knife, she pointed at the door with its tip. "You want to talk? Fine. I have some questions for you."

Boon stared her down. She stared back, refusing to be cowed. Eventually he scoffed and clicked his tongue several times.

"Anyone ever told you you gotta knack for giving orders? C'mon, then."

Boon shouldered open the door. The hut beyond looked and smelled like something a fisherman would live in, and Amaya wondered if Boon had happened upon it or if he'd driven the previous owner out. Or maybe it was just another casualty of an ash fever victim.

She stepped inside and wrinkled her nose at the sour odor. Boon muttered to himself and clicked his tongue in strange patterns as he lit a cracked lantern on a nearby table. The flames danced over broken furniture and trash littering the floor. Something crunched underneath her and she lifted a boot to reveal a small pile of fish bones.

"Would offer you tea 'cept I don't have any." Boon rummaged

through a cupboard and reemerged holding a mostly empty bottle of liquor. "Got this, though, if you want a nip."

"No thanks." Amaya lifted the ratty curtain over the window that looked out onto the street. "You said you wanted to talk. So let's talk."

"Right down to business, then." Boon collapsed onto a moth-eaten couch and took a swig of his drink, some of it dribbling into his beard. "What're you doing here, anyway?"

Amaya let the curtains drop and scowled at him. "What does it matter to you?"

"Curious minds and all that. Is that little fop with you?"

Amaya drew herself up to her full height—it wasn't much, but it was something—and resisted the urge to smash her boot into his face.

"His sister is sick," she said. "We came here to help her and try to put a stop to the counterfeiting."

"Ah." Boon drank deep and wiped a sleeve across his mouth, the tremor in his left arm even more pronounced than before. "Truth be told, I didn't think it would reach this far."

How could he be so calm about all this? "You and Mercado did this. And the Benefactor as well."

He tensed. "How do you know about the Benefactor?"

"I don't owe you any answers."

Boon smiled wryly. "Suppose you don't. Well, this so-called Benefactor is the reason I'm here."

"Do you know who they are?"

"No, only that they're in Baleine. Figured it was worth a shot to find out who they are, try to blackmail 'em."

"We think we already know who the Benefactor is," she said coldly. "Robin Deirdre."

229

Boon started. "Deirdre?" He contemplated this, the bottle in his hand forgotten. "Yeah, I guess that's a possibility."

"She owns nearly all the alchemists in the city." Her throat tightened briefly, painfully. "They're making the counterfeits while also trying to find a cure to profit from. She wants to weaponize the alchemists to fight the Sun Empire. To reclaim Moray."

"Hold on." Boon pinched the bridge of his nose. "Slow down. Why do you think this?"

"Again, I don't owe you answers." She took a step forward, fingers brushing her knife hilt. "There's nothing you can do that will help. You're part of the problem, and that's all you'll remain."

She thought he would bite back, turn it around as a joke. Instead, he stared at the bottle in his hand as his head twitched once, twice.

"Guess that's true enough," he muttered.

An uncomfortable feeling began to take over her. She didn't like seeing him like this, a reminder of how sad and pitiful he could be.

"What were you even thinking when you sent me to Moray with all that fake gold?" she asked.

"That I would poison the rich," Boon said immediately. He sounded oddly lucid, and it heightened her uneasiness. "That I'd punish the sorts of people who caused me to suffer. But then Mercado had to go and make his own, make it circulate 'round the Vice Sector and…" He made a circle in the air with his bottle, making its contents slosh. "Here we are."

"Well, congratulations," Amaya said. "You ended up becoming just like the man you wanted to take down."

She thought that, at least, would get him riled, but he only drained the last of his alcohol and let the empty bottle roll to the floor.

"Yeah," he muttered, "suppose I did."

Amaya couldn't decide what she felt more: pity or disgust. She could have easily turned around and left him here, let him fend for himself while she and the others continued on with their plan.

Instead, she sat carefully on the chair by the couch, half expecting it to collapse underneath her. It made a faint protesting groan but stayed put, so she leaned forward to rest her elbows on her knees.

"You mentioned something about a proposition." Liesl would be furious that she was even entertaining the idea of helping Boon, but perhaps he could do something in exchange that could aid their plans. "What were you thinking?"

Boon pulled himself up into a seated position with a grunt of effort. "Easy. I help you deal with the Benefactor, then you get me out of Baleine. I'll be out of your hair for good."

Amaya waited. When he said nothing else, she replied, "That's it?"

"Some unsavory sorts are eager for my head, and I'd rather it stay on my shoulders for the time being."

"Can't imagine why," she said dryly. "Even if I were to help you escape, you'd just run into the same problem again. The Rain Empire's navy will be searching for you, too." Remy had given his superior officers all the information they'd had on Boon. "And I doubt you'll find much refuge in the Sun Empire, seeing as they might use the fever to their advantage and strike at the Rain Empire or Moray. They'll close their waterways, if they haven't already."

Boon opened his mouth, but for once, it appeared he was speechless. His dark eyes flashed with anger, his entire face hardening with it, before his expression relaxed and he leaned back with a weak laugh.

"Gods, girl," he rasped. "I'd say I was proud if I wasn't in such a deep shithole."

"You put yourself there," she reminded him.

"Well. I don't blame you for turnin' your back on me. Should've told you the whole truth before."

"You think?" She stood, realizing that if she didn't kill him now, he would no doubt try to manipulate her in some fashion.

But as she reached for her knife, the weak lantern light caught the edge of her mother's ring.

She paused, staring at it. She had sought him out for answers, but the questions still sat churning inside of her without voice. Because she was scared. She was terrified of knowing the truth.

But if she was ever going to know something like peace, she had to ask them.

Knowing she would regret it, she turned back to Boon, whose eyes hadn't left her.

"You asked me about this ring," she said. "Why?"

Gone was any trace of the beleaguered rogue on his face. He wore an expression she had only seen a couple of times, something weary and somber and so unlike him that she had to wonder if she were still talking to the same man.

Boon slowly got to his feet, using the couch for balance as he leaned most of his weight against it.

"Because I gave your mother that ring," he answered.

So he *had* known her. The confession whisked the breath out of Amaya's lungs even as she curled her hand into a fist and pressed it protectively against her chest. It was another lie, another clever way to worm through her defenses. "No you didn't. My father gave it to her when they were married."

Boon sighed, raking a hand through his dark hair.

"Look, I—"

"No." She pointed a finger at him, walked a few paces forward with her shoulders squared and her jaw clenched. "My mother was an honest woman. She was a seamstress and happily married. You don't get to barge into my life, stomp around in the wreckage, and then tell me that you and my mother..."

She was breathing hard, satisfied by the muted horror in Boon's eyes. "She was a seamstress. She wasn't some...some sort of criminal alchemist! Why in the hells would she ever even be in the same *room* with someone as pathetic as you, let alone work with you? *Be* with you?" A sickening revelation opened in the pit of her stomach. "Is that why you killed my father? Because you wanted to be with her?"

Boon slowly sank onto the arm of the couch. He suppressed a cough, grimacing in pain. For a long time he didn't speak, and Amaya couldn't look away, could barely do anything other than force another breath in, another breath out.

"I..." He let out a huff of air and was quiet a moment longer. "I remember standing on my ship and looking out at Moray from the bay. I remember realizing that it was all gonna go away. That everything I'd done would be for nothin'. That Mercado would do anything to burn me out of existence, me and all that dirt I'd dug up on him and his illegal trade."

He coughed again, wheezing a little. "I did everything I could. Took out another loan. Sold the *Papaya*. Hells, I even tried gambling, which only made it worse. But Mercado was relentless. You wouldn't be safe. You..."

He fell into a coughing fit, and Amaya backed away, her heart a painful lump in her throat.

"How do you know that name?" she whispered. She had named her father's boat the *Papaya*, her favorite fruit, when she was four. Named it after the doll her mother had sewn for her.

Boon looked at her, his eyes wet from all the coughing.

"Amaya," he said, more gently than she'd ever heard him speak. "Come on."

She shook her head, backing away farther. "No."

"I didn't want you to find out. I didn't... want you to see who I'd become. But our paths crossed anyway—likely some god spitting on us from above. Ended up being more a curse than a blessing, huh?"

Her back hit the door, and she stood there, shaking, staring at the man she despised more than anyone.

Boon.

Arun Chandra.

Her father.

Tears fell from the corners of her eyes before she could stop them. She had been tricked, deceived, cheated, and yet none of it compared to this—the cruelest thing that had ever been done to her.

*Did you kill my father?* she had asked him.

*In a sense, I suppose I did.*

"Why?" It came out as a sob.

He rubbed a hand against his mouth, his gaze averted. "To protect you and your mother. I tried to pay off my loans to Mercado with the counterfeits, but he caught on. So I let myself get captured by the Port's Authority 'fore he could lay a hand on me. Thought they'd just plop me on a debtor ship, but instead they sentenced me to hang. Then Mercado came in and offered me a deal: the counterfeit recipe in exchange for being Landless. He didn't find out about the blackmail until I was long gone.

"But when I finally managed to get back to Moray"—he dug his fingers into the back of the couch so hard they paled—"I found out you were gone. Your mother was dead. I assumed she'd gotten

234

you out of the city so Mercado wouldn't use you to open the Vault. I didn't know you were on a debtor ship."

He forced himself to stand again, swaying slightly. The look he gave her was plaintive, regretful, but it did nothing to lessen the ache of betrayal within her.

"I'm sorry," he said. "For this. For all of it."

It wasn't enough.

It would never be enough.

Everyone around her lied and cheated and did terrible things, and she was the apex of it all, the eye of the storm that promised more disaster to come. She had learned it from this man who claimed to be her father. Perhaps it was in their blood, some awful, bitter thing that possessed them to ruin other peoples' lives.

She didn't realize she had taken out her knife until Boon's eyes flashed down to it.

Her father was dead. That was still true enough. Arun Chandra had been a good, loyal man, who had held her tightly and promised to never let go. He'd been a man her mother had loved, then grieved for. He had laughed at her jokes and taught her about sailing and bought her dumplings and cake whenever they could afford it.

That man was dead. The man before her was someone else entirely.

"Amaya," he began, but she kicked him back, made him topple onto the couch. She grabbed his shirt and held the blade against his throat. He smelled of alcohol and sweat, his body radiating an intense heat.

"You deceived me," she whispered. "You deceived me *twice*."

"I did." His throat bobbed against the sharp edge of the blade.

"When you were on the water the day I saved you…"

235

He closed his eyes briefly, as if in pain. "I was scattering marigolds for your mother."

She recalled the sight of marigold petals stuck to his jacket, like orange jewels. Her eyes stung, and she blinked hard.

"I didn't know you'd be on that ship," he said softly. "I didn't recognize you at first."

"But when you did, you saw fit to use me."

"Yes."

She held back the cry that rose up her throat, burning with all the rage and anguish that made her hand tremble. The knife he had bought for her nicked his skin, drawing a bead of blood to the surface.

"Give me a reason not to end it here," she said. Begged.

He smiled, or tried to. "Fresh out of those, I'm afraid. Suppose the only choice you have left is whether you want it to be quick or slow."

"What?"

Carefully, he reached for his right sleeve with his shaking left hand. She pressed the blade against him harder, but he didn't pull out a knife. Instead, he pushed the sleeve up.

All along his forearm was a patch of gray.

Amaya stared at it, wondering if it was real. But she could hear the rattling of his lungs, the fever turning his body into a furnace.

"All those years makin' counterfeits did its toll on me," he said. "Started out as little tics and tremors, now this."

Amaya's mind was wiped blank. The only thing that filtered through the void was: *unfair.*

A father who was dead then not, soon to be dead again.

*Unfair.*

He suppressed another cough as he looked up at her. She couldn't meet his eyes, so much like her own.

236

"So." He wrapped a hand around the one holding the hilt of her knife. "Do it or don't. I won't blame you either way."

Amaya struggled for breath. His hand was large and rough against hers, like when they had gone out on his ship and he had shown her how to pull on the sails. Like when he had held her hand as they walked through the park, or she had tugged him toward a food vendor selling confectionaries.

Tears blurred her vision. She could still remember the bone-jarring impact of her knife hitting Melchor, the hot blood that had spurted onto her hand. The way Zharo's eyes had stilled and dulled as he died on Liesl's blade.

Amaya backed away, stumbling over the detritus on the floor and falling. Her wrist snagged on a piece of broken glass. Boon reached for her, but she flung herself at the door, scrabbling at the handle until she was half tumbling onto the street.

That day on the *Papaya*, her father had caught her when she leaped from the mast. She had trusted him to save her, and he had, because he was her father and that was what fathers were supposed to do.

Now she was falling with no one to catch her, with no one to trust except herself.

*Unfair.*

She collapsed to her knees and finally let out the wail that tore up her insides, shredding her throat and numbing her mind. She screamed and let the night take the sound, making the stars tremble with the force of it. If she could extinguish every last one of them, she would. She would breed a playing ground for the dark, let it close in on the world until it was smothered and still.

Maybe then the gods would see fit to start over, try harder.

Or maybe they would consider it a blessing.

She didn't realize she had stopped screaming until she heard foot-steps on her right.

"Miss? Are...Are you all right? Do you need help?"

Amaya didn't bother to look up. She only gripped her knife and half lifted it, a silent warning to back away. The person swallowed a gasp and smartly left her to herself.

She pushed to her feet, the world hazy and dull around her. Her throat was sore, but her mind was clearer.

If she accepted the truth, she would be admitting that every-thing she had known until now had been a lie. It could unravel her, unmake her.

But she couldn't afford to be unmade, not when they had a mis-sion. Not when so many lives were at stake.

So she had to let it go. She had to keep going and pretend that nothing had happened.

Amaya took one step. Another. Kept moving forward, because it was the only thing she could do in a world that made no sense.

Then she looked up and saw the moon's position.

Midnight.

Her rib cage shuddered with horror, another cry wrenching from her torn-up throat.

Cayo was gambling without her.

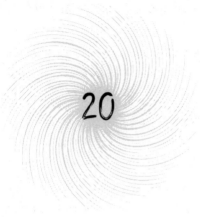

## 20

*What is the difference between winning and losing?*
*Sometimes, it's as small as a penny. Sometimes,*
*it's the cost of all you hold dear.*
*—THE INS AND OUTS OF TABLE BETTING*

Sweat ran down Cayo's neck as he studied the table. It was round and lined with blue felt, crowded with cards and a pile of coins, jewels, and bank notes. The gamblers seated around the table ranged from flinty to cocky, from blank stares to dimpled smirks.

He remembered this the way one remembers the feel of water, the smell of jasmine, the taste of wine. Heady and sensory, a fleeting pleasure. This was walking back into a dream of how things used to be—the way the crowd was hot and noisy, the way the air carried the scent of cigarillo smoke and perfume.

Cayo licked his lips and glanced at the woman two seats down from him. Robin Deirdre had dressed in green tonight, her sleeves gauzy, her bodice soft with crushed velvet. The collar was high, an echo of Rehanese fashion, with the double row of buttons down the front that was typical in Chalier suits.

Her eyes were bright and her mouth gave nothing away, not even the slightest twitch of satisfaction or displeasure as she studied her cards. Long, gloved fingers held those cards with the confidence of a woman who had been gambling nearly her whole life. It was no wonder she had been asked to participate.

The other gamblers were a mix of highbrow and commoner. They had all needed to confirm with the casino workers that they had enough to wager tonight; several had been turned away for not having sufficient funds, for having concealed weapons, or even for the amount of wear and tear on their clothing.

Cayo had only just gotten through, after a rather sour-mouthed dealer eyed the faded cuffs of his jacket. But his winnings from the other night had been more than enough. If they had found Jazelle on him, it would have been a different story.

There were two games slotted for the night. The first one, the one that Cayo had been assigned to, started at midnight. As he sat there and eyed his competition, his fingers twitched toward his pocket watch that was no longer there.

Amaya hadn't been in the apartment, and she hadn't been waiting for him here. Where in the hells was she?

His heart fluttered as the man beside him laid down a card. Cayo was not overly familiar with the game that had been chosen for the night, something called Both Sides. It relied on trading cards with the players to your left and right, but Cayo had a distinct feeling the woman on his right was cheating. How, he wasn't sure yet, but she had been quiet and withdrawn the entire time they'd sat here.

"Those earrings are exquisite, my lady," said the man who had just given Cayo his bad card. Cayo suppressed the urge to sneer as he picked it up and added it to his less-than-impressive hand. "May I ask which jeweler you commissioned?"

Deirdre shook loose curls from her shoulders, revealing more of the triangle-shaped earrings. They glimmered attractively against her soft brown skin. "Do you know of Bovrelle?"

"Ah yes, I've had some handsome cufflinks gifted to me from Bovrelle! I did not know their craft extended so far."

Cayo picked his weakest card and foisted it off on the woman to his other side. Her mouth tightened, barely perceptible. All the while his insides roiled unpleasantly at the syrupy, saccharine tone the man was giving Deirdre. She was no doubt used to it—hells, Cayo was used to it, having had no shortage of Moray gentry try to curry favor with the Mercados—but it seemed such a waste of time for a woman of her ambition.

Deirdre smiled through it all. She was an excellent actress, he had to admit.

How was he supposed to get anything out of her?

He received yet another bad card. Gritting his teeth, he glanced over his shoulder. The crowd watched while sipping their drinks and murmuring among themselves. Amaya wasn't there.

She had promised she would be here.

He forced himself to take an even, controlled breath, then put on his best smile.

"Forgive me if I'm wrong, but that dress is from Gohmer's collection, is it not?" he asked of Deirdre.

The woman's head jerked up, as if startled to find him speaking directly to her. Her black lashes framed dark blue eyes that studied him with an intensity he didn't like.

"My," she said with that small smile, "you've quite an eye on you. Are you familiar with Gohmer's work?"

"Only a touch," he admitted, being sure to employ his dimpled smile. "My sister is the true fan. She admires how Gohmer uses both Rehanese styles and those from the empires to create unique pieces."

"Indeed, that is what draws me to them as well." Deirdre received a card from her neighbor and barely looked at her hand before passing on another. "I'm also quite fond of Martisse."

Cayo did his best to keep his shoulders relaxed, his face from flinching. Was that a direct hint that she had seen him at Basque's gala with Amaya? Or was it simply small talk?

Sweat tickled the back of his neck as he received his next card. He had to suppress another flinch. He was receiving more bad cards than he could give away. If this kept up, his hand would suffer significantly.

"Martisse is quite lovely, although a bit too grand for me," he said carefully. "I think I prefer Gohmer."

"I see." She offered him another smile, which he returned. "You look and sound as if you come from Rehan. Is the way Gohmer meshes cultures together something you find particularly appealing about their line?"

His chest grew tight. He couldn't help but feel as if he were a mouse being idly played with by a cat.

"It does make for some unconventional designs," he said at last. "They're unique."

"I agree." Deirdre ran fingers along her high collar. "Though I can't say I'm particularly fond of Gohmer's political ideologies."

Cayo frowned. He knew about Gohmer's stitching techniques, yet nothing about their political ideologies; what could that possibly mean?

The man who had inquired after her earrings forced a laugh even as he handed Cayo another lackluster card. "Come now, my lady, where's your patriotism? Gohmer clothes the emperor himself, you know."

Deirdre's face barely altered, but Cayo was good at reading the subtle signs of gamblers. Her left cheek twitched just below her eye, so quick that he nearly missed it.

"Too true," she murmured, focusing once again on her cards.

Cayo studied his own, mind racing. Back in Basque's office, she had laid down claims of supporting the Rain Empire, of using the alchemists to create weapons for them.

But if she was this upset about a single mention of the emperor...

The woman beside him cleared her throat loudly, and he jumped before handing her one of his cards. His chest grew tighter; his hand was getting worse and worse. The pile of money before him gleamed innocuously—money that he had planned to use for Soria.

Glancing toward the entrance to the casino for the hundredth time, he swallowed a curse. Amaya *still wasn't here.*

*You promised*, he seethed, fingers denting the cards.

They had gotten to the point where players had begun betting their watches and jewelry in addition to what they'd put down. There was even a pair of gilded opera glasses.

Had this been worth it? Was there still time to bow out?

"Sir?"

He was so used to being called *my lord* that it took a moment to realize the server was speaking to him. She bore a silver platter upon which sat a variety of drinks.

He opened his mouth to decline, his hand moving to wave her away. But muscle memory made him grab the nearest glass instead, its liquid sloshing gently.

The server moved on, and Cayo stared at the drink. It smelled like vorene and citrus, sharp and familiar. He took a deep breath and closed his eyes, willing himself to put it down.

Instead he took a large gulp, the vorene burning down his throat. Amaya had told him not to drink, but she wasn't here, and he was losing badly, and what else was he supposed to do? He had a luck ritual to honor.

He could cheat—he wanted to—but he couldn't risk getting caught. Not when there were so many eyes on him. Not when Deirdre was here.

Cayo's leg jostled under the table, his temples damp with sweat as the feathery sound of cards overwhelmed him. The light was too bright in here, the room far too hot with the crush of bodies watching from the sidelines. Were any of them watching him? No doubt with pity, no doubt wondering what in the hells he was doing.

He didn't know. He didn't know.

Cayo finally managed to snag two good cards, but it wasn't enough. The man on his right handed him a lower card, and Cayo reluctantly took it. Cayo returned fire by handing the woman beside him his lowest card, but even that had been higher than the one he'd received.

*I can't lose*, he thought desperately, watching the other players reveal their hands. *I can't let this all be for nothing.*

He had to win. For Soria. For himself.

But then the cards stopped circulating, and the players were asked to show their hands. Cards fell to the table. They tumbled from Cayo's fingers.

"And the pot goes to Lady Deirdre," the dealer announced, bowing to the woman before raking up the money—including Cayo's pile—and pushing it toward her. Deirdre flushed prettily, almost as if on command, and inclined her head in gratitude. The crowd applauded as the other players sighed or swore or joined in on the applause.

Cayo was numb.

"The proceeds of tonight will be going toward a charitable cause," Deirdre announced. "The search for the cure for ash fever, headed by myself and Lord André Basque." The crowd clapped and murmured in appreciation, some even whistling their approval.

"The second game will take place in a half hour," the dealer called over the noise.

But he had nothing left to bet. All the money he'd won—gone.

He was back in his father's office, Kamon bearing down on him with all the force of his rage, demanding how exactly an entire life's savings went missing.

"Cayo!"

Amaya burst from the crowd, gasping for breath. Her hair was windblown, her clothes torn, and there was blood on her sleeve. She took him in as he sat there, with nothing before him other than the dregs of a strong drink.

"What happened?" she demanded.

Cayo didn't answer. He reached for his glass and realized it was empty.

"Cayo," she said again, her voice quavering.

"Sir," the dealer said, "if you're unable to bet, I must ask you to vacate your seat."

Cayo stared at the dealer, who shifted uncomfortably. Cayo grinned, then laughed, getting unsteadily to his feet.

"Yeah, I'll leave," he croaked. "I've got nothing anyway. That's what you bastards wanted, isn't it?"

"Sir—"

"*Fuck* you." Cayo turned and threw the glass on the floor. It shattered, making those around him cry out at the noise. Amaya might have yelled something, but Cayo couldn't hear it, his laughter drowning everything else out.

The casino guards grabbed him and pulled him toward the exit. Cayo fought against them like a panicked animal, growling and spitting until they threw him out the doors and into the street.

"Don't come back here," said one of the guards, pointing a meaty finger at him.

Cayo lurched to his feet, swaying. "You think I *want* to, you oversized boar? Fuck you."

"Hey, fuck *you.*"

Amaya pushed past the guards and approached him, her eyes alight with a furious fire. She said nothing, merely grabbed his arm and dragged him down the street, away from the noise and the heat and the humiliation.

She found a wide alleyway and pushed him against the brick wall.

"What happened?" she growled.

Cayo's head spun. He'd drunk that alcohol too fast, and nothing in the world made any sense. "I lost."

"That's obvious." Her nostrils flared—another tell, he thought distantly. "You said you could handle this. You *promised* not to drink, or to gamble without me there!"

"What exactly was I supposed to do, then?" he retaliated. "You promised me you would be here, and instead I was left to make an ass of myself!"

"You were supposed to *wait*. There's still another game, and we could have played that one. Instead, all your money is gone. You know what that means?"

"No, please, tell me," Cayo drawled. "Of course I know what it fucking means!"

His voice broke on the last word. Amaya moved away from him and began pacing the alley with her arms crossed tight against her chest. Cayo glared at a faded poster for a cabaret show on the wall, blinking hard against his blurry vision.

"Where in the hells were you?" he demanded.

She stopped pacing. She leaned a hand against the wall, her fingers covered in dried blood. Her entire body was stiff and trembling, her eyes wide, vacant. Spooked.

"I can't tell you." Her voice was strangled. "But it was important. I . . . I lost track of time. I'm sorry."

"Oh, you're sorry?" Once, he would have loved to hear it. Now it only fueled his rage. "You can't even tell me what was so important that it made you abandon me? I didn't know what to do; I barely even got anything out of Deirdre—"

"Which is why you should have *waited*." The faraway look morphed into something harder, and he could tell that Silverfish was coming out to speak. "You don't learn. No matter what happens, you always remain the spoiled, selfish boy who grew up with your father's influence."

247

Heat burned in Cayo's chest as he pushed off the wall. "Shut up."

"You've suffered. You've experienced hardship. But that hasn't made you better, has it?" She also pushed off the wall, her gaze wild, her mouth open, hungry for his suffering. "Face it. You don't know how to do anything on your own because you're pathetic without someone there to hold your hand."

"Shut *up!*" He turned and drove trembling fingers through his hair. "I wasn't doing this for me, I was doing it for Soria!"

"If you were really doing it for Soria, you wouldn't have—"

"Stop it, just—stop telling me what I should or shouldn't have done! I know I could have done better in there. If you'd just been here on time, this wouldn't have even happened! All those games I won the other night...you...you were part of my luck ritual." Although his vision was still hazy, he could make out the expression of disbelief on her face. "And because you weren't there, I lost everything."

"That's the most ridiculous thing I've ever heard," she spat. "You don't get to blame this on me. This is your fault, and you have to own up to it."

"This was *your* idea in the first place! This is *your* fault, but you're too damn proud to see it. You can't even see how the rest of it is your fault, too."

"What?"

"If you..." He tried to swallow, tried to get his breathing under control. "If you hadn't brought that counterfeit money into the city for your petty revenge, maybe Soria wouldn't be sick in the first place. How many cases of ash fever happened because of you? How many have died because of you?"

Amaya staggered back. Her eyes were wide and haunted, her face wan. It broke something inside him, but there was another piece of him already broken far beyond repair.

"Your father—"

"He's not the only one responsible," Cayo said. "And you know it. You're no stranger to pain, to death." He gestured to the blood on her sleeve. "All of this..." He laughed mirthlessly, flinging his arms out. "The world will be in ruins, and you helped bring it about. You let Boon pull your puppet strings, and now—"

"Stop it," Amaya growled.

"Maybe your mother knew," Cayo said. Nausea and vindictive pleasure roiled in his gut, returning all her verbal blows with interest. "Maybe your mother knew you would be nothing but trouble. Maybe she *did* sell you, if you were just as selfish then as you are—"

He didn't get to finish as her fist flew into his jaw. His head snapped to the side as he stumbled backward, pain exploding up the side of his skull. Amaya stood before him with hands clenched tight, panting.

He tested his jaw, wincing. "What, don't like it when I make implications about your family? Wonder how that feels."

Amaya yelled and charged at him again, sending him to the ground. The wind was knocked out of him as she drove her hand back for another punch, smacking him soundly on the side of his head. Cayo snarled and bucked her off him, remembering Liesl's training as he crawled onto his hands and knees, the alley swaying dizzyingly around him.

Amaya rushed him, and he grabbed her legs to take her down. He tried to pin her, but she was stronger and faster and more sober. She kicked him in the chest, and he was sent sprawling, coughing and sucking in air.

He made it to his knees before she grabbed a fistful of his hair and tugged his head back, pain alighting across his scalp. But that was nothing compared to the feeling of her knife pressed to the skin of his throat.

They both froze, their uneven breaths echoing off the brick walls. Amaya stared down at him, furious and vengeful, driving the tip of her knife in just enough to make a drop of blood roll down to his collarbone.

Her fingers tightened in his hair. He let out a quiet sound of pain, and her pupils dilated. Her eyes flicked down to his lips, as if she were suppressing some vulgar impulse, fighting against yet another mistake.

Even now, with anger sweeping through him and her blade pricking his skin, he wanted nothing so much as to crash their mouths together. To feel the heat of her lips and the thrumming of her heart, to know what it was to hate and love all at once.

He wanted her. He hated her, and he wanted her, and he didn't deserve her.

Finally, she released him. Cayo stayed on his knees as she backed away, knife glinting in her hand. Shaking her head in disgust, she turned and left him there.

He didn't blame her. He would have done the same.

But he wished she had just done the easy thing and killed him instead.

**21**

*What we search for is knowledge—the formulas and*
*equations to craft what others debase to spells. What if*
*an elixir of life is possible? What if gold can be fabricated,*
*instead of mined? There is no limit to what is possible.*

—WRITINGS OF ALCHEMIST BERNARD WILKES

Amaya didn't see Cayo when he came back to the apartment, or the day after. They only crossed paths when Avi made dinner and they both emerged from their rooms. She heard Cayo's small intake of breath as if to speak, but she left before he could. She couldn't even look at him. She was afraid of what she would do if she did, if she would resume their scuffle or slap him or simply feel nothing at all.

No—that was the problem, wasn't it? Where Cayo was concerned, she felt entirely too much.

Besides, she wanted to stay with her anger a little longer. She had a right to it.

And she wanted to ignore the guilt scratching up against her insides, telling her she had every reason to apologize, too.

She went by Boon's ramshackle hut again, wanting...well, she didn't know. She doubted there could be anything resembling closure between them. But at the least he could tell her what those papers from his Vault meant, what other secrets her mother had been keeping.

But the hut was empty. He was already gone again.

How was she supposed to contain the entirety of this truth within her? How was she supposed to go on living, talking, breathing, when the man who had created her was slowly dying somewhere in the city?

Amaya stopped by the hospital to check on Soria. The nurses somehow looked even more haggard than before, their hands shaking and their eyes deadened, as if none of them had gotten a single hour of rest in the last few days. Amaya slowed, wanting to ask what she could do, how she could help. But she lingered for too long, and one of the nurses snapped at her to move along.

Soria was lying on her side, weakly moving her pillow around to get comfortable. Amaya hurried to help her.

"Thanks," Soria whispered. She was pale and shivering today, despite the warmth coming off her body. Amaya grabbed the folded blanket at the end of the bed and covered her with it. "They said I have to keep changing positions. Don't want to get bedsores."

"Do you want to get up and walk around a little?"

Soria coughed into the pillow and shook her head. "Mother Hilas made me do that this morning. I'm exhausted."

She looked it, too. Amaya couldn't help the impulse to reach out and brush her hair back. Soria smiled slightly.

"You're surprisingly gentle for someone who gave my brother that bruise."

Amaya winced. "I—"

"It's all right. He already explained it." Soria's eyes fluttered closed. "If I wasn't in this bed, I'd be locking the two of you in a room until you came to your senses."

Amaya snorted softly. "It doesn't really work like that."

"No? It usually works in books."

Soria's voice was getting hoarser, her words slurred. Amaya's chest tightened as she thought of the nurses downstairs, the patients like Soria who had been cheated out of medicine. She wished she could be surprised that someone had been selfish enough to steal their treatments and their payments, but she wasn't. Seven years with Captain Zharo had taught her exactly what sort of greed people were capable of in even the most trying times.

"You don't have to stay," Soria whispered, her eyes still closed, her breathing beginning to even out. "I know it's boring...."

"I'll stay," Amaya said.

She watched the girl fall asleep and sat by her side for the entire two hours the hospital allowed her.

Liesl found her in the tenement's washroom later, a sad affair of broken tile darkened with mold. There were buckets for washing clothes and bodies, and a pump that delivered water from the bottom level. It always came out frigid and smelling sulfuric.

Amaya shivered as she scrubbed at her jacket, trying to get the bloodstains off. She hadn't even noticed she'd cut herself until Liesl had washed and bandaged her wrist. Amaya's hands were already numb and wrinkled, so she welcomed Liesl's appearance as an excuse to take a break.

"The boy looked rather banged up the other night," Liesl said casually, leaning against the doorframe. "Should I ask?"

"No."

"I'm assuming he deserved it?"

Amaya's mind was quick to say yes, but her gut clenched. She had abandoned him because of her desire for vengeance. Because of that, everything had spiraled downward, leading them back to who they were at their core: Silverfish and Lord Mercado.

He had messed up. But so had she.

Instead of answering, Amaya sat back on her heels and rubbed her hands together to get some feeling back in them. "Are you worried about Adrienne?"

Liesl smirked at the deliberate subject change. "She's strong, and she's smart, and she's not alone."

"That doesn't answer my question."

"You didn't answer mine." Liesl walked inside, crossing her arms. "She'll be all right. Jas will help her with whatever she needs."

"Did you know that he...?"

"Oh, there will certainly be an interrogation once I meet back up with them. But never mind about all that. There's an errand you need to run."

"What sort of errand?"

"We still have to look into the name Julien Caver gave us. Trevan Nicodeme. Cayo told me about what you two did, how you found the name of a den he likes to frequent."

Despite everything, Amaya's face warmed. She knew she should have gone to Liesl right away with the information, but that was when Liesl had been obsessed with Basque's code.

"What else did he tell you?" Amaya asked.

"Everything about the tournament." Liesl shook her head. "You two really should have cleared this with me beforehand."

"You couldn't have gone," Amaya pointed out. "In case someone recognized you."

Liesl briefly clenched her jaw. "Still. I could have told him what to say, what to do. And now he has no money to help Soria...." She sighed, taking off her glasses to clean them on her skirt. "In either case, he got something, small though it is. Deirdre tells others she's loyal to the Rain Empire, but her comment about disliking Wayan Gohmer's political inclinations doesn't match up with that. Gohmer is an imperialist through and through."

"What does that mean, then?"

"She could be working both sides. It's hard to say until we look into it more." Replacing her glasses, Liesl nodded to Amaya's jacket. "In the meantime, we have another lead to follow. Make sure that's dry by tonight."

Amaya and Avi crouched on a roof overlooking a side street of the Casino District, Amaya's shoulder pressed against the balustrade. The stone was cold, but her back was beginning to hurt from keeping the same position for an hour now.

Liesl had given them their assignments: Deadshot was stationed outside the Deirdre manor to watch for suspicious activity, Liesl had gone in search of information regarding Deirdre's allies, and Avi and Amaya were meant to track down Trevan Nicodeme.

Amaya knew she was supposed to be watching the street outside the building they thought Nicodeme was in, but she couldn't stop thinking about the way Boon had looked up at her as she'd pressed that knife to his throat, somber and heartbroken when he had no right to be. He had abandoned her. Molded her into a person she didn't want to become. Betrayed her. He deserved to be eaten up by the fever.

Didn't he?

"Counterfeit for your thoughts?" Avi asked.

"Not funny."

"It's a little funny." Avi grinned. "C'mon, what were you thinking about? The little lordling?"

"No." Amaya refocused on the street below, lit erratically with sputtering lanterns. A few people mingled outside a rundown card den called the Crown and Barrel, smoking what smelled like jaaga. The door to the den was open, filling the night with the sounds of clinking glass and boisterous laughter.

"I was thinking about Boon," Amaya said softly. "And how much I wish I could go back and do things differently."

Avi instantly sobered. "Such as?"

"Like how it would have been nice to push him into the harbor while he was drunk and watch him drown."

"Remind me to never piss you off." Avi stretched, relieving cramped muscles. "I get it, though. I knew Boon dabbled in alchemy, but I didn't know he'd used it to make all that gold. Or what the consequences would end up being."

"How did you know about Boon learning alchemy? He never talked about it."

Avi didn't answer right away. He rubbed a spot above his hip.

"He mentioned it a few times in passing," the man said eventually. "That's how I came to learn about his involvement with...your mother."

The truth banged its fists against her chest, wailing to be let out. To have someone, just one person, understand the churning grief inside her.

But before she could say a single word, Avi perked up. Amaya followed his gaze to the figure of a man leaving the den. He had a potbelly and a head of thick hair leading down to two wide, curly muttonchops, and the chain of a pocket watch glinted in the lantern light.

"I believe that is our man," Avi whispered. "All right, Trevan, let's see where you go...."

Trevan Nicodeme tottered down the street, away from the Casino District. Amaya recognized the gait of one who'd nursed a few drinks, but there was something else in his posture that hinted at anger, the way his fingers curled and his shoulders rose up toward his ears.

She and Avi tailed him, plotting a course across the rooftops to avoid being spotted. They used crow-stepped gables and the ridges of jutting windows to make their way from one building to the next. Amaya leaped onto a roof and nearly lost her footing, her boot scraping as she regained her balance. Trevan didn't notice, mumbling to himself as he wove through the dim streets.

Their mark led them toward a shopping district, then turned sharply onto a crossway street. As he tripped up to a strange-looking shop, Amaya and Avi dropped onto a balcony and watched from above.

Trevan pounded a fist against the door. "I need more!" he yelled in Soléne. "Hey!"

The door whisked open, revealing a furious man in his late mid-years. "Stop shouting! Do you want all of Baleine to hear you?"

"Need more," Trevan said again, thrusting his hand out with the palm facing upward. "I was on a streak and ran out."

"I don't have any more at the moment. You'll have to come back later in the week."

"I said I'm on a *streak*—"

"I don't give a damn if you're on a streak. I have no more, and that's that."

Trevan let out a flurry of curses that Amaya couldn't translate and spat at the man's feet before stalking down the street. The man in the doorway shook his head and closed the door, the windows turning dark a moment later.

Amaya's eyes traveled up to the symbol above the door: a star within a circle.

"This must be one of the places the counterfeits get distributed," Avi whispered. "Wonder if this is one of Deirdre's. Let's go back and report."

While they told Liesl what they'd overheard, Cayo wandered into the main room. Amaya did all she could to avoid his gaze.

"Was there a specific name on the shop?" Liesl asked.

"Not that we could see."

"No matter. Just point it out on the map."

When Avi marked the alchemist's shop on the map of Baleine they kept on the table, Cayo wandered closer with a bewildered frown.

"That can't be right," Cayo said.

Liesl pierced him with a sharp stare. "What do you mean?"

"That's Florimond's shop." He placed a shaking finger over the mark, horror etched across his face. "That's where I work."

They couldn't wait for Cayo to find evidence, not knowing how long it might take. The only thing to do was break in themselves that night.

Avi elected to stay behind, claiming he didn't feel well.

"Do you want one of us to stay with you?" Liesl asked, worry in her voice.

Avi shook his head and cleared his throat. "Just a stomachache. Nothing I can't handle on my own."

Cayo bit his lip, and Amaya wondered if he would volunteer to stay back with Avi. But he remained silent, surprising her. She allowed herself a brief glance at his face, lingering on the bruise on his jaw before turning away.

She couldn't let her focus stray. There would be time for words later.

The night was cold, hugging in on all sides. Amaya's sleeve had dried, but she kept checking it anyway, making sure the bloodstain was gone. Cayo hadn't even asked where the blood had come from. Was he that used to seeing her covered in others' blood? Was this what she was to him, a girl who spoke violence like a language?

*Focus*, she chided herself, waiting crouched beside Liesl as Dead-shot gave the all clear. Liesl crossed the street first, making quick work of the shop's lock before the door silently swung open. Cayo had warned Liesl that Florimond lived upstairs and that they had to be quiet.

"You never saw anything suspicious in the shop?" Liesl had drilled him earlier.

"I know he keeps letters locked up, but I've never been able to get to them," Cayo had said defensively. "I can't exactly snoop while he's a foot away from me."

"He never said anything strange? Met with anyone who seemed odd?"

"Not really. He said he was working on a cure for the fever. Deirdre isn't his patron—I made sure to ask him. I thought..." He'd let out a strained breath, wilting like a flower without water. "I suppose it doesn't matter what I thought."

Liesl now gave them the all clear signal. They carefully made their way into the shop, through the tables of wares on display, using only the moonlight through the windows. Amaya had no clue what to make of what she saw, baubles and metals and jars of substances that reminded her of her father's stories about Kharian witches.

"Dried salamander legs and bat eyes," her father would growl in a scary voice, making claws with his hands as Amaya giggled. "They'd toss 'em all together and make a poison so strong it could kill a god."

Amaya tried to ignore the ache in her chest as they ducked into a back room. *Focus.*

There were no windows here, so Deadshot lit a lantern. The back room was wide yet cramped with equipment and bookshelves, tables crowded with half-finished experiments and hastily scrawled notes.

Liesl peered into a barrel full of sand, even scooping up a handful and letting it trickle back down through her fingers. "There's a lot to unpack here. Let's split up and search. Look for anything incriminating—letters, notes, coins."

Amaya wandered toward the corner farthest from Cayo. She came across a table covered in jars and beakers and vials, filled with herbs both dried and soaking in colored solutions. There was a stone mortar and pestle beside them, stained green.

"Where's that box of letters?" Liesl asked. Cayo pointed to the shelves, and she got to work on unlocking it.

Amaya was riffling through a notebook when Cayo swore at full volume. Liesl whirled around to scold him but stopped at what she saw.

He had opened a burlap sack containing a mound of brinies. The scallop-like creatures were already dead and beginning to molt, their outer flesh hardening and tinged with a golden hue.

"This is it, then," Liesl said. "This is where the counterfeits get made. Or one of the places, at least. Who knows how many alchemists are in on it?"

Cayo stared down at the brinies, a hand over his mouth. Eventually he lowered it. "This... This isn't the bag I delivered to him." Relief made his voice shake. "But this doesn't make sense. He said Deirdre isn't his patron!"

"Regardless, he must still be in on the plot. Maybe Deirdre's not as involved as we thought."

"What do we do?" Amaya asked.

"We look for any other evidence and leave. We'll hand over everything we can find to Remy, who can report it to his senior officers."

Deadshot uncovered a workstation that had been hidden under a tarp, revealing a set of metal tools and a pile of black discs in the size of solstas. That in itself was damning, but even that couldn't compare to what Liesl found once the wooden box on the shelf clicked open.

"Here we go," she whispered, pulling out a letter. "The fool didn't even think to burn these."

"Who're they from?" Deadshot asked.

Liesl scanned the words, then looked at Cayo.

His face hardened in understanding. "My father," he said.

Liesl nodded and handed him the letter. Amaya couldn't help but creep closer, but the words were in Soléne, not Rehanese. She still recognized Mercado's signature at the bottom.

"It's addressed to the Benefactor," Liesl said grimly. "He says that he's sent the latest batch of brinies as promised, but that he's having trouble finding enough for the next batch."

Cayo looked up from the letter, barely concealed rage in his eyes. "That doesn't make sense. If he's making his own counterfeit money in Moray, why would he be sending the brinies here?"

"Brinies are only found in the south," Amaya said. Her father's notes had said as much. "Maybe he can't make it all himself, needs an alchemist to make it for him?"

"Or," Liesl said, already reading the next letter, "maybe it wasn't even his idea to begin with."

"What?"

Liesl read the letter out loud. " 'I'm tired of playing this game with you. I have done all you've asked and given you the recipe, so you must release me from my debt. I have done my part here in the city and have no more to contribute. Now I must watch Moray fall while you gloat half a world away.' "

Amaya bit her thumb, remembering what Remy had told them

about Mercado's debts to the Rain Empire. To the Benefactor in particular. "In the currency exchange offices we only found records of money being sent to Mercado, and not the other way around. What if he tried to use the counterfeits to pay off his own debts, and when Deirdre realized it she demanded the recipe for herself?"

Liesl nodded. "Which means the counterfeit money Mercado integrated into Moray didn't only come from him, it came from the Benefactor as well. Mercado was paying off his debt by spreading it for them."

"Why?" Cayo demanded, the letter shaking in his hand. "Why would my father do that to his own city?"

"Desperate men do stupid things," Deadshot muttered. "He likely didn't want to face the debt collectors, or a noose."

"Deirdre claimed she was going to use alchemy as a weapon," Amaya said softly. "To reclaim Moray. Setting off an economic crisis would give her an opening."

"But that doesn't line up with her comment about Gohmer," Liesl grumbled, beginning to pace. "Or that she's also working on a cure. And then there's the fact that Florimond said his patron isn't Deirdre. Could he be lying?"

"What if she wants to start a war with the Sun Empire?" Cayo ventured. "They both want Moray's trade routes. They want to profit off the casinos."

"No chance of that now that they're flooded with counterfeits," Amaya said.

She finally met Cayo's gaze. He was clearly shaken, but he still held himself solid and uncompromising. There were a thousand things left unsaid in his expression, but she read one thing clear enough: They had to put a stop to this.

Then his eyes slid to a point over her shoulder and widened.

It was all the warning she needed to drop and roll out of the way before a bullet crashed through the room. Amaya ducked behind a table and checked the others, but they didn't seem to be hit. Cayo and Deadshot had both whipped out their guns, training them on the figure of the middle-aged man Amaya had seen earlier that night.

Florimond shuffled inside, a gun shaking between his hands. "What do you think you're doing?"

Liesl kept her calm, standing slowly and lifting her hands in a show of surrender. "Trying to expose what exactly *you're* doing. Not a very legal trade you're in, is it?"

Florimond scowled. "That's none of your business. You have no right—"

Liesl continued as if he hadn't spoken. "You realize what your creations are doing to the city, yes? The fever, the overrun hospitals, the inflation of prices—"

"Shut up!" Florimond jerked his gun toward Liesl, making Deadshot growl in warning. He glanced at Cayo with a curling upper lip. "Who even are you? Who sent you here?"

"We should be the ones asking you that," Amaya said, sliding a knife from her sleeve. "You're working with Kamon Mercado, aren't you?"

Florimond's jaw dropped, but he didn't lower the gun or slacken his grip. "How...?"

"Are you the Benefactor?" Cayo blurted. Florimond blinked at him, mouth working desperately.

"N-no, I..."

"Who is the Benefactor, then?" Cayo demanded. "Is it Robin Deirdre?"

"Deirdre..." Florimond laughed, an unnatural sound. "Fucking

264

Deirdre. She tried so hard to recruit me. I kept denying her. I couldn't let anyone know."

"Deirdre is working with the alchemists to create weapons, isn't she?" Liesl asked.

His gun shook harder. "Yes."

"To reclaim Moray. To fight the Sun Empire."

Again that wild laugh. "No." He swung his head from side to side, eyes wide behind his glasses. "She's commissioning weapons, yes. But Deirdre isn't an imperialist. Her family was once royalty in Chalier, and she wants to be royalty again. She's trying to fight back against the *Rain Empire*. She doesn't give a damn about Moray."

Liesl reared back, visibly unsettled. Deadshot kept her glare on Florimond, ready to act as soon as Liesl gave the command.

"That's not what she's been saying to her business partners," Liesl argued.

"Of course it isn't!" Florimond cried. "She'd be arrested in two seconds flat if anyone knew her true motives."

"Then how do you know what she's actually planning?" Cayo demanded.

"She wanted me to help with the cure," Florimond whispered. "But I was already trying, and failing. I *tried* to find a cure. I did. I tried to undo what I'd done." Florimond had grown deathly pale, his eyes round and wild. "I'm sorry. I tried. I'm sorry!"

Unease pinched Amaya's gut, the same instinct as encountering a rabid animal. "Don't—" she began, but it was too late.

Florimond reached into his pocket and drew out a small vial of silver liquid.

"What are you doing?" Cayo asked, raising his voice as Florimond pulled the cork from the vial. "Stop! *Stop!*"

Deadshot vaulted over a table to reach him, but Florimond had already tossed back the liquid, swallowing it with a gasp. The effect was immediate—he began to seize and cough, foamy spittle frothing at his mouth. Deadshot caught him as he sank to the ground, where he convulsed a few times before his eyes rolled back and he lay still.

"Shit!" Cayo turned, gagging, as Liesl glowered over Florimond's corpse.

"The little cheat." She grabbed the empty vial from his hand and sniffed it. "He had a contingency plan in case people like us showed up. He really couldn't live with the consequences of his actions."

"The guilty always run," Deadshot said.

"Straight into death's arms this time." Liesl cursed and tossed the bottle aside. "We could have interrogated him more about Deirdre."

"But based on what he said, it sounds like Deirdre isn't the Benefactor," Deadshot said. "She's using the alchemists against the empire to reinstate Chalier as an independent kingdom. Why would she be working on spreading counterfeit money in a land she wants for herself?"

The muscle of Liesl's jaw jutted out. "I don't know."

"Does that mean..." Cayo seemed as if he were trying very hard not to look at Florimond. "Do you think *he's* the Benefactor?"

A moment of silence passed as they thought it through. "I suppose it's possible," Amaya said, "but why would your father be in debt to an alchemist?"

"I don't know, but we have evidence that Florimond was involved." Cayo indicated the bag of brinies.

"And we have evidence that something went terribly wrong here," Liesl countered, gesturing to Florimond's body. "Which will make the navy's sweep a bit more complicated."

"Then we get rid of the body," Amaya said. "There's no blood. They can think Florimond ran off."

Cayo glanced at her, and she tried not to flinch. *A girl who spoke violence like a language.*

"Agreed," Liesl said. "Let's get him wrapped in that tarp and make a trip to the harbor. We can theorize later."

Amaya stared at Florimond's wide, milky eyes as nausea stirred inside her.

*Pray to the star saints for forgiveness and mercy*, Amaya's mother had once told her. *The sight of death brings nothing but misfortune.*

## 22

*What is gained is lost. What is lost remains lost.*

—KHARIAN PHILOSOPHER SANJAY KORAPA

Standing in the pink light of dawn, Cayo fought down the urge to vomit.

He had stood watch last night as the others rolled the wrapped body of Francis Florimond into the harbor, where it splashed grotesquely. Deadshot had weighed the body with rocks so that it would sink, and Cayo had to stifle hysterical laughter as he imagined what would happen if the navy found Florimond floating on the water.

Cayo felt like a murderer. He hadn't killed the man directly, but he had taken his own life thanks to their interference. He had seemed decent enough when they'd first met, but now, knowing he had been working for the Benefactor... That he might in fact have *been* the Benefactor...

"At least we have evidence for the navy," Liesl said as they walked back to the apartment, silent and solemn. "We'll tip Remy off and they can examine the workshop."

"And then?" Cayo asked. "We're still no closer to stopping the counterfeit production."

"We'll have to stake out the other alchemists' shops," Liesl murmured, "keep watch over the Deirdre manor..."

She went on, but Cayo tuned her out. It all felt hopeless. His father was a criminal who had betrayed his home. Cayo had no money for Soria, and now his second employer was dead, thanks to him.

Everything was falling apart.

Which was why, as he reported for work the next morning, he barely paid attention to Victor's grousing. He performed his duties in a trance, transferring fish from net to ice, wondering if anyone in the fish market had helped his father deliver those brinies.

A commotion by the docks lifted him out of the fog of his thoughts. Victor turned as well, frowning as a scuffle began near a handsome galleon. Cayo couldn't hear what was being yelled, but he saw clear enough the naval soldiers trying to push irritated crew back onto the ship. A single word rose like a wave through the market: *infected*.

People in the market were beginning to point and murmur. Cayo caught a glimpse of yellow cloth as the sailors tried to get past the soldiers, their shouts escalating to a fevered pitch.

Then a shot rang out.

The effect was instantaneous: The market erupted into chaos, peddlers and shoppers alike screaming from the noise and making a mad dash for the city proper. Cayo leaped out of the way, barricading himself behind Victor's stall and trying to see what had happened.

One of the infected crewmembers had shot at a naval officer and made a run for it. The officers brandished their bayonets, yelling for the crew to get back on board while a couple branched off to chase after the runaway.

"He'll get everyone sick!" Victor was yelling in Soléne, covering his mouth with his sleeve. "Kill him before it's too late!"

The runaway crewmember dove into the crowd, making it harder for the officers to shoot at him. He shoved others out of his way, making them yell and brush at their bodies as if he'd poured ants over them. Carts and stalls were knocked aside and overturned as the crowd fanned out to avoid him, pressing Cayo and Victor up against the nearest building.

Cayo grunted as an elbow dug into his stomach, the smell of terrified people sharp and pungent over the fish. There was a gunshot, two, then more yelling from the docks.

"They got him!" people were crying.

Cayo could barely breathe in the crush of people. All he could do was keep his back to the wall and follow the stream as officers ordered everyone out of the market, heart thundering in the midst of the confusion.

When he finally made it out of the market, he had to keep following the others or else risk getting trampled. As soon as the streets broadened, he stumbled into the nearest alleyway and retched, nearly tossing up his puny breakfast of seed biscuits.

They had killed that man just for being sick.

How long would it be until they started doing the same for every other infected citizen?

Cayo shook so hard he could barely walk. He took a moment to collect himself, to breathe steadily in and out, before heading back to the apartment. There was no use finding Victor, not after what had just happened.

Although no alcohol was in his system, he found himself weaving anyway, as if the ground refused to stay still. The sunlight seared into his skull, his stomach cramping painfully. A thread of panic laced through the streets as the news trailed after him, and he saw more officers running toward the market.

He finally made it back to the apartment. His legs nearly gave out under him, and he had to lean against the wall a moment. "Damn it," he whispered. "Damn it...."

He was cold and he was frightened, and more than anything he just wanted someone to be near him, to tell him things would be all right. He thought of Amaya and his yearning nearly choked him.

But he couldn't forget the look of hurt and betrayal on her face. The hateful words he'd said had come pouring from some diseased pocket of his mind, an angry boil festering in his heart. Perhaps he hadn't actually forgiven her yet. Maybe he never would.

She certainly wouldn't forgive him after that.

Taking a deep breath, he opened the door and stepped inside. There was no sign of Amaya, but Liesl and Deadshot and Avi were sharing a pot of tea at the table.

"What in the hells happened to you?" Avi demanded.

"There was..." He pressed a hand to his clammy forehead. "At the harbor. They..."

But before Cayo could explain, to put the horror into words, loud footsteps thundered up the stairs. The three at the table tensed, Deadshot reaching for a pistol as the front door to the apartment banged open. Remy, disheveled and out of breath, hurried inside as Liesl stood.

"What's happened?" Liesl demanded. "Does the navy know what we did last night?"

"No—it's—" He leaned his hands on his knees, too winded to speak. A bedroom door opened and Amaya rushed out.

"Remy!" She took his arm, gripping a little too tight. "What's wrong?"

"Is it about the market?" Cayo cut in.

"What happened at the market? I was at the billet, I— Cayo, you have to go to the hospital. *Now.*"

An unpleasant jolt shot down into his stomach. "Why?"

"I got a note from Mother Hilas to find you immediately." Remy swallowed again, his eyes shining. "Soria. She—"

Cayo didn't wait to hear the rest. He shoved past Remy, out the door, down the stairs. His shakiness dissolved in a wave of adrenaline as he ran full tilt toward the hospital, following the scent of that cloying incense. He barely noticed the footfalls behind him, one or possibly more of the others chasing after.

He kept hearing the memory of gunshots in his head, that loud, lethal echo.

His mind was a constant mantra of *no, no, no* as he ran, pushing past the burning in his legs and lungs as he barreled down the incense-choked street and through the hospital doors. An administrative clerk jolted awake at her desk as he sped past, through the beds and the confused nurses.

*No, no, no.*

He barged into Soria's room and nearly toppled to the floor. Mother Hilas and another nurse were inside, their words quick and clipped as they loomed over Soria's bed.

"Move," he tried to say, but it only came out as a gasp. Mother Hilas turned and saw him, her lips drawn into a thin line.

"Mr. Lin—"

He reached the bed, nearly fell on top of it. Soria was struggling for breath, her inhalations weak and raspy, her eyes closed and sunken in her face. The gray had spread even more across her throat, like a possession.

"I'm afraid she's gone into a kind of shock." Mother Hilas exchanged a glance with the other nurse, who shook her head. "This usually happens when a patient either breaks the fever or..." She sighed. "We will monitor her, of course, but I'm afraid there's nothing else we can do now."

Cayo couldn't even understand the words. He just kept staring at Soria, at the struggle of her rising and falling chest, the faint sheen of sweat at her hairline.

The floorboards creaked behind him. "Can you give him some privacy?" Amaya.

"Of course." Mother Hilas touched his arm and left, but the other nurse stayed just outside the door.

Cayo crawled onto the bed beside his sister. Soria had done this when she was very little, deciding to come to him rather than their parents if she'd had a nightmare. He would put on plays with her toy animals, making her laugh, putting her back at ease.

But now there was nothing he could do. He gently wrapped his arms around her, brushing her hair back, feeling just how warm her body had become.

"Soria," he whispered. "I'm here." His words caught. He traced his fingers against the edges of the gray markings, wanting to soothe them away, to burn out the infection inside her.

He thought he saw her eyelids flutter, her lips twitch. As if she wanted to speak and couldn't.

"You can do this," he whispered, barely aware of the tears that fell against her cheek. Faintly he remembered his mother's nightgown dampened with his tears as she lay just like this, years ago, before she'd been lost to them forever. "You can fight this. If you do, I'll get you a new dress. A whole wardrobe of them. Just...please..."

He put his forehead against hers, whispering encouragement, whispering words of love, as if that could make up for the lack of proper medicine, make up for the pain their father had inflicted upon them.

He didn't know how long he lay there with her, how many memories and stories he told to give her company, to let her know she wasn't alone. The nurse came in to check on her once or twice, but he barely noticed. His lips were dry and chapped, his voice hoarse, but he didn't stop. He didn't dare stop.

Soria's breathing grew quicker. Shallower. Her body began to lose its burning warmth, began to shake.

"Hey," Cayo said, holding her face in his hands. "Soria, breathe. Soria, listen to me—just breathe, all right?"

He couldn't help her. He couldn't do anything. He was useless.

She shook and choked, the pulse at her neck jumping frantically, her fingers twitching, her limbs seizing—

And then she lay still.

It wasn't the slow transition from awake to asleep, but rather a violent letting go, all her strings cut at once. Her head lolled against his hand, her lips parted even though no breath came in or out.

At first all he could do was stare. He brushed a thumb against her cheek, waiting for her to look at him, to perhaps sigh or ask for water.

The world compressed around him. A single span of a heartbeat encased in glass, an impossible, intolerable thing, best not looked at directly. It had lingered in the corner of his eye, and he had kept his head turned away, refusing to acknowledge its existence. Because it wasn't *real*. It wasn't possible.

But then the glass shattered.

The impossible became real.

His sister was dead.

## 23

*When I think back to those black skies and gray waters,*
*I can't help but regret. He's down there in those depths,*
*waiting for him. I will join him soon.*
—DIARY OF AN UNKNOWN SAILOR, FOUND ON AN EMPTY BOAT

The scream that tore from Cayo's throat split Amaya in half.

She took a step back, pressing a hand against her mouth as if to stifle her own scream. It had happened so quickly, almost too quickly to process, but there could only be one reason Soria had grown so still.

She was gone.

The nurse rushed into the room, but there was no point. Cayo clung to Soria and buried his face against her neck, back heaving as he wept, refusing to let the nurse or Mother Hilas get near her.

Mercado had done this. Soria had been poisoned by her own father, left to die in a foreign country without any promise of a cure.

Amaya balled her hands into fists, baring her teeth against the sobs climbing up her throat. She would make him pay, him and Boon both. She wouldn't rest until their blood coated her blades.

But even that wouldn't bring Soria back.

"Mr. Lin, please," Mother Hilas was saying, trying to draw Cayo away.

"Don't touch me!" he yelled, clinging tighter to Soria's body. "Don't touch her!"

The nurses turned to Amaya, despairing. She felt weak and insubstantial as she approached the bed, her throat tightening painfully at the sight of Soria's still face.

"Cayo," she whispered, resting trembling hands on his back. He shook violently, each sob like a drum being struck in his chest and vibrating against her palms. She pressed her forehead to the space between his shoulder blades, tangled her fingers in his shirt. "Cayo, you have to let her go."

She couldn't tell if he'd heard her, if any of it had gotten past the thick shell of his grief. She was again standing on the deck of the *Brackish*, being told by Zharo that her mother was dead. That there would be no one greeting her in Moray. That her family was gone, with no one left to love her.

Her tears dampened Cayo's shirt as she took an uneven breath. Amaya reached for Soria's neck, just to be sure. No pulse. Nothing.

Gone.

She turned back to the nurses. "Can you just...give him a moment?"

Mother Hilas nodded and they left to wait outside the room. Amaya's legs gave out and she sat on the edge of the bed, mindlessly rubbing Cayo's back as he expelled the same furious heartache she herself had been through.

Cayo would never forgive his father after this, and she doubted Kamon Mercado would find any worth in that forgiveness anyway.

The two of them were alone now in this desperate, greedy world. At last, they had something in common.

The apartment was hushed the next day, the table coated with gray morning light. It swept over the chipped mugs and the open container of biscuits, which they vaguely nibbled on.

Amaya hadn't slept. She had stayed at the hospital with Cayo, sitting by his side while Mother Hilas helped them figure out what came next. There had been talk of cremation, of burial, of shipping the body back to Moray. Cayo had been blank faced and silent, staring at nothing.

"You have to choose one," Amaya had murmured.

Cayo had roused himself slightly, lips parted, but nothing had come out. His breath had hitched, his red-rimmed eyes filling with overwhelmed tears.

He should have never had to make a decision like this. Amaya hadn't even gotten the choice—didn't know what had become of her mother's body. The thought punched a hole through her, too dangerous to come near lest she risk being sucked into it.

But she knew which one she would have chosen. What the common practice was in Moray.

"Cremation?" she guessed.

Cayo had nodded, and he had signed the papers, and he had left to tell his sister goodbye for the last time.

"You can come back tomorrow to pick up the ashes," Mother

Hilas had told her, placing a hand on her shoulder. "I'm truly sorry for your loss."

Amaya appreciated the woman's efficiency. She had no doubt been through this too many times to count. But the pain in her eyes was not faked in the slightest. So Amaya had thanked her, and she had brought Cayo home, where he had taken to his bed without a word.

"I don't know what to do," Amaya whispered now. Liesl was gazing at the tabletop, holding hands with Deadshot. Avi sat with his hand around his mug, but he hadn't taken a single sip. "What... What do we do?"

Liesl stirred. "We continue with the plan. We take the counterfeits out of circulation. We try to prevent more deaths."

"But Cayo..."

Avi sighed, rubbing a spot near his hip. "He won't be able to help us in this state. Nor would we want to force him. Maybe it's time for him to go back to Moray."

"On his own? Where his father is?"

"I doubt he'll want to stick around here. Besides, he'll likely want to scatter his sister's ashes at home."

They fell back into silence. Amaya couldn't take any more of it and decided to spend the rest of the day wandering the city, letting the wind nip at her skin and remind her she was alive. That she *felt*, and that it was a welcome and terrible burden.

She even went by Boon's hut again, but it was still abandoned, and there were whispers that the Ghost Ship had mysteriously vanished from the harbor.

When she came back to the apartment, evening had fallen over Baleine. She opened the door to the boys' bedroom, wanting to check if Cayo had eaten anything.

But he wasn't there.

Her heart gave a sudden *thud*. Was he at the hospital? Had he gone back to the Casino District? She checked his side of the bedroom and found his pistol; he wouldn't have gone far without that.

She ran up to the roof, but it was empty. She scoured every floor of the tenement building, praying he was here somewhere, that he hadn't gone off unarmed to embrace a senseless night of debauchery to staunch the pain.

Then she remembered: the building had a basement.

She heaved the old, heavy door open and stumbled into the darkness. There was a lantern lit in the far corner, casting tendrils of orange light across the walls, piles of covered and broken furniture, and a floor in dire need of sweeping.

Cayo sat at the base of the wall with a bottle in his lap. Amaya held back a curse as she carefully approached him, as if he had turned into a feral tiger. But he barely acknowledged her. He barely did anything but sit there, cradling a bottle of what looked like lupseh.

"Cayo," she said softly.

His eyelashes twitched slightly. It was then she noticed the bottle wasn't open—none of it had been drunk. Relief washing over her, Amaya crouched before him and put a hand on the bottle.

"May I have this?" she asked.

He let go, and she moved the lupseh several feet away. Then she sat beside him, surrounded by the basement's damp, musty smell.

The lantern caressed Cayo's face with highlights of gold. His hair was limp and unwashed, his eyes red and swollen, but there was something untouchable about him, as if he had stepped out of a painting. Perhaps it was how he sat so still, the expression on his face unfaltering.

"You didn't drink anything," Amaya said. It was better than saying *I'm sorry* again.

Cayo took in a breath, let it out slowly. "What's the point?"

Amaya chewed her lower lip. She had woken up crying several times during the months she'd trained with Boon and the Landless, after dreams about her mother welcoming her home, or of Amaya finding her body washed up onshore. There were hardly any words to describe the unbearable truth of humanity—that people were there and then gone, and that you had to live on in the aftermath. That life would never be the same, and that's just how it was.

Unfair. Uncompromising. Unforgiving.

Liesl had tried to talk to Amaya about it, but Amaya had never been ready. Cayo was far from ready; only time would help with that.

So instead, she spoke of something else.

"We need to talk about what happened at the casino," she said.

Cayo actually turned to look at her, only a hint of confusion in his pain-deadened eyes.

"I'm sorry that I hit you." She twisted her mother's jade ring on her finger. "I'm sorry I wasn't there in time. That you were left to feel like you were on your own, or that I didn't care. I did. But I..."

Like on the rooftop with Avi, the words stuck in her throat, refusing to be voiced. How could she possibly tell him who Boon truly was when she hadn't even come to terms with it? When the pain was still so sharp she risked getting cut with one wrong move?

Cayo was silent for so long she thought he wouldn't bother to respond. When he finally spoke, his voice was low and hoarse.

"I shouldn't have said those things to you. I was upset. I..." He closed his eyes, tears rolling down his face. "I didn't realize how much I needed you."

The words were like a fishhook through her stomach. Amaya pulled her knees up to her chest.

"I understand why you did it," she whispered. "Everything you did was for Soria. I know how much she means—meant—to you." She rubbed at her damp eyes. "It's the only way you knew how to fight, so you fought. And you lost. I understand."

He exhaled a breathy, mirthless laugh. "I fought for her, and I lost her." A pained sound escaped his throat as he leaned his head back against the wall. "Now there's nothing."

"It feels that way now, but it won't forever." Amaya interlaced her fingers, clasping her hands so tight her knuckles paled. "There's still good to do in this world, Cayo. We can get justice for Soria."

"How?" The word was flat, almost cruel. "You saw what happens when I try to help."

"You're not the only one at fault here. I left you on your own. I used you again. Because you're right—I want to make up for my mistakes, and I thought that tournament was the way to do it. But I was wrong."

She had been going over their argument since that night, all the horrible words and accusations, the way causing him pain felt as if it were the only way to siphon off her own.

But she didn't want him to be in pain. If she could touch the bruise at his jaw and make it disappear, she would. If she could hold Soria's ashes and turn her back into a living girl, she would.

Cayo was looking at her now, studying her. She stared back.

"I still shouldn't have said what I did," he mumbled. "I'm sorry."

She twisted her mother's ring. "You were upset. I get it."

They sat in silence for a few moments, their heads turned toward each other, not looking at each other.

"Why is this so difficult?" Cayo whispered.

Tears had begun trailing silently down his cheeks again. He closed his eyes tight, face crumpling as the grief took over. Amaya remembered it always being heaviest at night, like a fever, or the ocean's tide.

He sobbed quietly, and she moved closer. She recalled the way her parents had once held her, wrapping her in their arms, shielding her from the world. Cayo's head dropped to her shoulder, and she curled an arm around him. Refusing to let anything near. Guarding him from whatever sought to do him harm.

She couldn't protect him from herself, but maybe she didn't need to anymore.

When they returned to the apartment, Amaya wasn't surprised to find Remy inside.

"I'm so sorry," Remy said. "I know that's not enough, but I am."

Cayo regarded him wearily. "Thank you. For telling me."

Remy nodded. "I wish things had gone differently. That the medicine had..." He sighed and ran a hand through his hair.

"It's not your fault."

"Has something happened?" Amaya asked to shift the focus away from Cayo.

"I used the information Liesl gave me about Francis Florimond as an anonymous tip. His shop was raided earlier today. They found letters implicating Kamon Mercado and the Benefactor, as well as a bunch of brinies, but that's where the trail goes cold again. We still don't know who the Benefactor is, and now Florimond's taken off, so we can't get more information out of him."

Amaya avoided meeting eyes with the others. Remy didn't have to know that Florimond had taken his own life.

"Deirdre—" Amaya started, but Liesl waved a hand through the air.

"I don't think she's the Benefactor," Liesl said. It sounded like it pained her to admit. "There's too much conflicting evidence."

Liesl spared a glance at Cayo. "Something has to change. The longer we're here, the deeper Moray falls into debt. The fever is rampaging worse than it was before, causing panic like what happened at the market yesterday, and Moray is practically hemorrhaging money."

Remy nodded. "And like the sharks they are, the Sun Empire's scented the blood. There have been reports of their ships near Crescent Bay. They're scouting Moray's waters and the land borders to determine if and when they can descend."

Amaya swore. "What do you think will happen?"

"I overheard some of the officers discussing it." Remy drummed his fingers against the table. "If this continues, both empires could make their bid for Moray, and the city will become a war zone. If ash fever continues to spread in the Rain Empire, then it's only a matter of time until it begins to fall as well. And there's no telling what sides Rehan and Khari will take, or if the fever will make its way to the Sun Empire."

Liesl began to pace slowly. Deadshot kept a hand on one of her pistols, as if to draw comfort from it. Avi merely stared at the floor.

"Any leads we've gotten about the Benefactor have now gone cold," Remy went on. "Whoever this person is, whether it's Deirdre or Florimond, they're clever enough to erase their trail completely. Which means we need to turn our focus elsewhere."

While the others argued over what the next step would be, Amaya slunk back to her room. Florimond had killed himself. Boon was gone again. Deirdre was a dead end. Soria had succumbed to the fever before a cure could be found.

What good had she done here? Had she hindered more than she had helped?

*I helped set the debtors on the* Silver Star *free,* she thought. *I helped Liesl save her sister.* If nothing else, that had been worth it. It had been worth it to use her skills to help others, to put aside her vengeance for once and focus instead on improving others' lives.

Amaya worried her father's papers out from under her pallet. She thought back to the way Boon had stared at her in that rundown hut, guilt and disgrace in his dark eyes.

There was so much he hadn't told her. So much her own mother had never told her.

*My greatest treasures in this life lie with my wife and my daughter.*

The breath caught in Amaya's throat.

The page crumpled in her hand as she hurried back to the others. They stopped talking as she made her way to the table.

"My mother knew alchemy," she said. "And I think she knew something about the counterfeits."

Liesl frowned. "How do you know she was an alchemist?"

"Boon told me," Avi said. "He knew Amaya's mother. But what makes you think she knew about the counterfeits?"

Amaya placed the papers on the table. Liesl read them as Remy's eyes tightened in recognition. "My father had a Widow Vault, right? I think...I think my mother had one, too."

Liesl looked up from the paper. "I thought your family didn't have the money for that?"

"I thought so, too." Amaya swallowed past her tight throat. "But my parents hid things from me. A lot of things. And I think she hid whatever wealth we had in another Vault, one not even Mercado knew about. If she really was an alchemist who helped my—helped Boon, it's possible she may have hidden something related to the counterfeits in there."

"Like a cure?"

"I'm not sure. But it's the only thing I can think of that she'd want to hide."

"That's a pretty big leap," Deadshot said.

"It is. I don't even know if it's true. But we can't continue to stay in Baleine." Amaya glanced at Cayo, his face lined with exhaustion and heartache, as if he had aged years in just one night. "The trail's gone cold here. We need to get back to Moray."

Liesl nodded. "I agree. We've done all we can here."

"But what if there's more we can dig up on Deirdre?" Deadshot asked.

"Well," Avi said, scratching his chin, "I'll be staying behind, so I can keep looking into it."

"You're staying behind?" Liesl narrowed her eyes. "Why?"

Avi sighed. His gaze trained on the floor, he lifted the hem of his shirt. A small patch of gray stood out against the brown of his skin near his hip.

Liesl gaped at him. "Avi..."

"I can't go back to Moray with you," he said. "I'd only slow you down."

Deadshot stood, looking furious. "You *fool*. You should have told us the moment you noticed it!"

"I'm sorry. I didn't want to worry anyone."

"Of course we'd be worried!" Deadshot glared at him. "How long?"

Avi swallowed. "I first noticed the mark a couple of weeks ago."

Liesl still hadn't said anything else, her eyes too bright and her mouth pressed into a thin line. Avi came to sit beside her, putting a hand on her arm.

Amaya had to sit down as well, too dizzy to keep standing. Everything was strangling her, drowning her, pushing and pulling like she'd been dropped into a storm-tossed sea.

A hand touched her shoulder.

She looked up at Cayo. His expression was bleak yet determined.

"There's too many questions and not enough answers," she whispered.

He nodded slightly. "Then we'll find some answers. I have to bring Soria home." His voice broke, and he took a moment to compose himself. "I couldn't save her, but we can still save others. If that means finding the cure, we'll find it."

Remy came up on her other side. "And you won't be alone. I'm coming with you."

"But the navy—"

"Gave me a three-month suspension after the stunt I pulled to save your ass, remember?" He gave her a lopsided smile. "You owe me *two* pastries, by the way." He then nodded at Avi. "And I can secure you a place in the military hospital until we find a cure."

"I'd much appreciate that. Thank you."

Liesl caught Amaya's eye. "You helped me rescue my sister. Anything you need from me, I'll be there."

"And where Liesl goes, I go," Deadshot said.

"Then I suppose it's settled," Remy said. "At dawn, we leave for Moray."

Amaya took a deep breath. Moray. Home. The place where she had lost so much.

She was terrified to learn what else she could lose.

## 24

*Though he nearly fell off the mountain, the magician*
*clung to it with all his strength. Inch by inch, step by step,*
*he ascended until he finally reached the stars. They cast*
*him in a cold light, demanded what he wanted of their*
*time. But he was so chilled, so tired, so defeated by the*
*mountain that all he could do was sit and weep, his tears*
*sprouting into white blossoms where they fell.*
—"NERALIA OF THE CLOUDS," AN ORAL STORY ORIGINATING FROM
THE LEDE ISLANDS

As the *Marionette* swayed beneath him, Cayo stared at the wooden ceiling of his cabin and wondered if his mother had lied to him.

When he was young, she would point up to the constellations and trace the familiar shape of a crown, the sign of Luck, the sign he had been born under.

"He who is lucky is a king," she had told him.

But Cayo was a pauper left to starve in the ruins of his kingdom. Perhaps he deserved to be so unlucky, but Soria hadn't. There was so much she had wanted to see and do. So much time now robbed from her, and from him.

*Nothing could stay; everything was temporary.*

That was something else his mother had said, and it rang truer to him now than it ever had before. They were returning to Moray, but there was nothing left for him there. Only memories and rage and regret.

Was this how Amaya felt when she'd returned all those months ago?

As if the thought had summoned her, there was a quiet knock on the door before it opened. He didn't have to look to know it was her.

"We're nearly at the docks," she said. "Remy says to get ready."

But he didn't move. He remained spread out on his back, staring at the ceiling, half wishing she would leave and half wishing she would stay. Everyone had given him a wide berth on the week-long voyage, almost as if he, too, were infected with a disease they were terrified of catching. But Liesl had explained they were merely giving him space to grieve, to take as much time as he needed before he welcomed company again. They all understood what it meant to lose something bigger than yourself.

Amaya let out a soft sigh. She closed the door behind her and sat on the thick wooden bed frame.

"Are you going to tell your father about Soria?" she asked.

His fingers twitched. The answer to that question kept changing. On one hand, Kamon deserved to be left in the dark, just as he had left Cayo and Soria for so long. On the other hand, he also deserved to know what had happened to his daughter.

What exactly he had done to her.

Cayo didn't answer, because he still didn't know. Nothing mattered the way it had before, when everything had been all desperation and reckless planning. Now he didn't particularly care what happened to him or his father, so long as they put an end to the fever.

Amaya hesitated, her body tensing slightly. Then, to his surprise, she spread out beside him on the bed. He moved over to give her room, but otherwise didn't acknowledge it. She joined him in staring at the ceiling, hands resting on her stomach. His ears crowded with the sound of their breaths mingling together.

Eventually she sighed again. "After my father died, we got condolences, but they always seemed empty to me. I felt like only my mother could understand, because she was going through the same loss, you know? We found comfort in each other." Her fingers curled inward. "And then I was taken, and while I was gone, she died. And I didn't get the chance to mourn her properly."

Amaya shifted onto her side, facing him. Slowly, he did the same.

"Words don't really mean anything, do they?" she asked softly. "Nothing can bring her back."

Cayo forced himself to meet her dark eyes. She knew loss the way he did, was still mired in her own. It made what he'd said to her before so much worse.

"It doesn't get easier," she went on. "Not really. It just turns into days where the pain hibernates and days when the pain is so bad you can't stand it." She blinked back tears. "I'm sorry if you wanted to believe something different."

"No," he said, his voice hushed. "It...helps. To not be lied to." He thought back to his mother's last days, the fury he'd felt at the unfairness of her weakening body. "I did want to believe something different, back then. When my mother passed, I kept the pain close to me, convinced myself it would go away eventually. It did, but only when I could distract myself from it."

"In the Vice Sector," Amaya guessed.

He nodded against the pillow. The two of them were quiet a long moment, a hint of Amaya's breath on his chin. Some of her hair had fallen across her cheek, frizzing and curled from the sea wind. Although Cayo's body felt heavy and burdensome, he lifted a hand to tuck the strand behind her ear, fingertips grazing her skin. She shivered, and his nerves reawakened in response.

He dared to rest his hand against her cheek. Her skin was dry, but she was warm, and it was intoxicating. Cayo had been cold every day since leaving Baleine. The heat of her body was a welcome beacon, a respite from the dark.

She must have felt him trembling, since she moved closer. Cayo pressed his forehead to hers, and the heat made him sigh in relief, made his body relax for the first time in days. His fingers had slipped into her hair, his thumb idly brushing the side of her jaw. She rested a hand on his shoulder, as if needing to anchor herself to him in some way.

His heartbeat was slow and even, but hers was fast, fluttering like a startled bird. His fingers trailed down her neck to feel her pulse, which jumped as if eager to meet his touch. Something dark and hungry opened in the pit of his stomach.

Nothing about this was right. Nothing about it was easy.

Maybe that was why he wanted it.

He carefully pressed his lips to her cheek. She stiffened, and he eased back, wondering if he had crossed a line. But her eyes were glassy, her lips parted, and she didn't run to the door. Instead, she slowly gripped his chin in her hand and brought his lips down to hers.

They were warm like the rest of her, feeding the hunger inside him, teaching him a new form of desperation. She was hesitant, unsure, so he let her be in control even as his hands ached to touch her. She kissed him again, her hand traveling to the nape of his neck and tangling in his hair. When she opened her mouth, it was like a prayer being answered. Cayo only gradually deepened the kiss with small, teasing swipes of his tongue, the hairs along his arms standing on end at the soft sound she made.

His veins were electric, his blood singing. He wanted to press his body against hers, to caress her skin with his lips, to make her cry out because of what he was doing to her.

Instead, he pulled himself back, panting for breath. Amaya's hair was mussed, her lips red from his. The hunger in him grew deeper, growling for more, but he had to let it starve.

He didn't want Amaya to regret any of this.

She avoided his gaze, steadying her breath as she tried to smooth her hair down. Cayo opened his mouth to speak, but there was nothing to say. Perhaps it would be better that way—to let the moment exist silently, being whatever the both of them needed it to be. A moment of comfort. A moment of distraction.

There was a call from above deck. Amaya slid off the bed, threw him one last glance, and left the cabin to help prepare for docking.

Cayo stayed behind and let the cold crawl back into his bones.

It took him three tries to lift the wooden box.

Not because it was heavy, or even all that large, but because the enormity of what it contained was almost too much for him to carry.

He had left it in the room Soria had used on their trip to the Rain Empire, but he couldn't avoid it any longer. Cayo carefully wrapped the box containing his sister's ashes in one of his old shirts, then tucked it securely into the pack Remy had given him. He stood there a moment, hollowed out just from the simple act.

But the others were waiting. He gathered himself and joined them above deck, the pack resting snugly against his back.

Moray lay spread out before them. Cayo held on to the railing as he took it in: the buildings rising up from the harbor; the swaying palms; the warm, moist air that smelled of salt and sun. Cliffs rose to their right, manors and estates dotting their summits like pretty cakes on stands. Cayo spotted a glimpse of his own through the thick foliage, wringing his heart with a sick kind of joy.

He had once stood on its balconies staring out at the sea, wondering where he would go, whom he would sail with, what he would discover. Daydreaming about coming home triumphant and sated, at least until the next adventure.

But that wasn't his home. Not anymore.

A ring of ships studded the outer edge of Crescent Bay. "What are those?"

"Sentries," Remy answered. "I had a feeling they'd be here, so I exchanged the colors." He pointed at the pennants flapping above the *Marionette*'s sails, which sported Moray colors instead of those of the Rain Empire. "They'll be checking for ash fever."

"And that's not all they're on the lookout for," Liesl said, jerking a thumb over her shoulder toward the west. "Some Sun Empire ships are lingering nearby. Probably waiting for the city to fall before they fight for scraps."

Sure enough, they were forced to stop and be boarded by a trio of guards who searched the ship from top to bottom. While he was inspected for ash fever, Remy made up some story about how they were migrants from a former colony. Cayo gritted his teeth as he was poked and prodded, until eventually they were all cleared.

"Once you enter the city, you won't be allowed to leave until the threat of the fever has passed," one of the guards warned them. "We can't risk it spreading any farther."

"We understand," Remy said.

Past the checkpoint, they all breathed a little easier. Amaya gazed out at the city, and Cayo tried not to think about what they'd just done. Similarly, she seemed to be avoiding looking in his direction; or perhaps she was caught up in nostalgia.

Then she straightened. "I can't believe it."

"What is it?" Liesl came to stand beside her. "Oh."

It took Cayo a moment to realize what they were looking at. In the harbor, the *Brackish* sat on the water, neglected and abandoned.

"It's still here," Amaya said, stunned. "I thought the Bugs would've taken it."

"Do you think...?" Deadshot began.

"Boon," Liesl finished for her.

"He could be hiding there," Remy agreed, narrowing his eyes. "We should at least check."

Amaya shifted at this, a tightness passing across her face.

Once the *Marionette* was docked, they made their way over to the *Brackish*. Its purple sails were gone, but the designs along the hull were still intact.

"The gangplank's out," Deadshot observed.

Frowning, Amaya led the way up to the ship's deck. Cayo followed after her, hoping they *would* find Boon here, that he could formally introduce him to Jazelle. The pistol's weight was as heavy against his hip as Soria's ashes were against his back.

But before they could start searching, the weight of another pistol nudged the back of his skull.

"What in the hells are you doing on our ship?"

## 25

*Away, away, the gods will play,*
*Leave them an offering they must repay.*

—CHILDREN'S RHYME FROM KHARI

Amaya heard the click of a gun and spun around, hand darting for her nearest knife.

Then she froze, taking in the young man holding the pistol to Cayo's head.

"Cicada?"

Cicada's eyes widened, and he lowered the gun. Amaya ran for him, and he laughed as he swept her off her feet, spinning her around in a circle.

"Silverfish! Thought we'd never see you again!" He set her down and turned to the companionway. "S'all right, it's only Silverfish!"

A few more familiar faces crept onto the deck, Water Bugs she had known from her time on board the *Brackish*. Matthieu, who'd been called Weevil. Jiana, who'd been Louse.

And Fera. Beetle. The little girl broke out into a wide grin when she spotted Amaya, showing off a couple of missing milk teeth. She crashed into Amaya's legs, wrapping her stick thin arms around her.

"Amaya! You're back!"

Amaya held her in a daze, staring at the Bugs. There were six of them, their ages ranging from Fera's eight to Cicada's eighteen. They stared at her in awe and disbelief, as if she were a myth come to life.

The last time she had seen them, Countess Yamaa's estate had been broken into by Boon's hired men. Nian and Cricket had both been killed in the scuffle. Amaya could still clearly envision Nian's small, crumpled body lying in his own blood.

Amaya sank to her knees before Fera.

"What are you all doing here?" Amaya demanded, speaking to Fera although the question was directed at Cicada.

"Ran into some complications." Cicada nodded in greeting to Liesl and Deadshot as they boarded the ship, looking just as stunned as Amaya. "All the other Bugs went home, but these ones...well, they didn't want to."

Matthieu shoved his hands into the pockets of his ratty trousers. "My da sold me. I don't wanna go back just to be sold again like cattle." There was some murmuring of agreement among the others.

Amaya couldn't blame them. But as Fera's lower lip trembled, Amaya knew it hadn't been an easy decision to make. To completely turn your back on your family when you were so young and helpless...

"And besides, the fever's been spreading like wildfire," Cicada continued, gazing solemnly at the city's skyline. "No one's allowed to take their ships outside Crescent Bay, so we couldn't leave now even if we wanted to. Not to mention the curfew and how the city guard's been crawling through Moray like agitated ants. Hope you don't mind we commandeered your ship, Silver—er, Amaya."

"Of course I don't mind."

Fera had begun to sniffle, rubbing at her eyes. To Amaya's surprise, Cayo crouched beside the girl and took a copper coin from his pocket. He held it up to catch her attention, then rolled the coin across the backs of his knuckles in one fluid motion. Fera stared as he walked the coin back and forth, then flipped it into the air with his thumb. He caught it, turned his hand over, and opened it to reveal that the coin was gone.

The girl gasped and grabbed his hand with both of hers. "Where did it go?"

"I can't tell you. It's magic." He winked at her, and Fera giggled. Amaya smiled even as her chest tightened painfully, wondering if Cayo used to do this for Soria.

But the sight of the coin also caused a sinking in her gut. Standing, Amaya turned to Cicada and lowered her voice.

"Boon's coins," she said. "Did you use it to send the children home?"

To her immense relief, he shook his head. "Didn't want to get in trouble or make a trail. We ended up tossing all the coins into the sea."

Amaya gripped his shoulder, weak with gratitude. When she had told him to use that fake gold, she hadn't known it was the cause of ash fever. "Then what did you use for money?"

"We sold all the countess's fancy dresses and jewelry and shoes. And the estate." He grinned. "Got a real nice sum for it, too. Trouble is we can't do much with it until this fever goes packing and we can leave."

"That's why we're here," Amaya said. "To hopefully find a cure."

"And find Boon," Liesl added.

"Boon?" Cicada's expression darkened. "The man who attacked the estate? We know where he is."

Amaya's heart tripped. "You do? How?"

Cicada glanced between them, a little uneasy. "He came by the *Brackish* and snuck on board a couple of days ago, but we drove him away. Matthieu followed him back to his hideout near the edge of the city, in the Shanty Sector."

"So he is in the city," Cayo growled. He met Amaya's gaze, the hardened look on his face no doubt a mirror to her own. "Let's go find him."

Amaya's fingers rested on the hilt of her knife. A knife that Boon had given her. A knife she had nearly driven across her father's neck.

She thought of Nian's and Cricket's bodies, the plague of the fever spreading through Moray and Baleine, Soria's ashes.

Boon would need to pay...but first, she had to speak with him again. One last time.

But even as they turned back toward the gangplank, Remy stood in their way.

"Have you forgotten the main reason we're here?" he asked. "Going after Boon now will be too risky. Our main focus should be breaking into the Vault and finding out if Amaya's mother hid any notes about the counterfeits. We're looking for a cure, not revenge."

"Why not both?" Liesl demanded.

"Both sounds good," Deadshot agreed, hand on her pistol.

Remy sighed. "We can discuss it later. Right now, we need to get into the city and start planning."

Amaya nodded to Cicada and the other Bugs. "I'll be back to check on you in a few days. Stay out of the city, all right?"

Fera hugged her again, and the others waved goodbye. As Amaya walked down the gangplank, she stared at the ship where she'd spent seven miserable years, finding it grossly unfair that the other Bugs had been forced to hide here. Although it had been renovated, there was no scourging those memories from their minds.

Something caught her eye, and she stopped. She walked back up the gangplank and leaned forward, bracing her hand on the hull as water sloshed below her.

Beside a porthole halfway down the ship was a faint engraving. The Water Bugs had only ever been allowed off the ship when they needed to dive, so she had never had much of an opportunity to study the outside the same way as the inside.

The more she stared, the more she realized it looked familiar: a circle with a diamond surrounded by ivy. Where had she seen it before?

Liesl called her name, and it clicked—the *Silver Star*. Liesl's sister had been on a debtor ship with this same engraving on the side. André Basque's debtor ship.

Everything was hopelessly twisted together, and she was no closer to unraveling the truth. Amaya had spent the entire voyage hoping her mother didn't have a Vault, that she hadn't lied to her daughter. But now she hoped the opposite was true, only so they could finally get the answers they were owed.

# 26

*The Business Sector is where weak men go to feel
important. They have so little else in their lives that
the mere sight of gold-veined marble and the whisper
of investment is enough to feed their ambition for days
at a time.*

—A COMPLETE GUIDE TO MORAY'S SECTORS

We're not splitting up," Liesl said.

Cayo had had a feeling she would say that. "Do you want
help or not?"

"We have no idea who this contact of yours is. For all we know,
they could expose our true purpose here."

"Or she can give us access to the Widow Vaults."

Cayo knew it was risky to return to Nawarak. To walk into the
Port's Authority as if no time at all had passed since he'd last been

there, when he had turned in his own father. He had gone to the Vice Sector after, unable to come to terms with what he had done, needing to numb himself. The next morning, Boon had taken him and Soria hostage.

He couldn't dwell on it now. The body count from ash fever was climbing, and they had to do *something.*

Liesl crossed her arms and stared him down. The five of them were in a ramshackle inn, the cheapest—and sleaziest—place they could find to lay low. Amaya was idly twirling a knife in her hands, Remy pacing, Deadshot leaning by the window to keep an eye on the street. Cayo found himself missing Avi's casual smirk.

"How many infected people do you think we passed on our way here?" Cayo demanded. Although they had seen sick people in the streets of Baleine, it hadn't fully prepared him for the sight of Moray. There were corpses huddled at the bases of walls, men in masks and gloves gathering them onto carts to burn their bodies. The sound of coughing seemed to be everywhere, and tattered white mourning flags waved from countless windows—not just for the prince, but for loved ones. The city was quieter than Cayo had ever heard it.

"This contact," Amaya said. "Is it Romara?"

The suspicion in her voice made him bristle. "No. I'm not going to *her* for help. She always has her own agenda."

"Then who is it?" Liesl demanded.

He sighed and raked a hand through his hair. "A family friend in the Port's Authority." Liesl opened her mouth, but he quickly spoke over her. "I won't tell her about any of you. I just need to know if she can get us access to the Vaults. It's worth trying, isn't it?"

"He's right," Remy said. "If there's any lead we can use, we ought to use it."

"How close of a friend is she?" Liesl asked.

Cayo shrugged. "Her mother was my mother's best friend. We grew up together."

"That doesn't necessarily mean you're close."

"Just let the boy try," Deadshot spoke up, surprising him. Cayo nodded to her in gratitude, and she winked.

Liesl threw up her hands. "Fine. But if you're arrested or the Port's Authority comes to collect our Landless heads, it'll be on you."

"Noted." Cayo stood and hesitated as he reached for his pack. He should leave it here, but . . .

"We'll watch over her," Amaya said quietly.

Their eyes connected, hers dark and steady. Something invisible stretched between them, a line pulled taut. He had held her on the ship, kissed her, but this was even more intimate—it was the beginning of trust, of handing over the last bit of himself that remained unbroken.

Cayo nodded and headed for the door, unable to say anything to her. He was afraid of what might come out if he tried.

The air smelled damp and musty, as if the city badly needed a wash. As Cayo roamed the streets he kept his eyes down, acutely aware of the shape of the pistol at his hip. Before, when his family had been wealthy and he had been able to wear finer clothes, he would notice people eyeing him as if determining whether or not he was worthy of robbing. Now he blended in with the rest of them, another citizen who had had too much taken away.

Was his father still in their manor? Did he stand at the top of the hill and look down at the diseased city he had helped ruin?

The Business Sector wasn't as crowded as Cayo was used to seeing it. People seemed to spend as little time on the streets as they could, rushing into or out of buildings or their carriages, covering their lower faces with masks and sleeves. He followed their example and slipped into the offices of the Port's Authority, the golden letters above the doors dull in the overcast light.

The wooden benches on either side of the receiving hall were full. Cayo spotted crying children, hollow-looking women, terrified men. Crime had likely gone up while the fever spread, thieves preying on unattended shops and abandoned homes.

"Fill out your name and take a seat," drawled the young man at the front desk, flipping a page of his book.

"I'm not here to report an incident," Cayo said. He was bemused by the sound of his own voice, the confidence that apparently came from having nothing left to lose. "I'm here to see Petty Officer Nawarak."

The young man looked up, blinking wearily. "You mean Lieutenant Nawarak?"

Cayo frowned in surprise. "I suppose I do. Tell her Cayo Mer... tell her Cayo wants to talk to her." He couldn't risk using his family name here, not when it was the equivalent of a red flag.

The clerk entered the offices and came back a moment later, gesturing for Cayo to walk through the doors. Usually the officers of the Port's Authority made all sorts of racket back here, but the din was more subdued today, the drone of a busy yet tired hive.

Nawarak waited for him at her desk. Her bluish-black hair was done up in a braid, and she wore a jerkin of boiled leather under the open jacket of her uniform. She crossed her arms and looked him up and down, a scowl on her round face.

"You disappear without a trace, and now you're back looking like a veritable urchin," she said. "Where in the hells did you go, Cayo? I went up to your family's manor and no one was there. Where's your father? How's Soria doing?"

He took in a breath to speak, but how could he tell her about all that had happened? Instead, he sat in the chair before her, bracing his elbows on his knees.

"I can't tell you," he said. "Not yet."

"What? Why?"

Because it was too much. Because it didn't matter. Because saying the words *Soria is dead* out loud would make it irrevocably true, like casting an unbreakable curse.

"You got a promotion," he said, deflecting her questions. "Congratulations, Lieutenant."

Her eyes narrowed. "You're acting strange. But thank you, I guess."

He glanced at the breast of her jacket, the silver bars denoting her new rank. "Is it because you've been working on the counterfeit case?" She had been on a task force until the threat of ash fever had reared its head.

"Not exactly. Although that's certainly been an interesting turn of events."

"I don't think interesting is the word I'd use. Have there been any more developments?"

"Most of it's coming from the casinos, which isn't a surprise. It spread through the lower classes like wildfire. We actually just got another report from the Rain Empire the other day." She leaned her arms on her desk. "They say the coating on the counterfeits contains some sort of virus? I don't know, I don't have the mind for science.

But the report said the coating can stay on people's skin for hours. If they come into contact with others with that shit still on them…"

Cayo swore under his breath. "So that's how it spread so much." It was all too easy to see the chain of infection now, the exchanging of coins between hands, the barest touch from one person to another.

His gaze went back to her silver bands. "If you're not on the counterfeit case anymore, then how exactly did this promotion come about?"

"What, don't think I have my merits?" She drummed her fingers on the arm of her chair—a tell. "You know we've got dirty officers, right?"

"Sure. What does that have to do with your promotion?"

"Because I caught the majority of them." She flashed him a grin. "Those officers were on the Slum King's payroll, did you know that? Double-crossing bastards. *Triple*-crossing even, considering some of them went behind Salvador's back, too. He wasn't too happy about that."

"How in the hells did you manage that?"

Nawarak lowered her voice. "Let's just say I have a contact who's very…influential."

Cold swept over him at the implication. He dug his fingers into his thigh, thinking of Jun Salvador, the Slum King, scheming behind his desk at the Scarlet Arc. How easy it would be for him to put someone as ambitious as Nawarak into his pocket for insurance.

He couldn't ask her for help with the Vaults. She was compromised.

"What's wrong?" she demanded as Cayo stood. "Cayo—"

He turned and fled. This entire city was rotten, molding from the inside out. Even the people with the best of intentions became corrupted by the merest whisper of power, of money.

God and her stars, he had been one of them.

He slipped into an alleyway and caught his breath, choking on the fumes of stale vomit. He couldn't go back to Nawarak, and he couldn't go back to the others and admit he'd failed. Again.

They had to find some way into those Vaults.

Cayo cursed and held his head in his hands, his heart speeding up the way it always did before he made a terrible decision. But what other choice did he have now?

Fighting against the tide of his better judgment, he turned like a compass pointing true north, following the well-worn path back to the Vice Sector.

Cayo expected to find Diamond Street emptier and quieter than it usually was, especially considering the curfew the authorities had put in place here. He did not expect to find it bustling with activity and merriment, as if the horror of the rest of the city were a door that could be easily closed and locked.

It wasn't even fully dark and the lanterns were already lit, hanging like fat, glowing apples above their heads. He stared at the people drinking and dancing and laughing as if nothing could touch them. Some chased one another with playful screams, and couples kissed in the open without shame. One girl even took off her top and spun it in the air above her head while others cheered and threw coins at her.

If anything, ash fever had turned the Vice Sector even more depraved.

Cayo numbly walked through it all, absorbed by the noise and the raucous movements around him. Someone tried to put a necklace of seashells around his neck, but he batted their arms away with a snarl.

"Just trying to give you a protective spell," slurred the young man as he bent to retrieve the necklace. "Asshole."

Cayo kept his head down until he found himself on the Gauntlet, the string of casinos and dens reserved for the more serious gamblers. The Slum King owned the biggest one: the Scarlet Arc, a beacon for felons and con artists who eventually became nothing more than lapdogs for Salvador.

He had never wanted to come here again. Had nightmares about walking through those red-painted doors and seeing the Slum King's scarred face. Salvador usually held a jar in those nightmares, Bas's eyes staring accusingly at him from within.

Cayo had turned in his father, exposing Mercado's dealings with the Slum King. If he were caught here, the Slum King would do a lot worse than pluck out his eyeballs.

He lingered outside the doors, and it was only then he noticed that the sign above him no longer read the Scarlet Arc.

*The Black Lily?* He frowned at the name; it didn't sound like the Slum King's style. Keeping a hand on Jazelle, he carefully slipped inside.

At first he thought he had the wrong place. Everything was... dark. No longer the malignant, dripping red of the Arc, but painted top to bottom with flat, oppressive *black*. Silver lanterns hung from the ceiling in a pale imitation of stars, and the walls sported strange, unnerving paintings of abstract shapes and haunting beasts.

The Slum King's regular crowd wasn't here. In their place was younger, fresher meat, gathered around the bar and the dice tables and even dancing to the music of a four-piece band in the corner. Cayo wandered farther inside, confusion overcoming his trepidation. Had Salvador decided to switch things up? Or had he moved the Arc and left this one for the newer recruits?

"Excuse me!"

Someone ran into him from behind, making him stumble. A bag fell from the person's arms, scattering the floor with mushrooms.

The young man cursed, crashed to his knees, and began shoving the mushrooms back into the bag. "Now I'll have to give these an extra hard scrubbing! She'll be so upset I'm late again...."

"Uh." Cayo looked around, wondering if someone, anyone, could tell him what exactly was going on. "What is this place?"

The young man blinked up at him. He was roughly Cayo's age, perhaps a little older, with a swoop of black hair and eyes so dark they appeared just as black in the dim lighting. His nose was crooked in an otherwise disturbingly symmetrical face.

"If you have to ask, perhaps you shouldn't be here." The young man hugged the bag of mushrooms to his chest, blowing a stray lock of hair off his face. "Now please get out of my way before I lose my job. Again."

"I—"

The young man hurried away, but Cayo gave chase. "I thought this was the Scarlet Arc. Does the Slum King still own it? Where is he?"

"Oh, you *definitely* shouldn't be here," the young man said, throwing him a wide-eyed look over his shoulder before disappearing through a door.

Cayo sighed and pushed in after him. "I'm looking for someone. Can you help me find her?"

They had entered a kitchen, the counters covered with crates of food. The young man set down his bag of mushrooms and turned to a knife block, pulling out a blade and twirling it expertly in his fingers. Cayo smartly took a step back.

"I should be asking *you* for help preparing these mushroom dumplings," the young man said. "Say, you're not the new recruit, are you?"

"What? No." This was clearly a dead end; he would have to try elsewhere. "Never mind."

"Just as well," the young man sang, beginning to snap the stems off the mushrooms. "Her Majesty'll be in a right fit if she doesn't get her dumplings in time."

Cayo froze. Turned back around. "Her...Majesty?"

The young man paused with his knife in the air, gaping at him. "Have you not yet paid your respects to the Slum Queen?"

"The Slu—" It was like a blow to the head, making him sway. He barely even heard the door open behind him.

"I thought I heard yapping back here," said a slick, familiar voice that made the hairs on the back of his neck stand on end.

She wore a form-fitting dress of black silk and lace, her arms sheathed in elbow-length gloves. A fat opal sat at her throat, a sibling to the gems glittering at her earlobes. Her lips were painted black, the kohl tracing her eyes so thick it likened itself to war paint.

Romara's grin was the promise of a dagger in the dark, silent and purposeful. "Welcome home, puppy."

# 27

*Your world and mine were built with different tools.*

*I do not know if a land exists on which we may stand*

*side by side.*

—INTERCEPTED LETTER FROM AN ANONYMOUS LADY OF MORAY

Cayo was taking too long.

Remy had gone out to find something in the way of food, but Amaya wasn't hungry. She kept walking around their small room, the old floor creaking beneath her weight as she opened empty drawers and inspected the sparse furniture.

"That's the fourth time you've checked the window," Liesl said.

"Like you're one to talk," Amaya shot back. "You didn't want him going in the first place."

What if he *had* sought out Romara? What if he'd run into the Slum King?

What if he had gone to find his father?

"Where are you going?" Liesl demanded as she headed for the door.

"I don't know," Amaya said. "Anywhere that isn't this room."

It was too small, too crowded for her right now. Remy would be agitated to find her missing, but he would just have to accept that this was her city and she was entitled to some freedom within it.

Amaya padded down the street, wondering if she could follow Cayo, wondering where he was most likely to go.

*You need to trust me*, Remy had told her back in Baleine. But his face was replaced with Cayo's in her mind, the somber look he'd given her just before he left. The expression he'd worn after they had kissed, awe mixed with doubt.

Amaya traced the shape of her lips. What was so tempting about them? What was it about his touch that sparked something awake inside her?

She couldn't think about this now.

She stopped in the middle of the street. The lanterns here hadn't been lit; there was no point, abandoned as it was. The last time she had been in Moray, she had been Countess Yamaa, powerful with wealth and rage. But both of those had dried up. She felt empty, aimless, her insides scraped raw.

Amaya gazed at the jade ring on her finger.

*I didn't want you to find out. I didn't want you to see who I'd become.*

A bitter heat crackled in her chest. Standing in a city devastated by the greed of men, she came to a swift decision and turned in the direction of the Shanty Sector.

She was owed an explanation. She was owed far more than that, more than Boon could ever afford.

Amaya followed the street signs, hollowed out by purpose. She passed through a residential district, the buildings gradually changing to gable-and-hip roofs with curling eaves in the Rehanese style, statuettes of the star saints looming over doors for prosperity and protection. There were mourning flags strung along the street; ash fever had visited this place as well.

*Your fault*, she seethed as she kept her eyes forward, a hand on her knife hilt. *This is all your fault.*

She had never been to this sector before, and it was difficult to make out what it looked like in the darkness. The buildings she passed were peeling and cracked, with broken windows like eyeless sockets and doors sitting off their hinges. The distant sound of coughing echoed down alleyways, and the few people she saw were like wraiths, quiet and vacant.

She searched up and down the streets, keeping an eye out for a familiar head twitch, the bark of a laugh, a curse. There was no sign of him. As the night crawled on and her stomach writhed with nerves, she realized there was one other place she had yet to check.

So she turned in the only direction that made sense. She turned toward home.

It didn't belong to her; it never had. But she and her parents had lived there, and they had been happy for a time. That was all that mattered.

She found Guen Street and hesitated. The last time she had come here, she had been surrounded by ghosts. Visions of her mother's smile, echoes of her father's gruff laugh. It had been so long that she couldn't exactly recall what they had looked like, just a vague impression she could point out in a mirror. There, her mother's chin. There, her father's nose.

Could she still find pieces of herself in Boon?

She could see it up ahead—the red door, the broken owl statuette on the roof. The place where she had fallen and scraped her knee. The wall her mother had leaned against while talking to the neighbors.

And the figure of her father sitting where she had sat not too long ago, a bottle in his lap and his eyes closed against the starlight.

Amaya sat a good few feet away from him. They were quiet for several moments, only the sound of his labored, wet breaths between them.

"How did you get out of Baleine?" she demanded at last. "Or get into Moray, for that matter?"

Her father cracked open one bloodshot eye. "Wouldn't you like to know?" He coughed, not bothering to hide it in his sleeve.

"What are you doing here?"

"Saw some folks sniffin' out my place in Baleine. Figured it was time to get going before I lost my head. What're *you* doing here?"

The questions she hadn't been able to ask him last time rose like a swell, the first warning of a storm. Amaya swallowed and looked away.

"My mother," she said softly. "She was in on it, too, wasn't she? The counterfeiting?"

Boon stiffened. Glanced at the ring on her finger.

"Rin and I . . ." He exhaled shakily, rubbed a hand over his weary, craggy face. "Once I started gettin' into alchemy, she took up an interest, too. We did research together. Did a couple of experiments. Had a feeling she was planning something on her own, but she wouldn't tell me what." The hand that bore the tremor lifted, then fell. "Never got to find out. But the discovery of the brinies . . . the counterfeits . . . that was all me."

A knot in Amaya's chest released. The situation was far from

315

good—her father was a criminal, a murderer, worse—but at least he hadn't roped her mother into his deeds.

She took out the papers she had carried from Baleine and tossed them onto his lap. He peered blearily down at them.

"Mercado raided your Vault," she said. "But you probably already knew that."

"Aye." Boon squinted at his own words in the dim moonlight. "Burned all the evidence. I take it this's the only thing left?"

She nodded, her skin feeling too tight for her body. Sitting beside her father after all these years, discussing matters of crime and alchemy so calmly, casually, was almost enough to make her start laughing at the ridiculousness of it.

"That last line," she said. "What does it mean?"

Boon handed the papers back to her. "Since you've come back here, I'm guessin' you already know what it means."

"So it's true. My mother had a Vault, too."

He nodded, just a slight dip of his chin. "She told me she was gonna open one."

"What's inside?" She realized she was sitting up straighter, leaning toward him.

"No clue. Couldn't open it without revealing who I am."

She deflated again. If her mother hadn't been a part of the counterfeit scheme after all, did that mean there was no cure waiting for them inside her Vault?

Even if that were the case, she knew they had to look regardless. Her mother wouldn't have gone through the trouble of obtaining a Vault if there wasn't something extremely valuable to place inside.

"Surprised the little fop isn't with you," Boon murmured, taking a sip from his bottle.

"That little fop's sister died," she whispered.

Boon paused with the bottle halfway to his mouth. He stared at her and saw the truth in how she pressed her lips together to keep them from trembling.

"Shit," he said. "Mercado basically killed his own daughter. I knew the family was cracked, but..."

"Really? That's all you have to say? As if your counterfeit scheme didn't have a part to play in all this!"

"It was *Mercado's* coins what poisoned her," Boon replied fairly. "I'm sorry to hear of it, but I'm not at fault for that."

"What about the rest of it?" She threw her arm out to the side, indicating the ruined city around them.

He took a deep breath that ended in a deep, rattling cough. "I had my part to play. I won't deny it. Suppose you think this is justice, huh?" He lifted his wrist, the one where she knew a splotch of gray was spreading.

She didn't think it was justice. She didn't know what to think—how to process the churning of her stomach, the way her eyes stung at the reminder of all the unfair ways in which the world worked.

If she were a different person, she would have turned to the man beside her and wrapped her arms around him and told him what he needed to hear. But the pain written in her bones spoke of a grief too deep to mend with words alone, the years of abandonment, loneliness, and desperation whittling away her capacity for forgiveness. Even for herself.

Especially for herself.

It was no one's fault and everyone's fault, and she sat at the heart of it like a lodestone surrounded by sharpened metal.

Amaya stood, her legs and heart aching. Boon looked up at her in surprise, and in that moment she saw the pieces she had taken from him—the thick eyebrows, the slant of his nose.

She had to get back. She had to discard these small pieces, leaving them in the gutters and the alleyways until she could emerge as someone new, someone who didn't understand betrayal and the way it felt to have love and hatred tangled together in her throat.

"Amaya," Boon said, struggling to get to his feet. "Wait—"

She didn't wait. She hurried away, ignoring her father's frantic calls at her back.

## 28

*What is a queen, really, but a woman who refuses*
*to be controlled?*

Romara had fashioned herself a throne.

She had completely stripped her father's old office of its desk and bookshelves and crowded it with chaises and rugs and pillows for her subjects to recline on. There were a few lazing about inside who immediately jumped to their feet when Romara strode in.

"All hail the Slum Queen!" one shouted drunkenly as the others laughed. Romara patted them on the cheek and continued on to a raised dais against the far wall, atop which sat an elaborately sculpted chair painted black with red velvet cushioning.

"Like what I've done with the place?" she asked. Cayo couldn't help but stare at his surroundings, remembering what the room had been before. Remembering the jar containing Bas's eyes. "It used to be so dingy when my father owned it. I think I've made quite the improvement."

Cayo had no idea where to begin. His entire world had been flipped upside down in a mere matter of weeks, and this certainly wasn't helping. Romara, seeing his struggle, reached up to a golden rope dangling beside her "throne." When she pulled it, a bell sounded somewhere in the casino, and a few seconds later the young man who had run into Cayo rushed inside.

"Yes, Your Majesty?" he panted. He was wearing an apron dusted with flour.

"Jacques, please fetch another chair for my friend."

"Right away, Your Majesty!"

The young man, Jacques, took off. Cayo raised an eyebrow at Romara.

"Don't you think this"—Cayo gestured to the chair and the bell pull—"is a bit much?"

"I'm going to tell you a little secret, Cayo." Romara crossed her legs, revealing a slim ankle. "I've been planning for this day since I was ten years old. I kept notes of how I would run the place once my father was out of the picture. I spared no expense to realize every detail."

"Ten-year-old Cayo wanted to be a pirate, but you don't see me plundering ships."

"Oh? Then what *have* you been doing out on the sea?"

He would have taken a step back if it didn't mean falling off the dais. "How did you know?"

"Please. I can smell the salt on you."

Jacques rushed back in, panting as he hoisted a similar chair up beside Romara's. There were flour fingerprints all over it. When

Romara cleared her throat, Jacques quickly used his sleeve to wipe them off.

"Good boy," Romara purred. "Now where are those dumplings you promised?"

"Coming right up!"

"What's that all about?" Cayo asked as the young man retreated to the kitchens.

"One of my more...overzealous followers."

Cayo carefully sat in the chair beside her. "Why keep him around?"

"He's loyal. Unlike some." Romara leaned an elbow on the arm of her chair, resting her chin on the backs of her fingers as she gave him a slow smile. "So. What exactly has my ex-fiancé been up to, hmm?"

A sudden wave of uncertainty gripped him. What was he doing here? Why had he decided that Romara, of all people, would be willing to help him?

But he had no other choice—or at least, none that he could see. He had to bring back the old Cayo, the one who knew what to say, how to appease her.

"I'm far more curious to know how *this* happened." He indicated the casino beyond the door. "The Black Lily? What happened to the Scarlet Arc?"

Romara scoffed and leaned back. "A relic from my father's time. It was outdated, ready to be turned into something new."

"Like the title of Slum King?"

She peered at him from the corner of her eye and grinned. "Don't tell me you're not relieved my father isn't here. That I'm the one calling the shots instead."

It galled him that she was right. "But where is he? What happened?"

He doubted Salvador would simply hand over his entire empire to Romara.

"I *tried* to make him see reason," she said with a sigh. "What with the whole counterfeit fiasco, his followers were getting antsy, frightened. Some of them caught the fever. Some of them died. They began to turn on him, one by one." She tapped her chin with a finger, the nail filed to a sharp point, painted black. "I may have convinced some of them to mutiny."

"You..." Cayo gripped the armrests of the chair. "You deposed your father."

"That's certainly a nicer way of saying it. Wish I could've stomped him out of existence, but the man's like a cockroach." Romara smiled as one of her followers approached, a girl holding a cigarillo with a smoking end. Judging by the smell, it was jaaga. Romara took it and allowed the girl to kiss a ring on her hand, which she did giddily before returning to her friends, giggling.

Romara took a deep inhale and breathed out smoke. "Old ways have a habit of dying out, Cayo. The people were hungry for something new. They wanted fresh blood, and I'm here to give it to them."

"They adore you." Cayo watched as the girl who'd given Romara the cigarillo kept glancing up at the dais. Romara winked at her. Blushing, the girl looked away with a fresh peal of giggles.

"Because I give them what they want," Romara said, handing him the cigarillo. He silently declined. "My father was selective with his jobs, his resources, but I won't be. Everyone has a fair chance until they mess up."

"And if they mess up?"

She grinned, smoke purling from the corners of her mouth. "Follow me."

Reluctantly, he followed her out the door and across the casino. The rattling of dice passed through him like bone striking bone, the feathery shuffle of cards running down his spine like a whisper.

He yearned, but the yearning was weak and half-formed, not so much a compulsion than an idle thought. A dream he could hardly remember. It would be easy, too easy, to sit at one of these tables and play, to forget about why he was here and what had led him to this moment.

But what good would it do? It would change nothing, only prolong the pain until it ripped him apart like a wild animal let off its leash.

Romara led him down a short flight of steps to the basement. When she opened the door, a wave of cooler air rushed out carrying the scent of sweat and old blood.

Cayo had never been down here when he had worked for the Slum King. The others had said it was merely a cellar where he kept his alcohols and spirits, but that was far from what it was being used for now.

There were bodies strung up along the stone walls. Their hands were tied above their heads in chains as they were forced to stand, unable to rest their full weight on the ground lest they put unbearable strain on their wrists or risk dislocating their shoulders. All of them were weak and shaking, a few of the men shirtless and bleeding from shallow cuts.

"Romara, what in the hells?" Cayo's stomach clenched at the sight of them, at their pleading groans.

"These are the people who deserve punishment, Cayo." Romara walked up to a man in his midyears, taking a stiletto knife from her thigh holster and pressing it against his stomach until he winced.

"This one was still loyal to my father. I caught him sneaking into my room to garrote me in the middle of the night." She backed off, leaving a thin trickle of blood on the man's stomach. "That one over there? Tried to cheat me out of thousands of senas—real ones, not counterfeit. That woman at the end? Put poison in my food. She didn't bet on me knowing exactly what hemlock tastes like."

Cayo swallowed and looked away, unable to stand the sight of them anymore. "So, what, this is your form of justice?"

"It is. If you have a problem with it, puppy, you can leave."

But he couldn't leave, not until he asked her about the Vaults.

"They'll all be handed over to the Port's Authority soon enough," Romara assured him, putting her knife back. "A full day and night here, then on to a cell. This step is crucial. It tells them not to fuck with me in the future."

"Whatever you say, Romara."

She was still holding the cigarillo, and she took a hit off it as she narrowed her eyes at him. "I think I've answered quite enough of your questions, Cayo. It's time for you to return the favor."

She led him back upstairs, through the casino with its hair-raising noise, and then up to where he knew her living quarters were. He had been here only once before, when she had roused him the morning after he'd lost himself to the Vice Sector. Right before everything had fallen apart.

A room in the back of the apartment had been converted into an office. It was quieter here than it was downstairs, but Cayo could still hear the thin melody of music, the quiet roar of the crowd.

Romara sat behind her desk and took one last, long inhalation before snuffing her cigarillo in an ashtray. Cayo looked around and wondered if this used to be her father's bedroom. There were knife and bullet marks in the walls, and a dark stain in the corner he didn't want to examine too closely.

"Where exactly is your father?" he asked. He felt jumpy in his own skin, the uneasiness of knowing there was a spider in your room but unsure where exactly it was hiding.

"You're done with questions, remember?" She was no longer the smirking Slum Queen, but a businesswoman who was ready to negotiate. "You're going to tell me where you went and why. And then you're going to tell me what you're doing here and what you want from me."

He tried not to flinch. He should have known she would guess.

"It's . . . a long story."

"We've got time."

Cayo sighed. He couldn't tell her everything—he didn't want to compromise Amaya and the others. So the story came out of him in ribbons, how he had gone to Baleine, how he had found out about the Benefactor, how the counterfeits and sickness were spreading. He didn't say Soria had gone with him. He didn't want to know what would happen if he said his sister's name out loud.

"I came back because I believe there's something left in a Widow Vault that could help," he finished. "It might give me some clue how to counter the effects of ash fever."

Romara stared at him while tapping a finger against the desk. Cayo had never been good at figuring out her tells, but perhaps this was one of them.

The door flew open and Jacques rushed inside. "Your dumplings, Your Majesty!" He tripped in his haste, spilling a couple of dumplings onto the floor. "Oh, drat."

Romara sighed loudly. "Jacques. I'm in the middle of something."

The young man turned back to the door. "So sorry, Your Majesty, I'll just—"

*"Leave the dumplings."*

Jacques scurried forward to put the plate on the desk before bowing his way out and shutting the door behind him.

"You wouldn't believe how difficult it is to find good help around here," Romara muttered as she picked up a steaming dumpling between two of her sharp fingernails. "Help yourself."

"I'm all right, thanks."

"So you want a way to gain entry to the Widow Vaults." Romara leaned back in her chair, raising the front legs off the floor as she nibbled at her dumpling. "It's very difficult to pull off a heist like that. Even my father was reluctant to try it."

"That doesn't mean it's impossible."

Romara laughed. "Now you're getting it. But really, Cayo, I don't think you have the right skill set for this sort of thing."

"I won't be alone."

"Even still." Romara finished her dumpling and rocked her chair forward, the legs thumping against the floor. "If I help you, you'll be on your own from this point on. Anything that happens to you won't be on me, understood?"

"Does that mean you know a way inside?"

"Perhaps." Again she showed him that wide grin, all teeth and ambition.

"What do you want?" He had done this song and dance with her before, knew she wouldn't merely help him in the name of whatever passed as friendship between them.

"Something fairly simple, all things considered." Her expression sobered. "I'm looking for a man who goes by the name of Boon. And I have reason to believe you've been in contact with him."

Cayo couldn't hide his surprise. "Boon?" he repeated. "What do you want with him?"

"Many here in the Vice Sector know my father was working with Mercado—because of you, I might add—but my father made it known that Mercado was also working with this Landless man, Boon, to help bring counterfeit money into the city. And now there's been a statement from the Rain Empire claiming that the counterfeits are the source behind ash fever." Romara's eyes flashed. "The people are angry, Cayo. They want justice."

He thought of the bodies strung up below the casino and shuddered. "Real justice, or your version of it?"

"Either way." She stood and began to pace, her arms crossed. "If I can find this man and deliver that justice, the people will bow at my feet. My father's reign will be well and truly over. It'll be the final nail locking him in a coffin of his own making."

"Why do you hate your father so much, anyway?" He had never asked her before, only because he'd been terrified she would flay his face off if he dared.

Romara paused, fingers tightening on her arms. "Isn't it enough that he's a terrible man?"

"Not for this level of payback."

She snorted. "Fine. He..." Romara looked away. "He got my mother exiled."

"What?" Out of everything he had expected her to say, this was at the very bottom of the list. "How?"

"She was a con artist. Or she used to be, until partnering with my father. I refuse to believe there was anything like love between them, but she gave him three children anyway, my two older brothers and me. Then one day he found out she'd been skimming money from his private coffers to send to her home village in Rehan. He told her if she cared about the place so damn much, she should just go back and stay there. He exposed her location to the Port's Authority, and they exiled her from Moray. I was ten at the time."

She had said she'd started planning her father's downfall when she was ten years old. Cayo knew Salvador was a callous man, but that seemed particularly cruel, even for him. "I had no idea. I'm sorry."

"Once I gain a bit more influence, I can hopefully convince someone to revoke her Landless status and bring her back." Her face hardened. "If she's even alive."

"I'd say you're more than influential enough."

"You've seen how many still oppose my rule, Cayo. I've done my fair share of hustling, trust me. I even infiltrated the Port's Authority and leaked the names of the officers secretly working for my father."

Nausea clenched his gut. "Nawarak. *You're* her contact in the Vice Sector."

"And she's been quite diligent in weeding out some of my father's biggest supporters, which got her a lovely little promotion on her end." Romara threw him a wink. "Keep your enemies close, right?"

Cayo laughed hollowly. Could he trust no one in this damn city?

Then he berated himself; of course he couldn't. He had already learned that lesson.

"If I show the people that I can do what my father can't," Romara went on, "I'll gain their loyalty forever. A public trial for Boon, the man who brought ash fever to Moray."

"And my father?" he demanded, lifting his gaze. "Will you put him on trial as well?"

"I'm waiting to see if he has any other uses first."

In other words, she wanted to keep Kamon Mercado around just in case she needed leverage.

"Speaking of which, have you gone to see dear old daddy yet?" she asked, leaning against her desk as the slit in her dress revealed the length of her thigh. "Or your sister?"

Cayo's throat tightened. He tried to swallow, thinking of the pack he had left back at the inn. The words he hadn't been able to say before now.

"She's dead," he whispered.

Romara was silent as Cayo stared at the floor, longing to be anywhere but here. When she finally moved, he expected her to return to her seat, or to open the door and tell him to get out.

He didn't expect her to lay a hand on his shoulder. He looked up, startled by her grim expression.

"I'm sorry," she said. "You should have led with that, Cayo. Shit."

He exhaled shakily. "Yeah, well. That's why I'm here. I've got to do anything I can to put a stop to this, Romara. That's why I need to know how to get into those Vaults. If there's a chance a cure is waiting there, I need to take it."

Her hand tightened on his shoulder. "And that's why I need to know where Boon is. Don't you want vengeance for your sister?"

Soria wouldn't have cared about vengeance. He could almost see her shaking her head at him, telling him not to go down that road. But the burning in his chest told him differently.

Cayo clasped his hands together. "He's on the outskirts of the

Shanty Sector." That was what Amaya's friend on the *Brackish* had told them.

He could practically feel Romara's smile as she squeezed his shoulder. "Thank you, Cayo."

Perhaps it would be better this way, he thought as Romara dug through a cabinet. Now Amaya and the others wouldn't have to get their hands dirty with Boon.

But it still left him uneasy.

Romara handed him a rolled-up length of parchment. "Blue-prints of the Widow Vaults. They're not entirely up to date, but it's the best I've got."

Cayo stood and took it from her, the parchment heavy and glossy with wax. "Thank you."

"The least I can do." She hesitated, and for one terrifying moment Cayo thought she would hug him. Instead, she gripped his jaw and shook his head a little.

"I'm sorry for your loss," she said. Her sharp fingernails dug into his skin. "But that doesn't mean you get to be careless. Whatever your plan is, make sure you're careful. All right?"

"Worried about me, Romara?"

"Always." She let him go and turned back to her dumplings. "You're not a big dog yet, Cayo. And we all know puppies get into more trouble than they can handle."

Cayo took a deep breath before walking into the room at the inn. Everyone's heads turned in his direction, and he lifted the parchment.

"I have blueprints of the Vaults," he said. "Will that help?"

Liesl laughed in delight and grabbed them. "How on earth did you manage *that*?"

"I told you I had a good contact."

"The one from the Port's Authority?" Remy asked with a frown. "She would just give something like this up?"

Cayo carefully skirted the truth even as guilt stabbed him like a knife. "I have it, don't I?"

Liesl spread the parchment on the table. Cayo spotted Amaya sitting at the edge of one of the beds, staring blankly into space. There was something off about her, a hollowness that made his unease return.

He went to sit beside her. She stirred and looked at him.

"I take it the meeting went well," she said. Even her voice was devoid of emotion, all flat and unfeeling. "Good job."

He should tell her the truth—that he had gone to Romara even though he'd said he wouldn't, that he'd had to give away Boon's location to get the blueprints. But he had finally done something useful, something that could benefit everyone. He didn't want to tarnish that, even if it meant denying Amaya her vengeance.

"Yeah," he said with a forced smile. "Looks like we're finally on the right track."

Her faint, echoing smile twisted the knife in him further.

## 29

*What's the best way to find out what a man is truly like?*
*Easy: Open the safe he keeps under heaviest lock and key.*

—A SAYING FROM MORAY

The next night, they were ready to hit the Vaults.

Amaya almost asked why she couldn't just say she was the rightful heir to her mother's Vault, but that would do no one any favors. Amaya Chandra was supposed to be on a debtor ship, for one thing. For another, the city had no doubt learned the scandalous true identity of the erstwhile Countess Yamaa by now.

So she let Liesl cobble together a plan using the blueprints Cayo had retrieved. He'd seemed a little off last night when he returned, just half an hour after Amaya had. But she had no right to question him about it, not when her mind was still spinning after her encounter with Boon.

The moon was hidden behind clouds when they set out. Amaya felt as if she were moving through a dream, all observation and no consequence. Remy must have noticed, because he wrapped a hand around Amaya's wrist.

"Are you ready for whatever we might find?" he asked. "Or not find?"

"I'm ready. I just want this to be over."

Her father had already disappointed her more than she'd ever thought possible. Whatever her mother was hiding, it surely couldn't surpass that.

The Business Sector was quiet this time of night. Then again, the whole city was quieter than usual. But that didn't prevent guards from attending to their patrols, pacing up and down the streets, standing before the building that sat above the underground Vaults.

The structure was done in the style of the Rain Empire, with columns and marble and senseless adornments. A set of shallow, wide steps led up to the main doors, which were closed and locked for the night. Under a triangular pediment carved with statues read a long yet simple phrase: *Blood to blood, name to name, bone to bone.*

Amaya swallowed. Her mother's blood sang inside her, her father's name forsaken, her bones formed from the dust of her ancestors.

The five of them lingered in a dark alley as Liesl counted the guards. "Remember what we agreed on," she whispered. "If anything happens, we split up. We find new safe houses. We only send word once things calm down."

"And if we're caught?" Cayo asked.

"You said you have a contact in the Port's Authority, didn't you?"

He shifted. "Yes, but..."

"Patrol coming," Deadshot announced softly.

"Go," Liesl hissed.

They raced across the street and around the back of the building.

According to the blueprints, the Vaults were built underground and spread out far more than the office building above them. Drawn on paper, it had looked like an ant colony. But in order to find out which Vault was her mother's, they needed access to the offices.

"No back doors," Liesl had said while hunched over the blueprints, "but look at what we have here." She had pointed above the building's cornice, to a parapet flanked by marbled lanterns. "Windows leading into the attic. And see this little square? There's a panel that opens and closes, likely for a water hose in case a fire breaks out. That's our only way in. And out."

Amaya didn't like putting all their hopes in a small slab of stone, but there was no other way, short of strolling up to the front doors.

Despite there being no back door, a trio of guards stood at attention along the back of the building. One of them held a long, sleek rifle, the other two adorned with swords at their hips.

Liesl nodded at Remy, who breathed out and rolled his shoulders back before slipping out of the alley and toward the guards. Amaya's heart lodged in her throat at the way the guards' attention immediately snapped to him.

"Evening," Remy said in his best Rehanese. Although he had grown up speaking Circíran, most of the Bugs had spoken Rehanese, and he had picked up the language quickly.

So Amaya was fairly certain that wasn't the reason why the middle guard swung his rifle up, aiming its barrel at Remy's chest. Remy immediately raised his hands to show he was unarmed.

"Shit," Liesl hissed. "The uniforms."

Amaya saw it. The uniform Liesl had managed to snag earlier that day—she didn't reveal how, only mentioned something about visiting the nearest laundering facility—didn't match the uniforms of

334

the Vault guards. The color of Remy's was more of a middling blue whereas the guards wore deep navy, the crest on Remy's lapel silver and theirs gold.

Deadshot quickly broke off from the others as Cayo reached uncertainly for Jazelle, sweat already lining his brow. Amaya had no idea what Deadshot was doing until they heard a shot ring out nearby.

The guards around the front of the building yelled in surprise. Making the most of the distraction, Remy leaped forward and got the guard with the rifle in a headlock. Amaya took care of the one on the right, knocking his legs out from under him and letting him crumple to the ground, where she choked him into unconsciousness just like Avi had taught her.

The remaining guard was halfway to unsheathing her sword when Deadshot returned and whacked her with the butt of her pistol. The guard collapsed.

"They're going to feel that tomorrow," Liesl said as she motioned for them to drag the bodies into the alley. "Let's hope you didn't do any permanent damage."

"I'm very skilled at knocking people out, thank you very much," Deadshot said, grabbing the guard under the armpits. "A bad headache, a minor concussion. Some bed rest and they'll be fine."

"I thought for sure it was the right uniform," Liesl growled as she knelt and stripped down one of the guards. "Sorry, Remy."

"No matter." Remy quickly shed the uniform to replace it with the new one. It was too big for him in the shoulder, and he had to roll the sleeves up. "Cayo, you take the other."

Cayo started. "Why me?"

"It looks like it'll fit you."

Despite the nausea in her stomach and the storm in her head,

Amaya still felt her skin prickle as Cayo began to unbutton his shirt. She turned around as the rustling of his clothes echoed against the alley walls.

The guards seemed to have settled back at their stations in the front, calling an all clear.

"All right," Liesl whispered once he was done. "Let's move."

Liesl jiggered the lock on the nearest administrative building and gestured everyone through. It smelled like parchment and ink as they quickly ascended the stairs and found themselves on the roof, a good four feet away from the Widow Vaults' marble balustrade.

Deadshot made the leap first, landing gracefully. She peered down to check that the guards below hadn't heard anything, then signaled the rest of them to join her. Liesl jumped after, stumbling a bit as she landed. Remy jumped next, then Cayo, after taking a deep breath and a running start. When Cayo landed, he wobbled and nearly fell to his knees, but Remy caught him.

Amaya again had that dream-like sensation where everything was fuzzy and made no sense. It took her a moment to realize she was just standing there while everyone else motioned for her to jump across. With a jolt, she took a few steps back before running and leaping.

She drew up too short, her foot landing on the railing of the balustrade. She gasped loudly and slipped, and would have fallen and cracked open her skull if Remy and Cayo hadn't reached for her at the same time, each of them grabbing an arm and hauling her up.

"What was that?" came the voice of a guard below.

"Something's going on. Go make a perimeter check."

Amaya's heart beat a frantic rhythm as she caught her breath. Liesl shot her a disbelieving look, as if to ask, *What's wrong with you tonight?*

"Sorry," she breathed.

They crept through the rounded windows beneath the marble lantern towers, entering into a short, empty colonnade. Liesl waited for the guards to complete their perimeter check before she tapped her foot on the roof panel. Deadshot lifted it, stifling a grunt at how heavy it was, stone dust falling like a snow flurry as she set it down as carefully as she could. One by one, they hung off the lip before dropping inside, onto a wooden landing overlooking the ground floor.

Amaya briefly returned to the night when she and Remy had infiltrated the currency exchange offices in Baleine. He must have as well, because he gave her a quick grimace.

But unlike that night, there were no trips or traps to outmaneuver. As they crept along the second-story landing, they soon saw why: There were guards inside the building as well. There were two sitting at a desk playing a card game as they carried out a murmured conversation. Along the far wall, through a window lit with yellow light, two employees were hunched over their desks working late into the night.

"Damn it," Liesl muttered. "The one thing blueprints can't tell you."

"What do we do?" Amaya whispered.

"Let me think. In the meantime…" She pointed to a room up ahead. "Records in there. Remy and Amaya, go."

Cayo tried to follow, but Liesl wagged her finger at him and pointed to the end of the landing for him to keep an eye on the guards. He scowled but did as he was told.

Liesl used her lock picks on the door, going as slow as she dared. A faint *click* sounded from the lock and they tensed, but the guards didn't hear it over their conversation. Once the door was open, Amaya and Remy slipped through.

"Cr-, Ci-, Ca-…" Remy whispered as he scanned a shelf of ledgers. "Ch-, here we are." He wormed a record out and flipped through the pages. There were no windows, so Amaya fumbled in her pocket and took out the few matches they had stolen from the inn.

She struck one, and the tongue of flame it produced danced between her fingers. Remy turned the pages quickly, then went back a couple and stabbed the page with his finger.

"Chandra," he whispered, his finger sliding down the page as he read. "Arun Chandra has a record here. And so does Rin Chandra."

"That's her," Amaya said, voice shaking.

"She purchased the Vault the same year we were sold to the *Brackish*." They exchanged a meaningful glance. "Vault number fifty-seven."

The match's flame kissed her fingers with a sudden, bright pain. Amaya hissed and dropped it. Remy snuffed it out with his heel, then pocketed it.

"Are you all right?" he demanded, but she knew he wasn't talking about the fire. "If you're too distracted—"

"I'm *fine*." She led the way back out once they had replaced the records, closing the door softly behind them. They told Liesl the Vault number, and the girl took a moment to think back to the blueprints before nodding.

"I know where it is," she whispered. "But first we'll have to get past these fools."

She pointed down to the guards, who occasionally raised their heads to check on the employees. Deadshot touched her pistol and raised her eyebrows, but Liesl shook her head. The less evidence that they had been here, the better.

Remy leaned over and whispered in Cayo's ear. Cayo grimaced but nodded. The two of them went down the stairs to the bottom floor, looking out of place yet trying their best to seem like they belonged here this late at night. Amaya couldn't help but think how odd it was to see Cayo in a uniform, stiff and austere against such an expressive face.

"Gentlemen," Remy said with that disarming smile of his. "We're to relieve you for the night."

The guards jerked in surprise, glancing from Remy to Cayo to the stairs. Liesl pulled Deadshot and Amaya down.

"Where did you...?" One of the guards shook his head, setting down his cards. "It's only midnight. There's no shift switch for at least another hour."

"Sorry. They told us twelve." Remy shrugged, affecting casualness despite the sweat glinting at his temples. "Simple mistake."

The guards were tense, their shoulders stiff and eyes pinched. Amaya's hand drifted to the knife up her sleeve, ready to throw it, to leap down from the banister—

"You really want to stay here when you could be getting a drink at the Shy Clam?" Cayo blurted. "They close in about an hour."

One of the guards hummed in his throat. "Always wanted to go there, but they close right when our shifts end."

"Well, don't let us stop you," Remy said. "We'll watch over the candle burners." He jerked a thumb in the direction of the lit office.

The guards hesitated before finally scraping their chair legs back.

"Get the Salted Oyster," Cayo told them. "Nice and strong."

"Will do. Be sure to lock up after the clerks are done."

They all waited in tense silence until the two guards left. Cayo let out a shuddering breath and wiped his forehead.

"Good thinking." Liesl patted Cayo's shoulder. "Now we only have to get past these clerks and find the code to the Vault."

"Yes, very simple," Remy muttered. "Should we tell them to head out?"

"We might need one of them to access the codes for us," Liesl said. "Get in and distract them. Leave the rest to us."

Amaya worried out a knife as Remy took the lead again, he and Cayo entering the office while the others crouched under the window.

"Afraid you need to pack up for the night," Remy said.

There was a rustle from beyond the door. "What? Why?"

"Security measures. There were a couple of suspicious noises outside, so they want to evacuate just in case."

More rustling, the dry whisper of paper. Amaya tried to keep her breathing quiet as the clerks grumbled and yawned. Cayo's shadow fidgeted.

As soon as the first clerk crossed the threshold, Deadshot moved like a whip and grabbed them from behind, slapping a hand over their mouth before they could scream.

"No sudden movements," Liesl ordered the other one, who stood gaping with wide red-rimmed eyes as Deadshot pressed her pistol to the clerk's temple. "We only want one piece of information. You give it to us, we'll let you go."

The other clerk twitched suddenly. Amaya acted without thinking, throwing her knife into the clerk's shoulder. The woman screamed and Remy grabbed her, hand over her mouth. A small bottle fell from the woman's hand, and Cayo picked it up with narrowed eyes.

It had to be poison. No doubt those who worked here had been trained to protect the Vaults at whatever cost—the finest riches of Moray were more important than their very lives.

Cayo briefly met Amaya's gaze. She wondered if he, too, were thinking about the way Florimond had tipped a bottle of mercury down his throat.

"There's no need for that," Liesl said, nice and calm. "Just give us the code to Vault fifty-seven, and we'll let you go."

The woman was crying, trying to shake her head around Remy's hold. The clerk with Deadshot's pistol trained on them—who wore a pin in the shape of a diamond on their lapel, signifying their pronouns—took a trembling breath.

"I know the code," they whispered. "Just…leave her alone. Please."

Liesl nodded to Remy, who guided the woman back to her desk and ripped a swath of fabric from his uniform to tie her to the chair. She was outright weeping now, blood spilling down her front, and Amaya avoided her glaring eyes as she carefully retrieved her knife and wrapped a tourniquet around the woman's shoulder.

"I'm sorry," Amaya whispered. She knew it wouldn't do any good.

Remy stuffed another wad of fabric into the woman's mouth and closed the office door behind them. The remaining clerk was pushed gently toward the stairs leading down to the Vaults, Deadshot's pistol trained on their back.

Amaya remembered going down these steps. She had run down here after finding out her father had a Vault and that Mercado had seized control of it and all the incriminating blackmail within. She could almost sense that other Amaya walking alongside her, the ghost of a girl who didn't know who she was, who had been lied to, manipulated, kept in the dark.

In some ways, she was still that girl.

"Amaya." Cayo was beside her. The heat of his hand hovered above her back, close to touching but keeping his distance. "Are you sure you're all right?"

Nothing was all right. She wanted to smash down the walls. She wanted to tear out of her own traitorous skin. She wanted to tell Cayo everything.

"I'm fine," she said.

They followed the clerk down corridors lined with Vault doors painted gold. After a while, the doors became dingier, the golden paint discarded to display only simple metallic doors.

The cheaper Vaults, Amaya guessed, if any Vaults could truly be called cheap. The ones kept in the back, smaller and uglier and easier to afford. This, at least, did not surprise her.

They stopped at number fifty-seven, the number inscribed on a plaque above the door. The locking mechanism was connected to two dials, one on either side.

"A dual combination lock," Liesl murmured. "Interesting." The clerk was guided to one of the dials, and Liesl made for the other.

Then she paused. "You should be the one to do it," she said to Amaya.

Amaya just stood there, staring at the other dial. A few simple turns, and that door would open, and there would be no going back.

"Amaya," Liesl whispered.

She clenched her jaw, welcoming the ache in her teeth. It helped her focus. She took a step forward and placed her hand on the dial, the numbers already blurring in her vision.

The clerk gave the code slowly, both of them turning the dials in synchronicity. Amaya tried her best to exist outside her body as she turned the knob, hearing the clicks and catches, until finally the tumblers inside gave way.

The last secret, she hoped. The last time she had to confront the terrible legacy her parents had burdened her with.

She heaved open the door. The air inside the Vault was stale and musty; it hadn't been opened in years. The smell, strangely, reminded Amaya of being on the *Brackish*, and nausea rushed through her.

There was a sconce on the wall with an unlit torch. Liesl took one of Amaya's matches and lit it, casting the small room in a pale orange glow. Amaya held her breath as she finally looked around, expecting piles of fake gold, or perhaps an alchemy laboratory like Florimond's, or a chest filled with schematics and plans.

Instead, there was a large pile of cloth.

And that was it.

Everyone was silent as they stared at it, confusion giving way to incredulity. Liesl picked up a handful of the cloth—it was thick and tan, like canvas—and even shook it out, but there were no secrets to reveal. Nothing written or sewn into fabric, no papers hidden within its folds. Just neat, even rows of thick white thread, stitching the cloth together into a shape they couldn't fathom.

No experiments. No clues.

No cure.

"This doesn't make sense." Cayo crouched and touched the fabric. "Why would she spend so much money just to store away some cloth?" He looked up at Amaya. "Do you know?"

She shook her head, silent. Trying desperately to suppress the horrible ache in her chest.

Liesl made a poor attempt to mask her disappointment. "Well. Let's take it with us anyway, just in case."

As Liesl folded the cloth and put as much of it as she could into the pack they'd brought, Remy came to stand beside Amaya.

"Maybe it had some sort of value to her," he said. "Maybe, I don't know, she wanted to make something for you?"

Amaya appreciated what he was trying to do, but at the same

time she wanted to push him and everyone else away. To just sit in this room her mother had once stepped foot in. To wait for understanding to crash down on her.

She slowly raked her eyes around the Vault, as if her mother had scrawled some note for her on the stone.

She didn't find a note, but she did notice a small, rectangular shape leaning against the wall near the door. She picked it up and turned it over.

Three smiling faces stared back up at her. A painted portrait of a bygone family.

Amaya's hands tightened against the canvas. She remembered this. She had been five years old, and her mother had insisted the three of them go to the Arts Sector for a festival. Her father had been reluctant, but eventually they'd all been coaxed out the door—mostly with the bribe of festival food.

While they were there, her mother had spotted an artist taking commissions. She had been so excited despite her father's grumbling. Amaya had been fussy, squirming on her father's lap and asking for more fried sugar buns. The artist had been patient and quick, and her mother had fawned over the portrait for days afterward, proudly displaying it in their home.

Amaya's gaze caressed the shape of her mother's smiling face. She looked so startlingly young that Amaya realized for the first time that she had no idea how old her mother had been. She was holding a five-year-old Amaya's hand, her former self soft with baby fat, her mouth hanging open in an excited child's grin.

And her father. He had worn his hair a little long then, his chin sporting a short, well-trimmed beard. He didn't look as young as her mother, but he was certainly younger in this, his face not yet lined with crags and ridges. His smile was calmer, smaller, but there was still something in the way his eyes crinkled that proved he had been happy despite his complaints about having to sit still for the artist.

The longer she stared, she more she saw the man who would one day become Boon. They had the same dark eyes, the same broad forehead, the same solid frame.

He was her father. And despite everything, she loved him still.

Amaya's shoulder hit the wall as she pressed the portrait to her chest, closing her eyes as they watered. She bared her teeth against the pain clawing up her throat, her back jerking with the effort to not let her despair overwhelm her.

It had been so easy, once, to look up at the sky and believe the stars shone for her. That nothing bad could ever happen and that love would always save her.

But stars were cold and distant things, and love was too abstract to ever hold on to.

"Amaya?" Cayo's voice, his presence warm at her back.

Half of her wanted him closer, and the other half wanted him to look away, to let her be. She didn't want to be alone, and yet that was all she craved. Just a moment, her and her family, in the only way they could be reunited.

Before he could say anything else, a shout rang down the hall.

"Here!" yelled the clerk, struggling against Deadshot's grip. "In here!"

Amaya spun away from the wall and lifted the portrait just in time. A bullet embedded itself into the wood and canvas, peeking through the space between her mother and father.

She tossed the portrait to the side as the two card-playing guards from earlier came at them. Deadshot was faster, taking one out with

345

a bullet to the leg while Remy grabbed the other in a headlock. With both guards down, they wasted no time fleeing the Vault, leaving the rattled clerk behind.

"I didn't even hear them," Liesl panted as they ran for the stairs. "They knew something was wrong, I could tell—"

"Save your breath," Deadshot snapped as another guard hurried down the corridor. She barely paused to aim as she got him in the shoulder, making him stagger and fall.

At the stairs, Liesl shoved the pack at Amaya. Its sides bulged from the cloth that had been stuffed inside.

"You should be the one to hold on to it," Liesl said as Deadshot and Remy ran up the stairs to check if the floor was clear.

"But—"

"We don't know why it was in there, but it's your mother's, right? That means it has value, even if it's a value only you can see."

Amaya slipped the pack on with a nod. "Thank you."

"More coming!" Deadshot shouted down.

They followed the other two up. Deadshot moved away from the window and used her gun to point to the open roof slat.

"It's the only way out," she said.

Cayo cursed under his breath as they raced up the stairs. When the front doors banged open below, he nearly stumbled into Amaya.

"Up, up, up!" Deadshot cradled her hands together. Liesl pushed Amaya forward first, so she placed her foot in Deadshot's hold and let her hoist her up to the roof. Amaya grabbed the ledge and pulled her upper body through, arms shaking at the strain. Once she was secure, she reached down to help Cayo crawl up after her. Liesl came up next, Amaya and Cayo helping her through.

Amaya extended a hand down for Remy. He was reaching for her when a dark shape appeared behind him, snatching him away from her grasp.

"Remy!" Amaya made to jump back inside, but Liesl and Cayo held her back.

"Go!" Remy yelled as the guards wrestled him to the floor. Deadshot punched the guards coming at her and jumped for the opening, pulling herself through before closing the heavy roof slat down.

"No!" Amaya screamed, lunging at the slat and trying to hoist it up, tearing her fingernails against it. A bullet whizzed over her head, and Cayo pushed her down.

"We can't help him if we get caught, too!" Liesl yelled.

Amaya sobbed and struggled against Cayo as he forced her away. He grunted as she elbowed him in the ribs, but he pulled her after Liesl and Deadshot with surprising strength. The guard on the opposite roof was taken out with a spray of blood at his shoulder, and Deadshot didn't even bother to holster her pistol as she led them across the gap between the roofs.

But even as they hurried down the stairs and spilled back out onto the street, they were greeted with a new bevy of guards.

"Split up!" Liesl yelled.

Cayo pulled Amaya after him. He turned into a nearby alley, the sound of the guards right behind them. A bullet crashed into the wall on their right and Cayo stumbled. She nearly tore free of him, but his grip tightened.

"We can't go back there!"

"They got Remy! Of course I have to go back!"

"And have the entirety of the Port's Authority on our asses? Not a chance."

Amaya was lost among the streets, but Cayo knew them better

than she did. He turned right, left, crossed a main thoroughfare until they were out of the Business Sector, the guards falling away one by one until they'd lost them entirely.

Even then the two of them didn't stop running until they found their way back to the inn. Gasping for breath, they hurried to their room, but Liesl and Deadshot weren't there.

"Damn it," Cayo panted, running his hands through his sweat-slicked hair.

As soon as Amaya caught her breath, she turned back to the door. Cayo blocked it with his body.

"I have to help Remy," she insisted.

"Remy will be fine until we can figure out what to do. He's part of the Rain Empire's navy. The Port's Authority won't harm him."

"What about your contact?" Amaya asked desperately. "She's the one who gave us the blueprints, right? Can she help us get him back?"

Something in Cayo flinched, and he looked away from her. Amaya's chest seized up, her lungs still on fire from running.

"Let's wait for Liesl and Deadshot to return before we make any plans," he said.

She was too tired, too stunned to argue. She took off the pack and opened it, running the fabric between her fingers.

Had this really been worth losing Remy?

The two of them waited in tense silence as the night crawled on. Amaya's heartbeat wouldn't slow despite forcing herself to take deeper, even breaths. She paced the room, glancing out the window every time she passed it.

Hours slid by. Still Liesl and Deadshot didn't return.

"What happened to them?" Amaya whispered. "What if..."

Cayo sat on the bed with a hand over his mouth. He had changed out of the uniform into his normal clothing. He looked haggard and hollow, eyes bloodshot with exhaustion and a hint of stubble shadowing his upper lip and chin.

Amaya stood before him, forcing him to look up at her.

"We need to do something," she said. "We can't wait around any longer. Let's go to your contact."

Cayo breathed out, defeated. "We... We can't use my contact at the Port's Authority. She's been compromised. But there is someone who might be able to help us."

Amaya's hands curled into fists as she realized her suspicion had been right. "Cayo."

"I had no other choice," he hissed, standing so they were only a couple of inches apart. He glared down at her, as if daring her to admonish him again. "I told you, my contact in the Port's Authority was compromised. We needed a way into the Vaults, and I found one. I did my part."

"By going to *Romara*," she spat back. "She's dangerous, Cayo!"

"You think I don't know that? You barely even know her!"

"I know her style well enough to guess she probably wanted something in exchange for those blueprints."

Cayo hesitated, and something in her twisted. She had thought there would be no more secrets between them, that the last of their barriers were in the process of being demolished. Apparently she had thought wrong.

She grabbed the front of his shirt and pulled him in close. "What did you give her, Cayo? What did she want in exchange for the blueprints?"

The muscle at his jaw twitched. They stared at each other for a silent moment.

"She wanted Boon's location," he said at last, his voice hoarse. "She knows he was part of the counterfeit scheme. Now that she's the Slum Queen, she wants to show her followers that she can deliver justice, unlike her father. And from what I saw, her justice is slow and thorough."

Amaya let him go and backed away, her head pounding. "You... You told her where he was?"

"What else was I supposed to do?" he demanded. "Boon ruined our lives, Amaya! Yours most of all. I'm sorry you're not going to be the one to kill him, but I'd think you would be glad he was finally getting the punishment he deserves."

Amaya was going to be sick. She turned away from him, the horrors of the night building up inside her until it was all poisonous black bile. She gagged and caught herself against the wall as the room spun around her.

"Amaya—"

"Don't touch me," she growled before he could take another step toward her. "You have no idea what you've done."

"What are you talking about?" His voice was rising, growing more and more agitated. "Have you forgotten what *Boon* has done? The city is like this partly because of him! You were just as ready as I was to make him pay. So why in the hells—"

"*He's my father!*"

The words rang against the walls. Cayo took a step back as if they had physically shoved him.

"What?" he whispered.

"He's my father. Arun Chandra." Saying it out loud was like taking a hammer and chisel to her heart, breaking it open even more. She thought back to her family's portrait, to the man he had been—the one she still wished was inside him. She blinked tears from her eyes as she stared Cayo down. "You told Romara where he is. You lied to me. *Again*."

Cayo struggled for words. "You... You didn't tell me. When did you find out?"

Guilt finally began to gnaw at her. "In Baleine. The night of the high-stakes tournament."

His eyes widened before an incredulous laugh escaped him. "And you didn't think this was important to share?"

Amaya shook her head, not to answer him but because she had no idea what she should have done. She wanted to blame Cayo, *did* blame Cayo, but this was her fault, too.

Maybe they would never learn what real trust was. Maybe this was their curse, to forever fall back into their old ways.

Amaya snatched the pack from the bed and slung it over her shoulders.

"Where are you going?" Cayo demanded.

"To warn Boon. To find Liesl and Deadshot and save Remy."

Cayo reached under the bed to retrieve his own pack. "I'll go with you."

"No." She turned back to him, her heart twisting at the careful way he held his pack to his chest, the same way she had held her family's portrait in her mother's Vault.

"No?" he repeated, as if he'd never learned the word.

"There's..." Her voice broke, and she forced herself to swallow. "There's no way this can work, Cayo. How can we stand beside each other when we can't even trust each other?"

He held his pack tighter, as if afraid she would snatch it away. She expected him to protest, to be angry, to plead, but he said nothing. He knew the truth of it, too—that there could be nothing good between them so long as they remained the merchant's son and the girl with too many names.

With the last of her strength, Amaya turned away from him, leaving the inn and Cayo Mercado behind.

She scoured the Shanty Sector until she found a small crowd outside of a run-down hut.

Muscling her way past them, she burst through the door and knew immediately she was too late.

There were signs of struggle everywhere, from the overturned table to the broken wine bottle on the floor. A splash of dark blood had puddled near the door, cold and dry. The smell of old sweat and sea water permeated the room, familiar and unmistakable.

Romara had already gotten her hands on Boon.

Amaya sank to the floor as the curious citizens began to meander away. Remy was taken. Liesl and Deadshot were gone. Cayo had lied to her. Their mission had crumpled all around them.

And all she had to show for it was a bundle of cloth.

She opened the pack and stared at the tan fabric, wondering what to do. How she could fix this.

But maybe this was how it was always supposed to be: her alone, abandoned by her own city, just like her father. Loveless and betrayed, hatred hardening her until she became the worst version of herself.

When her tears came again, she let them run freely, her chest shaking with sobs. She had no one left to hide them from.

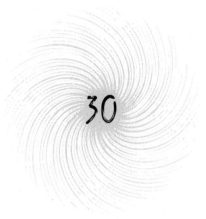

# 30

SOLAS: You cannot deny you owe me more than you can pay.

BRAEGAN: What, then, would you have from me?

SOLAS: Your blood, sir.

—*THE MERCHANT'S WORTH*, A PLAY FROM THE RAIN EMPIRE

As Cayo climbed the hill to Mercado Manor, his nose began to bleed.

"Damn it." He held his sleeve to his nose, catching the thin trickle. His head had been fuzzy since they'd returned to Moray, a pressure in his ears and in his chest that threatened to turn into a headache.

If Soria were with him, she would tell him it had something to do with the weather. That his body was simply acclimating to the humidity of Moray again. She would have taken a handkerchief from her sleeve and pressed it to his nose, fussing even while she teased him.

But Soria wasn't here, and Cayo's sleeve now bore a red stain. Sniffing, his mouth and throat tasting of copper, he continued on to the manor.

It was dark still, the sky a couple of hours from lightening to dawn. It was difficult to believe he had been involved in a heist tonight, that just a few hours ago they had been running for their lives. His legs prickled with an unpleasant ache as he climbed the hill on sore feet, the only thing he had to show for what they had gone through.

Remy had been taken, and Liesl and Deadshot had either been caught as well or gone off to secure a safe place to hide. Amaya's mother's Vault had led to nothing but another dead end, more questions without answers.

And Amaya had left him for good.

Cayo's hands tightened around the straps of his pack. He couldn't say what he felt more, anger or shame. He'd had his role to play in this, same as her. Again they had arrived in the place they always found themselves: bitter, scorned, uncertain.

He tried to tell himself it was a good thing, cutting himself away from her. But Soria's ghost shook her head and sighed at him, told him he would never learn.

At the crest of the hill, he paused to catch his breath. The manor was dark and silent. He'd expected to feel something more, looking at it—to be flooded with memories, to have his heart swell with all the things that were no longer his.

He didn't expect to feel nothing at all. To gaze upon his childhood home with a blankness that terrified him, as if it were a thing already long dead.

Cayo wasn't entirely sure why he had come here. When Amaya had left him in that inn, he'd spent a long time contemplating what to do. He could go back to Romara, but what was the point? She had what she'd wanted from him; he had nothing left to offer.

If only Amaya had told him about Boon, he could have understood why she hadn't shown up to the high-stakes game. He could have talked to her about what it was like to have a father who wasn't who you thought they were. He could have...

Cayo sighed and closed his eyes, let the night breeze play with his hair. He was so tired. There were too many things he could have done, and hadn't. What was the point of brooding over them?

When he opened his eyes, he knew what he *should* do: He should scatter Soria's ashes into the sea, like he had intended.

But the manor called to him like a grave marker with a name he couldn't make out. He approached the front doors, taking in the white marble columns, the unlit iron chandelier hanging crookedly above his head. He expected the doors to be locked, but they opened easily.

As soon as he stepped inside, his foot connected with the bottom of a cracked vase. It rolled away from him, curling an arc across a floor littered with debris.

Cayo reached for Jazelle. He held his breath and listened, but the manor was silent. Even the tall clock against the right wall was quiet, its glass shattered and its gears left unwound.

Who had done this? Enraged citizens? Romara? His father?

He carefully picked his way across the antechamber, stepping between piles of broken pottery. It was as if someone had taken all the plates from the kitchen and smashed them here, where they would make the most noise. The art on the walls was crooked, a couple of the lower pieces thrown to the floor and snapped down the middle. He spotted Soria's favorite: a painting of a mermaid curled on a rock, calling to a distant ship.

Cayo crept up the stairs, his footfalls muffled by the green carpet runner. The hallway above was dark and quiet. He went to the left first, his body automatically taking him to his bedroom as if he were merely sneaking in after a night in the Vice Sector. He eased the door open, and his chest clenched at the familiar sight of his bed, his wardrobe, his bookcase. Empty.

The last time he had been here, Boon had taken him and Soria hostage. Frowning, Cayo closed the door behind him and backtracked down the hall.

Just the idea of returning to Soria's room was enough to weaken his knees. Cayo took a deep breath and walked in that direction anyway, wondering if there was anything left of hers.

He slowed to a stop. A faint light flickered from under the closed door of his father's office.

Heart hammering, Cayo turned the knob while his other hand rested on Jazelle.

The lanterns were lit, casting an erratic glow over the room. The light gleamed against the bottle of alcohol on his father's desk, already mostly empty.

And in the chair behind the desk, Kamon Mercado sat staring at the opposite wall, not even bothering to look up as his son stood before him.

His father was far from the man Cayo remembered and had respected, the one who was always put together, pristine, powerful. Now Kamon's hair was in disarray, his clothes stained and torn. His face was harder, leaner, and there was even a smudge of dirt on his cheek.

He looked...broken. Pitiful.

Cayo waited to be acknowledged. Waited to know what to say to him. His hand never left the gun, the pack he wore suddenly twice as heavy.

"Soria is dead," Cayo said at last.

Kamon gave the slightest flinch, closed his eyes. But still he said nothing. Hatred boiled in Cayo's chest, burning up his throat.

"You killed her," Cayo whispered, blinking back sudden tears. "Your counterfeits are what did this. Did you know?"

Kamon reached halfheartedly for the bottle on his desk, dragging it closer. "Not until it was too late."

Cayo's teeth chattered, and he clenched his jaw so tight he thought something might crack.

*Murderer. Monster.*

"You really have nothing else to say?" Cayo demanded, his voice hoarse. "Your daughter is ash, and all you can do is sit there and ignore me?"

Kamon raised the bottle as if to drink, then lowered it again, not even having the energy for that simple action. A tear fell down his cheek. "What is there to say?"

Cayo's vision flared crimson. His mind went blank, and when he came back to himself he was grabbing his father by the collar and punching him in the eye.

Kamon toppled over along with his chair. The bottle fell from his hand, spilling its contents onto the floor. Cayo grabbed him again and drove his fist into his temple and then his jaw. His knuckles barked with pain, splitting open and leaving smears of blood on his father's face.

When Cayo released him, Kamon slumped to the floor, hair hanging in his face. Cayo staggered to his feet, panting.

"Now do you have anything to say?" Cayo growled.

Kamon spat out blood and finally looked at him. One of his eyes was already swelling, the other dark and bloodshot. If there was remorse in his expression, Cayo couldn't see it. All he saw was a broken man who had already accepted his fate.

Cayo grabbed Jazelle and pointed the barrel at his father. He cocked the hammer back with his thumb, marginally satisfied by the widening of Kamon's uninjured eye.

Then Kamon laughed, a low, faltering sound.

"Go ahead, then," his father whispered. "Finish it."

Cayo breathed hard, trying to still the tremor in his hand. He sighted the barrel on his father's chest, wanting nothing so much as to strike his heart and be done with it, give Soria the vengeance she was due.

But his sister's ghost was still with him. She put her hands on his shoulders, pressed her forehead to the space between his shoulder blades, where her ashes rested. A silent plea.

Tears ran down his face, but Cayo didn't lower the gun. "Why did you do it?"

Kamon sat up with a wince. "You wouldn't understand."

"Try me."

Kamon breathed out, resigned. "Gaining status...doesn't come easily. I wanted a better life than my parents had, scrimping and scraping by. They spat at even the mention of the gentry, but I was smart enough to know it was the only way out. I became a merchant. I made the right connections. But it wasn't enough. Not for me."

His father stared out the wide window beside them, at the sea's endless horizon. "I broke the rules. I traded with the Rain Empire. Brought illegal goods to Moray. I infiltrated waterways that belong exclusively to Sun Empire. I built a small empire of my own, enough to give out loans with interest rates that would fill my pockets. *Our* pockets. It still wasn't enough."

Cayo shook his head, wondering how he could still be so surprised at the depths of his father's greed. He had always thought he and Soria were lucky to live the life they'd had, cushioned and gilded, hiding the rot underneath.

*Do what has to be done*, his father had been fond of telling him.

"And then came Arun Chandra." Kamon's upper lip curled, a flicker of emotion finally crossing his face. "He took out a loan from me for his pearl business. A ship, perhaps—I can't quite remember. He was late making payments, and I was about to double the interest when all of a sudden it was paid in full."

But Amaya had told him what had happened to her father—or at least, what she thought had happened—and it involved Arun Chandra not being able to pay off the loan in time, digging himself further and further into debt.

"I'd never had a client pay in full like that before," Kamon went on, ignoring the gun Cayo kept trained on him. "So of course I was suspicious. After a while, I realized how he'd done it. The gold was fake. He had crafted an alchemical counterfeit."

So Boon *had* been the one to start all of this. "And you somehow ended up with the recipe?"

"He evaded me for a long time, gathered all sorts of incriminating evidence to use against me. But in the end, the debt collectors got him before he could unleash it. So I gave him a choice: the recipe for the counterfeits and Landless status, or a hanging. He chose wisely. Or so I thought. Should have just lobbed his head off then and there."

That, at least, Cayo had to agree with. "Then you used the recipe to create your own counterfeit."

"At first. But I was also in debt to my contact in the Rain Empire. They supplied me loans, ships, illegal goods. I tried to use the counterfeits to pay it all back, but I was found out. And my contact wanted the recipe."

Cayo's mind raced back to infiltrating Florimond's shop, the letters in that wooden box. Even half a room away, Cayo had recognized his father's handwriting. "The alchemists made the counterfeit coins. And then it was sent to you to distribute."

Kamon's eyebrows lowered in surprise. "Yes."

"Why would you do that?"

Kamon sighed. He looked older than Cayo had ever seen him. "Because money and power are the same thing, Cayo. And we needed more and more of it. This manor...most of my ships...I had my own debts to pay, and this was the only way to pay them. It was either do as I was told or have all my secrets exposed."

Cayo's hand tightened on the gun. "By the Benefactor, you mean. Who is it? Who's been sending you the counterfeits?"

Kamon laughed hollowly. "I wish I knew."

"How can you not know?"

"They always kept their identity a secret. Didn't want their name to be known in Moray, in case anything were to happen with the Sun

Empire. The less of a trail, the better. I only communicated with an alchemist named Florimond, a sort of middle man between us."

"Shit." Cayo turned away from him at last. If they couldn't expose the Benefactor, the counterfeits would continue to spread. Moray was a hair's breadth away from falling into one of the empire's hands. If the Rain Empire claimed the city state, it would doom them all to war.

"There's only one person who might know who the Benefactor is," Kamon said behind him. Cayo turned back, waiting, and his father smiled mirthlessly. "Arun Chandra. He dug up mounds of blackmail on me. If he was able to figure it out..."

Amaya said she'd seen Boon in Baleine; he could have investigated Deirdre on his own. Boon might be able to tell them for sure if she was the Benefactor.

And Romara was set on making an example out of him, just like those poor bastards in her dungeon.

The gun was heavy in Cayo's hand. He lifted it again, wondering what he would feel if he pulled the trigger, if some of the pain would ease once his father was taken out of this world.

*Do what has to be done.*

But he already knew the answer. If there was anything he had learned from Amaya, it was that vengeance was an empty, hollow thing. If he allowed himself to give in to it, he would be no better than Boon and his father.

Soria had always wanted him to be better. So he would be better.

Cayo lowered the gun. Kamon visibly relaxed, and it flooded Cayo with shame.

Turning to the door, he expected his father to call him back, or perhaps even say he was sorry. But he did none of those things.

So Cayo left him there, in the wreckage of all he had built—and all he had lost.

There was only one place Cayo could think of that Amaya would go.

The gangplank of the *Brackish* had been pulled up, so Cayo stood on the dock and called out as dawn infused the sky with a light, pearlescent gray. A moment later, the young man named Cicada looked down from the railing, locs spilling over his shoulders.

"Coin trick boy," he greeted.

"Is Amaya with you?"

Cicada studied him a moment, considering. "Why do you want to know?"

"I have news she'll want to hear." When Cicada didn't move, Cayo sighed in vexation. "It's *urgent*."

"Oh, well, if it's urgent."

Cicada left the railing with a smirk. Cayo paced the dock, clenching and unclenching his hands for what seemed like an hour. Finally, the gangplank was rolled out and he hurried onto the deck.

Amaya and a couple of the other children stood there waiting. Amaya had her arms crossed, expression carefully blank. The little girl beside her grinned when she saw him.

"Can you do another trick?" she demanded.

"Maybe later." Cayo approached Amaya. "We need to talk."

"Whatever you need to say, you can say it here."

Cayo took a deep breath, trying to ignore the others' curious eyes. "I found my father," he said softly. "He doesn't know who the Benefactor is either, but there's a good chance that someone in this city does."

"Who?"

"Boon."

He saw it click, saw it in the way her spine straightened and her arms lowered.

"I spoke to him," she said slowly. "Here in Moray. But I left before... He was calling me back, but..." She rubbed a hand over her mouth, cursing softly.

"I'm sorry for not telling you the truth about Romara," Cayo said, holding out his hand. The other children watched on, fascinated. "That you felt as if you couldn't tell me about your father. I don't know if I can promise to never lie again, though I can do my damn best to try. And to do whatever I can to help you get him back."

Amaya stared at him, stared at his hand. A chasm had opened up between them, widening more and more with pain and rage and loss. The bridge across was only half-constructed, unsteady. He wouldn't blame her for abandoning it.

But she didn't turn away. She reached across and grasped his hand, their palms pressing together.

"Let's go pay our respects to the Slum Queen," Amaya said.

# 31

*Although the people cheered, Trickster knew his time was drawing short. He felt always the watchful eye of Protector on him, counting his every step, his every cheat, his every lie. It would not be long now until the gods turned, forcing him, at long last, to stay quiet and still.*

—KHARIAN MYTH

D o you really think Boon can say for sure if Deirdre is the Bene-factor?" Amaya asked, watching as Cayo rolled a coin between his knuckles. Fera watched on with round eyes. The three of them were sitting against the railing of the *Brackish*, waiting for evening to fall. One of the Bugs, Matthieu, had stolen into the city to keep an eye on the Black Lily in case Romara did anything rash with her new prisoner.

"I don't know, but finding out what he knows might be our last shot," he said. "If he was able to dig up all that evidence against my

father, I'm sure he could have done the same against the Benefactor."
He extended his hand to Fera, giving her the small coin he had taken
with him from the Rain Empire. "Do this." He showed her how to
hold it between her thumb and pointer finger, how to roll her hand
just so. She tried to copy the movement, tongue poking out in con-
centration, but the coin clattered to the deck.

"That's all right," Cayo said when she made a dejected sound. "It
took me lots of practice, too."

Amaya watched them silently. She wanted to be mad still, considering what Cayo had done, but her anger was burning off like morning fog. They had both lied. They had both been betrayed. They both
had fathers who had shaped them into who they were.

Running footsteps came up the gangplank before Matthieu
barged onto the deck.

"You better go," he panted. "There's somethin' brewing in the
Vice Sector."

Amaya glanced at the darkening sky and shared a look with Cayo.

"Wait here," Amaya told Cicada when he moved to join them.
"The others need someone to watch over them." Cicada reluctantly
nodded before Amaya and Cayo crept into the city.

The Port's Authority had issued a mandatory curfew, and those
who were still out and about were beginning to hurry home. Amaya
kept checking the points where she kept her knives: sleeve, hip, boots.
Cayo similarly kept his hand on his pistol, gaze burning.

She wondered if he had fired any bullets yet. As if he had heard
the thought, Cayo said, "I couldn't do it."

"Do what?"

"Shoot him." Cayo clenched and unclenched his hand. "My
father. I was ready to. I *wanted* to. But I couldn't."

Amaya thought back to her knife pressed against Boon's throat.

"Why not?" she asked softly. The streets around them were dim and dark, the people no more than shadows. It made her feel as if she and Cayo were the only ones alive.

Cayo took a deep breath, keeping his strides long and quick. "Death isn't the worst punishment for him. To be heirless, penniless— that's always been his nightmare. So I let him stay in it."

Something dangerously close to pride stirred in her chest.

They were silent the rest of the way to the Vice Sector, but the closer they got, the more they heard the distant din, saw the blur of people running to get to Diamond Street despite the curfew.

They soon saw why. The broad street was crowded and messy with people shouting, yelling, laughing. It wasn't the usual boisterous crowd; this was something on the verge of feral. Domesticated animals now adapting to the wild.

Amaya's hand came to rest on the knife at her hip. Her heart tapped nervously against her chest as she and Cayo scanned the street, letting themselves be absorbed into the crowd.

And then Amaya saw her. Romara stood on the roof of the building before them, decadent and deadly in black trousers and a Rehanese high-collared tunic. Her hair had been tied up, all the better to reveal the ravenous expression on her face. She wasn't addressing the crowd; she was merely gazing down at it with a small, satisfied smile, a queen surveying her domain. Beside her stood a young man with wide, excited eyes, holding a drink in his hands like a human side table.

*Sometimes it's wiser to bend a knee than lose your head,* Liesl had once warned them.

"What have you done, Romara?" Cayo muttered beside her.

*You helped her do this,* Amaya thought, but the resentment was there then gone. There were so many other factors, so many other things to worry about.

The cage sitting in the middle of the street, for instance.

"Shit," Cayo hissed as Amaya hurried forward, using her elbows and shoulders to shove people out of her path.

The cage was tall and narrow, comprised of thick, rusting bars. It looked to have been dragged out of some old-fashioned dungeon. In the middle of the cage knelt Boon, hands tied behind his back, face bleeding and bruised. The crowd jeered around him, shaking the bars, throwing rotten food through the gaps. Someone banged a metal cup against the bars, making Boon flinch.

Amaya grabbed the man with the cup and pointed her knife at his chest. "Keep rattling if you want to lose a hand."

The man backed away quickly, tripping over his feet. Amaya knelt before the cage, Cayo standing protectively at her back, glaring at anyone who got too close.

"Boon," Amaya called. She couldn't call him *father*—her mouth refused the word.

He looked up in surprise. Romara's people had given him a thorough beating; his clothes sported darkening blossoms of blood, his lip split, one eye ringed with a bruise. Romara had taken out all her frustrations on the man who had made Moray what it was now, and she was giving her followers the chance, too.

"What are you doing here?" he rasped.

"Getting you out."

Boon tried to bark that laugh of his, but winced and shook his head. "I don't think so."

"He's right," Cayo said behind her. "If we take him from Romara, I don't know how she'll retaliate. She has too much power."

"Terrifying girl," Boon murmured. "She'll go far."

"I don't give a damn about what Romara will do. We're getting you out."

But Boon just shook his head again. She had never seen him so defeated. "Don't bother. Whatever she plans to do with me, I deserve it."

"Well, for once you're not calling the shots," Amaya snapped, already searching for the lock to the cage. "I am."

"Amaya—"

"No." It came out louder than she wanted it to. Amaya forced herself to meet Boon's eyes. Her eyes. "I know you messed up. You caused a swell when all you wanted was a wave. You're not perfect, and you never were."

She took a deep breath. "But in your own way, you gave me a second chance by turning me into a countess. So I'm giving *you* a second chance. It's not mercy, it's what I owe. And I refuse to be in debt anymore."

Boon opened his mouth, ready to disagree, to work his words in that manipulative way of his.

"I'm not leaving you here," Amaya repeated, her voice stronger. "You're my father. I'm not done with you yet."

His shoulders shook in a silent, humorless laugh. "You've got your mother's voice, you know that?"

Now she did. Swallowing back the lump forming in her throat, she stood and turned to Cayo.

"She left the roof," he said. "She must have seen us."

"Then we don't have much time. Quick, find the lock—"

But Cayo was already drawing out his pistol. The crowd around them scurried back, startled by the sight of it.

"What, may I ask, are you doing?"

Romara. She strode to the front of the crowd, her heeled boots making sharp statements against the cobblestone, her lackey still carrying her drink. Her eyes darted from Amaya to Cayo.

"What's the meaning of this, Cayo?" she demanded.

"I should be asking you that," he said. He sounded different than Amaya was used to, as if confronting his father had given him something new—or perhaps had taken something away. "First your little makeshift dungeon, and now this?"

"I told you the city is out for his blood," Romara said. The people around her yelled in approval, and her lips curled into a smile. "I'm doing what my father couldn't. I'm giving them exactly what they want."

"You don't have to do this," Cayo said. "Let's talk, you and me. We can make a deal."

"You have nothing to offer me."

"I can give you my father."

Amaya froze, and Romara actually let her surprise show. But then she grinned, shaking her head.

"I can get to him in my own sweet time," she purred. "He's no longer a threat."

Cayo swore and pulled back the hammer of his pistol. Romara frowned.

"Oh, please," she drawled. "You wouldn't shoot me."

"You're right." Instead, he turned and shot the lock on Boon's cage.

Amaya's ears rang as the ruined lock fell to the ground, the cage door creaking open. The crowd around them cried out in protest, recoiling.

Amaya grabbed Boon and dragged him out. He lurched to his feet, his breathing shallow and wet.

"The Benefactor," Amaya said quickly as Romara started forward, Cayo interjecting himself between them. "You were trying to tell me before, weren't you? Did you find out if Deirdre—"

She was cut off by the sound of gunshots peppering the air.

Romara whirled toward the commotion as the crowd yelped and screamed. At the far end of Diamond Street was a cadre of people wearing red fabric tied around their arms. They carried guns, knives, and daggers, their faces intent on bloodshed.

At the center of the pack was the man Amaya had met the night she had come to the Vice Sector on her own, his face handsome and scarred, his voice smooth and scheming. He strode forward, unhurried, confident, already playing the role of victor.

The Slum King.

"Of course he chooses now to attack, the dramatic bastard." Romara turned to Cayo, and for an instant she wasn't the Slum Queen but rather a girl searching for a friend's help. "Did you have anything to do with this?"

"Nothing," Cayo promised. "What do we do?"

Romara pulled a wicked-looking dagger from her sleeve as the crowd broke out into chaos, a kicked anthill unprepared for invasion. Even her lackey looked ready to bolt, his mouth hanging open as the Slum King's small army advanced.

"We finish them for good," Romara said.

Amaya took her knife to the bindings on Boon's wrists, freeing his arms. He hissed and rubbed the raw, red skin.

"You're not seriously planning on taking on Salvador, are you?" Boon demanded.

"This isn't my fight," Amaya said simply.

But Jun Salvador was quickly making his way down the street, knife in one hand and gun in the other. His expression was murderous as he mowed down Romara's followers, those who tried to stop him or were simply unlucky enough to be nearby. Romara stood waiting for him, her lackey sending up prayers to the sky god and her star saints for protection.

There was an alley nearby they could duck into. Amaya grabbed Cayo's arm, but it was tense under her hand, and he stayed put.

"Cayo," she said, "you can't help. This is beyond us."

"She shouldn't face him on her own." He pulled the hammer back on his pistol. "He's taken things from me, too, Amaya."

"But—"

A man broke through the crowd and crashed into Cayo, ramming him against the wall. Cayo grunted as the man's knife plunged into his shoulder, blood splattering his chin.

Amaya started forward, but Cayo had already fired the gun. The man staggered back with a hole blown through his hip, screaming. Amaya knocked him down and rammed the hilt of her knife against his temple.

Cayo stared down at the man, gasping for breath, face speckled with blood. Their eyes met, and for a brief moment they spoke the same language without uttering a single word.

A rough hand grabbed Amaya's arm. "Get out of here," Boon growled. "It'll be me he wants."

"Then why aren't *you* running?" She pointed at the alleyway, where some of the crowd was already fleeing.

Boon grunted. "Had enough of that. Besides—"

Amaya didn't see the man coming in on her right. He held a long knife already dripping blood, the look on his face twisted, ferocious. Boon turned, quicker than she thought possible, and punched the man senseless. Boon immediately dissolved into a coughing fit, lips wet with blood. She helped him sag to the ground, leaning against the cage.

"Just stay out of the way," she ordered. "Then we can talk."

"Aye, Captain," he mumbled.

The Slum King loyalists continued to advance. Many of Romara's followers fought back, producing hidden weapons, getting between them and the newly crowned Slum Queen. When some of the red-clad men reached Romara, Cayo rushed forward before Amaya could stop him. He fired his gun into the air and the people near him yelped in distress, some even smart enough to run away. He aimed at the ones who lingered.

"Get away!" he yelled, cocking back the hammer. "I swear I'll shoot!"

Amaya stayed in front of Boon, sunk into a defensive stance, her knife flashing in the low light. The crowd continued to beat against one another, against the walls of the dens, wanting—needing—to take their aggression out on someone, something, *anything*.

A smoke bomb was tossed and unfurled like a noxious flower, tendrils of odorous fog obscuring the melee in the street, covering the smell of gunpowder and blood.

The Slum King emerged from the fog like a demon out of her father's stories. His front was stained red, a trail of bodies in his wake.

"Romara," the Slum King called. "You can stop this. The Vice Sector is mine, and always has been. Relinquish it, and I'll allow you to leave the city."

Romara yanked her dagger from a downed loyalist with a

sickening squelch, drops of blood making a constellation against her cheek. Her grin was the opposite of surrender, her stance anticipatory, eyes sharp with a promise she had likely made to herself a long, long time ago. Amaya suddenly understood Romara a lot better—a daughter in the shadow of her father, pinned down by all his mistakes, desperate to fix them.

"Just like you did to Mama?" Romara called sweetly. "Force me into exile rather than muster up the balls to end it here?"

The Slum King smiled coldly, lifting his gun and aiming it at her. "I didn't want to do this, Romara."

"Really? I did."

"Obstinate child." The Slum King's smile fell into a scowl, his finger curled decisively on the trigger.

The shot rang out and Boon grabbed Amaya from behind, pulling her back even as he jerked at the earsplitting sound. Amaya flinched; it had sounded close, far closer than where Salvador was standing.

And then she saw why: Cayo's pistol was smoking, held steady between his hands even as the wound at his shoulder trailed blood down his arm. His eyes were wide, his lips pressed into a thin, grim line.

The Slum King let out a choked scream and collapsed. He dropped his weapons, scrabbling at the mangled, bloody mess of his knee.

Romara stared at him, then at Cayo. He stared back with a wildness in his eyes that Amaya knew intimately. It was the same wildness that had clawed up her guts after killing Melchor.

But the Slum King was still alive, wailing in agony over his ruined leg. Romara barked a quick order, and her uninjured followers hurried forward to grab hold of him and kick his weapons away. Bodies clogged the street, most of them wearing red. The fight was finally winding down. It had taken only minutes, but it had felt like hours.

Romara marched up to Salvador, her nostrils flaring, dagger still in hand. "How dare you point that gun at me. You're *weak*, Father. You deserved to be usurped."

The Slum King breathed hard, his carefully styled hair falling into his eyes. "You'll run it into the ground. The city is doomed, anyway. It'll fall through your fingers like sand."

"We'll see about that." She changed her grip on her dagger, ready to plunge it into his chest.

"Wait!"

Cayo hurried forward. The Slum King sneered at him.

"Mercado's whelp," he drawled. "How fitting for you to follow in your father's footsteps."

Cayo spared him a cool look. "Be grateful I didn't do worse, considering what you did to Sébastien." He turned to Romara. "Don't kill him. We can still use him."

Amaya expected Romara to lash out. Instead, she lowered her dagger. "I'm listening."

But whatever Cayo said next, Amaya couldn't hear it. It was drowned out by the sound of Boon's gurgling cough behind her, the hitch in his breath.

She turned, and the center of her went ice cold. Boon held a hand to his stomach, his shirt drenched in blood.

The Slum King. When Cayo shot him, Salvador's aim must have gone wide.

"No," she said, or maybe she only thought it. Boon sank to his knees as blood poured out of him, staining the street below.

"Not the worst I've gotten," Boon wheezed, then weakly clicked his tongue. Red stained the corner of his mouth. "Then again...not the best, either...."

"Shut up," she snapped, grabbing him by the shoulders, forcing him to lie down. The bullet had gone into his upper abdomen, and blood continued to well up and over, cherry dark. She ripped at her shirt, tried to press the strip of fabric to the wound, but it only made Boon groan in pain.

"Cayo!" she screamed. He was at her side in a second, ashen faced. "We need a compress or—or something," she babbled, her mind going blank. "The bullet's still in there, we need to get it out—"

"Amaya." Boon struggled to grasp on to her wrist. Blood trickled down his cheek, dampening his beard. "That's enough."

"I..." She looked to Cayo, but he turned his gaze down. "No. *No.*" She had found her father, and now she was losing him all over again. *Unfair.*

"It was either this or the fever," Boon reminded her, voice wet and ragged. "Amaya, listen. What you said about givin' me a second chance..." He stopped as a shudder rolled through him. "Didn't realize... how much...I needed to hear it."

Amaya shook her head, her mind still blank, her limbs numb. Her mouth worked, but no words came out.

"'M sorry," he whispered. "For not...telling you 'bout me sooner. Who I was. I'm not..." His face tightened briefly, his breaths coming shorter, faster. "Not proud of who I became. Didn't want... you to see me...like this."

How much time could they have had to work it out, if he had told her?

The blankness gave way to horror, to heat, to the blinding force of her sudden rage. She grabbed him by the shoulders.

"You can't do this," she seethed. "You can't just tell me the truth and then die! You can't—" Her words caught on a sob. "You can't leave me again!"

He exhaled shakily, reaching up to cup her face in his large, callused hand. Blood smeared against her jaw.

"I hate . . . disappointing you," he said, his voice weaker, his chest struggling beneath her. "One more chance, yeah? To make . . . things right." He suppressed a cough, grimacing. "The Benefactor. Not Deirdre."

Cayo leaned forward. "Robin Deirdre isn't the Benefactor?"

Boon's voice faded even more, but they could both hear the name that fell from his red-stained lips.

"No. It's André Basque."

Cayo sat back with a curse, but Amaya didn't care. Her father was dying.

"Amaya." His hand fell to her shoulder, tried to squeeze it. "Thikha. I'm sorry."

"Don't," she sobbed, curling her fingers in his shirt.

But his breaths came quicker, one after the other, until eventually he let out a small sigh and laid still. His eyes were still locked on to hers, as if she were the last thing he wanted to see.

Her throat ripped apart as Cayo's arms went around her. The knife dropped from her hand. The world was falling out from under her again, like it always had, like it always would, because nothing stayed and nothing was easy and nothing was hers.

She let Cayo hold her as she screamed into his chest. The street was full of the dead and injured, and they were in their own pocket of misery. The stars overhead watched on and said nothing, and Cayo said nothing, because what was there to say?

Her father was gone. There was no one left in the world to love her.

Amaya didn't know how she found herself sitting in an alleyway in the Business Sector, waiting for Cayo and Romara to return. She just kept staring at the wall before her, stained and dark. Refusing to look at the shrouded body beside her.

Romara had done that. Wrapped him up in cloth, given Amaya this one last piece of him to do with as she wished.

Footsteps. Cayo and Romara were coming back, a third person tagging along beside them.

"Remy," she whispered.

He rushed to her and threw his arms around her. She clung to him like she was drowning, and maybe she was.

"I'm so sorry," she whispered against his shoulder.

"Don't be. You needed to escape. Besides, I'm not hurt." He eased back, and she noted the way his eyes flickered to the body, the exhaustion lining his face. "Cayo told me what happened. I'm sorry, Amaya."

She only nodded, too empty for words.

Thankfully, Cayo cleared his throat. "It worked, obviously." He gestured to Remy. "Nawarak agreed to exchange him for Salvador."

"After some minor negotiation," Romara said darkly, arms crossed.

"You deserve it," Cayo told her. "If you're going to be Slum Queen, you'll need your fair share of allies."

"At the cost of increased patrol in the Vice Sector?" She scoffed.

"I should have just stabbed my father and been done with it." She glanced at Amaya. "Sorry."

Amaya swallowed. "You owe me, Romara."

The other girl scowled but nodded. "I suppose that's fair."

"I need you to find two people for us. And I need..." Her voice faltered, but Remy slipped an arm around her, securing her. She forced herself to look down at the shrouded body. "I need him...to be burned."

Romara sighed. *"Jacques!"* she barked.

The young man hurried around the corner. "Yes, Your Majesty!"

"Write down these descriptions, then go find a cart."

Amaya told him what Liesl and Deadshot looked like, and then he took off. A little while later, she was watching Remy and Cayo carefully lift the body and settle it into the back of a cart.

Her hand hovered above him until she placed it on his chest.

"I forgive you," she whispered. It would have to be enough.

The next day, Romara's lackey came to the *Brackish* with Liesl and Deadshot in tow.

"Thank goodness," Liesl said as she threw her arms around Amaya. She squeezed tight, Amaya returning the pressure. "We weren't sure what happened to you two, so we chose to lay low for a bit."

"I'm just glad you're all right."

Liesl held her by the shoulders, her face solemn. "We heard about what happened in the Vice Sector."

Amaya's gaze strayed to Cayo, who bit his lip. "There's...a lot to talk about."

Romara's lackey, Jacques, stepped up with a short bow. He presented her with a box, larger than the one Cayo had.

"The Slum Queen sends her condolences," he said.

Amaya carefully took the box from him. It was heavier than she expected.

She put the box under her hammock and joined the others in the galley while the Bugs kept lookout above deck. Despite his bandaged shoulder and red-rimmed eyes, Cayo did most of the talking while she stared at the far wall, feeling the others' glances from time to time. Liesl's hand covered hers, and Amaya gripped it tight.

"André Basque," Remy repeated after Cayo explained why they had gone back for Boon, what had happened on Diamond Street. "Do you think we can trust what he said?"

Amaya looked to Liesl. "That seal I saw on the *Silver Star*? It's also on the *Brackish*. André Basque owns a fleet of debtor ships, right? Mercado must have bought one of Basque's ships, and that's how they came to work together. Basque saw an influential merchant in Moray he could use for his own benefit, and Mercado played right into it."

Liesl sat back, dark satisfaction on her face. Deadshot rubbed her back as she processed the information.

Remy swore. "And Basque is wealthy and respected enough in Baleine that the authorities wouldn't dare look at him too closely."

"But you have to convince them to," Amaya said. "You need to go back to Baleine anyway, Remy. You can expose him."

"We'll go with you," Liesl said, gesturing to herself and Deadshot. "You'll need help, and I've waited a long time to be able to bring Basque down."

"I'm all for it, but how are we supposed to expose him?" Deadshot

379

asked. "Like Remy said, he's rich and respected. We would have run into the same problem with Deirdre."

Remy snapped his fingers. "The currency exchange offices. We need to take all the counterfeit coins from them and find a way to link it to Basque."

They began to plan. Amaya only sat and listened; she was exhausted, hollow. Across the table, Cayo watched her. He didn't try to smile, or even look triumphant. He was just as hollow as she was, and it was a cold comfort.

Remy and the others couldn't leave by boat. The sentry was still stationed along the edge of Crescent Bay, prohibiting anyone from fleeing Moray. They would have to go on foot and slip past the guards patrolling the city's border, travel to the nearest port town, and procure a small boat. Then they would sail to Viariche and enlist Adrienne and Jasper's help, reclaiming the *Silver Star* for their plan.

No one had any idea how long they would be gone.

In the darkness of predawn, Amaya held herself as the three of them prepared to set off. She and Cayo had decided to stay behind; a larger party would be more difficult to sneak around. Besides, Cayo was injured and in no state to travel. She didn't want to leave him by himself.

And beyond all that, Amaya was tired. Her mind, her heart, her bones. All she wanted to do was lie down and let the earth claim her.

Her eyes pricked with tears as Liesl and Deadshot hugged her goodbye.

"Please don't do anything I wouldn't do," Liesl begged. "You've had enough trouble for ten lifetimes."

Amaya only worked up the barest smile. "I'll try, but only if you remember to be careful."

"Of course. I'm always careful."

"And if not," Deadshot said, touching her pistol and leaving it at that.

"Send word as soon as you can. And when you see Avi..."

"We'll tell him what happened." Liesl squeezed her arm and gave her a trembling smile. "We'll see each other again, Amaya."

She hoped so. But Amaya had stopped believing in promises.

Remy slung his pack across his shoulder and came to hug her. She held on for as long as she could. For a moment she returned to the day she thought she would leave the *Brackish* for good, before Zharo had shot at her. The same bittersweet mix of relief and regret, knowing there was more waiting for her, but that it came at the price of being separated.

"I don't know when I'll be able to come back," Remy whispered.

Amaya tightened her arms around him. "Don't bother. I'll find you this time."

His laugh was quiet. "Good." He stepped back, his eyes over-bright as he gave her their salute. She returned it, knowing it wouldn't be the last time. Not if she could help it.

She and Cayo watched them disappear down the docks, toward the far beach, where they would scale the cliff face and slip into the thick foliage of the jungle. Above them, the sky began to vein with silver. Below them rested her father's ashes.

And between them, too many words they still couldn't say.

# 32

*The magician appealed to the stars. He begged of them*
*to bring Neralia back to her kingdom in the clouds, to give*
*her the reign that was her right. But the stars said no. "She*
*has killed one of our own," they said, "in an attempt to*
*take that light for herself. She is no longer welcome here."*
*They cast him out, and he fell just as Neralia had, straight*
*into the sea. But she waited for him there, and though he*
*had failed, they were together at last and decided they did*
*not need the stars. They had all the sweetness of the dark,*
*the beginning of their own kingdom.*

—"NERALIA OF THE CLOUDS," AN ORAL STORY ORIGINATING

FROM THE LEDE ISLANDS

The first week on the *Brackish* was difficult.

Cayo was a stranger to the Bugs, so it took a while for
them to adapt to his presence. There weren't very many of them,

but sometimes the children got so loud it felt as if the entire ship were full.

It used to be, he reminded himself. When his father had owned it. He decided to think as little of his father as possible.

Instead, he acquired a barnacle named Fera, the girl who wanted to learn all his coin tricks. He often saw her concentrating with a coin in her hand, and it made him smile despite everything. It reminded him of Soria, sighing and complaining it was not fair that Cayo had inherited the good hands of the family.

Her ashes still rested in his pack. He was back in Moray, but he couldn't bring himself to do what he had to. In the quiet, bleak moments, he sat with the pack in his lap, staring out at the ocean that shifted from dark gray to crystalline blue. His mother had often done this with Cayo or Soria in her lap, just staring out at sea, staring at something they'd never been able to perceive.

And then there was Amaya.

He did what he could. He gave her space, letting her navigate herself the way she wanted. He practiced making tea and left steaming mugs beside her hammock when she was too weary to visit the galley.

She didn't speak much. Didn't have to. Her father had died underneath her, his blood dried and flaking on her skin. It had drained something out of her, just as losing Soria had drained something out of him.

This was the thing about grief: It was always there. It would always take something out of him, out of her, carving its initials into their hearts. The pain would flare bright until it dimmed, until it needed kindling in order to grow again.

Amaya flared, and Cayo could hardly look at her. He knew if he tried to speak to her, he would flare, too, until they were burnt up to nothing.

So they both hugged ash to their chests and stayed silent, listening instead to the waves in the distance, their rhythm steady, unbreaking.

During the second week, Matthieu came back with reports that soldiers from the Sun Empire were beginning to infiltrate Moray by land, setting up a barrier to the west. Plumes of smoke rose from different points in the city, and Cicada said they were from massive pyres for those who had been claimed by the fever.

Cayo stole into the city to assess what was happening, but the streets were too choked with guards wearing masks and herding people away from closed-off sectors. Gunshots echoed farther down.

They sometimes heard wails and alarms in the distance. The children grew tense at the sound, eyes fixed on the skyline. But then they would relax again and play a card game, or try to roll coins across their fingers (Fera had recruited the others), or simply talk about impossible and fantastical things.

There was a night where the air was balmy and sweet, and Cayo closed his eyes and turned his face toward the wind. The deck was lit with a few lanterns glowing like watchful eyes in the dark. Cicada was teaching the children a new card game, and they sat in a circle to watch, yapping like a herd of puppies.

The wound at his shoulder ached. He had never been stabbed before; he hadn't been prepared for the sharp cruelty of it, the way the shape of the knife lingered even now in his flesh. It was mostly healed now, though moving his arm in certain ways proved difficult.

Someone joined him at the railing. Cayo didn't need to open his eyes to know it was Amaya. He knew how she moved, like a blade through the water.

"I'm worried," she whispered. It was the most she had said to him in days.

He looked at her then. Her face was wan, her hair tangled. She was thin—they didn't have much food, but Cicada got what he could from the city—and it was as if she were trying to disappear off the earth entirely.

Cayo had already determined that he wouldn't let her.

"I'm sure they're still traveling," he said. "It takes a week just to sail to Baleine, and they had to go on foot for the first few days at least."

She bit her lip, eyes dark and moonlit. She twisted the jade ring on her finger. Cayo thought of taking her hands in his, to make her look at him, but he made no move to do so.

"They'll be all right," he said.

Her breath hitched. Ever since he'd known her she had been closed off, sewn up, but now she was breaking open, practically snapping her ribs away to reveal what lay beyond.

Cayo may have shied away from it once. Now he accepted it like an unfinished gemstone, rough and heavy and worth more than he could imagine.

"I'm tired," she whispered, gazing out at the dark water. The lighthouse atop the nearby cliff flashed its light in a steady tempo. "I'm tired of feeling like this."

"I know."

"Why did he have to keep it from me?" A tear fell slowly down her cheek, gleaming like a pearl. "Why couldn't he have just told me the truth from the start?"

Cayo was afraid of touching her, of being burned alive by the pain that raged around her. But still he reached up and brushed the tear away with his thumb. It spread across his skin, warmth and salt.

"He was scared," Cayo said. He hadn't known Boon the way Amaya had, but he could understand that, at least. The truth was often horrifying—it was difficult to know when to divulge it or keep it close.

"So was I," Amaya whispered. Then she turned her head slightly, resting her cheek against his hand. His heart kicked in his chest, so sudden and hard that Cayo wondered if it had been beating at all before now.

He stepped closer, and she let him. He thought it would be difficult, but it was simple, really: just the two of them standing together, bodies close, sharing heat and breath and light.

By the fifth week, he was woken with a shake as Amaya leaned over his hammock.

"News," she said simply.

He followed her out onto the deck, where the early morning light was being filtered through thick, heavy clouds. A stranger stood waiting by the gangplank with an envelope. Amaya tossed him a coin, which the stranger bit before handing over the envelope and taking off.

Amaya drew out the letter inside. Cayo read over her shoulder.

*A.—*

    *It's been done. R. had the brilliant idea to raid the currency exchange offices across the city, to pile up the counterfeit coins.*

*My sister kept the* Silver Star, *and so she and J. helped us navigate it back to Baleine. Once we had all the counterfeits we could find, we put them on the ship and left it in the harbor. R. said he was inspired by the Ghost Ship incident. He put in a report to his officers. The ship was confiscated, and the counterfeits discovered.*

*All of it, of course, tied to Basque, who owns the* Silver Star. *His manor was raided, and he was brought in for questioning. You wouldn't believe the secrets in that house of his, double rooms and compartments and even a laboratory. Deirdre and her alchemists found a few useful reports and ingredients in that laboratory, all contributing to what they believe to be a cure.*

*This whole time Deirdre was just trying to seduce him for his money so she could funnel more funding into her research, to mobilize the alchemists against the Rain Empire and drive them out of Chalier. Believe it or not, she and I are on the same side. I might consider working with her in the future.*

*Basque was arrested. His debtor ships are being recalled, the debtors' contracts now null and void. My sister is a free woman and doesn't have to run anymore. And what's more: His ties to Moray are now severed.*

*They sentenced Basque to hang on the Sinner's Shelf. I made D. row me out there to see it for myself. He made a pretty corpse. I spat on it. At least now R. can work with his superiors to revoke my Landless status, thanks to my contribution in Basque's arrest.*

*The cure is still in development for mass distribution here, but Deirdre's alchemists and the doctors are working together to* bring it into circulation as soon as they're able. Avi was in the first testing group to see if it actually works. He tells you hello, and that he feels like he can do a dozen backflips. (I tried to convince him to perform those dozen backflips, but he made up some paltry excuse and made me leave.)

Now for the bad news, because of course there must be bad news. Although the cure will surely come to Moray, and although Basque is done, the city will remain ravaged for quite some time. We're already seeing it here in Baleine. The loss of the counterfeit money is putting it under financial strain, and I can only imagine the impact it will have on Moray. It may take years, even a generation, to recover from this.

But at least this is a beginning. The worst of the nightmare is over, or so we hope.

I cannot tell you what to do, but I hope whatever path you choose now, you know you have a place with me and A. and D. in Viariche. (And J., if he survives my interrogation.) R. says he has to stay in Baleine for a while yet, but I trust the two of you will reunite soon enough.

I'm proud of you. I don't know if I've actually said it. You and C. both. Please be safe, and remember who your friends are.

—L.

Amaya's throat worked as she swallowed. She read it through again, then one more time, before folding it carefully.

"A cure," she whispered. "André Basque had the components for it all this time."

A bright, burning rage grew in Cayo's gut. He desired nothing more than to travel to Baleine so he could follow Liesl's example and desecrate the man's corpse.

"He was weeding them out," Amaya said softly.

"What?"

"The poor. The hospitals in Baleine were filled with those who could afford treatment, remember?" She turned to him, her face contorted in grief and the same fury that sat within him. "They left the poorer citizens to die in the streets. He didn't bother to make a cure because he wanted to weed them out."

Cayo held on to the ship's gunwale, taking deep breaths of briny sea air. It did nothing to staunch the damage. He hung his head, choking on a sob.

If the cure had been found just a few weeks sooner, Soria could have been saved.

Amaya held him from behind, and they swayed together, the flare building and building until it burned brighter than the hidden sun.

"I want to bury my father's ashes."

Cayo looked up from reading the news sheet that Matthieu had stolen. Cicada had read it out loud for the Bugs who didn't know their letters, breaking the news they already knew from Liesl: A cure had been found, and the Rain Empire was sending shipments of it to Moray in good faith, but it was more likely a favor they expected to be repaid in the future. So long as the Sun Empire decided to let them pass, it would circulate within the city shortly.

But that still didn't relieve Moray from its financial sinkhole. It didn't take care of the counterfeit money still running through the city.

Cayo had been reading through the details—and then rereading, his focus slipping—when Amaya showed up beside him, her pack heavy on her shoulders.

"Bury?" he repeated.

She nodded. "I thought about scattering them, but I don't want to. He already spent so much of his life away from home." She turned to the gangplank. "Will you come with me?"

A simple question that wasn't simple at all. He wondered if he should grab his own pack, if today was the time to say goodbye, but he decided against it. This was Amaya's day, not his.

He did make sure to take Jazelle with him as they left the ship. There were still dock workers performing their duties, because what other choice did they have? The city had to go on even as it decayed. Some of the workers were coughing, and Cayo spotted splotches of gray on their skin.

The two of them carefully navigated the streets to avoid the ones that were closed off. The air smelled of smoke and soot, growing stronger and stronger as they walked. Cayo pulled his shirt over his nose and mouth, Amaya doing the same.

Eventually Amaya led him to one of the residential districts. Cayo instantly recognized it. They had passed this street before, back when they had been a countess and a merchant's son. She had gotten mad at him for...something. He couldn't quite remember. It was a lifetime ago, when he had worn a different skin.

She stopped in front of a humble-looking house with a red door. She stared at it for some time, arms hanging at her sides, face giving nothing away.

"This is where you lived," he said.

She nodded, then led him around the house, through the narrow space between buildings. In the back was an overgrown garden fenced in with rotting wood, the small plot of land studded with weeds and wild herbs. Bushes had been left to turn wild, and morning glories snaked across the fence, up toward the house.

Amaya climbed over the fence and Cayo followed, half worried the wood would give out under them. In the middle of the garden, Amaya sank to her knees and set her pack down. Then she began to dig.

Cayo knelt beside her to help, but she took his wrist with a dirt-smudged hand and shook her head, so he sat back and watched as she scraped out as deep a hole as she could make. The beds of her fingernails turned dark, the earth clinging to her, fresh and soft.

When she took the box out of her pack, Cayo spotted a glimpse of her mother's cloth. She still hadn't taken it out, hadn't found a purpose for it yet. It felt right for it to be here, though; for some part of her mother to join them for the ceremony.

Amaya took a deep breath. Another. She opened the box, revealing the gray ash studded with bits of bone, all that was left of the man who had raised her—destroyed her.

"I meant it," Amaya whispered, and Cayo knew she wasn't speaking to him. "When I forgave you. The world ruined you, and it ruined me. I understand." Her voice broke, and she gripped the box tighter. "I loved you. Maybe I still do. I hope you know that."

Cayo watched as she tipped the box over, letting the ash pool into the hole she had made.

"You're home now, at least," Amaya said.

She covered up the hole, patting the earth back into place. Cayo

391

watched on, a silent witness, until a rustle made him turn. He jumped back at the sight of a dozen spiders in the overgrown bushes nearby.

"Don't worry about them." A weak laugh escaped her. "That's what my mother would tell me. She was fond of spiders."

"Don't know why she would be," Cayo murmured, taking in the blue triangle on the spiders' bulbous bodies.

"Something about how their silk is special." Amaya rubbed a sleeve over her eyes, then placed her hand over the disturbed dirt. "Say hello to her for me, all right?"

It almost broke her, made the tears come again, but she brushed them away and got to her feet. The two of them climbed back over the fence, returning to the main street.

"I thought I would feel different," she admitted as they walked through the quiet streets. "But it's more like the ending to a story I already knew."

Cayo didn't know if he could relate, if it would be the same for him when he finally let Soria go. Instead, he held out his hand and she took it in hers, grave soil pressed between their palms.

# 33

*Blood is more costly than any coin or jewel.*

—REHANESE PROVERB

Y ou're bleeding."

Amaya pulled Cayo to a stop. They were still a ways from the ship, but she had just noticed the cut on Cayo's hand, blood tickling her skin where it dripped between them.

"Must have snagged it on that fence." Cayo reached for the hem of his shirt as if to rip off a makeshift bandage, but she stopped him.

"That's too dirty. The wound will get infected."

She made him sit as she dug through her pack, but most of her supplies had been taken out to make room for the cloth. Hesitating, Amaya ran her fingers over the fabric before using a knife to cut a strip away.

"You didn't have to do that," Cayo said, watching her wrap his hand.

"It's fine. Not like it has any other uses."

But as she tied the bandage securely, she realized for the first time that there was something off about the fabric. The parts that weren't already stained pink with blood were...shimmering.

The clouds had parted, the sun beating down on them. The longer the sun shone, the stronger the fabric glowed. Amaya gathered more of it in her hands as the shimmer took it over, a strange buzzing sensation making her palms itch.

The cloth was *absorbing* the sunlight.

A cloud skidded across the sky and cut off the connection, but the cloth still shone, still humming with that unexplained energy.

She and Cayo exchanged a bewildered look.

"Well," he said weakly. "That's new."

It was Cicada who figured it out.

They spread the fabric out on the deck of the *Brackish*, a huge square of canvas-like material that began to glimmer when the sun hit it. The children gasped and squealed in delight, but Cicada rubbed his chin and frowned in perplexity at the reaction.

"Never seen cloth do that before," he said.

"It somehow absorbs light," Amaya said. "The longer it's out in the sun, the longer it glows."

"It feels weird!" Matthieu exclaimed, his hand pressed against the cloth. "Like bugs crawling up my arm!"

"Eww," Fera said.

Cicada walked around it with a thoughtful frown. He lifted the edge to fan it out, the cloth rippling.

The *Brackish* jerked beneath them, throwing them all off balance.

"What in the hells?" Amaya peered over the railing, but the water below was calm.

Cicada did it again, and once more the ship jerked forward, kept tethered by its anchor. He shared a look with Amaya.

"That's not possible," she said.

"You said it's alchemy," Cicada said. "Down on the Islands folks think it's witchcraft, and now I'm beginning to suspect the same thing."

Amaya ran the cloth through her hands, watching as she left trails of darkness with her fingers that were quickly eaten up by the light.

She thought back to what Avi had said about her mother helping Boon—her father—with alchemy. How her mother had told her not to be afraid of the spiders in their garden, that their silk was a gift.

"They're sails," she said at last. "Or at least, they can be used as sails. They'll store the sun's energy and keep a ship going when the wind can't."

Cicada whistled and shook his head. "Your mother must've been one powerful witch."

Cayo had been silent until now, merely observing. When he finally spoke, he said the one thing she least expected.

"Get Romara."

The Slum Queen was not thrilled at the summons.

She barged into the galley as Cayo was setting a mug before Amaya, nearly startling him into spilling hot tea across the table.

"What is this?" Romara demanded. Her lackey, Jacques, hovered behind her. "I was enjoying a nice breakfast when some ragamuffin urchin comes in practically demanding I come to this ugly heap of a ship."

"Nice to see you, too, Romara," Cayo muttered as he sat beside Amaya. "Have a seat."

"I'll pass. What happened?" Romara eyed the bandage around his hand, then Amaya. "You finally decided to stick him?"

Amaya growled, and Romara had the decency to look unnerved.

"I'm calling in one final favor," Cayo said. "After all, I *did* help you secure the Vice Sector."

"Which I repaid by handing over my father in exchange for that lanky boy." Romara crossed her arms, leveling a glare at him. "You want a favor, there's going to have to be payment of some sort, Cayo. You know that."

He and Amaya exchanged a quick glance. She nodded.

"Fine," Cayo said with a weary sigh. "But once we let you in on this plan, there'll be no backing out of it."

Romara quirked an eyebrow, intrigued. "All right."

They told her about the cloth, and what they wanted her to do with it. At first all she did was let out an incredulous laugh.

"You're running a con?"

"It's not a con," Cayo said.

Amaya showed Romara the small square of cloth she had cut from Cayo's makeshift bandage. It was glowing with the sunlight she had exposed it to this morning.

Romara held it, lips parted in wonder. Even Jacques couldn't help but stare, glancing from it to Romara and back.

"Thirty percent," Romara said suddenly.

"Five," Cayo countered.

"I don't think so, puppy. It'll be thirty or nothing."

"Then you won't be leaving this ship."

She tensed, but one look at Amaya's hand drifting toward her knife made her huff.

"Twenty-five percent," Romara said.

"Seven."

"Fifteen."

"Ten."

"Twelve."

"*Ten.*"

"Eleven!" Jacques shouted, then shrank back at Romara's glare. "Sorry. Didn't know if I should be contributing."

"Ten," Cayo said firmly.

Romara scoffed and threw the square of cloth onto the table.

"Fine," she said. "But only because I feel sorry for you."

Once they drew up the plans, Romara left the ship with most of the cloth. Amaya stared after her, her fingers twitching as if she longed to run after her and get it back.

It had been her mother's. It was *hers*.

But she had kept some for herself, because she knew this alone wouldn't be enough. There was one final step, one more attempt to fix things.

Amaya headed back into the city, the last of her mother's cloth folded in her pocket. It took hours to find an alchemist's shop, the same symbol above the door as she'd seen in Baleine.

It took even longer for her to convince the woman who owned the shop that what she held was real, and how it had been accomplished.

"Rehanese Blueback spiders," the alchemist repeated, running her fingers along the shimmering cloth, inspecting the thick, glowing thread. "They only live in southern Rehan. If we make this public..."

"You can make them a protected species," Amaya finished for her. Which meant having access to a product that only Moray could manufacture, and therefore having leverage against the empires. The alchemist's eyes gleamed with possibility, even a hint of greed.

Amaya twisted the jade ring on her finger. This was for the best, she reminded herself. It was what her mother would have wanted, her parents' true legacy.

A way to save the city that had brought them together, broken them, rejected them, and ultimately reunited them.

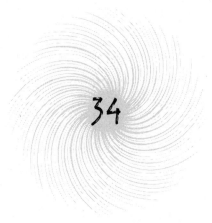

# 34

*I've taken what you showed me and made it my own. Using the silk for thread, soaking the cloth in the solution I made. I think you would have been proud. I wish I could hear you say the words.*

—LETTER FROM RIN CHANDRA TO ARUN CHANDRA, UNSENT

*L* andless.

Cayo had expected something grander, something worse. Sentenced to a debtor ship, or a hanging.

But as he watched his father being marched out of the Port's Authority, he knew this was how it should have been. How many people had Kamon Mercado made Landless? How many had he forced into exile just to protect his secrets?

Amaya touched his shoulder, but Cayo shook his head, telling her he was all right. He had needed to come here today. To hear the sentence for himself.

They took a long walk down to the harbor. Amaya kept his hand in hers, staying quiet. Allowing him to be with his thoughts.

Romara's auction for the sails had gone better than they had anticipated. She had made sure the word spread, even going so far as to draw in bidders from the Rain and Sun Empires. Amaya had gone to witness it, had told him all about it in detail afterward, but nothing had prepared him for the sum the sails had gone for.

It wasn't nearly enough to buy back the counterfeits, but it was a start. Enough to at least delay Moray from falling to either empire.

And when she told him the second part of her plan, Cayo knew it was only the beginning.

"The alchemists got together and agreed to petition the state," Amaya told him. "They're going to make the Rehanese Bluebacks a protected species in Moray, use their silk to make more sails and goods."

"Which will help chip away Moray's debt," Cayo realized.

He had almost cried in relief, knowing they had done all they could to fix their fathers' mistakes.

The sentry ships were no longer patrolling the bay now that the cure had arrived thanks to Deirdre's efforts. Emergency clinics had been situated throughout the city, giving out free doses to rid citizens of ash fever once and for all. Cayo had worried they might charge for the medicine, but the people were already so on edge, so ready to riot at the smallest grievance, that they had likely thought better of it.

He and Amaya made their way to a small ship being loaded with prisoners. His father stood with a guard at either arm, his wrists and ankles shackled. His hair fell in ragged locks, his jaw dusted with stubble. Cayo had never seen him so disheveled.

Kamon's eyes flickered to Cayo as he approached, making sure to stop a healthy distance away. Amaya stayed behind.

"Father," he said. "I can't say I'm sorry to see you go."

Kamon breathed out and looked away. Said nothing.

Cayo pretended that it didn't hurt. "I only came to say goodbye. So…" He stepped back, nodding once. "Goodbye, Father."

He was turning when Kamon finally spoke.

"I didn't mean for her to die."

Cayo clenched his hands into fists. "But she did. Because of you."

His father shrank back from the words.

"I hope our paths never cross," Cayo said. *Because I don't know what I'll do if I see your face again.*

Kamon met his gaze with something that put a pressure on Cayo's chest. Cayo refused to think of it as love. This wasn't what love looked like. He had known enough of it to tell the difference.

He returned to Amaya, leaving Kamon to board the ship that would sail him out of Moray forever. She wrapped an arm around his waist, and he leaned some of his weight against her.

He didn't bother looking back.

With Kamon Mercado arrested and made Landless, the manor was now up for sale. Cayo went to the Business Sector to discuss what all had to be done, only to learn that he didn't have access to the deed. It was now the property of Moray, and they would sell it to the highest bidder.

He stood before the manor on a clear morning and watched

movers take out what remained of the furniture, the artwork, all the pieces and bits of him that still hurt to look at. There—the chair his mother used to sit in as she read. There—the books from his room, adventures and romance and action. There—Soria's favorite painting, the one of the mermaid calling to a distant ship.

Cayo almost stepped forward, a hand squeezing his heart. But what would he even do with it? He let the mover carry the painting away, never to be seen again.

His home, dismantled piece by piece, as if it meant absolutely nothing at all.

Cayo closed his eyes, felt the emptiness gaping larger within him as if the movers were taking out his bones and organs instead, piling them next to the furniture.

"I've lost everything," he whispered, and it hurt more than he thought possible.

Amaya's hand circled his upper arm, and she leaned against him.

*So have I,* that gesture said.

Cayo took her around the back of the manor, down the bluff, toward the cliffs. Amaya followed, silent and sure. He wondered if she was remembering the day they had swum in the inlet, the first unbinding of their masks.

The sun was beginning to set as they stood there, wind blowing past them toward the sea. The water was a bed of orange and red, warm and glowing.

He lifted the box from his pack, held it one last time between his hands. He rested his forehead against it.

"I'm sorry," he whispered. "You deserved so much more."

His throat closed, tears escaping past his closed eyes. Amaya's hand settled on his back.

"I love you, Soria. Always."

He opened the box, steeled himself before reaching inside. He lifted his palm and opened his fingers, letting the wind carry her away, blowing her into spiral patterns and scattering her like stars.

Amaya reached into the pouch she had brought with her. She took out a handful of marigold petals—a Kharian custom, she had explained, when one is mourning. The bright orange petals tore from her hand, eaten up by the wind.

They let ash and petals fly, blending together. Eager for the water, for the open sky.

# 35

*I'd like to sail, one day. To have my own ship and discover new islands and make friends with sea monsters. I want to feel like the world belongs to me. That I have a place inside of it.*

—DIARY OF CAYO MERCADO, AGE TEN

There was enough money left over from the auction to buy provisions for a long voyage.

Amaya and Cicada made the necessary preparations while Cayo plotted out their path. First to the Lede Islands, where Cicada and the Water Bugs would stay. There they would sell the *Brackish*, and Amaya would get a ship of her own; something smaller, something two sailors could manage.

She and Cayo would sail up to Viariche and stay with Liesl and her sister for a bit. Maybe up to Baleine to check how things were coming along and to see Remy.

And then, when she was ready, she would set out to free as many debtor ships as possible. To grant as many second chances as she could.

The day they set off, the *Brackish*'s sails finally unfurled, the children cheered and waved goodbye to Moray. Strange, how this ship had once been their prison and was now their ticket to freedom.

The city fell away behind them. Amaya pressed her thumb to the knife tattoo at her wrist, watching Moray grow smaller, knowing it would be the last time she ever laid eyes on it.

She had known it as Amaya, as Silverfish, as Countess Yamaa. She had seen it at its best and at its worst. It had taken from her, and she had given back. There was nothing left for her there.

When Moray finally fell out of sight, Amaya turned and spotted Cayo at the bow. She took in how the wind played with his hair, how he stood as if waiting for something to rise out of the depths and swallow them.

As she came up beside him, he relaxed. Even let out a little laugh.

"It's funny," he said. "I always wanted to be a sailor, to go on adventures. I didn't realize they'd be so exhausting."

She couldn't help but smile. "I could have told you that the first day we met."

*Do you regret meeting me?* she had asked him in Baleine. He had never answered.

"Mm." He glanced at her sidelong. "I should have guessed, that first time."

"What do you mean?"

"You had stuffed snacks into your pockets. Hardly ladylike."

"One has to adapt to survive."

"True." He took a deep breath, and there was something fitting about him here, framed by the sea and the rigging above his head. "We'll have to adapt a lot, won't we?"

"We will. Are you prepared for that?"

"Honestly? Probably not." The way he looked at her this time was different, a warmth that made her blood feel fuzzy in her veins. "But we'll figure it out. We always seem to."

*We'll figure it out.*

They would, she realized. The unexpected would always come, carefully laid plans gone awry. The wind would change, and the skies would darken with storms.

But that was all right. They didn't have to weather it alone.

Cayo brushed back a lock of her hair, fingertips skimming across her cheek. A silent question, a quiet pleading.

She drew her hands up his chest and around the back of his neck. When he kissed her, it was soft and slow, as if they had an eternity to savor it. Time enough to forgive, and to learn. To go at whatever pace they set.

His next kiss was more urgent, drawing heat up through her chest. She tangled her fingers in his hair and savored the rhythm of his heartbeat against hers. A reminder that they had survived, that some part of the world was theirs alone.

They leaned their foreheads together and swayed with the ship, letting it carry them on to whatever waited for them next.

"I'm glad I met you," Cayo said, and she knew it was the truth, worth more than any sum of gold.

# ACKNOWLEDGMENTS

When I first drafted *Ravage* in early 2019, I had no idea that a year later a pandemic would be rampaging across the world, and that so much of what I put into this book would come to life. Even as I write this, we're still in the thick of it. So, though they had nothing to do with this book directly, I want to say thank you to the health-care workers, first responders, grocery store employees, postal workers, retail workers, and delivery people who have sacrificed so much of themselves during this difficult time.

This book has gone through the careful hands of several editors. Hannah Allaman, thank you for your incredible insight and helping me shape the rough draft into something that actually resembled a book. Hannah Milton, thank you for making sure that all the nooks and crannies were filled. Patrice Caldwell, thank you for being the one to launch this series in the first place, and for your support ever since. A big, BIG thank-you to Kat Cho, without whom I would have perished long ago.

Thank you to the teams at Disney and Little, Brown, especially Melissa Lee, Morgan Maple, and Alvina Ling. A book's cover is super important, and I'm so glad to have had Sammy Yuen and Jenny Kimura's vision for making Amaya even more badass, as well as Tom Corbett's stunning photography.

Thanks to the folks at Glasstown who supported me and these books, especially Jenna Brickley for helping me navigate *Ravage* through choppy seas.

Traci Chee, Emily Skrutskie, Jessica Cluess: Somewhere along the way we went from being not just author friends but *friend* friends who throw insults and *Cats* content at one another, and I think that's pretty special. Thank you for your love, jokes, and Crack Pie.

To the Cult—Akshaya Raman, Katy Rosé Pool (yes, Rosé), Kat Cho, Mara Fitzgerald, Christine Lynn Herman, Amanda Foody, Amanda Haas, Axie Oh, Alex Castellanos, Meg Kohlmann, Melody Simpson, Janella Angeles, Ashley Burdin, Claribel Ortega, and Maddy Colis—thank you for always being there for me and one another, for Zoom happy hours, and hilarious TMI stories.

Thanks to Margaret Owen for being patient while I scream in her texts and for reading my terrible rough drafts. Thank you to Ellen Gavazza, Meagan Cupka, and Jamie Lynn Saunders for *Animal Crossing* dates and letting me sell my cherries on your islands.

Thank you to my Patrons, especially those who've pledged five dollars and up: Ash Hardister, Susan Hamm, Mae Nouwen, Sen Scherb, Caitlin O'Connell, Amanda Wheeler, Carolyn, Sylph, Ellen, and Common Spence.

Thank you to *The Untamed* for getting me through some very difficult times.

To the readers, reviewers, BookTubers, bloggers, fan artists, etc.: a million thank-yous. Your support means the world.

And last but not least, thank you to my family for always having my back and making me smile. Like Amaya, my parents taught me the value of love and stories, and that is something I will always carry.

# T A R A   S I M

can typically be found wandering the wilds of the Bay Area in California. She is the author of the Scavenge the Stars duology as well as the Timekeeper trilogy, which has been featured in *Entertainment Weekly, Bustle*, and various other media outlets. When she's not chasing cats or lurking in bookstores, she writes books about magic, murder, and explosives.